A Certain Persuasion

Modern LGBTQ+ fiction
inspired by Jane Austen's novels

An anthology from

Published by Manifold Press

E-book ISBN: 978-1-908312-44-0
Paperback ISBN: 978-1-908312-75-4

Proof-reading and fact checking: F.M. Parkinson

Editor: Julie Bozza

For further details of Manifold Press titles both in print and forthcoming: manifoldpress.co.uk

Dedication

In loving memory of Alan Rickman, 'our' Colonel Brandon.

> *What though the sea with waves continuall*
> *Doe eate the earth, it is no more at all;*
> *Ne is the earth the lesse, or loseth ought:*
> *For whatsoever from one place doth fall*
> *Is with the tyde unto another brought:*
> *For there is nothing lost, that may be found if sought.*

Edmund Spenser
The Faerie Queene

Table of Contents

Introduction

Julie Bozza

I have found that many of us reading and writing in queer fiction and romance cite Jane Austen as one of our favourite authors. On one hand, this isn't a surprise, as Austen played a fundamental role in the creation of the modern novel as we know it today. On the other hand, mainstream readers might find it very surprising, as Austen's novels are generally seen as entirely heteronormative. A quick Google, however, brings up several instances of useful applications of Queer Theory to her work.

I think one aspect of her novels that explains this is the stubborn independence of her main characters. They never consider choosing to live outside the genteel society of their times, but they are determined to make their own choices and negotiate their own terms within those structures. Related to that notion is that while her main characters outwardly conform to the gender roles of the times, inwardly they are all as capable and as fallible as each other. Her society might place more value on Fitzwilliam Darcy than Elizabeth Bennet, on Frederick Wentworth than Anne Elliot – but Austen knows that as individual people they are all equally worthwhile.

How can readers and writers of queer characters resist such a humanist?

I'd like to thank Fiona Pickles, Editor-in-Chief of Manifold Press, for her faith in and support for this project. The Press's colleagues and friends have been delightfully enthusiastic likewise.

The indefatigable F.M. Parkinson served once more as proof-reader, for which the authors and myself are eternally grateful.

The authors have been creative, diligent and professional though the long process of pulling this volume together.

And now the results are in your hands and before your eyes, dear Reader. If we entertain, provoke and charm you even a tenth as much as Austen does, we'll consider it work well done.

A Charming Marine Prospect

Lou Faulkner

Mr William Elliot, of the younger branch of the Kellynch family, being obliged to travel through a part of the country in which that family had its residence, elected to take the route least convenient to Sir Walter's home; in short, to travel along the coast. Since he was journeying from Plymouth to London, he took the southerly road, and, jolting along the rough lane that took its course between Seaton and Lyme, had cause before very long to regret his choice. The lane was deep rutted and badly-made, and the mud of early spring made it slippery under his horses' hooves. A passing donkey, switched along by a boy and laden with samphire, compounded his difficulties at a sharp bend; the curricle was overset, and Mr Elliot and his groom found themselves on the ground and the distressed horses thoroughly tangled with their harness.

Cooper, his groom (in fact his name was Colquhoun, but Mr Elliot saw no reason to bother himself with remembering such an outlandish name), went to help his master, and thence to the horses; but he fell back, his handsome face distorted in sudden pain, and could not speak even when Mr Elliot addressed him sharply.

Aid there was none; the boy and his donkey had made themselves scarce. Mr Elliot, having had time to right his thoughts, cursed once but with feeling, assisted Cooper to a seat on a stone in the hedgerow, and went to the horses. After freeing them from the tangled harness, he led them back one by one to Cooper, who spoke to them softly, albeit through clenched teeth. The next difficulty facing Mr Elliot was the pole of the curricle, which had been badly cracked in the upset.

He glanced back at Cooper. The man was obviously in severe difficulties; any help would therefore have to come from Mr Elliot himself. A walk to the nearest farmhouse beckoned, not something he would particularly enjoy at the best of times, and certainly not considering the muddy state of the ground. There was nothing for it, though, and he was preparing to set out across the ploughed fields to a house, the position of which could be guessed at from a plume of smoke ascending from beyond a sheltering belt of trees, when the small boy, reappearing cautiously, volunteered the information that his mother was at home in the farmhouse, and that assistance could be brought should it be needed.

Mr Elliot agreed to this plan, and informed the child that there would be a shilling in it for him if he would be quick about it, so, encouraging his donkey to a trot, the messenger departed across the fields.

Thereupon, Mr Elliot turned his attention back to the upset curricle; a careful inspection shewed that beyond the cracked pole, there seemed no irreparable damage. A couple of days' stay in Lyme should see the pole replaced and the body of the curricle refurbished, and then he could continue to London, on better-made roads – or, if necessary, hire another vehicle. He knew that a public coach stopped at Lyme, but was not inclined to make use of it. The company to be met with on a public coach was not to Mr Elliot's liking, and was to be avoided if at all possible.

The first task to undertake was to remove his baggage from the back of the curricle; he unroped it and dropped the large valise to the ground. "No, look after the horses," he snapped at Cooper, as he made to rise and help, and the man subsided once more. Then Mr Elliot set his shoulder to the vehicle, and heaved with the strength of suppressed anger; it balanced for a moment on one wheel, before tipping upright. He stood back, dusting off his gloved hands and regarding it with satisfaction. His predicament was beginning to look less severe.

At this point a young man, some eighteen years of age or so, Mr Elliot guessed, appeared beyond the seaward hedge, tossed a heavy bag over the stile, sprang onto its topmost rail, balanced easily there for a moment, then jumped lightly down into the road.

"Good day to you, sir! I thought I heard a smash. A thorough one, too. Are you in need of assistance?"

Mr Elliot, not at all pleased to be found in such a situation, replied shortly, "It is a most confounded nuisance. What may be done to help, I do not know."

The young man walked round the damaged curricle, and said, "My brother has one very like this. If the pole is all the damage there is, I believe I may be able to repair it, with the use of some of that line." He indicated the back of the vehicle, where the rope lay in a tangled pile on the ground.

"You are a repairer of carriages, then?" Mr Elliot was surprised; the young man's voice was a little too refined to suggest any such occupation.

"Not I! Richard Musgrove, midshipman of His Majesty's sloop *Callisto*, at your service." That would explain his dark blue breeches and round jacket. "We have little to do with carriages, more's the pity! But much ado with the repair of spars, and if you wish it, that smash will only take a few minutes to set right. Or right enough for you to continue your journey to Lyme, at least, if that's where you're headed."

"You are very kind, Mr Musgrove. William – Walters, of London, at your service."

The two horses were between Mr Elliot and Cooper, so he could not see the groom's expression, but was confident that it would be schooled to indifference. He paid the man well, and required his silence, and if, from time to time, his master made use of a nom de guerre, that was none of his business. So Mr Elliot, too close to Kellynch to wish to make his real name known, was able to give this alias with confidence, and turned his full attention to the newcomer.

The young man was fair-haired under his hat, and his eyes very bright. His complexion was a little tanned, to be sure, but altogether he presented a pleasing picture. Mr Elliot might stand on ceremony, but William Walters was not inclined to deprive himself of his company.

Within ten minutes, the rope was disentangled from the baggage, the broken pole of the curricle laid straight, and Musgrove was engaged in "'splicing'" the split halves which William held firmly together.

Help for Cooper was now at hand. The urchin's mother was approaching, driving a cart, with a young woman – her daughter, judging from the resemblance between them – at her side. The woman surveyed the scene briefly, and brought the cart to within a pace of the injured man, then set her shoulder under his, and between herself and Musgrove they had him onto the cart-bed in a trice. Her daughter arranged a rug for Cooper's comfort, while William opened his purse.

"This is for your trouble, madam. I will arrange for an apothecary, or a surgeon if there is one, from Lyme, and, depending on his opinion, Cooper may require your hospitality for a while."

"You'll want Mr Atkins, on Broad Street, sir," said the woman. She had an air of competence which was reassuring, though William was chagrined when she continued, "Westport Farm. He knows the way. That's a nasty bend and we often have folks upturned."

So he had been victim to a common circumstance. William sighed inwardly, but thanked her for the information, touched his hat in conscious courtesy, and left them to drive away.

"Easier to do this on solid ground than up in the rigging, with the yard trying to throw you into the sea," said Musgrove, with an easy grin, as he took a final turn with the rope and contrived some form of complicated knot to finish all. "That should hold." They both surveyed it, William anticipating disaster, Musgrove with an air of satisfaction, and since it did not collapse into its component parts, William turned and shook the other's hand.

"You have saved me from an uncomfortable walk, or a ride in a farmer's cart at least," and William indicated his driving-coat and glossy boots, already spattered with mud from the road. "If I can offer you conveyance to the town, or to some point nearer, I will be more than glad to do so."

"That's handsome of you, sir. Since my bag is heavy, I'll take you up on the offer. I wasn't looking forward to hauling that lot to Lyme."

"Let us harness up the horses, then, and be on our way!"

The baggage was reloaded, they climbed into the curricle, and William took up the reins and encouraged the horses to a cautious walk. When it became apparent that the pole would hold, he glanced at his passenger and said, "You are an excellent repairer of carriages, sir. Once again, my thanks."

He received a grin in response. Not one to approve such familiar manners as a rule, William was nevertheless ready to let this pass; the youth was possessed of an undeniable charm.

"This ride is all the thanks I need, sir! It's a very considerable walk from Axmouth, especially with my finds to carry." He nudged the satchel with his foot.

William cast his mind back to Axmouth, some five miles to the west. There had been a small ship tied up at the wharf there. "I believe I may have seen your sloop as I came by the town."

"Yes, that's the *Callisto*, come in to provision. Some of us were given shore leave, and since there's always a market for fossils in these parts, I set about obtaining some."

"You are a natural philosopher, then!" William glanced at his passenger, smiling.

Musgrove met his eye with great frankness. "I am on the rocks, sir, like many a midshipman! So I go to Lyme, where I may obtain the best prices for my curios. I noticed a new collapse in the under-cliff as we came in, and it seemed likely that it had not been picked clean of specimens, so I got there with all speed once I had leave. It was hard going, though – the under-cliff is rough country!"

"This under-cliff – is that the land along the shore line? I caught a glimpse of it now and then as I came along the road. It seems to me that a whole portion of the cliff has fallen away, trees and all."

"Yes. That happened before I was born, but more rocks are always coming down. Very romantical and overgrown it is too – visiting gentry are fond of it for expeditions – but I'm there for the fossils."

William said, as if he had just had the idea, "Since I have a day or two to spare while this carriage is repaired, or the pole replaced, I've a mind to explore this under-cliff a little way – though not today, since the light is beginning to fail. Perhaps, if you know the path, you would be willing to show me the route where I may least expect to break my neck?"

"Gladly, sir, though the rocks shift constantly and the path shifts with them. It's a puzzle sometimes to know how to get along."

"An exploration, then! Which will be a novelty to me, though doubtless you've undertaken many such."

"Oh, I've been mostly in home waters: no far-flung voyages for me! Damned uncomfortable it would be too, sailing to the Indies or the Arctic, though blockade-duty is dull enough, and little chance of prizes; a few days on land don't come unwelcome. I'll go to the curio stall in Lyme today, and see what prices I may expect. Trouble is, they know their fossils, and it's not as though I can sell elsewhere."

"I must visit this stall. Fossils are of some interest in London, I believe, and a present or two for friends and family would not go amiss."

"Come with me, sir, if you wish. I can lead you straight there."

"You are familiar with the town, then?"

"I'm from Uppercross, further north. I've visited Lyme once or twice, with the family. We searched for fossils on the beach, and there are always more being uncovered."

Good God. Uppercross. He'd been right to be cautious; it was only a few miles from Kellynch. This he understood from Sir Walter's endless tedious remarks about his ancestral seat, and those of his chilly, designing daughter. He would have to tread carefully; and yet, Musgrove's strong, lithe body ... and since he had no intention of further contact with the Kellynch branch of his family, nor of going anywhere near their residence, he could perhaps indulge himself a little.

"Uppercross is not far from here, I believe? I feel sure I heard the name at Sidmouth, where I changed horses."

"Oh, aye, my father's the squire there." Young Musgrove was letting him know that he was not without connections: a wise precaution which William mentally applauded. It did not mean that he might not be inclined for a little dalliance, though.

"You are close to home, then! I am not: on my way from Plymouth to London, and my friend at Exeter has been called away, so I find myself with a day or two at my disposal before I'm expected."

"There's plenty of interest around Lyme, sir. You'll not be bored." Another grin, almost a wink, tossed over his shoulder. "For me, I'm giving Uppercross a wide berth. They're not bad, my family, but there are such a devil of a lot of them! And my brother and his wife have just been blessed –" his voice took on an ironic tinge "– with a baby boy, thereby securing the succession. Mama will be clucky as a mother hen, and my father not much better. I'm staying out of it. They've already given the happy couple a whole house to themselves. That's money that could have gone to me, and the Devil knows I need it."

"We could all do with more money," murmured William, all sympathy. "So that's why you go to search for curios to sell. That shows admirable enterprise."

"Oh well, a fellow must live a little, and has expenses he doesn't want his father to know about! Especially if his father's a magistrate." *Good boy*, thought William. "I prefer to go my own way when I can. Though Lord knows Charles don't do anything to earn his keep, apart from marry the daughter of one of the local bigwigs. Miss Mary Elliot of Kellynch Hall, as was!" William pursed his lips in a silent whistle. "But all Charles does otherwise is shoot – nothing to deserve being the favourite. Apart from my youngest brother, of course. I'll wager they don't send Harry to sea! Not that I'm complaining. I like my freedom and I wouldn't get that at Uppercross. And my next younger sisters aren't bad brats, for girls – always up for a lark!

8

If I find a few fossils I might spare some for them. They're at school, and I don't see much of them, or I might be back at Uppercross now."

"Well, I'm glad you have some congenial company at home! Now, here's a conundrum: does our road take us left or right?" They had arrived at a hamlet, and William deflected the conversation from any reciprocal revelations of home life that might be expected.

Their way bent to the right – Musgrove and the signpost agreed on this – and the road sloped down into a warm, sheltered coomb full of frisking lambs and their mothers.

The travellers soon arrived at the steep little town of Lyme. William negotiated the narrow streets carefully, Musgrove talking the while about the *Callisto* (though if one were to talk of Jove's lovers, *Ganymede* might be more appropriate, thought William, by now quite determined to see what seduction might accomplish).

"Here's the place I told you of!"

They had fetched up in Broad Street, outside a small, dark shop, at the same time as the public coach. This made for a crowded and uncomfortable few minutes, as some passengers alighted and identified their luggage, and others bustled aboard, intent on securing the best seats.

William reined in to allow Musgrove to descend while the confusion was resolved, and turned the curricle into the yard of the Golden Lion almost opposite. Shortly he had made arrangements for the horses to be stabled and the curricle repaired. He secured a room, and the hostess promised to send a boy to the surgeon with news of Cooper's injury.

This necessary business done, he returned to the street, glimpsing Musgrove over the head of a spry old woman with a basket of preserves on her arm. He was conversing with a young girl, perhaps twelve years old, who had self-possession beyond her years.

"They'll need a deal of cleaning up, sir, but you know that. Couple of snake-stones, a devil's toenail, a few nice crocodile's teeth …" She was laying them out rapidly on her stall. "Will you wait a few minutes while I have a closer look at them, or will you come back? Ma will give you a receipt, don't you worry."

William listened to this very assured young person with some amusement, while he glanced at the rest of the curios on the stall. Some were very fine indeed: a doubled shell with the nacre still on it, what looked like a fern frond, all its leaflets wonderfully preserved, and a wickedly curved claw almost as long as his hand. He picked the shell up and it was heavy and smooth in his hand, a pleasure to hold, and the claw might well appeal to his wife.

"What is your price for these, Miss … ?" He ended on an interrogative note.

"Anning, sir." She bobbed slightly, but with self-possession; here was a young woman who knew her worth. "A crown."

He paid it without a murmur and with some amusement. A woman of middle years – Mrs Anning, he assumed – had emerged from the shop and was writing out a receipt for Musgrove's finds, for this young man had decided not to wait on the crowded street.

"I will take my parcel now, I thank you," said William to Miss Anning. It was small enough, and he could carry it himself.

"Don't forget to note that one of the snake-stones is left-handed. They're rare," Musgrove was instructing Mrs Anning.

"Aye, I'll write it down. Mary here will have a glance at them. There you are, young sir." This, in motherly tones, to the point of some irritation. "We should have a price for you by half past the hour."

The bustle was subsiding as she handed over the receipt. The way to the Golden Lion was now clear, and William said to young Musgrove, "I am thoroughly indebted to you, sir. I have an expedition planned for tomorrow, and have purchased some most interesting fossils. I hope you will be my guest for dinner," and he gestured at the Golden Lion, hoping that it ran to dinner at short notice.

Fortunately, the inn prepared its set dinner to coincide with the arrival of the coach. William and Musgrove were shown to a table by the window, through which William observed with amusement that Mary Anning was studying Musgrove's fossils with a magnifying lens.

"Your expedition was successful! I think your prizes have met with favour."

"A midshipman needs all the prizes he can lay hands on!" said Musgrove. "The King's Service don't pay well for us lowly fellows. It'll take more than a sea-fight or two for me to set up my carriage; the captain has the lion's share of the profits of any action, and any admiral within sight may claim a portion. Still, it's a living, when all's said and done – and there's less study than being a parson, or a lawyer."

"As it happens, I'm a lawyer myself." William observed with amusement how Musgrove mentally reviewed his words to ascertain that he had not been disparaging, and on satisfying himself of this, took a sip of coffee to cover the awkward gap in his conversation. "But I agree with you about the study that is necessary. No longer for me, though; my wife and I have a more leisurely existence. At the end of the week I will meet her in London; she is visiting old friends at the moment." Now why did he suddenly feel the need to mention his wife? But a little truth was easier to maintain than a wholesale lie, any lawyer knew that, and at some point soon, perhaps, he would reveal that he saw no need for strict – or even any – fidelity.

Indeed, this information was met with a guffaw. "So you're off the leash for a few days, then?"

William poured himself more coffee. "I am indeed off the leash."

"Well, there's not much of *that* sort of entertainment in Lyme!"

"Nevertheless, I find myself intrigued by the place." William regarded him over the rim of his cup. "These fossils of yours, and the mysterious under-cliff! I look forward to our expedition tomorrow. I wonder where I may procure a sketchbook?"

"The host will know – or the Annings. I believe the young girl is quite the natural philosopher already, and makes drawings of the better fossils. And if you've a mind to sketch, why, Pinny is your destination. A very romantical scene, and I thought to go that way tomorrow, since there's been a new rock fall; it may not have been picked clean as yet. I'll see what I can find there, and be your guide at the same time."

So simply was the assignation made.

The meal finished, Musgrove departed to speak to the Annings before going on to a smaller inn; and after a final stroll down to the Cobb to observe the tide lapping at the shore among the fishing-boats, and the nets draped against the clear evening sky, William went back to the inn.

The morning saw him waiting at the Cobb as the sun climbed beyond a thin white haze overlying the eastern horizon. The weather, he had been assured, would be mild and fair.

He was dressed in clothes suitable for walking, and armed with a sketch block purchased from the circulating library. This was stowed in a satchel, which would also hold any finds he might make. A couple of bags had already been sent on a carrier's cart to Pinny, for it had been decided over dinner that they would stay there that night, the walk there being so rough.

He employed his time while waiting for Musgrove by sketching a prospect of the under-cliff from his seat on a bench placed for the convenience of visitors. A whole quarter-hour passed, and he was beginning to wonder if the assignation was a failure, when the sound of a rapid approach reached his ears. On turning his head, he observed the latecomer trotting along the Cobb.

"Your pardon, sir! I overslept a little. Well, to be honest, I may have had a tot too many last night. It's hard to resist temptation, when you're not going to be roused out of your bunk at some godforsaken hour!" Musgrove's grin was rueful.

"It is of no moment, sir." William could have spoken this with a coldness that would freeze its hearer to the core, but his smile was friendly and his tone amiable. "Our gallant defenders deserve their rest! And I have been passing the time profitably: observe!" He turned the sketch block so that Musgrove could see his drawing of the under-cliff stretching away along the coast into the hazy distance. "It would be improved by the addition of a person for scale; if you will be good enough to stand just there ..." and he added the young man's figure, its lankiness fined down to elegance, and rose to his feet to show the result. Then he snapped the sketch block shut, and placed it in his satchel. "Now, sir. You are my navigator on this expedition; where do we go?"

"There's the path to Pinny." Musgrove pointed to a breakneck thread of a track, winding up the western headland, which gave William pause.

"You may call it a path, but I do not." He said this with his most charming and rueful smile.

Musgrove grinned and shook his head, plainly thinking that such a path was nothing to one who had spent time in His Majesty's navy. "I don't doubt you'll manage well enough." And his eye lingered for a moment on William's form.

Well, well, thought William.

Half an hour later they stood on the headland, looking down into the tumbled under-cliff, its boulders showing plainly through the budding trees and shrubs which found unsteady footing there. The onward path fell steeply away past a great spire of rock; the first step down was a good couple of feet.

Musgrove seized a branch, tested his weight upon it, and swung down onto the first tread of the giants' staircase. He turned, hesitated a moment, and extended a hand to William, who was standing above and regarding the descent with a rueful expression. Their glances met for a moment; Musgrove raised one eyebrow, head tilted to one side, and William took the hand.

That was most unusual in him, in any gentleman of the day. But he might as well nail his colours to the mast, to use a nautical metaphor, and now, as they descended into the warm, sheltered dimness of the under-cliff, was as good a time as any.

Musgrove's hand was strong, calloused, and warm; he steadied William with little apparent effort, and William retained hold of it for a moment longer than was strictly necessary. Musgrove smiled as he let go, turned away, and resumed his descent.

Their progress took him westwards along the under-cliff, a long strip of farmland which had descended abruptly and in thunder one night some forty years ago, and which had since become thoroughly entangled and overgrown, making it a place of great interest for visitors such as himself.

Now and then they stopped to survey the route onwards. It was a scene that would delight any artist: the cliff itself, its grey stone gleaming in the morning sun; the broken land along its foot, comprised of great blocks and spires of the same stone; the budding trees, draped with ivy and suchlike trailing plants and leaning drunkenly here and there; ferns everywhere, and the trilling of birds enough to delight any lady's heart. His wife, for instance, would be in transports were she to see it, and indeed he might bring her here at some point, since he bore her no particular ill will; but for now, he was very glad of her absence.

Musgrove was ahead of him most of the time, and in his round jacket, his thighs and shoulders working as he scrambled from rock to rock, he was a sight to distract anyone not made of stone. As fine an arse as William ever had the pleasure of beholding. All that running up and down the rigging, no doubt, or whatever it was that midshipmen did.

"Aha!" The sudden exclamation brought him out of his indulgent thoughts. Musgrove crouched over a scatter of rocks that had seemingly fallen very recently. William cast a thoughtful eye at the cliff-face; but there were no more rocks poised to fall, so he stopped beside Musgrove and watched his strong hands rake over the stones.

"This. D'you see? That's a fish, if I'm not much mistaken."

It was a perfect impression, in reverse, of such a creature; about three inches long. Musgrove was not satisfied. "If I can just find the fossil itself …" He reached here and there, and rapidly turned over all the rocks at hand, and William, close by, did the same in a more leisurely fashion. He was pleasurably aware of Musgrove's warmth, right next to him, and of the faint smell of sweat and tar emanating from his clothes; and thus distracted, it was no surprise that it was Musgrove who picked up the obverse of the fish, in a piece of stone the size of a volume of a novel, and held it in both hands, smiling widely.

"It's like no fish that I've ever seen," said William dubiously; not that he was about to dispute the nature of the animal, but simply to continue the conversation.

"The Annings had one just like it on their stall yesterday, right at the back," said Musgrove. "Ten shillings, too! The girl – Mary – wouldn't bargain, but that'll keep the price up for this one. I wonder! Are there are more like this? It'd be a capital thing if there was a shoal of 'em!"

So saying, he left William holding the stone and scrambled up the slope a little way, where he rummaged around, not unlike a questing spaniel. A short while later, he emerged from the scree, the trails of loose ivy and the burgeoning wildflowers with a triumphant cry. "Here are a couple more! Will you catch 'em, sir?" Without waiting for an answer, he tossed the stones down, one after another, and William caught them and set them down next to the first.

Musgrove launched himself back down the slope in a single leap, staggered as he landed, and William caught him before he could overbalance. For a moment, he tottered on the edge of a fall himself; the slope to the sea beckoned, but an out-flung foot saved them both. Musgrove's leg was hard against his inner thigh, his shoulders braced against William's arm, and they laughed into each other's eyes from a distance of less than a foot.

"Whew! Haven't quite got my land legs yet. Your pardon, sir!" His thigh flexed against William's as he stood upright again.

"Not at all. It's a steep spot, for sure. And wait, you have ivy leaves and God-knows-what on you." William's hands swept over Musgrove's shoulders and back, while keeping their stance close enough to be called an embrace. Musgrove, seemingly nothing loath, turned slowly while his coat was divested of the imaginary foliage. "Let me look at you. Yes, that will do. You are fit to be seen."

"I'm obliged to you, sir! Now, where are those stones?" And having spied them on the ground close by, he stooped to pick them up, giving William a very fine view of that arse, and stowed them away in his satchel. "Onwards!"

"How far is it to Pinny?" asked William, once he had his breath back, as they continued along the path, which now gave a good view of the sea to their left.

"Oh, two-three miles, I'd guess, from the charts. You'd think we could do it in an hour or so, but since the country's like this we'll be all morning at it," was the careless response.

"I'll make a sketch or two, if the prospect is as fine as this one." A remark that could be interpreted two ways; Musgrove was taking a long step up at that moment, and using his hands to steady himself. But out at sea there were ships to be seen, fishing-vessels, he presumed, and two larger ones passing half a mile from the shore. "Tell me, are those members of your – squadron, I suppose you'd call it?" He hesitated as if the word were unfamiliar, and Musgrove took the bait.

"Those are *Dido* and *Plassey*, which came in with us. They took some damage in the last blow, like us, so they're in home waters for now. We've brought dispatches in, and will take provisions out when the repairs are done. Life on the Western Squadron: we have our excitements, for sure!" And his tone indicated that it was anything but exciting.

Musgrove, engaging youth as he was, had an undeniable inclination to chatter.

So it went for the next hour or two, for they were much exercised to get themselves along the chaotic under-cliff. There were fresh falls of rock here and there. William, observing them, said, "A few days' rain and more will come down, I have no doubt."

"That would be the time to look for fossils!" Musgrove glanced around, seeking his route, and William pointed upwards to a place where the path they were on continued, with great nonchalance, at head height.

Musgrove surveyed the climb with some perplexity, and William said, "This will take both our efforts, I believe." He stooped a little, like a groom offering a leg-up to a rider, and Musgrove, with very little hesitation, placed his bent leg in William's hands. And then it was a matter of tossing him up – his lessons at the pugilist's salon in London had paid dividends in strength – and with a grunt of surprise, Musgrove found himself able to get his arms over the lip of the path. He paused there a moment, and tottered slightly as the earth and fine roots gave way under his hands; a firm grip on his thigh steadied him, and after a moment's pause, the muscles flexing in William's grasp, he hauled himself onto the upper level. Then he slewed round, his head of a height with William's, and laughing, eyes bright and hair all disordered, reached down.

"There's nothing for it, I'll have to pull you up," said he.

"You will need to take the bags first," William reminded him, and handed them up one by one. Then he jumped, caught Musgrove's shoulders, and scrambled up the declivity and up and onto Musgrove's prone body.

There was a confused moment in which his hands grabbed at whatever hold they could find – belt and hip and calf – while Musgrove's grip travelled from under his arms to his torso and somehow to his inner leg. And then he was up, perspiring, dirty, and laughing, and in the sorting out of a strange juxtaposition of arms and legs, came face to face with Musgrove, lying under him, and looking delightfully abandoned.

William propped himself on his elbows over the young man, but made no other move. "We appear to be closer acquaintances than a mere day would warrant," he murmured.

"Closer yet, if you fancy it."

"Oh, yes. I fancy it. I fancy *you*, Richard Musgrove." He dropped his head down for a kiss: all was delicious warmth and wetness, eagerness and little moans, especially when he got a leg between Musgrove's thighs and bent it upwards. Musgrove squirmed beneath him.

"Oh God, that's good. Just there. Yes, that's right. God. You know what you're doing."

"I should hope so." He hitched himself higher over Musgrove, as far as he could, for his leg was now firmly gripped between Musgrove's strong thighs, anchoring it just so, and delved his tongue deeper yet, bringing a

16

groan up from within the young man's chest.

"Here. We'd best get off the path." William suddenly remembered caution.

"I just need to fire my shot. *Now*." Musgrove was not interested in prudence.

"You can wait a few seconds."

A growl of frustration beneath him, but William rolled them into a kind of ferny bower beside the path, got their breeches undone somehow, mounted again and dug in his hips. The taut body beneath him gathered itself, arched hard against him, held for a moment, and fell back.

"Oh. Oh God. That's good." This was a breathy murmur against William's neck, which had somehow become divested of its cravat, and he could only grunt something in response before he too lost all awareness.

This blissful state could not, did not, last for long. Ferns dripped their moisture down William's exposed neck; a hitherto unsuspected branch was digging into his side; good God, was that a *leech* inching towards them along the damp ground? He scrambled to his feet and stamped on it with alacrity, and the two of them hastily adjusted their dress.

"We must get to Pinny immediately, and remove any of these creatures that we find." William moved his shoulders within his clothing uncomfortably.

"Aye, I'll search for them on you, if you like! And you can do the same for me. Salt is the way to deal with them." Musgrove was calmly knowledgeable.

"To the salt cellars of Pinny, then!"

The inn at Pinny was rustic, but sufficient to their needs, and their baggage had already arrived. The landlady was all solicitude, the more so when she heard of their encounter with the leech, and provided a battered but mercifully large salt cellar, which they took with them to their apartment. There they removed all their clothing, and in the close inspection for more leeches became quite at ease with each other's nakedness.

At the end of their hunt the last of the loathsome parasites dropped to the piece of sacking provided for the purpose. William, who had been inspecting Musgrove's back, said, "That's all of them, I think. We are both clear of them." He rolled up the sacking, and tossed it into the fire. Then he put his hands on Musgrove's shoulders, and whispered in his ear, with all the seductive power which he had cultivated over the years, "You are a very well-set up young man, you know."

"So I've been told," replied Musgrove, and leaned back against William, and arched, cat-like, in response to his stroking hand. "You're no weakling yourself."

"A gentleman's pursuits only. I have not climbed a ship's mast."

"Nor me, if I can avoid it! But sometimes there's no help for it, and *up* you must go."

William smiled, bit on his ear lobe, and his free hand slipped around the hard chest to play there. Musgrove gasped, and then there was silence for a while – but it was a busy silence.

A couple of hours later, in their private parlour, the inn's fare was found to be plain but adequate. "Yes, sirs, we're used to gentry like yourselves walking along the under-cliff – though not so much at this time of year! But come spring and summer, there are people arriving all the time with bags full of spars. Do you want the use of a hammer and chisel? My husband keeps some tools in the outhouse especial."

Six o'clock was certainly too early to go to bed, so for the space of three hours, Richard tapped and chipped at their fossils, though after an hour or so William took up his sketch block and pencil again and began to record some of their finds. Though no portraitist, he also essayed a sketch or two of Richard, a profile and a three-quarters face, and handed them to him with a slight smile as the clock struck nine.

"Oh, very fine – you've made me quite a handsome fellow!" said Richard, breaking into a smile. This gave his words a truth they had only slightly lacked before.

"No, keep them – they are yours," said William, as Richard made to return them.

"I'll tell the lads my sweetheart drew them," said Richard, folding them into his pocketbook. "A dark-haired lass to break your heart."

"Any more of the 'sweetheart' and I'll show you otherwise," said William, in mock threat.

"I don't believe you could," said Richard, with a martial glint in his eye, so William pounced on him, picked him up, not without a grunt of effort, and carried him over his shoulder through the connecting door to the bedroom.

The following day, William breakfasted alone, at ten o'clock or so. The hostess even provided a copy of *The Times* only a week old with a look of pride; brought in by a traveller from London, he presumed. Truly, the modern age was full of wonders, when news could be disseminated so quickly. He glanced through it, and a notice caught his eye of a philosophical meeting at Great Russell Street, with the display of a saurian fossil found at – good Lord – Lyme. Seemingly, the finding of fossils hereabouts could distinguish a man in London society.

His musings were interrupted just after eleven o'clock by the arrival of his young friend. Richard had the expression of a cat who had got the cream, and he smiled lazily at William, who gestured to the ruins of his excellent breakfast.

"I was up betimes, you observe; you will have to ring for more."

"Without more ado!" Richard pulled the bell-cord, and helped himself to William's coffee-pot while he waited.

When even Richard's pangs of hunger were assuaged, the pair left the inn, having sent their finds ahead to the Golden Lion. So they were but lightly loaded when they walked down a winding path beside a boggy stream, that descended by degrees into a valley and thence a rocky declivity, and found themselves once more in the strange country of the under-cliff.

After an hour or so of scrambling, they paused while William made a sketch of a particularly interesting prospect of rocks and leaning trees around a spring, from which issued a pretty waterfall; Richard meanwhile found a spot from where he could look out to sea. After that, they resumed their progress – and were very quickly lost. They stood beside a ruined cottage, quite bemused.

"I am sure we did not pass this on our way here," observed William.

"Nor I – though I did not mark our way closely: too shagged out, me!" Richard had taken off his hat and was scratching his head.

"It is all my fault, I see. Well, we shall simply have to search for the onward path; I will go this way, and do you go the other. We can convene here in half an hour, if not before; did you remember to wind your watch last night?"

"Of course I did. I'm not a complete noddy!"

On these words they parted, William going upwards and Richard down, and soon William found himself walking a narrow path at the base of the inland cliff. In another ten minutes he halted in astonishment. For there, in a boulder split in falling from the cliff, was a fossil the likes of which he had never seen. It looked like the offspring of a crocodile and a porpoise, with paddle-like limbs, and its skull possessed a long jaw full of teeth and a huge, staring eye socket.

For a moment he had the notion that the creature was about to turn and swim out of the rock in pursuit of him – which notion he swiftly dispelled. The thing was æons dead, after all.

But it was like nothing he had seen before, even in London. In a twinkling, he had a vision of himself at Great Russell Street, surrounded by admiring society, and giving an account of its discovery and removal. Perhaps it could even be named after him! *Pseudodelphinus ellioti* – no, that would never do. *Pseudodelphinus williami* would be better.

His dreams had taken him thus far in the space of a few seconds when he heard a crashing in the undergrowth, the sign not of some monster come to life, but of Richard, returning from his own scouting expedition. "That way's a dead end!" was his cheery shout, and William hastened to call back, "This, also!"

It would never do for Richard to know of the *Pseudodelphinus*; he would have it out of the rock in a trice and sold to the highest bidder, and there would go William's chance of distinction in society for the present. He hastened back to the main path. "We need to try further on." Through fern and entangling ivy he pushed, and made sure to let drop the curtain of ivy after him; though the fall of a stone drew Richard's eyes there for a moment. "Come, let's be off; that cliff-face is not over safe!"

He hustled – yes, that was the only word for it – the young man before him, down a sharp slope and into a green hollow ringed by slanting trees, in which a small pond gleamed through the gloom. On the far side of the hollow a path rose and turned around another fallen boulder.

"That's the way – we'll be fine now!" Richard seemed to have forgotten his interest in the cliff-face behind them, and ran light-footed down and around the little pond, and up the opposing slope. "Yes, there are boot-prints here, leading onwards."

"We are lost no longer, it seems." He must mark their way carefully in his mind, and keep Richard diverted; so, a while later, seeing a kind of natural amphitheatre above them, well concealed by shrubs and yet more ferns, he said solemnly, "This would be good place to stop and rest, do you not think?" And when Richard stopped to glance back at him, he let his hand stray around the young man's waist, and then slide lower and grip, and Richard said with feeling, "By God, you make the Commodore look chaste." But he pressed into William's hand, and was undoing coat buttons in a moment, before turning and scrambling up into the dell above them, which fortunately was lined with fern-fronds rather than rocks, and provided a very satisfactory bed when the coat was flung down upon it.

Further diversion was provided when, through a pleasant haze, William heard voices approaching. Reluctantly he opened his eyes, and caught Richard's merry regard. He had surely heard the voices too and was hard put to it to stifle giggles, judging by the ripples that ran through his body beneath William's. More listening convinced William that the voices were approaching along the very path from which he and Richard had scrambled up.

He made a stern face, and placed a finger on Richard's lips, which was, of course, a mistake, for it was instantly sucked in and nibbled. He hurriedly removed it, and waited for the inevitable.

Yes. The footsteps paused. "You'm willing, then?" came a young man's voice, and to this latter-day Corin's question came his Phyllida's reply, "Certain sure I'm willing!"

They were about to climb up. Richard raised his voice. "Friends, allow us a little privacy, if you don't mind!"

A moment's startled silence, and a girlish giggle. "Sorry, sir!" She had identified him as a gentleman – which was unfortunate but unavoidable. Richard curled under William's shoulder and shook with laughter.

The girl, now also laughing openly, called, "We'll leave you in peace. You enjoy yourselves, now!" The four of them, regardless of station, were caught in a moment's conspiracy, although each pair was invisible to the other. Then the footsteps moved on, and William lifted up slightly to let Richard breathe.

"Your expression!" said that young gentleman. "If ever I saw a look a fear on a man!"

"I have a name to lose, if you do not!"

"Mine was lost long ago. Come on, I'm getting cold." He sat up, flung aside the second coat, which had been draped sketchily over them, and reached for his shirt. "It'll be dinner time before we get back to Lyme."

"You are a youth of animal urges," stated William, dressing likewise, with some haste, for the air was truly chilly. "Am I to suppose that I will be paying for dinner?"

"Aye, indeed. And I'll pay you back later." This was spoken with a grin that left William in no doubt as to the nature of that recompense.

The journey back to Lyme was accomplished in an exhausted silence, though familiarity with the path made it seem somewhat shorter than had been the case the day before. Now in front, now behind, William continued to make mental note of the lie of the tumbled rocks, of a tilting tree here and the opening of the view onto the sea there. Richard, looking through such a kind of window in the tracery of branches, said knowledgeably, "Wind's on the change. Give it a day or two and there'll be a storm."

Out over the Channel, and in the upper airs, streaks of mares' tails were beginning to extend from west to east.

"What will that mean for you?"

"Nothing to the purpose, not while I'm on shore leave. But the poor devils in the Channel will know about it. I wouldn't be aloft tonight for all the world."

"The officers go aloft in storms?"

"Oh, aye, rain or shine, day or night," said Richard, with a casualness which astonished William. "I wonder how that scrub Johnson will manage? And MacArthur – he ain't too keen on the t'gallant yard at the best of times, ha!"

"You seem remarkably unfeeling, if I may so say, young Richard."

They had turned away from the sea view, and were continuing along the narrow path, but Richard, now leading, stopped short and looked back. "I've been at sea five years now, Mr William Walters. I've seen it all. You learn to get like that."

William, assailed by a surprising feeling of shame, was silent for a moment or two, before reaching out to clasp the youth's shoulder in apology. Richard nodded just slightly, and they continued on their way.

At last the familiar headland came into sight through the trees. They toiled up the final slope to its crest and looked down on Lyme in its bay, and the embracing arm of the Cobb.

"All downhill from now on," said Richard, with a new access of cheer; he had been noticeably quiet for the last half hour or so.

"I have taken the apartment for one more night; you see I have the gift of foresight. You will join me for the night, I hope, unless you have other accommodation arranged."

"A cheap bed at the Three Cups," said Richard. "Frankly, sir, your bedroom will suit me very well indeed!"

William's plans for the morrow were already well advanced. *Pseudodelphinus* could wait for the single day that it would take him to reach Bath; London was, unfortunately, too far to undertake the journey so quickly. But he would not entrust the fossil to the Annings. It would demean him to consult in any such capacity two females, and these were of such a lowly station in life. No, Bath was his best destination; there would be someone at the Rooms who would take a keen interest, and who would, moreover, establish William as the discoverer of the beast. And from there, London, and the notice and admiration of society, even if only for a day.

These thoughts occupied him as they gained the harbour, the town, and the Golden Lion, and as they changed for dinner; and to begin with, he steered the talk towards Richard's career, past, present and future.

"Do you plan to rise through the ranks?"

"Little chance of that! There's too much book-learning needed. If I get a thousand or so in prize-money, I'll leave the Navy and set myself up on land."

He might even do something for the young man, thought William. A frigate would give him a better chance at prizes than blockade-duty. Surely there was an acquaintance in London who had spoken of a friend at the Admiralty?

Their dinner over, their conversation turned back towards their finds.

"Not a bad haul, though the Annings will take their cut; as bad as prize-agents, be damned to them!"

"You cannot sell the fossils elsewhere? I would be happy to take them to London for you."

"No! but my thanks. Everyone goes to the Annings, and they're the best at preparing the fossils, so in the end you get a better price through them. I'll take 'em along in the morning," and he swept his fish and leaf-prints together and stowed them away in his satchel.

"You may take these as well, if you like." William pushed forward his own finds. "No, they're a gift. Only I will reserve a few of the better sort; my wife and her acquaintance will appreciate them as objects of conversation, if nothing else."

"Well, that's handsome of you! Every penny counts to one of His Majesty's midshipmen. And tell me, sir, how may I express my thanks?"

The candlelight on the table glinted on silver and glass, and gleamed on the youth's fair hair and sea-blue eyes, lighting up half a knowing smile; the fire crackled; from the taproom downstairs came a murmur of voices and a burst of song muted by the intervening walls. William smiled back. "You know very well."

It was a night such as William had not had in a long while. Richard did not even consider going back to the Three Cups, but stayed with William in the Golden Lion's best bedchamber. There they fully indulged their animal urges, as primal as the waves on the hard stones of the Cobb. As the clock struck midnight, William was poised, braced and rigid, on his hands, over Richard on all fours beneath. A couple of hours later, with the moon flooding in through the unshuttered window, he gazed down at Richard's fair head, busy at his most private parts, and involuntarily arched his own head far, far back as the most delicious sensations engulfed him. It took a while for him to near his consummation; and then Richard simply hauled him over onto his belly and whispered rough and intimate in his ear, "My turn now."

William, in no mood to resist, waited, panting, to be entered, and that was something he had never had before, but by God he would want it again. He cried out; Richard's arm slid under his face to muffle his mouth and he bit down on it; together they convulsed in sublime pleasure, and fell among the tangled sheets.

A while later, William mumbled, "Get off me, you great oaf. I cannot breathe." His face was crushed down among the pillows, his back protesting at the solid weight that lay inert upon it. But his tone conveyed only a token irritation.

Richard gathered himself, rolled off him, and blinked at him languorously in the moonlight. "That was good, was it?"

"You know damned well it was good. Where did you learn all that?"

"Here and there around the Med. You should go there sometime."

"One day I will. Not today. Or tomorrow." He was drifting into sleep; he had a dim sensation of a damp cloth cleaning him up in a perfunctory manner before being tossed to the floor, then was lost to the world.

A couple of times more in the night he woke, faintly aware of a warm body next to him, limbs flung wide in abandon and taking up far too much of the bed. The sea hushed just yards away; he could not tell the difference between its sound and the soft, steady breathing beside him, and fell back into slumber himself. The next time he woke, the moon had set and all was dark, the tide going out, he supposed, since its murmur was further off. He slept again.

And woke to an empty bed.

The room met his gaze with indifference; all was as it had been last night, but of his companion of the last two days, never a sign. Clothes gone, possessions gone, with only the towel and the rumpled and stained bedclothes to speak of his presence.

William felt an unexpected pang. He had been ready for more, knowing that this would be their last opportunity; indeed, had been hungry for more. But the lack of any sign of Richard meant that this was not to be. The weather was on the turn, rough seas were presaged; perhaps that had called him away.

Having woken, he might as well get up and be on his way. So he left the warm bed, and began to dress himself as best he might, and, halfway through that task, wishing to freshen the air in the bedchamber before the servants arrived, opened the window and leaned out. The sky was almost clouded over, the air was chill and breezy, and fitful gleams of sun fell here and there upon the roofs of the town and the headland beyond.

And on one other thing. Going down the street was a small procession, comprising a cart, a couple of rough workmen, and a woman and young girl – surely Mrs Anning and her daughter. At its head was a lanky figure, leading the way as if entitled to command.

"A cutting-out expedition, by God!" William pushed the other casement open and leaned out, the better to watch Richard Musgrove striding out towards the Cobb.

The cries of the seagulls mocked him. But some noise must have alerted the object of his regard, for he glanced back, and over a hundred yards of cold air their gazes met for a brief moment. William could swear that a grin crossed the young man's features, and certainly he lifted a hand in amiable greeting and salute which William, leaning in his shirtsleeves from the window, acknowledged. Then Richard turned back to resume his stolen march to dig *Pseudodelphinus'* bones from their resting-place.

"You've played and won, my fine sailor-man. I wish you the best. May you make all the money you could want from this!"

He turned back into the room, smiling a little as he donned his coat. That half-wave had warmed him, surprisingly; perhaps the young man had some kind of regard for him, since no acknowledgement was necessary. Certainly they had both acquitted themselves well over the last couple of days.

William could distinguish himself among his London friends some other way, and maybe he would speak to someone in the Admiralty and get the young man transferred to a better ship. Such determined self-interest deserved its reward, after all.

Two years later, in chilly and unprepossessing weather, he stopped again at Lyme, this time accompanied not by a midshipman of the Navy but by Cooper, his groom; and he stayed once more at the Golden Lion. He had followed, idly and at a distance, the career of Richard Musgrove; and the final sad report of his demise at Gibraltar had left William downcast for a surprising period. For some reason he had kept the sketch he had made that morning at Lyme, of a young man standing on the Cobb and looking out along the under-cliff, and he kept it still.

So he paused at Lyme on his present journey, as a kind of tribute, and reading in his bedroom that evening heard the noise and good cheer from the apartment next door which had been his. A night of unrefreshing slumber drove him out onto the Cobb early next morning, from where he looked across the grey waters of the bay to the indifferent under-cliff, and along which he now perceived a group of ladies and gentlemen proceeding toward him.

A remarkably pretty lady, one of them: not in the first bloom of youth, but she had a certain elegance about her. He touched his hat to her, and went on his way.

It was just a couple of months later, after making better acquaintance of that lady and her family, that he was passing through Bristol. In a tavern in the lower part of the town, in the midst of negotiations with a working woman, he caught a glimpse of a lanky, fair-haired young man so familiar to him that he was given pause. Richard Musgrove had mentioned that he came from a large family, but unless he had a twin brother, that was surely he. For a moment William stared; the noisy tavern seemed to fall silent, and the young man turned his head. Their eyes met, with a start of recognition on either side. Then, with almost a wink on the young man's part, he was gone, and William returned to his transaction with half his mind entirely elsewhere.

Author's Notes

The Undercliff is one of the strangest and most significant landscapes in Britain. Jane Austen herself was moved to lyrical writing about its romantic appearance; and when she stayed in Lyme she had dealings with the father of the great fossil hunter, Mary Anning.

The museum's website is here:
lymeregismuseum.co.uk/collection/landslips-and-landscape/

Lou Faulkner

I live in a little house with a big garden in the far south of the world, and most of my life has revolved around books: selling them, lending them out, and more recently, writing them. Apart from bibliophilia, I've done a variety of different things, including years spent learning falconry, and I enjoy trying hands-on pursuits that might give me material for my stories: blacksmithing, tall-ship sailing and flying. I will attempt things in my writer's persona that I would never contemplate as myself: this does not, however, extend to bungy-jumping.

One Half of the World

Adam Fitzroy

Emma Woodhouse, handsome, clever, and rich, and possessing not the least disposition in the world to enter the married state, had for some years past devoted herself to humouring the whims and fancies of an ailing father. Her steadfast intention had been to remain single as long as he should be in need of her support – and when, at last, he had passed beyond her power of comforting, she was confident of being old enough to have removed her far from the notice of any intending suitors with pretensions to eligibility.

The dispositions of Emma's parents had assured her of her independence. A substantial inheritance from a mother who had died when Emma was four years old, and a life interest in Hartfield reversionary upon her eldest nephew, were hers so long as she continued unattached. Indeed, whether in Emma's mind any man living could transcend the attractions of Hartfield and an income must always be open to question, and her marrying could therefore be considered neither advantageous nor disadvantageous, with nothing save personal inclination to influence her in one direction or the other.

Such a question, however, was rarely in Emma's thoughts; daily attendance on her father, together with a wearying round of paying and receiving calls, left little opportunity for philosophical reflection had she been inclined to it. Moreover there were servants to be directed, meals to command, the management of Hartfield to be overseen; these accomplishments she had acquired from Miss Taylor, who had but lately departed to become the wife of Mr Weston. Indeed, Mr Woodhouse had not yet left off mourning the loss to the household of 'poor Miss Taylor' – just as, at an earlier period, it had wanted two whole years and the baptism of a grandson before he had reconciled himself to his daughter Isabella's marriage with Mr John Knightley – and it was not to be expected that he would be inured to Miss Taylor's leaving any sooner.

The parting from Miss Taylor had afflicted Emma differently. Since Isabella's marriage, her governess had been Emma's sole and most constant companion; with Miss Taylor she had been accustomed to converse about books, art, poetry, flowers, everything that was not commonplace and workaday and dull. With her father she could sometimes talk of literature, it was true – of Shakespeare and the Bible, or *Paradise Lost* or *Robinson Crusoe* – but latterly, as the power of his eyesight had begun to decline, it had become Emma's duty to read to him from whatever book or journal took his fancy. And sometimes to read over again the passage she had read the previous day, and to discuss it in the same terms, because he had forgotten ever having heard the words before.

Society at Hartfield was necessarily circumscribed, although Emma's brother-in-law, Mr George Knightley of Donwell Abbey, could be counted upon whenever he was in the country and so could the invaluable Westons. Beyond them a few county families might sometimes be prevailed upon to travel to dine or sup, but Mr Woodhouse's dislike to evening parties – and his superstition of anything involving inclement weather – were so well known in the neighbourhood that the number of invitations received as a result was small, and these were necessarily often declined. Serle's cooking was of such celebrated excellence, however, that when company was wanting at Hartfield there were single ladies enough living nearby to make up any party; Mrs Bates, the widow of a former vicar; her daughter, a garrulous old maid whom Emma could not but think absurd; Mrs Goddard, the proprietress of a school for young ladies of the middling sort. And Mrs Goddard had lately asked if she might be permitted to introduce to the Woodhouses a pupil of hers, a certain Miss Harriet Smith.

Miss Smith's origins were unknown – even, it appeared, to herself. Mrs Goddard had received her from a lawyer acting for someone with charge of her upbringing, and could say only that nothing had been wanting in Harriet's education which money could supply. She had learned drawing and music, had read, had acquired what graces and deportment a provincial establishment could impart, and – now that she was becoming of marriageable age and the discharge of her guardian's duty lay ahead – nothing lacked but such polish as could only be furnished by example. Mrs Goddard urged the benefit of Harriet's meeting with a society superior to her own and praised Emma's value as exemplar, which overture was so complimentary it could not possibly be denied. Accordingly, shortly thereafter, Miss Smith and Hartfield each made the acquaintance of the other.

In truth, Harriet was of more decorative value than intellectual. Demure and respectful, her discourse fell something short of inspiring; however she was flatteringly inclined to attend to whatever she was told, her guileless blue eyes widening prettily as she weighed and digested every treasured syllable, and Emma did not at all object to being admired by her.

Mr Woodhouse, too, was much taken with Miss Smith. He thought her a good sort of little girl, who might well be forgiven the ill-considered conduct of her parents. He approved of her, too, as a friend for Emma, now that she was deprived of the company of Mrs Weston.

"She is so appreciative of your notice, my dear," he told her, more than once. "The encouragement of Miss Woodhouse of Hartfield can only be beneficial to her. You might bring her out a little, you know. You might be of inestimable assistance in establishing her."

That the idea was attractive Emma could not deny; she believed it would be delightful to be the means of further perfecting one who already possessed such charm of person and character, and had that been the sole inducement for cultivating Harriet she would still have given the project her ready acquiescence. The notion of standing in the place of Miss Taylor to a pupil of her own, however – of winning from her the love and affection Emma had felt towards her governess – why, such a duty was one from which in all conscience she might not voluntarily excuse herself.

Nor would she willingly surrender the society of a girl as lovely as Harriet. Unformed and incomplete as she was, she had the advantage of a cloud of fine-spun golden hair and eyes of an unsullied sapphire; small, pink-cheeked and healthy, quick to laugh, light of foot, with a natural elegance which wanted only a little refinement, she would be a worthy object of Emma's attention – and in due course, if a suitable opportunity should present itself, Emma would undertake to secure a match for her with some unexceptionable husband. Few men in Highbury, she acknowledged, could equal the amiability and distinction of a Mr Weston or a Mr John Knightley, but it should not be beyond the wit of an Emma Woodhouse to lay hands upon a worthy partner for her friend.

It was Emma's proud boast, indeed, that she had made the marriage between Mr Weston and Miss Taylor, and its subsequent happiness had confirmed her in the belief that she was uniquely accomplished in this regard. It seemed to her that she enjoyed an understanding of human nature others lacked, an ability to judge people to a nicety and conjure for them matches that were both rational and expedient. For Harriet in course of time, therefore, she determined upon Mr Elton, a dressy young man of a certain agreeableness, not long installed as vicar of Highbury. Small endeavour was required upon her part to convince Harriet of Mr Elton's love for her, although Mr Elton himself was not so easily to be influenced. Moreover, so far was he from a consciousness of Harriet's qualities that at Christmas that year he even ventured to propose marriage to Emma herself – a predicament from which she was extricated only at the expense of some great personal mortification and embarrassment.

Mr Elton was lowered irredeemably in Emma's judgement by his actions on this occasion; she had discovered him to be driven solely by considerations of wealth and consequence and no true feeling towards herself; she had seen through the lustre of his deportment to the base alloy which lay beneath it. And yet, when she could spare time to reflect further upon the matter, it was not merely as the unwilling object of Mr Elton's advances that Emma felt the enormity of his conduct; it was also, and chiefly, for the sake of Harriet, on whom she had come so alarmingly close to inflicting him as a husband.

The night that followed Mr Elton's proposal was both long and dark. Alone in her room Emma turned his declaration over in her mind and considered its meaning, deprecating her own unwitting collusion in the scene. His impertinence in itself might almost be tolerable, she conceded; she was of an age and position in the world to which adventurers must inevitably be drawn, as Mrs Weston had been at pains to caution her, and small blame could attach to him for that; it was no worse than many another young man might have ventured in his place. Yet Emma would not have allowed herself to be alone with Mr Elton even for a moment had she received any presentiment of his wishes; she had thought his passions to be directed solely towards Harriet, and had never once acknowledged that she herself might be his object.

How narrowly had they both escaped catastrophe! Had his conduct been only a little less venal, his ambition only a little less vaunting, Mr Elton might have made his proposal to Harriet instead; she would not be without a modest marriage portion of her own, her unknown guardian would see to that, and a less determined man might well have reckoned it sufficient. But, had he married Harriet, how quickly afterwards must Mr Elton have shown his true colours – and how profound must have been her subsequent disappointment! He would surely have run at speed through whatever fortune she brought him, indulging his taste for all that was new and fashionable and pleasing to the eye – and what would have been the end of it? A child a year until Harriet was quite worn away, supposed Emma, because a man like him would never be denied his posterity; afterwards, a long rest in a corner of the churchyard while her husband scoured the county for a successor. Clearly, to Mr Elton, a wife's value lay only in such social advantage as the marriage could convey; he did not, she concluded, place any importance on affection in domestic life.

That Emma had been mistaken in his character she now saw. She had come close to consigning her friend in marriage to a man wholly without scruple, and in doing so had risked compassing Harriet's utter destruction – and Harriet herself had been wholly unaware of the peril she was in. This was a circumstance, felt Emma, which could not be borne with a moment longer than was necessary, and as soon as the weather might be propitious – as soon as Christmas should be over and the guests departed – she had determined to go to Harriet, to unburden herself and beg forgiveness of her. She had erred, she knew, and gravely, but with timely action was sanguine of amending matters so far as might be possible to do – although Harriet's heart, she was afraid, might well have been broken beyond her power of restoring it.

Emma found her friend pale, red-eyed and weak, as if she had already endured a month of weeping; Harriet had been excluded from the Christmas festivities at Hartfield by a cold which had obdurately refused to leave her, and although she was now once again in health she still bore upon her features the emblems of its passing. She was sitting in her bedroom at Mrs Goddard's house, wrapped warmly, a newspaper and a pile of letters readily to hand, and when the servant brought in Emma she sprang up and greeted her eagerly.

Emma declined Harriet's invitation to seat herself beside the fireplace;

she must be the bearer of bad news, and to be comfortable at such a juncture was insupportable to her feelings. Instead she stood watching the flames that flickered in the hearth.

"Harriet, my dear, you must prepare for a disappointment," she began. "Mr Elton is gone from Highbury – and gone, I am afraid, quite out of countenance with me; I have offended him too far and too greatly soon to be recovered from, I think."

Harriet's astonishment was great, and her foremost inclination to demur. "Oh! – but I'm certain you could never – I mean, Miss Woodhouse, surely it must be impossible –" However she was unable to reconcile denial of her friend's guilt with the discourtesy of rejecting her confession altogether, and stumbled inarticulately into silence. "I am sorry indeed to hear it," she continued, recovering. "I am confident there must have been a misunderstanding. I cannot believe that you had any intention of offending him."

"Oh, but I did!" exclaimed Emma, warmly. "When I learned what it was he wanted, I said whatever I could to prevent him speaking to me any further. He had asked, you see – He had asked me if I would be his wife."

"Good heavens!" It was the strongest expression ever to have passed Harriet's mild lips, provoked as it was by astonishment rather than sorrow or despair. "Oh, but it demonstrates such excellent judgement on his part; indeed, I would hardly have thought him equal to it!"

Taken aback at this response, Emma could say little to the purpose but "Indeed, Harriet? Surely what it demonstrates is ambition coupled with an absence of refinement?" She explained to her friend how Mr Elton had intruded himself upon her in her carriage after visiting the Westons at Randalls, and how he had declared himself in love with her and evidently expected her to demonstrate a similar devotion in return.

"But if he loves you – ?" began Harriet, and then could find no words with which to continue.

"*If* he loved me," said Emma, "the strength of my answer would surely have wounded him, but I believe he is not and has never been in love – except, perhaps, with himself! He is not a man of emotions, Harriet; he is calculating and entirely concerned with his own advancement, and he thought a few syrupy words and hackneyed sentiments would induce me to accept him. He was too presumptuous, too forward, and esteems me too little if he imagines I can be taken in by such obvious hypocrisy! It does him no credit that he thinks so meanly of me – or indeed of any woman else!"

Emma spoke more vehemently than she had intended to. Having begun by offering comfort and commiseration to Harriet upon the loss of Mr Elton, she had gradually become so conscious of his impertinence in making an advance towards herself that it fell to Harriet, now, to offer her such consolation as she could.

"Oh, Miss Woodhouse, how could we ever have been so deceived in him? He always seemed so perfectly amiable! But then –" Harriet stopped, appearing to weigh her words with greater care. "Mrs Goddard says men always do seem amiable until they have what they want, and after that they change. How dreadful it must be to marry a man, and to love him dearly, and then to find him altered! There would be nothing certain any more, and nothing safe – truly, I wonder that any woman ever has the courage to marry at all, if that is how men are."

"Not every man, Harriet," said Emma, feeling that notwithstanding her present despondency it was incumbent upon her to defend the generality of her male acquaintance. "Mr John Knightley is as good a man as ever was; he is kind to my sister and their children, and so is his brother. And as to my father –" It would, perhaps, be appropriate to make some commendatory remark concerning her father's qualities as a husband, and yet she had been afforded very little opportunity of observing his conduct towards her mother and perhaps she had better say nothing at all about that. Nor did he ever, now, make allusion to Mrs Woodhouse or to the life they had known together. "Well, at least he did not marry again after my mother died, and no doubt he could have had his choice of ladies. He might easily have married Miss Bates, after all."

"Yes, but he had learned, do you see – At least," continued Harriet in confusion, "Mrs Goddard believes that when he came to understand how sorely Mrs Woodhouse had been tried during her confinements, and how greatly she suffered, he could never be the cause of inflicting such distress upon anybody ever again. She honours him for it, truly she does – but she says that, if he had not been half so anxious to be the father of a son, your mother might still have been alive today."

This sentiment indeed was justified, as Emma could not help admitting, although Mrs Woodhouse had never truly been strong; Isabella had confided as much to her, and had expressed misgivings of her own when the birth of her first baby was imminent. Young Henry Knightley, however, had made his way into the world without inflicting an excess of travail upon his mother, and Isabella had learned never again to be afraid of her children's coming.

"Marriage is not an unmixed blessing for everyone," agreed Emma. "Mrs Weston is at present very happy indeed, and Mr Weston seems the very model of a husband, but that need not always be the case. If he should change, or they suffer some reverse of fortune, she would be the sufferer and not he. Indeed I wonder, Harriet, whether any two people can ever live in harmony where a man enjoys sovereignty over his wife and she none over him. People who are married can never be equal as long as a wife must always promise to obey her husband."

"Oh, yes, indeed, and that is so truly to the purpose! Whom does a man ever promise to obey, after all? His commander, I suppose, if he is in the Army, or his employer, or his father – but he may part from those whenever he chooses, and then he need never be obliged to obey anybody's orders ever again."

Emma might have questioned that a man could leave either his family or his occupation entirely at will, but she was compelled to admit the general justice of Harriet's pronouncement.

"God," Emma said, uncertainly. "He promises to obey God, does he not?"

"So do we all," countered Harriet. "And why should a man's service to God be greater than a woman's, except that men wish it to be so?"

"Goodness, Harriet! If you continue to talk like that, I may begin to wonder how you ever came to hold such radical opinions. Have you been reading about politics in the newspaper?"

"I have, a little, but that has not been half so interesting as some letters Mrs Goddard has been good enough to show me. They are from two friends of hers who –" And there Harriet paused, as if a presentiment of alarm had come upon her suddenly and she could not quite determine how it might be wisest to proceed.

"Why, Harriet, whatever is the matter?" For there could be little doubt that some feeling of momentary discomfort had interrupted her companion's discourse.

"Dear Miss Woodhouse! But I'm not sure whether I may say or not; they are two ladies, you see, who live their lives entirely without gentlemen."

It wanted a moment or two before Emma could fully comprehend the substance of Harriet's utterance, and then, "But so do Mrs and Miss Bates," she said, in some confusion.

"Yes, but it was not always so – and they are mother and daughter, so it is not at all the same thing; there was, at one time, Mr Bates at least! Mrs Goddard's friends live together because neither of them has ever wanted to be married to a man; they eloped when they were quite young," said Harriet, the words bringing a very pretty colour to her cheek. "Think of it, Miss Woodhouse: one dressed as a gentleman and stole the other away through a window, and her father was obliged to go after her and bring her home – and said she must go as a nun, but she told him she would not!"

"Oh!" Tangled and disorderly as this speech had been, Emma had extracted from it the sense of some adventure, absurdly romantic in nature, concerning the elopement of two women, and believed she had heard something of the sort before. "Do you mean the two Irish ladies? But that was thirty years ago or more!"

"More, indeed! Mrs Goddard knew them when they were in Ireland, and has been their friend in all that time, and they are still contented in their choice – and what marriage between a man and a woman could truly be more felicitous than that? They can choose the company they keep, and manage their own purses, and they need not be troubled by any unpleasantness –"

"Unpleasantness? Why, Harriet, do you think there is anything unpleasant in the company of men? Do you dislike their talk, or is it perhaps the aroma of tobacco? I will admit that there may be objections to the society of individual men – such as Mr Elton, for example – but on the whole I find them perfectly unobjectionable as a species."

"Oh, no, indeed, in general society men may very well be charming, and may flirt and give compliments and suchlike, and there may be no offence given in the world and none taken I am sure – but in private – when they want children – and when it is our duty as wives to do whatever they require of us –" Here confusion again seized Harriet, halting her maladroit stuttering with the sentiment only half-expressed. "Were you never afraid of it, Miss Woodhouse? Of being at the disposition of a husband who might ask too much of you, I mean? I am, and I confess I think I always shall be."

This was dangerous ground indeed. Emma herself had raised a similar question when Isabella's marriage had first begun to be spoken of; how could her sister or any woman be assured of being treated by her husband with consideration and respect?

"Surely," she said, "if the gentleman is honourable he will never try to enforce his will upon his wife counter to her own inclinations, and never be the cause of giving her any inconvenience in the world?"

"Well enough," exclaimed Harriet, "if he is! But he may just as easily be a dissembler or a cheat, or be a gambler or keep actresses – and he may run through his wife's money and grind her reputation into dust, and she may end by being no happier than if she had stayed at home and looked after her mother instead like poor Miss Bates."

"But Miss Bates is living very reduced," replied Emma. "Think, Harriet, how much better it would have been had a husband presented himself when she was younger; he could have cared for her and for her mother both, and they would never have been short of coals or meat or tea or anything else ever again."

But Harriet could not easily be consoled. "If it were a choice between marriage and poverty," she said, "I believe I would rather be poor, and then I need not be beholden to the whims and fancies of a husband! If one must marry, a pleasant gentleman like Mr Weston is to be preferred – but how much more romantic must it be to be stolen away in the night by a lady dressed as a man, to be thrown across the saddle of her horse and to be galloped off with across the moors by moonlight? Think of it, Miss Woodhouse: boots and spurs and ruffles, and carrying a whip!"

"Oh!" And there was no denying that such a notion provoked in Emma a singularly powerful sensation, although whether she would prefer to have been the one carried off or to have done the carrying herself she could not truthfully say. However, the fallacy of Harriet's argument was soon apparent to her, and she did not neglect expatiating on the point. "And live on what, pray? 'apricocks and dewberries, purple grapes, green figs, and mulberries'? There must be money, Harriet, for whips and spurs and ruffles – and more for horses and carriages and wayside inns. Romance, and dreams, are all very pleasant, but the world is not made of dreams; the world is made of rules, and rules are made by men, and whatever a woman possesses of her own is only hers because some man or another has permitted her to have it. There are few women capable of supporting themselves by respectable means," she added, "although Mrs Goddard is among them, and Mrs Weston was before she married. A woman might run a school, but there may be little money in it – and it would be hard work, I think." And, if it could be considered unkind of her to have trampled upon Harriet's romantic dream, Emma was consoled by the conviction that it would be crueller still to allow her friend to be led astray by the power of some elusive but enchanting chimera.

"Certainly," admitted Harriet, with complaisance. "But there are some women who have money of their own. They, at least, have the freedom to pursue romantic objects their parents may not approve of. The Irish ladies are somewhat supported by their families, I believe, and they also farm in a small way."

"Do you know anything about farming, Harriet?" There had been, earlier in their acquaintance, uncomfortable talk of a sojourn with the Martin family of Abbey-Mill-Farm; Harriet had been their guest for two months, and had settled so very happily among the Martins that Emma had begun to fear an attachment between her friend and young Mr Martin. Wiser counsels had prevailed, however; it had become clear that Mr Martin's regard was not nearly so necessary to Harriet's continued happiness as Emma's own.

"No. That is to say I have collected eggs, and picked beans and apples, and brushed a horse's coat, but I could not well say what to do to feed a chicken or to grow a bean or shoe a horse – but the Irish ladies do not concern themselves with such commonplace matters either; they employ men and boys about the village to do the work for them – or so I have been told."

"Doubtless," said Emma, wishing that the example of the Irish ladies might never have been adduced in the first place, so tiresome had mention of their circumstances become. "And have they any society that could justifiably be called polite? For that is another disadvantage of romantic elopements, I am sorry to say – that nobody of any quality will be able to recognise them, and they will be obliged to live their lives among people of a very different sort. Indeed they might just as well rake their own hay and milk their own cows, for those who do such things daily will be their only friends. To be born to consequence and wilfully to put oneself into the position of an inferior is not merely a degradation, Harriet, it is rejecting the kind family which has provided everything for the happiness and security of its members. If she turns her back upon it, she chooses what will make her relatives and herself thoroughly miserable ever after."

"Oh, but it is only because they are both ladies that they lack the power of rising in the world!" returned Harriet with spirit. "A man who marries a woman against her family's wishes may end by earning their regard, but such a course is not open to a woman who cannot prove herself by entering Parliament or the Church – or distinguish herself in the Army or medicine, or bring honour to her name in any other way. A woman who has once fallen from her family's esteem can never recover her position, it seems to me – and so, surely, if she has any discrimination, she will never take an extraordinary course of action unless she believes it is her truest chance for happiness. If one of those Irish ladies had been a man, Miss Woodhouse, or you or I …"

"Why, Harriet, whatever are you saying? Do you consider our situations to be in any particular worthy of comparison?"

And could any comparison indeed be possible, thought Emma, between herself and the two Irishwomen – who must now, she supposed, be of considerably advancing years? They had been born to gentility – and one to a noble name – but had, quite recklessly and as it seemed in the throes of an inexplicable passion, chosen to forsake the benefits and protections of a comfortable existence in order to pursue an attachment which lay wholly beyond the confines of society. Did anyone doubt that the two lived, as it were, in a state of marital harmony? It had long been whispered that one or other, or both, had sometimes dressed in masculine attire, and that they were generally considered frights and unnatural creatures. For herself, beyond a certain prurient and – she acknowledged it! – *vulgar* curiosity concerning the nature of the intimacies that might pass between them, Emma had devoted very little thought to any minor points of correspondence between the circumstances of the Irish ladies and her own.

"Oh, no, indeed! – that is to say, yes, in some respects, it is very like! You have said that you never will marry, you know, unless you can better your condition – like Queen Elizabeth, who said that she was happy in the single state and persuaded herself there was no other kind of life comparable to it – and you are already Emma Woodhouse of Hartfield, which is not a condition capable of being improved upon unless some husband of extraordinary distinction should chance to recommend himself."

"You suggest, do you Harriet, that I have set myself too high a standard, and that like Queen Elizabeth I will never be presented with a husband who is in any way capable of meeting my expectations? You believe I am in danger of dying an old maid?" It was a criticism with which Emma was only too familiar, and to which she had on many occasions been subjected by those who felt certain they understood what would be best for her. Had it not been for her father's particular desire to keep her at his side, and his morbid aversion to change in any form, Emma might easily have found herself under considerable persuasion to accept a proposal of marriage even less attractive to her than that of Mr Elton.

"I believe," said Harriet, "that there is hardly a man in England who could fairly consider himself your equal, and I myself have not so far been privileged to encounter one. Would it not be reasonable to suppose that no such man exists, and that he can therefore never be expected to address himself to you? And if that is acknowledged to be the case, dear Miss Woodhouse, could not you and I instead live together in affection after the manner of Mrs Goddard's friends, and resist whatever temptations may come our way of marrying anybody *else*?"

There was no denying the extravagance of such a sentiment, although its meaning fell somewhat short of perfect transparency. That Harriet was unwilling to be separated from her was easily comprehended, but the exact quality of her stated devotion remained obscure.

"You would like me to take you as my companion?" asked Emma, cautiously. "Truthfully I had not considered making any arrangement of the sort quite yet, although I have long ago concluded that, when my father no longer has need of my attendance, yours would be the company I sought. You will understand that Hartfield is not mine at present, Harriet, and the power of invitation must therefore remain with him, although it is conceivable that perhaps – in time – I might be able to persuade him to it."

That this declaration was a source of satisfaction to Harriet was apparent in the pinkness of her cheek and the brightness of her eye, and also in the fulsomeness of her rejoinder.

"Oh yes, indeed – and, if Providence is kind, dear Mr Woodhouse will be spared to us for many seasons yet! But how delightful it would be, would it not, to live together as one – under one roof? Just think how congenial it would be never once to be parted from one another – not even at night-time, and not even in bed!"

Emma found herself almost at a loss to answer. She had thought that such utterances, when they came, would fall from the lips of men rather than of women, and had never once entertained the likelihood of receiving a similar proposition from the distaff side of her acquaintance, yet here was Harriet very nearly declaring herself in proper form – omitting only the bended knee and the unaffected summary of her material prospects, which calculation was of no particular interest to Emma who was more than capable of supporting a dozen Harriets if need arose. It would be as well, nonetheless, to remove from their discourse anything which tended to misapprehension, and to have their meanings clear.

"These words, Harriet, if they had been spoken by a gentleman, would no doubt be the preliminary to a formal offer of marriage. Indeed, if *a certain person* had spoken so to me, it would not have been as simple a matter to reject him as it was."

It was half in her mind to scold Harriet for her forwardness, to tell her that her suggestion was no less presumptuous in its way than that of Mr Elton – but what in him had manifestly been ambition, and perhaps pardonable speculation, had become in Harriet a matter of singular gravity. Emma had been certain that the gentleman's emotions were not engaged, and there had been little danger in rejection of doing any damage to his heart; that it was otherwise with Harriet could scarcely be gainsaid.

"Why," exclaimed Harriet, "if there could ever be such a marriage, I should scarcely have anything resembling a rightful claim to proffer it – and yet, perhaps because I know it is nonsense, I believe it may not be improper to advance the suggestion. Have you never in your life, Miss Woodhouse, desired to do something utterly shocking, to fly in the face of what is accepted and even – if it must be – to invite ridicule? Must one always be safe and never be extraordinary? Have you never once considered the merits of – of *adventure?*"

"Good heavens!" An upwelling of spirits unsettled Emma's composure, and she moved to stand beside the window. Harriet remained seated, but continued to observe her closely. "Do I understand you aright, Harriet? You would live, would you, without society – and without money – for the sake of a woman who would woo you as a man? Would you have me dress in breeches and steal you away out of a window? Out of this very window, perhaps, although we would need a good long ladder? Elope with you, in short, contrary to the wishes of our families and our friends, and retire with you somewhere quite out of the world?"

"Oh, no! That is to say – it is perhaps not necessary to assume male attire, although the notion of it is an intriguing one, but I feel sure that a woman must always be happy as long as she is with whomever it is she loves. If she is fortunate enough to marry a man and love and trust him, so much the better for her – but if she is devoted to her mother, as Miss Bates is, or to her child, or to a friend of her own sex as I am to you, then surely it is better for them to be together than apart! Do you not agree with me, Miss Woodhouse?"

"My dear Harriet, you have such romantical notions! And you would never be lonely, would you, having the companionship of that one person who was dearer to you than any other in the world?"

"Dearer than all the others put together," affirmed Harriet. "Surely you cannot be unaware of it?"

"I am not unaware," replied Emma, for it had begun to feel to her as if she had known it all along. Harriet, having made a most deliberate accumulation of her feelings, had exposed them with honest and delicate care and laid them at Emma's feet in little expectation of return. As to her own emotions, it would be foolish to pretend that they were disengaged. That she had encouraged Harriet's friendship less from a genuine spirit of benevolence and more from a desire to fashion for herself a constant and devoted companion Emma was no longer able to dispute, and yet she had also learned to value the refreshing innocence of Harriet's conversation and to enjoy the undemanding warmth of her affection. That Harriet was prepared to adore her had always been an important consideration in Emma's appreciation of her friend, but now she understood, too, that Harriet had both courage and spirit and was prepared to defy convention for her sake.

There appeared to Emma, as she considered it, not the least reason in the world for refusing Harriet; that she was female and the expectations of society would have her partner with a man seemed wholly insufficient – could she feel for any husband half, even a quarter, of what she felt for Harriet? It did not seem possible.

"If it were only as simple as that. And you in turn – Harriet, please!" For her friend had started, and would have made to move towards her had Emma's outstretched hand not stayed her. "My dear, of course – But it is not enough merely to love, is it? One must always be practical. I shall have you as my companion one day, when – when we are older – if some young gallant does not steal you away from me beforehand – but until then –"

"Until then it will be necessary to wait. Yes, indeed, I fully apprehend your meaning; there can be nothing more between us while your dear father is so happily in health." And Harriet had never, perhaps, sounded quite as wise nor as sensible in her life before – nor as reduced in spirit. "And we will still have our friendship, will we not? Oh, but waiting is always such a trial!"

Emma's first instinct was to acknowledge the righteousness of this complaint, although it was not a subject upon which she had ever been given cause to expend much thought before. Harriet's idea of an elopement, however, having both alarmed and delighted her, she now began to wish that she might have been the sort of bold, impetuous creature who would be capable of contemplating such a scheme. To be galloping across farmland in the dark with Harriet pressed tightly against her would be a thrill beyond measuring – and yet her rational sense scolded that it wanted only a rabbit-hole and a misstep by the horse and down they would tumble, neck and crop, into cabbages, or nettles, or worse.

"But wait we must," she acknowledged, "nevertheless; Hartfield does not belong to me – nor will it, perhaps, for many years. To do the honours of a house is not at all the same thing as owning it."

"Yes, I know. But we may make a promise to each other, may we not? A pledge that we will marry no one else, at least?"

"Of course we may, although there is nothing to warrant the keeping of such a pledge. There is no law to govern promises that may be made between two women, after all."

"We need none!" declaimed Harriet robustly. "What can law accomplish that true affection cannot? I assure you I should never give my word on this or any other matter without wholly purposing to keep it."

"And nor should I, but I have made many good and well-meaning schemes before which have come to nothing – and I meant to keep my word on every one! I am a fanciful, troublesome creature, Harriet, and I do not altogether know if my word is ever to be relied upon."

Harriet looked as if she might very well have disputed this, but she did her friend the justice of acknowledging the true purport of the sentiment – that Emma was honestly in doubt of her own capacity to honour any promise she had made.

"Very well. But if I must choose – between such as a Mr Elton who will swear one way and act another, and a Miss Woodhouse who will not swear because she is afraid to break her word – then I will choose Miss Woodhouse, and trust to the operation of her good conscience. If my feelings are to be hurt and my heart to be broken, I had rather the suffering were accidental than deliberate – and rather at your hands than his! I would a hundred times sooner apprehend my peril beforehand than be deceived at the outset and learn about it afterwards, dear Miss Woodhouse – dear Emma, if you will allow me to call you that? – and I know that I can never love any gentleman as dearly as I will always love you."

Much affected, Emma returned to Harriet and took both of her friend's hands between her own. "Why Harriet, I am thoroughly astonished! How could I ever have thought of you as meek and complaisant when you are a creature of such decided opinions? I should never have made your portrait as a classical virgin as I did; I should have painted you as a cavalier instead, with jewels and ringlets and a sword!"

"Oh, do you really think so? How exciting! I have never thought of myself as a cavalier before, although I do think I should enjoy to be one!"

The picture these words created in Emma's mind was an enchanting one, but one to which she knew she could never do full justice with her paints and pencils. Only through the medium of speech could she ever hope to depict the magnificence of the vision as she saw it.

"My own dear Harriet, in lace ruffles and silk breeches, her fingers rich with jewels and a bold expression in her eye. How you would stare down all the stout, hook-nosed Puritans who despise ornament and wish to make everybody look the same! I believe you would even fight a duel in my honour, my dashing suitor, would you not?"

"Of course. I would do anything, anything at all, for my lady!" But Harriet shivered and looked conscious, and could not immediately continue in the same confident manner.

Emma drew her close. "My dear, you're trembling; are you really so afraid of me?"

"Afraid of you – no, never! – but to be saying aloud things that may hardly even be thought of without a qualm is more than enough to make anybody fearful, don't you think? Oh, but I have been so fortunate to have had dear

Mrs Goddard to guide and instruct my conduct, and to teach me that it is not at all improper to desire to declare oneself head over heels in love! I believe –" continued Harriet, "– indeed I know – that she truly understands the affection one woman may have for another."

The source of Mrs Goddard's knowledge – if such it were indeed – was not immediately obvious to Emma, although she was under no difficulty in accepting that there could exist looks, glances, indications of attachment passing back and forth between people in love and imperceptible even to themselves. The reader who could interpret signs such as these would not be unlike an ancient man with a hazel twig, who had long ago walked over the fields and closes of Donwell Abbey looking for water; Emma had been told the story by her father who himself had been a witness to it, and had often mentioned – laughing – how the Reverend Bates had spoken so strongly against the practice but had later privately recalled the man and set him to searching out a new well in the vicarage garden.

"There are many things we may not understand," had been her father's patient response when Emma had once challenged him upon the matter, "and we should leave them to those who do." This commandment of his was inducement enough, now, for her to acknowledge the infinite superiority of Mrs Goddard's apprehensions. Mrs Goddard's experience of the world so greatly exceeded Emma's own that she could arrive at no other conclusion than that; Mrs Goddard had understood Harriet's heart – and Emma's, too – and had, by carefully adducing the example of her Irish friends, inspirited Harriet to act in accordance with her feelings.

"Dear Mrs Goddard!" exclaimed Emma, conscious of her extreme goodness in assisting the progress of Harriet's suit. "That *she* should prove to have been the foremost matchmaker of Highbury after all! My father has often told me that I should leave off making marriages, but never until now have I understood the reason for his saying so: that I have no aptitude whatever for the sport, and any marriages that I may consider to have been made by me were truly made by others, or by chance, or solely by inclination, and this has proved him to be truer than he guesses! That I should ever have thought to find a husband for you, Harriet, or not to have seen what was so plainly under my nose; it is a particular kind of blindness, I think, and one for which I am most heartily sorry. Can you ever forgive me, my dear?"

"Oh yes indeed," replied Harriet, "and readily, but I have never really thought of being married to anyone but you! And whether I am to be a husband or have one, or to be a wife or have one, or to one day be a husband and the next day be a wife, it will scarcely matter as long as I may always be with you. Nor will it matter that it must be kept the most close of all secrets and that half of the world will never comprehend our pleasure in each other; I would rather live in poverty with you, if it must be so, than go to bed on silk sheets with Mr Elton or any other of his sort."

"It will assuredly not be poverty," said Emma affectionately, "but neither will there be silk sheets. It will be, I hope, a sweet retirement from the world such as the Irish ladies have shared for all these years – and if our felicity lasts as long, my Harriet, as that between Miss Ponsonby and Lady Eleanor Butler, you will not find me unappreciative of my good fortune. And neither of us," she added in conclusion, "will ever be required to climb out of any window anywhere unless she really feels inclined to it – and then she may choose for herself whether she does so dressed in masculine clothing, or feminine, or indeed without the benefit of any clothing at all."

Harriet Smith's laughter in response to the outrageousness of this remark became, in the estimation of Miss Emma Woodhouse of Hartfield, quite one of the loveliest and most delightful sounds she had ever been privileged to hear in all her life.

Author's Notes

This story grew out of a coincidence of names and dates which was just too felicitous to ignore. The Ladies of Llangollen knew a Mrs Goddard – a friend of Sarah Ponsonby's family in Ireland, described as 'a sprightly and ambitious widow with an eye to the main chance' – who corresponded with them faithfully. There is no record of her ever moving to England, however.

Adam Fitzroy

Imaginist and purveyor of tall tales Adam Fitzroy is a UK resident who has been successfully spinning same sex romances either part-time or full-time since the 1980s, and has a particular interest in examining the conflicting demands of love and duty.

adam-fitzroy.blogspot.co.uk
twitter.com/AdamFitzroy

Hide nor Hair

Atlin Merrick

Adam Ashford Otelian began to suspect something when he saw Miss Mary Hay's beard.

Not that Adam had not noticed many interesting things about Mary Hay before then. It was just that he had said nothing about what he saw because Adam was that sort of man.

He was also the sort to ask friends to call him his childhood nickname of Ash, though of friends he had few. It was Adam's misfortune to be considered among the chosen and the best and, without once insisting on his place in society, he found himself constantly put there by others. Of course these others were anxious to acknowledge his social elevation so that they could then be acknowledged by him.

The problem was, Adam had always had a problem with that.

For down in his bones Adam Otelian was a tradesman's son. Born to wealth, yes, but into a family that had earned their fortune through a century of effort. As such, Adam had a natural diffidence and a contentment with simple things, tendencies his doting parents dotingly encouraged.

So, when his mother had twins the year Adam turned sixteen he was, to no one's surprise, delighted. After Isabel and Isaac came into his world, Adam was even less inclined to place himself forward. Instead he always made time for the twins when he returned home from university and, far more importantly, they always made time for him.

Though ever-busy with the hectic intrigues of four-year-olds, Isabel and Isaac slowed down long enough to enjoy garden-meandering tea parties with their indulgent big brother. With the aid of elderly Annie – who had cared for Adam's mother when she was little, then cared for Adam too, before happily taking charge of the twins – the three siblings would wear their finest attire, eating with dainty forks the candied fruits Adam brought back from Oxford's fancy shops.

When the children turned five, they abandoned tea parties and took up tatting with their mother. No one said anything about Isaac having a finer eye for detail and a more delicate hand with the shuttle. Instead the family expressed delight when the twins, side by side and with little tongues poking from the corners of their precious mouths, whiled away long afternoons engaged each with their own bit of lace.

When the children were six, Isabel fell in love with insects and then so too did Isaac. This meant picnics by a Heath pond, though which pond depended on which creatures could be found hatching, mating, or moulting at that time. Isabel became highly proficient on the subject, and announced bug breeding facts as she thought pertinent, no matter the company.

It was just as the children turned seven that everyone's interests shifted. The twins wished to do nothing but play battledore and shuttlecock; the father wished his eldest son would find a wife; and Adam – Adam stayed silent on wishes of his own.

And then it was too late for wishes.

For in quick succession Adam's lovely mother succumbed to consumption, then Annie followed from the same disease only four months later.

Their amiable father wilted, weakened, then died the winter after, "of complications from pneumonia," his doctors said. Adam was not the kind of man to tell these men that they were wrong. So "Father died of heartbreak" was something Adam said only to himself.

This was how Adam Otelian found himself a twenty-three-year-old father to seven-year-old twins, and then the employer of their new governess, Miss Mary Hay.

Miss Hay was dark-haired and a tiny bit tall, of a lively and curious temperament, as inclined to listen as to speak, and accomplished in the instruction of natural history and philosophy, as well as reading and writing. These were the things acquaintances knew about Miss Hay. What they did not know was that Mary had been born Martin, the son of a French teacher and a milliner. For all her growing-up years home was to be found in the corner of her father's library, where she was always free to attend to her own entertainments and studies.

And oh the things you can study when you are a teacher's child are interesting things indeed.

So by the age of thirteen Martin learned why she was in head and heart always Mary, and she learned she was not the only one who thought in this way. She especially learned that there were people like her in London, where she moved as soon as she was able. Free from her family's judgemental eyes, Mary could at last dress, speak, and live correctly in this busy city of strangers, and took a position in north London, tutoring two girls.

Though her work kept her busy, the rare times time permitted Mary would attend the parties and picnics to which she was invited, though she was never quite sure why as she did not much like parties or picnics.

No, that was not true, and Mary Hay was always truthful with herself, as she could hardly be truthful with anyone else.

Mary went where she was asked because Mary wanted to understand the world and where special people like herself moved in it. So she dressed in her smartest spencer and wore her best-fitting gloves, and she looked for people with whom she could belong. The problem was that sometimes special people hide so well that they became invisible, even to those as special as themselves.

Then Mary's students married and a mutual acquaintance introduced her to Adam Otelian. Mary felt an instant sympathy for the grieving young man and though she did not know there was anything special about Adam the day they met, Adam knew there was something special about Miss Mary Hay.

And by *something*, Adam meant *everything*.

He could not have told you exactly what. Adam only knew that the twenty-four-year-old governess was … she was … that is to say she emphatically *was*. That, though slim and of a height, though serene and sometimes quiet, he found himself over the next months looking at Miss Hay the way he had only ever looked at the prettiest boys in his class.

Of course, from the start Isabel and Isaac adored her, perhaps a bit giddy with Miss Hay's ability to run and shout, pleasures arthritis had long taken from their much-missed Annie.

And run with the children Mary did, when not teaching them the things they ought to learn about geography and arithmetic, Shakespeare and natural history.

No longer the perennial student himself, Adam was as often working at home as in his father's City office, and so, on those early spring days when the sun shone brightly over the nearby Heath, Adam would find himself 'accidentally' sitting in on the children's lessons. These 'accidents' were often quite difficult to achieve, what with geography taking place by the rocky rose bower, natural history near where the bees buzzed busiest, and arithmetic and reading happening in any place that took Miss Hay's fancy.

Yet despite these complications, Adam managed many accidents, and so Miss Hay and he managed many conversations.

"– and it's a relief you think so, for I did worry. I dare say some have said it's peculiar that Isaac has won a tatting competition and Isabel collects dead bugs."

Perched together on the back garden's low wall, watching while the children captured dragonflies by their tails, Mary replied, "Well, those things don't seem so very peculiar to me. Or perhaps I have always done peculiar things."

"Oh," said the man to the woman, "like what?"

Just then Isabel brought over a bright blue dragonfly which Miss Hay surrounded with her large hands. She then held those hands in turn to Isabel's ear, Isaac's, and finally Adam's. Everyone smiled at the tiny buzz of the trapped insect, then all four waved it off as Mary set the dragonfly free.

'Like this," replied the woman to the man.

Watching the children run after the insect, Adam reflected that Mary's hand was very soft, but what he said was, "Is a lady loving dragonflies all that peculiar? I was not aware."

Mary threw back her head and laughed, hand resting against her throat. "Well," she said a little later, voice now raspy-deep, "I thought you might think so."

"You'll never know unless you ask, Miss Hay, and should you ask, I would tell you it was I who showed Isabel how to capture dragonflies, and how to do it so gently that they're never any worse for wear after."

Mary hummed happily and Adam now understood why she had picked this spot for natural history lessons. The humming bees buzzing everywhere were as soothing as sweet wine. "Do you think," he asked, "that this means we are both peculiar?"

Mary's grin faltered. "Some would think there are peculiarities far greater than a love of nature. I have …"

Their conversation ended then for business called when one of Adam's father's old partners showed up to talk of City matters.

But because small children take up a large amount of a governess's time, there were always ample opportunities for 'accidents'.

The rocky rose bower provided the next and there Mary asked, "Is a love of capturing dragonflies your only peculiarity then?" She tried to hide a smile by turning away, which let Adam admire how the sun cast her cheekbones and jaw in sharp relief.

"Oh, not at all. I am a treasure trove of surprise and intrigue."

"Do tell."

Months later Mary asked Adam why he said the next thing he did, for it was a risky thing. Adam answered, "Because you never made me afraid."

So without fear Adam confessed, "I've an old stuffed horse Annie gave me when I was small. His name is Christopher and I still tell him my deepest secrets."

At this revelation Mary blushed scarlet, and much later Adam asked why she had become so flustered. Mary answered, "Because suddenly I wanted to be as brave as you."

Bravery came later, after seven months, then eight, passed, until autumn was ending and the rain came back, then the snow. The children played rumbustiously until suddenly everything was boring, and they wondered if winter would ever end. Meanwhile, a man wondered if he should tell a woman how much he loved her, and a woman wondered if she should leave before her heart had completely finished breaking.

Then all that any of them wondered was how, how, *how many* prayers it would take for God to spare a sick child.

Isabel did not know many prayers, so when she sat on her brother's sickbed – again the doctors said pneumonia, and this time they were right – she made up her own. "Please make Isaac well and I will be good. I will give him the best plums, I will show him where the honeybees live by the bird bridge, I will learn all my French. Please make Isaac well and I will be good, I will give him the best plums –"

Each time Isabel fell asleep beside her brother, one adult would carry her to bed and the other would stay with the suffering little boy, each praying their own desperate prayers.

I will give my life for his. I will forever hide what I am. I will be a normal man and I will marry as Father wished …

I will give my life for his. I will forever hide what I am. I will leave this good family and go somewhere far away …

And so it went on for days that seemed like weeks, and it was on Isaac's very worst night, when both Mary and Adam had not slept or eaten or changed their clothes, that Adam finally noticed an unusual thing about Mary Hay.

She had a beard.

He saw this fine, rare thing when he came to change places with her that night the fever broke. Entering the sickroom he found that Mary had fallen asleep in the chair beside the smouldering fire, and it was in the gentleness of that light that Adam saw Mary had lovely ginger stubble from neck to cheek to jaw.

Giddy with delight, Adam ran his hands over his own unshaven face, judged that Miss Hay's beard was definitely thicker than his and that it contrasted so prettily with her dark hair. He remembered she had once said her grandmother had been "red-haired as a copper penny," and despite his promises to a silent God, Adam longed to know if Miss Hay's shoulders had freckles to match that pretty beard, if her limbs were reedy with slim muscle, if her voice would go deep when she moaned.

Maybe desire had weight, maybe hope did too, for what else would explain Mary waking just then, catching Adam's eyes, and sharing with him a gentle smile?

It was as she brushed hair from her temple and her cheeks that Mary's smile faded and her hands, one on either side of her face, went still.

Maybe guilt had weight too, and maybe fear accounted for why neither woman nor man spoke just then nor hours later, when Mary returned to help Adam, her face as smooth as it always ever was.

That had to be it. Fear and desire, guilt and hope had to weigh an awful lot to keep lips bitten between teeth, to make it impossible for gazes to meet, to rob intelligent people of their words.

Fortunately the needs of a small boy weighed much more, and so Mary and Adam continued to care for a sick child until that child was fully well.

It was on a spring day, when Isabel and Isaac were noisily practising their French in the back garden, that Adam 'accidentally' came upon students and governess, and then in a panic quickly excused himself away.

Mary followed, until woman and man found themselves in the conservatory, a half-dozen feet apart. Adam looked at Mary and said nothing. Mary looked at Adam and also said nothing. Adam said more nothing. Eventually Mary got impatient with all of the nothing.

"If you want me to go, you must ask me to leave."

Adam tugged at his waistcoat. Took a deep breath. And he asked … nothing.

Suddenly tired of all the things unsaid, Mary said, "Stop it."

"What," Adam said softly, "should I stop?"

Mary's jaw worked and worked, as if her mouth were full up with words, words she had rehearsed well and needed only provocation to speak, but now there were too many in her mouth, so in the end she said just a few. "Stop *tolerating* me."

Mary had not known she would say that, for that was not what she had rehearsed. Those words had been about responsibility and duty, but those had fled the moment she looked at Adam looking so gently at her.

"Is it toleration to love someone? Is that what they call it where you're from?"

Mary ran the back of her hand over one cheek and then the other, an instinctive gesture, a reminder of something of which neither needed reminding.

"You never asked me about the things I tell Christopher."

Mary's cheeks flushed, remembering a day when she should have been braver. "Your … stuffed horse?"

Adam smiled ruefully and nodded. "Oh my, yes. I've told Christopher perhaps more than I ought over the years. I think I whispered my first secret to him when I was five. I told him that spinach was very awful and I would rather piss my drawers than have to eat it."

Mary Hay barked out a low laugh. She covered her mouth, then uncovered it, then placed her hand over her throat, then removed it. There was no longer any use in hiding what was easy to see if you really looked. So Mary threw back her head and laughed, her voice deeper than she wished, and yet happy for all that.

Eventually she took a step closer, whispered, "What else?"

Hope bloomed in Adam's chest. "Well, some years later I told Christopher that I found dances very boring because I move like a frog, full of ill-timed leaps and bad landings."

Mary's body shook and her face went a bit pink, then very pink, then she just let loose and giggled high, low, and everywhere in between. "You lie, Adam Otelian!"

"I do not!"

Mary tried to sober because this was a serious conversation, but she had had about enough of seriousness and if her life was going to fall to ruin in a minute, she would rather laugh than cry. She took a step closer and said, "I've seen you dance and I would say you're more puppy than frog."

Bravery bloomed in Adam just then and with a glance toward the back garden – where two children's voices could clearly be heard – Adam Otelian said the one thing that changed everything.

"And, Miss Mary Hay of the large hands and the ginger beard and the sometimes-deep voice, I told Christopher the threadbare horse about the first person I ever wanted to kiss. I told him that William Douglas Billings was in my class and that surely he had the prettiest mouth in the world." Adam looked at Mary's mouth. "About that I now know I was very wrong."

They drifted closer, did Mary and Adam, close enough to whisper, close enough to feel the weight of their desire, the wonder of their shared need. And in that sun-filled conservatory, two people who had made desperate promises to a God in whom they no longer believed, made better, sweeter promises to one another.

In stories like this, the tale is usually quite done by now, but Mary Hay hates that sort of story – for it is Mary telling this one, writing a memoir she intends to give to Isabel's girl, Annie, to show her that there are many different ways of living in this world.

Above all, Mary would most like to say that scandals are rare things, and the men and women who come to public notice for not conforming to society's standards, are but the smallest fraction of such people in this world. The reason we do not know of the others is that their stories are *boring*.

Beautiful and fine as the stories might be for those living them, people who are different in one way are nevertheless usually gloriously ordinary in most others.

Like Mary Hay and Adam Ashford Otelian, who married one year after they met and who went on to be so incredibly boring to most, that most never knew they were quite different.

That Mary had soft hands, fine cheekbones, the prettiest lips, as well as a penis: none of those things were what made her different really. And Adam's gentle hands, the lovely curls he would keep well into old age, and the fact that his penis was very partial to his wife's penis: those were not what made *him* different either.

No, what made the Otelians unusual to others was the couple's quiet and constant devotion.

A devotion expressed by their always-linked arms as they walked about town. A devotion shown by the frequency of the husband murmuring near his wife's bonnet ribbon until she laughed, by the wife replying softly against her husband's ear until he blushed. A devotion shown by their disinclination to dance with anyone at the rare ball they attended though dance they did, always with each other, covering the floor in charming, puppyish steps.

When Mary and Adam were at home, their devotion took other, more private forms.

Words were always there of course, whispers of *hard* or *want* or *beg* when the children were near, giggles of *spend* and *in my mouth* and *yes oh please yes* when the children were asleep.

There were midnight devotions where they explored one another's body, learning that Mary liked to be ridden and Adam liked to ride, that each loved to suck, and that the quieter they were when the pleasure came, the harder their bodies shook.

When the children each married, Mary and Adam took a house closer to the Heath, and on harsh winter days they would curl up lazily by their fire and fingers would push in, tongues would probe, and on her belly on the carpet Mary would rut and moan, or spread-legged on his back, Adam would keen and plead.

Come the heat of summer, they would lounge indolently on the balcony and under cover of the old weeping willow they would reach under each other's dressing gown and drag out the pleasure as long as they could stand. Mary loved the splattery mess they would leave on balcony tiles and Adam loved to tell her she was terribly depraved.

As is the way with these things, Isabel and Isaac grew into rather conventional people, each with two children, though it was to the very eldest that Mary gave her memoir. Though it would take Annie quite some time to be honest with herself, she eventually grew tired of hiding, and at last set up house with her dear friend Julia. After a while life went on as it had been. It went on in all its boring, beautiful, and ordinary glory.

Atlin Merrick

Atlin Merrick is the author of *The Night They Met* and the upcoming *The Six Secret Loves of Sherlock Holmes*. As Wendy C. Fries she's written *The Day They Met*, hundreds of features on high tech, finance, and health, and is fascinated with London, lattes, and theatre.

atlin.merrick@yahoo.com
improbablepress.co.uk/

Outside the Parlour

Andrea Demetrius

Part 1

In truth, Darcy knew he could not overcome his fate. Marriage news and prospects of it kept closing in on him, and a decision was to be made soon. He was, after all, a single man of eight-and-twenty and in possession of a good fortune.

When Bingley announced he was looking for an estate and then – true to his disposition – proceeded to lease it the same day he saw the property, Darcy kept silent about the feasibility of his friend's prospects, confirmed it was a short-term agreement, and assented to accompany him and provide advice when needed.

They were both fleeing.

Darcy had heard only rumours about his young friend's latest entanglement, but Bingley said enough – warm protestations and eyes distractedly studying the quarters' furnishing – to know that this season's 'angel' had rejected his offer. Darcy felt a twinge of regret for not being there to support him, but several events had converged and had not permitted him to act otherwise.

Having to bear being reduced to a mere bystander, maintaining his carriage while feeling useless, mortified and undone, until his Pemberley housekeeper – recalled post-haste to London to tend his sister's situation – proclaimed the matter resolved, was almost causing him to become distempered as well. The normal way of his world appeared now to light his shade strangely and it felt almost as if he were wearing a disguise.

Georgiana was acknowledging their presence, but her written apologies were long and rambling, and barely alluded to the summer's events, after an initial outburst defending her virtue in a shocked rejection of her full ruin. Mrs Reynolds believed her, and attributed her poor health to the nerves, and the absence of her menses to the lack of appetite and the subsequent loss of weight. These were things Darcy had not expected ever to learn about.

And then there were the other happenings. The news-sheets, the dark whispers in the corners at his clubs, acquaintances leaving the city, or suddenly announcing their betrothals.

He winced internally and firmly avoided unravelling any more of that poisonous thread, and as such he focused on Bingley's new establishment.

The main thing about Bingley's sisters was that they could provide good company and were engaging and witty enough to distract both men when the gentlemen's pursuits were falling short.

Bingley threw himself into this new endeavour in his typical fashion, with candour and energy. He favoured meeting his neighbours, though, rather than following through with his decision to take the reins and begin his initiation in estate owning. Darcy, though grateful to add more distractions to his share of business, was nonetheless worried that now his friend was provided with a good house and the liberty of a manor, he might decide to spend the rest of his days at Netherfield and leave to the next generation the task of purchasing a property. After only two years of being of age, Bingley showed signs of quiet resignation about gaining the place his father, and his sisters, claimed he deserved in society. Theirs was a respectable family, but their fortunes came from trade.

Darcy had wondered about his friend's choice of settling near this small market town, especially when his friend was praising the barely tolerable local assembly rooms they had to resort to. Nothing of interest happened, but Bingley spoke of everybody being kind and attentive to him, of enjoying the absence of formality and stiffness, of having met the pleasantest people and the prettiest girls of his acquaintance. Darcy was baffled; he had not received from any either attention or pleasure. He considered the young man's effusions an effect of the arts and allurements of a new 'angel', but consoled himself with this re-emergence of his friend's usual easiness and ductility of temper, signs of already improving spirits.

Darcy's musings were interrupted when a parcel arrived from his house in Town. It contained not only his steward's usual account of business and housekeeping affairs, but also, unfortunately for his good spirits, the latest broadsheets his manservant had dutifully sent along. He rearranged those at the bottom of the pile and quickly perused the forwarded letters, dreading the news when he saw Mrs Reynolds' and Georgiana's handwriting, but also releasing a disappointed sigh when another letter proved not to be in the bundle.

Some moments later, though, he could not quite suppress his loud imprecations as the words of several journals and gazettes began chasing through his normally ordered mind. *Charged with committing, or attempting to commit an unnatural act … committing sodomy on the body of … for unnatural crimes sentenced to stand in the pillory … unnatural attempt … solitary confinement … against Lieut. Colonel and another soldier … anonymous letters … sentenced to be hanged …*

He hastily supressed another strangled curse, automatically checking the door, but words were still roaring inside his head. The Bow Street Runners were coming down hard on crimes lately, and an endless wave of prosecutions against sinners was, unavoidably, recorded in the newspapers.

He berated himself each time for purchasing the gazettes, but could not bring himself to quit it either. John had said …

Darcy caught the thought in time. He did not want to think about him.

Despite his admonishments, his mind importuned him again with the image of John, heated by the wine and silhouetted against the dying fire, adding to the shadows of the study's walls closing in on them, carefully and blandly enunciating the names of twenty-seven men, captured and then released publicly, after examination, amidst an enraged multitude, the majority of whom were females – and that *it was with the utmost difficulty the prisoners could be saved from destruction.* Only seven were actually convicted, but all their names were printed in the newspapers.

There was not a single gentleman amongst them, of course.

Darcy saw it in *The Morning Chronicle*, but John had more gruesome details because of his intimate acquaintance with Lord D., who had been there. Even in disguise, the noble had managed to bribe someone, and he and his other well-born friends left without being remarked upon.

In defiance of his own counsel, Darcy's blood thickened and his reason weakened in remembrance of that last night. It had surely been the fumes of the contraband French brandy. There was no sense to be found in those solemn, passionate protestations of affections. The only merit in that disgraceful occurrence was John's warm vows of forsaking such a disloyal, cowardly sort as Lord D.

Fearing to become undone again by the force of his memories, Darcy searched for a distraction to save him. He did not want to dwell on the wicked longing that burdened him and made him not want to submit to his fate, but to yield to a conduct certain to lead straight to his ruin.

He went to the sitting room where he found that one cannot outrun the hellhounds once they have your scent. Miss Bingley was fervently exclaiming over a friend's letter detailing an encounter with Lady A., whose engagement to Lord D. – 'the ultimate bachelor about town!' – was the latest 'most astonishing' news causing uproar among the Ton.

Darcy left then to check upon the horses.

Anyhow, it was time to put together their first shooting party in this county. He focused his mind on the small game and the birds in great need of population control and despaired of the character of a landowner who had left his property this long without tenants. Of course, considering a busybody neighbour had offered his own for after they finished shooting 'all' of Bingley's birds, Darcy was less inclined to consider the neglect of hunting duties as a hopeless failing.

His efforts at distraction paid off. With each new encounter, the faceless people crowding him began to form into individual entities.

It was country fare to be sure, confined and limited, but Darcy found some interest in a pair of uncommonly intelligent eyes belonging, surprisingly, to a young lady. Made curious by the novel discovery he willed himself entirely to it, avoiding his own turmoil and postponing his decisions. Although Miss Elizabeth Bennet was not a beauty by the normal classical standards – she had hardly a good feature, her body symmetry was a failure, nor were her manners fashionable – Darcy found her pleasing.

He shuddered in remembrance of a bountiful cleavage 'accident' in his first season in Town. He was thankful this young lady was light on that type of 'female accomplishment'.

Darcy was usually drawn toward lively, cheerful conversations – a talent he was often told that he himself lacked in society, perhaps because he had never made an effort to improve upon it – and the young lady now receiving his consideration was not an exception amongst his exclusive and carefully cultivated inner circle.

Admittedly, the content of her conversation was on occasions somewhat lacking – he was still astonished by the amount of energy the ladies exerted when the subject of a ball was brought forth – but nevertheless, Darcy found the impertinence of the lady in question quite refreshing. Flirting and self-deprecating, those dark eyes seemed to betray her playfulness behind every attempt at severity. These female arts, when employed by her, appeared quite entertaining, safe as they each were within their different stations in life.

Darcy was also grateful for her sufficiently imperfect music display. It distracted his mind from his sister's latest performance at the request of their aunt, Lady Catherine de Bourgh, before the summer's events. And his subsequent discovery of one of Bach's cantatas. His understanding of music was now forever altered by that forgotten slip of paper, annotated by the hand of the late Sir Lewis de Bourgh.

A supercilious fellow approached him, bringing an end to those perilous thoughts, and the distraction was sufficient to focus Darcy on the moment, allowing him to voice his disapproval of the dancing taking place.

It was yet another reminder of the French influence upon traditional English society, as if the number of militia officers milling about in their bright, red coats was not enough. He was disgruntled with this wave of assimilation and the extension of the social circle to include the public assembly rooms. Private gatherings like this one, unwisely allowing dancing, seemed to forecast an even deeper downfall. *Society has its claim on us all,* he had often been told. It did not make it any easier to bear.

Miss Elizabeth appeared sensible enough not to care to dance when he offered. Her relaxed country manners did not extend to the breaking of etiquette, and he was pleased by her behaviour, awakening his good humour enough to allow him to tease Miss Bingley quite fairly in return. He was content with his display of gallantry and not even her barbed references to marriage – that spectre always looming on the verges! – could affect his perfect indifference.

Apart from these necessary social engagements and his usual affairs, Darcy also dedicated himself to Bingley's – which proved to be intricate enough to keep Darcy occupied.

His friend's relatives, the Hursts, seemed to have settled themselves in Bingley's new house, even sending their hired horses away, deeming the expense too much. There was also the matter of Bingley's unmarried sister overspending. Milliners' boxes from London, and too many newly employed housemaids and footmen crowded them in a display meant to impress. Darcy thought Bingley was leaning more and more toward putting off the purchase of an estate – he found enough substance in his worries to consider approaching the younger man with this delicate subject and discussing the advisability of returning to London.

Matters were complicated further when the two eldest Miss Bennets became guests of the manor, uprooting the household's established routine, and causing frictions between the ladies.

Darcy found himself affected by the situation, especially when Miss Bingley's wit and barbs hit too close to his troubles with his sister. He was growing doubtful of his previously stated – quite modern – views regarding the independence, education, and decorum of ladies.

Knowing that John Brindley would be disappointed by the re-apparition of his more conservative thoughts did not help Darcy's conflicted frame of mind.

They had spent nights in heated debates over the French situation, or the new ideas spreading from fellows such as Jeremy Bentham, William Godwin – even, shockingly to some of his own circle, the latter's wife – or arguing about new inventions and machines, or about the importance of acknowledging the existence of a very rich and powerful middle class. The memories waited for any unguarded moment to spring to life in Darcy's mind, bringing the shadow of his absent friend, and throwing him off balance, despite his resolve to distract and distance himself.

Darcy's failings were never better displayed than when his turmoil grew with every post-rider coming short of one much expected letter.

Thankfully, Bingley continued to recuperate his spirits.

Darcy was content for his friend, even when he ended up subjected to the man's improving mood. Usually careful and considered with the fairer sex, in the private circle of his own home Bingley was at liberty to display his sharp mind and humour. Even Miss Elizabeth – self-proclaimed 'studier of character', and much more suited to the sort of duels bandied about in parlours – fell into his trap in a conversation about disguises and false outward appearances, despite having successfully recognised the reference to Shakespeare's *Twelfth Night*.

Of course, a poorly educated young lady of the country was no match for Bingley when he cared to put his mind to work. Unfortunately, it also affected Darcy's own composure.

Bingley's and John's names were associated in Darcy's mind. Normally, Darcy was proficient in avoiding thinking about the beginning of their relationship, but on placid evenings like these, with nothing much to occupy one's mind or body, and confined indoors, Bingley's barbs and wit were free to play havoc with certain memories.

A previous encounter in the study during which Darcy brought to Bingley's attention his concerns about the younger man's lack of diligence in managing his affairs, left his friend bristling and in need of retaliation. Bingley made the drawing-room his arena and swiftly pitted the young lady currently residing with them against Darcy, then stepped back to enjoy the results.

By the time Bingley spoke of his so-called deference for Darcy, and the awful object Darcy made on particular occasions, in particular places, at his house especially, on Sunday evenings when he had nothing to do, Darcy had forgotten the letter writing and the audience, and was bewitched by the combination of Miss Elizabeth's arguments and spirited countenance and delivery, and his dear friend's evident mischievousness.

He endeavoured to focus on the lady, hoping to avoid the pitfalls of being faced with Bingley's rarely displayed bite. Despite Darcy's best intentions though, the memories came to life.

John Brindley, long past his university days, had asked Darcy to look after this young fellow whose respectability, like Brindley's, was tainted by trade.

John had never mentioned his first weeks at school, but Darcy knew what courting the favour of a peer really meant in a certain context. Afterwards, he had learned more than he had ever wanted to know about Lord D.'s entourage.

Thankfully, Bingley had never had reason to encounter that kind of situation. Before Darcy met him and offered him his friendship, Bingley had managed to defend his position and integrity by showing there was steel beneath his easy manners. That fierce, strong young man had impressed Darcy at their first meeting, and, ever since then, those feelings had solidified into a worthy friendship.

Turning from the wandering paths of his mind, Darcy renewed his interest in the evening's proceedings, much to Bingley's amusement. But the lady upon whom he was bestowing his considerable attention was safe from him. From him, and from the shade in his character.

Thankfully for the soundness of his mind, their inner circle soon returned to its previous composition as the ladies departed.

But then news of a private being flogged for dishonourable conduct in the garrison stationed near Meryton quickly chased away Darcy's illusion of peacefulness, and caused his worries to reappear.

It did not help his disquiet when the post continued to lack even a simple note from John Brindley announcing he had indeed left the city. The man had planned his return to Liverpool shortly after their last encounter – that fretful night when John had disavowed his friendship with Lord D. after the latter's close encounter with the Bow Street Runners and the ensuing announcement of his engagement.

That confusing night kept circling Darcy's thoughts, distracting him with relentless memories of late hours, merry disorder, and fired-up appetites that both men usually strived to keep from undoing them. Once more their resistance dissolved, and they yielded to it. But giving in between the sheets was not the worst of his burdens. His bewilderment, and the inverted world he now inhabited, came from the intimation and the protestation of affections. Unbelievable testimonies that, surely, could not bear scrutiny in the crude daylight.

Darcy knew that no amount of atonement could clean up their blindness and impudence. He repented. And he was still waiting for that letter and hoping absurdly for some absolution or relief from it.

In the letters that Darcy did receive, Mrs Reynolds continued to express her hope and belief in Georgiana's quick and complete improvement.

Another correspondent was his uncle, the Earl of M., who blessedly just sent brief notes, usually commenting on matters of business or politics. The subtext in the nobleman's increasing worry about the country's economic and social situation was not veiled though, and his personal troubles were easy to discern. His uncle talked about the cost of the wars, and of wealthy and increasingly vociferous bankers, ship- and factory-owners claiming the vote for themselves.

He never asked directly about Darcy's marriage plans, only sent along his wife's enquiries.

Darcy felt he still could deflect it all silently, just as he did with his other aunt's much more overt presumptions.

"It never rains but it pours!" denounced Darcy under his breath, fuming at the unbelievable apparition interrupting his pleasurable ride with Bingley. "What is Wickham doing here, of all places?"

Bingley noticed his distemper, and stopped his enquiries after hearing that scoundrel's name. Darcy, grateful for his friend's perceptiveness, took off, needing to distract himself until his conduct could follow his reason and not his impulses.

Darcy could confide in Bingley, but the prospect of one day having him for a brother-in-law made him refrain – at least until it became an unavoidable disclosure. It was too much having his cousin Richard brought into his confidence – their conjoined guardianship of his sister made it unavoidable – despite the precarious balance of influence between the earl and Darcy. Before the summer's events, Georgiana had been a prospect for Richard. His sister's dowry – at one time it had been the dowry of the earl's sister – a last resort for the younger son of an earl, unspoken compensation if Richard could not have Rosings when Darcy married his cousin, Anne de Bourgh.

Previously incomprehensible fragments from his childhood, relating to the earl's and Lady Catherine's single-minded pursuit of the exact terms to be included in Sir Lewis's will, resulting in the subsequent exclusion of every other de Bourgh relative from the inheritance and favouring exclusively his only daughter, to the effective eradication of Sir Lewis's existence and name, were now lit by a terrible meaning.

This year, Darcy's habitual Easter visit at Rosings had produced a terrifying clue about Sir Lewis. Darcy had come upon the gentleman's handwritten annotation on a Bach cantata. It said the cantata possessed the most amazing and enlightening verses. The lyrics it referred to was 'The Quarrel between Phoebus and Pan', and the underlined text comprised a damning reference to Hyacinth that Darcy could recite by heart, despite having read it only the once.

> *With longing*
> *I press your tender cheeks,*
> *Lovely, beautiful Hyacinth.*

And I like to kiss your eyes,
Because they are my morning stars
And the sun of my soul.'

His aunt's husband wrote about finding in the myth a validation for the unnatural inclinations he and others like him were afflicted with. He justified a love poem to a man just as if the recipient were a lady, and dressing up the wicked lusts just as handsomely and courteously as if the shadows of Newgate Prison could never touch him.

To Darcy's damnation and peace of mind, he understood all too well that short exculpation.

Darcy wanted to erase this insight from his mind. He wanted to scourge those sweet-evil verses from his memory, and remove their power. They were haunting him at the most inopportune moments – such as when he was waiting for a certain letter from Liverpool and trying to dismiss his discomposure as mere restlessness about his silent investment in Brindley's schemes.

Darcy's evasive mental detour did not ease his fury at having just laid eyes upon Wickham, but, as intended, it did get him away from the man and dispersed some of his shock.

The free rein on the previous summer's repressed rage and shame resulted in a weary animal and a fine mist rising from the black hide.

He had come to this little town to escape the constant reminders of his failure with his sister. At barely fifteen years old, he had agreed to take her out of school, deeming her prepared for her own establishment and trusting the wrong person with her safety. He had not been diligent enough. He had been distracted with selfish, evil preoccupations.

Shame blanched his already pale complexion. He realised he had only one of his gloves, the other probably removed to salute the ladies, and forgotten somewhere in his agitation – his wan hand was a taint against the moist, dark animal skin.

He had been relieved when his sister had asked for a separate establishment after Easter. He had relished his continued liberty in his comings and goings. He intended to continue his bachelor status until she was ready to marry and then he would simply discharge her to her husband's care.

How utterly and irredeemably selfish he had been.

"Above all else, I abhor deceptions!" he had said not so long ago, thinking about the agreeable countenance and manners of Wickham, his one-time childhood friend. How fittingly it applied, though, to his own follies and vices! His own self-willed blindness.

This last understanding of his own character, and Wickham's written apologies offered the day he received Darcy's letter demanding satisfaction, were the only thing keeping him from following through with the vindictive plan his mad dash through the country had fabricated against the perpetrator of his sister's private ruin.

"Good old George Wickham and his lucky escapes! Damn the scoundrel!"

Skilfully, the man had been publicly, and occasionally, calling on his sister's companion. There was no hint of rumour associating their names. There were no expectations raised; only a broken heart unable to claim being jilted, since the only witness, the companion, had confessed in writing to being the sole recipient of the man's calls, and had withdrawn herself from society in compensation for any slight.

This solution had been costly. Darcy had in his possession several notes of paid debts, and his family's good name had suffered a heavy blow, but the alternative offered – the marriage – implied an even greater cost, a public one. Wickham had not seemed overly fond of being a husband, either, when it meant no access to the dowry, and being cut off from the very society he had been striving all his life to be part of.

Darcy was still unsure what had most influenced this arrangement: having been connected at one time in the closest manner with the man, his father's fondness for the boy, or Georgiana's disgrace being made public. Or his own guilt.

He wondered where the last of his sins would end, and how to begin to atone for them anew in the face of his continued retreat from the field.

Having lost the last thread of relaxation achieved in this country detour, Darcy decided it was time to stop running away and go back to London to face at least some of his failings.

On the way back to the house he was accompanied by black clouds bringing about the very rain invoked in such a careless way. It poured until the much anticipated Netherfield Park ball.

Wickham had been invited to the ball, since he could hardly be excluded from the general invitation made to the officers, but Darcy had given leave to Bingley, knowing the scoundrel had not enough courage in him to accept.

"There was such a truth in his looks," his sister had said. "It all seemed so true and pure ... like in the poems!"

It seemed more likely the man was the embodiment of a Shakespearean comedy of masques.

The discreet inquiry made by Darcy's manservant informed him that Wickham had indeed invented a task to remove himself from the neighbourhood on the evening of the ball. Bingley had snorted in his liquor when he heard the news.

Not very fond of the marital market that a ball represented, and remaining preoccupied with the lateness of the post – presumably caused by the rain – contributed to firm Darcy's resolve of heading back to London after fulfilling this barely tolerable social obligation.

As a farewell gesture, he indulged his fascination for the unusual Miss Elizabeth and applied for a dance, secure in the knowledge that his subsequent departure would aid in dissipating her hopes. He exerted himself enough to caution her about the peril of happy manners, alluding to Wickham's presence in Meryton, and stretching the limits of propriety in addressing her directly over a matter not fitted for young ladies and better left for the province of men.

The rest of the ball proved to be as dreadful as he had feared – even more so, considering the quality of the local attendants. There was unbecoming conduct from young ladies, impertinent freedom of manners in general, and the usual greed and marital schemes from industrious mothers.

It was almost more than he could bear but he managed to finish the meal with the utmost civility.

As it usually happens, the very next day after the ball, Darcy received the delayed post.

And, as it usually happens with careless invocations and impatience, a man should take care, lest he suffer having his wishes fulfilled.

Darcy's reaction to the unexpected letter from Lord D. communicating his recent betrothal, despite them not frequenting the same sphere, had the dubious honour of being surpassed by the shock of being urgently summoned to his sister's side.

Darcy spared Miss Bingley the bare civilities in his haste, and, distracted, agreed to enquire of Bingley about his future plans on the way to Town, presuming his friend wished to ride alongside him, and not be confined in the carriage.

Darcy never remembered what they spoke of on the road to Town.

His sister's loss of consciousness was at last pronounced not life-threatening by the physician, who said it was caused by her weakened body and her usual womanly bleeding. Despite the fright engraved forever on Darcy's mind, he decided to give in to her entreaties, and retire early to their country home in Derbyshire. He reasoned that the roads were easier to navigate at this time of the year, and that any further care she would need could be better provided away from the prying eyes of the Town.

Perhaps they were both running away.

In any case, he expected to find solace in their childhood home, counting upon the solitude offered by the scarcity of neighbours, and the inclement weather.

Whenever he caught himself thinking that Liverpool was much closer to Derby than London, Darcy savagely redirected his mind and body with business and sport, hoping exhaustion would help keep his resolution of daily penance for his failings and vices.

Besides, it was only sound to give some precedence to his dealings with his sister, and as such Darcy spent a great part of his time in her company.

As they had wished, they ended up being alone even for Christmas.

His cousin Richard could not attend them because of 'grave state matters'. His uncle and the viscount also announced their intention of staying at their country houses, resolving only to call for a short visit if and when the weather permitted it.

The letter from Liverpool did not arrive.

It followed that, with a single-minded purpose and utter absorption, Darcy dedicated himself to his sister. He attended on her slightest desires, and all the time he could spare from his business was hers: he read to her, he even accompanied her sometimes in her music – though he had always avoided it before – or he pestered Mrs Reynolds for childhood treats – in which the cook was only too happy to oblige.

Sometimes it appeared to be some kind of mourning period, but, slowly, Georgiana's spirits rose, and for her, Darcy found peace a little easier to achieve too.

After he had lost hope of the riders ever making it through the worst of the snow with the post, Darcy received several letters at once from Liverpool.

"What is eighty miles of good road, even in winter?" one of the men asked.

The letters contained a careful report on the management of his investments overseen by John Brindley, who was acting as his man of affairs given the necessary anonymity Darcy's status demanded. His friend mentioned that his family was looking to exchange their part in the slave trade in favour of new factories, and entrusted Darcy with his thoughts concerning the health of their workers or the troubles with some of their merchant ships. He cautioned Darcy about a wave of machine-breaking extending through the country in the name of Ned Ludd, and asked about Darcy's progress in agricultural experiments.

John carefully mentioned that he did not envisage leaving Liverpool for the next season in Town. The Brindleys, unlike the Bingleys, had no intention of ever becoming gentlemen of idle occupation, and John also felt absolved of the need to provide an heir to his aging father, since his brother – with three sons – proved to be quite fruitful in that particular duty.

The last careless lines came as a surprise. They mentioned a respectable recent widow with two children who, apparently, had trouble facing the change in status and the neglect of her new legal guardian. John debated calling on her once her mourning period ended.

Letters in hand, Darcy finally let go of the breath that felt as if it had been lodged in his throat ever since their last ill-advised night together. He let his spine straighten up, and eased his shoulders from the alleviated burden: his own duty was waiting for him.

He did not acknowledge any regret, and if some twinge persisted it was only because he, like his sister, had been used to consider poetry as the 'food of love', and was now mourning, on her behalf only, the loss of that illusion.

Part 2

Darcy was studying the bottle of citrus liquor his cousin Richard sent him – definitely a Spanish trophy of war – with a note announcing his impending arrival in London, when the gentleman's father was announced. Darcy eyed the decanters for a stronger beverage.

The greetings barely out of the way, his uncle promptly made himself comfortable with a glass of gin and then, uncharacteristically, hesitated.

A moment later, the earl began a quite animated monologue about the unfashionability of still serving gin, about the necessity of introducing another ban on distillation, quoting the increase in coarseness and excess brought by the drunkenness and his fear for the pious principles of their society – "Just look at what happened in France!" He drank, then pointed out to his nephew in an authoritative tone that the high number of crimes, the poverty, and the infant mortality the lower class was suffering was caused solely by their alcohol consumption.

Darcy inferred from his fervour that he was in Town for the session of Parliament.

"That Brindley fellow is in town."

The brusque change of topic froze Darcy's neutral countenance.

"Do you maintain the acquaintance?" The nobleman's tone held its characteristic disdain at having to acknowledge 'that kind' of person, but Darcy observed something new lighting his eyes.

Darcy looked intently at the town house accounts spread on his desk, searching for an answer. Perhaps his manservant had misplaced the note bringing that bit of news between the cards and letters waiting still for Darcy's perusal.

"Yes." No matter his surprise, Darcy felt compelled to fend off further enquiries. "I have no plans to attend to any social obligations before leaving for Kent, though."

"But he is still a friend, is he not? Not of our sphere, true, but very well connected, and –" the earl gulped the rest of his glass, and promptly poured another one. "Frankly, nephew, the fact that they opened the marquess's house just for him …"

The marquess's house? John was staying at Lord D.'s townhouse? Again?

Darcy managed to maintain with some effort his reserved mien, and when the blankness in his mind retreated, the conversational topic had thankfully changed. "I intend to go to the Academy after I return from Kent. My fencing practice has badly suffered this winter ... Brindley, though, is a boxing practitioner."

His uncle made a pitiful display, trying to disguise his disgust at such an uncouth form of exercise. "They still have family in the Peak District? The baronetcy will be capital for them!"

Ah. What baronetcy? "Of course."

"Right. Right." His uncle eyed the decanter, but refrained. "It is a great honour, of course. Not a peerage, but, well. I hope you will remember to introduce him some day. At the club. The marquess's family must have sponsored his admission, must they not?" He absently peered into his crystal glass. "A leviathan of wealth." Darcy was sure he was not supposed to hear that part. "This business of canal mania is finally winding down, but the Brindleys are still connected with them."

"The connection with the late Duke of Bridgewater – and his trustee – was through John Brindley's uncle, the canal's engineer, dead some forty years now. I do not think there remains much of a connection, but then I do not mingle socially with either."

"Hmph," conveyed only too clearly his uncle's opinion of that. "There is word that the coal prices will rise again now that the new heirs are taking charge of the Worsley and Manchester mines. There are also voices rising against the use of the canals, and something about how it affects the new factories. And these new steam machines." He paused. "The Brindleys are still in the canal-building business, are they not? Are they behind these new schemes? They must know the cause of this unrest. The Crown needs ..." 'Funds and support' went without saying. Hence the baronetcy.

"I am not in their confidence, Uncle." Which was a truthful, if somewhat incomplete answer.

Darcy calmly waited out his uncle's renewed tirade about the war with France, and the Treasury coffers, and, of course, about the increasing worry stirring amidst the noblemen and landowners forced to face the reduced profitability of their estates in comparison with the new emerging industries.

Darcy firmly refused to dwell upon other matters.

Despite Darcy's efforts, some unruly thoughts escaped his careful control, and he found himself wondering about John's silence. Did he come to Town to accompany his father for the ceremony? But why then choose to accept Lord D.'s hospitality, considering his previous determination to forsake the nobleman?

Aware of his lapse, Darcy reined in his thoughts, and concentrated on the earl's words until he could politely deflect the thinly veiled enquiries into his future plans and schemes.

He knew this stance meant he would have to pay a price, but he was willing to pay it if it meant not taking part in the political and social games his uncle preferred. Their families' connections had to produce a benefit, he accepted it as his duty, and as such he felt no surprise when his uncle overcame his scruples, and carefully sounded him out on his plans to marry Anne.

"Nephew, you know I respect you greatly. Darcy was an excellent man, of course, and he ensured that you are also of independent fortune and means." He paused. "Your mother, my dear sister, confided in me her dreams and hopes for you, and as you are aware she considered her godchild, Anne, a handsome prospect for you. You are your own master, of course, and as such you have no ties and obligations, but I hope you will choose well for your family's sake – at your own convenience, of course. But not too late either! – the situation with Anne's health being what it is …"

Darcy heard the words, but only realised his composure was not as imperturbable as he thought when he checked his hands to see if his normal pallor reflected the warm-and-cold feelings alternately flowing through him. He was impressed that he remained seated when he felt like pacing the room. He struggled for the appearance of composure, and only opened his lips when he believed himself to have fully attained it. Then, with great endeavour at civility and a tranquil tone, he thanked his uncle for his interest. With gentleman-like manner he allowed the reunion to end with cordial feelings on both parts.

When alone, Darcy wistfully found himself longing for a boxing match. Instead, exercising some of his considerable control, he went back to his household accounts, and concentrated on business.

He allowed himself to leave the house for a single visit – not that he acknowledged his waiting about – and it was only because Bingley had preferred to remain in his rented rooms. Fortunately, their visit was cut short by a mysterious appointment cited by the younger man. Darcy noted his friend's low spirits, and almost offered to accompany him, certain that the type of establishment they were emphatically not talking about and the release it brought to men, could serve him well also.

For better or worse, he postponed that outing, and when he got home he found John's calling card waiting for him.

He deliberated on his answer, but decided he was too busy preparing his departure for Kent to attend the club they usually frequented. Or to receive visitors.

He did receive his cousin Richard who was to be his companion for the annual Easter visit to their aunt.

"… blind and short of one arm." After Darcy's neutral grunt, Richard continued what was always a favourite topic when returning to English soil. "Then the vice admiral said, 'You know, Foley, I have only one eye. I have a right to be blind sometimes.' He then raised the telescope to his blind eye and said 'I really do not see the signal'." Richard let go of a full belly laugh, but was careful nonetheless of the contents of the glass in his hand.

Darcy did find the stories fascinating, but, as with the man's father, Darcy was waiting for what his cousin was really setting up to say.

"… Sir William Hamilton's death is still deeply felt! Ignore the gossip about the town …" He lined up his billiards cue for his shot. "I care not for Lady Hamilton's need or joy for the Ton – she likes to *dance*, and to have several partners for it, if you know what I mean – but I know that till his death, Sir William opened his house and heart to Lord Nelson." Richard admired his shot, and salaciously said, "That's the three of them! Balls, I mean." He laughed again, and Darcy thought he should watch out for the alcohol in which they were indulging.

The loud impact of a ball echoed in the room.

"Each time I came home, I was appalled by the – Did you hear about my sister? She came to my mother to complain – hear this! – about the viscount's mistress! There they were, talking about gentlemen's business and my brother's bastard as if they have a say in these matters! My father said it well when he denounced the appalling masculinity some women displayed in their behaviour. Most disagreeable affair …"

Darcy hummed to acknowledge the misappropriation of Dr Fordyce's *Sermons to Young Women*, and much later, when the alcohol had warmed them enough, Richard finally approached the business at hand, and mentioned the strain on his father's household caused, in part, by his sister's recent marriage and the subsequent loss of a considerable amount of funds for her dowry. Unfortunately, his older brother had also lost a considerable sum of money in some dangerous schemes.

Richard was indignant at having to pay for the bad management, since his father also used the portion settled upon him from his mother's dowry to cover up his own debts and habits. Richard had been thinking about his retirement. He was already well past thirty, and while he was grateful for the war and its perks, he felt it was wearing heavily upon his health.

"I admire your power of choice, Darcy. You know not what self-denial and dependence can do to a man."

When Darcy did not speak, Richard, with the harshness of a drunk, said, "Did my father tell you he had Cousin Anne examined at last by a doctor? He said he will avoid Aunt Catherine for a while: their confrontation was violent … It's very doubtful she can conceive."

Even addled, Darcy knew this was the real purpose in his uncle's last attempt to show he was most definitely not interfering with his nephew's 'independence'.

He remained non-committal, but the pressure in his head grew, almost driving away his inebriated languor.

Richard was too impaired to stop though, and too humiliated not to vent, "You need an heir, Darcy. Georgiana's ruined. No, let me finish –" He covered his eyes, but continued. "I will offer for her. For Anne. My father will give his consent, since I am the spare one. With your agreement, of course. We are family. I can –" He trailed off in thought. "There is no entail on Rosings anyhow, and Anne can be prevailed upon to pass a bastard as hers …"

Darcy topped up their glasses, and the topic was closed, never to be mentioned again.

Darcy was intrigued to learn upon their arrival at Rosings Park that his aunt's clergyman was currently having as houseguests a party including Miss

Elizabeth Bennet.

Richard, of course, jumped at the occasion of more entertainment, and left Darcy to indulge their aunt and cousin, while he went to seek his enjoyment elsewhere by way of dusting off his best arts with the ladies. That is to say ladies other than Anne.

As for Darcy, even knowing his path and duty admitted no failing in this matter – the survival of his ancestral family depended solely upon him – he still had enough heart to reproach himself for indulging his aunt, and letting her and her daughter hope for an outcome that was but a last recourse. He needed an heir, and Anne had been poor of health since childhood thus making her an unlikely prospect for him since the beginning.

In regards to Richard, well, he was his own man, and Darcy considered it improper to interfere in how the gentleman chose to employ his time – previously stated intentions notwithstanding.

Darcy's contemplation of his future plans was barely interrupted by John's sudden prolific renewal of correspondence. Lady Catherine's overt allusions to marriage did not help Darcy's humour, especially when coupled with effusive exclamations about Lord D.'s imminent match.

Despite Richard's offer to take Anne off his hands, his cousin ignored the lady and cheered himself with almost daily visits to the nearby lively and outspoken Miss Bennet.

Perversely, Darcy applied his will and went searching out the same young lady. The calls gave him an unlooked-for insight into the Parsonage's new marriage. Darcy became impressed with the complicated, yet satisfactory dance of it. He began envisaging a terrible, shocking idea himself. His past admiration of Miss Elizabeth returned with renewed strength, and Darcy found himself confused and fascinated by the unique position she was quickly gaining in his estimation. She seemed a lone, miraculous exception to his usual disenchantment with female company.

Deeply intrigued, he began an enquiry of the lady's qualities and character. He was conflicted enough by this novel occurrence that he had postponed the decision about their departure once already. He reasoned himself first one way and then the other, and tried to appease his pride. He was wounded by her inferiority and the degradation it would bring him in light of the connection he was contemplating. His character, his judgment, his will pulled him in several directions, and his struggles were so great that he could barely spare time to attend to his written communications.

His scruples proved to be almost insurmountable. Only the deep conviction of his own faults and sins – the shade that he was always trying to escape and to atone for – gave him the strength to conquer them.

It was an inescapable fact that this young lady had managed to catch his attention, when others had failed, and he took it as a sign of the respite he had wished for, as an end to the turmoil and the sickness inside him. He truly felt that he could be a good husband for her – he had never felt such an inclination for a lady before! If he had been of a more religious inclination, he would have called it an absolution. He was able to relax in her presence, he could forget, and not feel torn and tormented, a failure of a man, a perverse and evil joke.

He truly could stand up with her on his arm, a husband, and not have it be an abhorrent disguise. He could fulfil his duty, and his self-respect and honour would be appeased.

In the end, Darcy concluded that his strong feelings of affection for her could surmount any obstacles, and a feeling of euphoria came over him. He was proud, at long last, to be able to relate to his fellow man; he was proud to have won the battle for his soul, because, surely, only the utmost force of passion he had read about in poems could put aside the strong objections against such an imprudent match.

Determined at last, he spent the rest of the night until sleep claimed him, practising the most ardent declarations of love he knew, grateful to enter the long line of romantic fools his gender was known to become when in front of the fairer sex.

Part 3

Darcy did not remember the specifics of how he came to be in his town house.

His anger and stupefaction made him reply harshly to Richard, "As you said, cousin, I have the power of choice. I am my own master. Behave like a gentleman and do not pry into other gentlemen's affairs."

Irritated, he clarified for his baffled cousin, "I did not propose to Anne. It was your choice whether to pay her court or not. You apply yourself so much better at dancing and flattering the ladies than I could ever hope to, after all."

Sadly, his gratification at the colouring his words provoked did not last long, especially after his cousin decamped for the rented accommodation his fellows in the army used when in London.

Darcy's mood did not improve either with Bingley's visit the next day.

A combination of late night hours, wine, Bingley being morose over some lady, and a heavy dose of remorse with just a touch of bitterness, contributed to loosening Darcy's tongue, and telling Bingley that his character was being abused around Meryton for having jilted a young lady.

He offered what information he possessed about the lady's current situation, and her continued esteem for Bingley, but his friend's outrage and precipitate departure only added to the boiling, far from vindicated, fury inside Darcy. He began to fear it would prove to be too much to bear for a lone man.

Soon he found out again that it was not wise to keep tempting fate.

The following morning brought to his doorstep the very person who had most tormented him for this twelvemonth: John Brindley.

The unwittingly invoked apparition pinned Darcy's body to his chair, provoked his mind to become void and his mouth to freeze up impolitely, his lips unwilling to utter even one single word of greeting.

His inanimation felt eternal.

At long last, and in a hurried manner, he recouped, and uttered an enquiry after his friend's health. He remained seated, not really attending to the answer, until he could no more, and then he got up, and began walking the room. After another bout of silence, he approached the other man's chair in an agitated manner, and said, "Your resolution to cut ties lasted only till the next visit to Town."

He saw the confusion on his friend's features, and dispassionately thought he should experience shame for bringing up such private, unspoken matters in the crude, unforgiving light of the day.

"I do not quite get your meaning, Darcy."

He came to himself, at last, as if that voice were finally penetrating through the thick fog in his head.

He could read the sincerity behind the question, but could not work out a reason to stop talking now that he had begun. That struck him as out of character. "You have taken lodgings at Lord D.'s."

His fingers twitched as if adjusting to his favourite rapier. At the last moment he avoided falling into advance-lunge position.

John's nostrils flared, and he deliberately rose from his chair and faced Darcy. For a moment it almost felt as if the maestro's Italian-accented voice talked in the space between them, "One-two-three. Like a dance move, gentlemen. Like a dance, but thrust with all your vigour."

John broke that tempo by quizzically arching an eyebrow, and then he followed the movement with an inclination of his head – perhaps an acknowledgement of the touch. He was already mounting the counter-attack.

"I have not." And it was not a hit, but a parry.

Enthralled, Darcy remembered that while his good friend always claimed a dislike of fencing, it was a fatal mistake to assume that meant he did not excel at it. It only meant that the man preferred other types of exercise.

Darcy changed colour at the thought, but the emotion was short-lived. With a smile of affected incredulity, now that the moves of the game were finally in his possession, he continued, "Where are you staying then?"

It felt as if he had woken up after a long bout of inactivity. He felt the need and the want in his body urging him to move, to conquer all obstacles. His burst of animation compounded his sudden need for verbal sparring, and was enlivening his normal stoic and controlled demeanour.

"At the marquess's. They insisted."

The mischievous tone and laughing dark eyes only inflamed him further. "How can you deny it, then?"

"I meant Stafford House, of course." John's pause let Darcy feel his indignation. "The heir finished remodelling the house and he honoured my father as his first guest. He arrived in Town while you were in Kent. I come to convey his greetings and an invitation to dinner."

"I was misinformed."

"So it seems."

They stared at each other in silence.

He regrouped. "I convey to you and your family my heartfelt, although somewhat belated, congratulations. I will, of course, accept your father's, the baron's, invitation."

This time he had the satisfaction of seeing the other man's composure slip. John took a few steps back, and the chair ended up between them. "I thank you, of course. This baronetcy business ... We are not as free to dispose of our own destiny as we think. I intended to talk to you about this last curious development. I was sure you would be interested. There are rumours about town of schemes and alliances, did you hear about them? There's talk of increasingly vociferous bankers, ship- and factory-owners claiming the vote for themselves. The gall of these upstarts!"

Darcy stared transfixed for a moment at the sardonic curl of lips, and then smiled back. "I heard something about it, yes. In fact, my uncle, the earl, is most interested in making your father's acquaintance. At one of his clubs. And yours, of course."

"Of course."

What followed was a much calmer repartee between them, but Darcy had one last shot left. "When am I to congratulate you on future happiness?"

John took several quick steps in Darcy's direction, and looked him straight in the eye. "Next year, I think. Once the mourning period has run its course ... She is my eldest sister's good friend."

It was Darcy's turn to start. Ah. "You did not mention the heir's age, did you?"

With a faint smile, and – at long last – a trace of warmth, John replied, "The boy is but fifteen, and the daughter is about sixteen."

Oh. She was not what he had imagined. "I, too, made a proposal," he confessed.

His friend's smile became fixed. "Allow me, then, to con-"

"She refused me."

"I beg your pardon?"

Darcy was compelled to bare all to this man. "I am the last man in the world whom she could ever be prevailed upon to marry." The absurdity of that statement made it easy to speak, but the next part was something else entirely. It struck too true and it hurt too greatly, but he found the strength to say the words, "I did not behave in a gentleman-like manner."

John paled, and his hand gripped the back of the chair. "What happened?"

"I do not know."

"Tell me."

And he did. Patiently, John sat and heard the whole sad recount.

"… I must confess, this unfortunate affair does nothing to convince me of the soundness of this much sung-about business of lovemaking, and –"

John interrupted his perusal of the copy of the letter Darcy had handed to him, and said, "Lovemaking, you say. Do you fancy yourself crossed in love?"

"Disgruntled, more like."

John smiled. "Do tell me more about the ardent and romantic display you made to court the lady?"

"You are strange by way of a friend. Are you mocking me?"

"Teasing, more like."

"You cannot deny the romantic gesture of simply asking for her hand! Have I not explained to you the vast separation in rank and consequence between the two of us?"

"If it were to be known about town, I concede, it could be interpreted as an example of a truly passionate and romantic affair. Scandalous, and foolish, but we can perhaps trick them into thinking it is simply a chivalric example of old. Explain to me again about the horrid dragon of a mother, and the family you were saving her from."

Without pausing in his discourse, the tall, dark man rose from the chair, and declaimed laughingly, "*Let not one spark of filthy lustful fire Break out, that may her sacred peace molest.* Truly, Fitzwilliam, the poet was right! This is but the embodiment of the most romantic poem ever." He paused. "It loses the poetic star-crossed air when one hears your account, though."

John sat again in one of the chairs placed in front of the fireplace, so Darcy took the other one. "Tease all you want, your turn will come, my friend … She seemed less inclined to frivolity than the normal fare. I think now that her turn for independence, and the appearance of valuing reason over trifling emotions came less from deliberate understanding and more from a lack of structured education aided by a confined but lax environment."

"I beg your pardon, then." The serious tone was softened by the laughing eyes, and Darcy was hard-pressed to look away.

"I concede that the retelling revealed the error of my approach." When the enthralling dark gaze faltered, eyes widening comically and letting him breathe, Darcy added, without really following the conversation, "I credit her with reason and sense, but I failed to consider the influence of – my own inadequate –"

"It is hard to face certain truths in the harsh light of day." John's words absolved him from having to conclude his thoughts. The fog had cleared completely from Darcy's mind. Or perhaps this man's presence enabled Darcy to hide better the turmoil, giving free rein solely to the peace.

For a beat, Darcy completely lost the thread of the conversation.

With some throat clearing, John looked down at the forgotten letter. "I do think it best you crossed out the name of Georgiana from your explanation." John folded the paper, and put it aside. "It was improper enough to write to the lady."

"I felt that I could sustain the public disclosure if it came to the rest of the content." He stared at his friend's hand resting on the letter. "I am very careful of mentioning private matters in my correspondence."

"As am I." John's warm eyes confirmed his words. "You know I prefer to address my personal affairs in person."

Darcy looked to the fireplace, and felt his memories stirring with ghosts of other nights spent before in this same place.

Somewhere in those moments the letter found its way into the fire.

"Are you staying for dinner?" Darcy resolutely occupied himself in organising the papers and documents on his desk.

"I am free of obligations this evening ... And tomorrow morning too."

A smile tugged at Darcy's lips, and for a moment he knew not what purpose the pen had in his hand.

"Would you like help mending your pen?"

"I always mend my own," was the automatic reply, but his hand pushed the object across the table.

He felt the heat warming his face at the soft laugh he received in response.

"What is the schedule for the rest of your visit in Town?" Darcy clung to the polite veneer with all his might. At least, till he felt able to look back at the other man and not become undone again.

"This visit has not been easy on my father. We will try to keep it free of unnecessary appointments."

Mustering his most neutral mien, Darcy could only mutter, "Of course," before a treacherous smile was tickling his lips again. "Let me send for my housekeeper, and ask her to prepare your usual room. It is quite late and dreary outside already."

Darcy dispatched his errands with utmost diligence and speed, and then he led the way to the dining room.

The dance of silverware on fine porcelain did not falter with each nonchalant remark flying above. "Is that coffee? ... Did I tell you that Bradshaw was talking about his new green coat? The latest in fashion, I am told."

"And I thought Bingley's blue was extravagant."

"A gentleman of fashion has to compete with the sea of common red invading the society ballrooms and parlours. So, blues and greens, my friend. Nothing of that dreary dark grey, dark blue and occasional brown of yours."

Somehow they finished a meal they barely could remember tasting, and continued to the billiard room with the brandy and cigars. It was a short stay, though, what with the hour being late.

"Are you ready to retire?" one of them asked.

The other took his last sip of brandy, and lined up the last shot of the game.

"Quite."

The billiard ball struck true.

Andrea Demetrius

Andrea Demetrius lives on the island of eternal spring, or so the brochures say. She cannot confirm that statement since she is often unable to put down her books to step outside and check.

Margaret

Eleanor Musgrove

Margaret Dashwood had never been as enthusiastic about the prospect of marriage as the rest of her family. Oh, she adored Edward, and she had come to be very fond of Colonel Brandon, but though her mother and sisters had now begun to talk of Margaret's own marriage, she could not bring herself to take any real interest in the prospect.

She found herself in rather a predicament, however, when it came to understanding her feelings on the subject. She longed for a confidante, but for various reasons neither her mother, nor either one of her sisters, could be counted on to give satisfactory advice. After all, she already knew what they would say.

Elinor, of course, would tell her that, unfortunate as it was, a woman's financial security was tied to her marriage. She and Edward did not have much but, carefully managed as it was, they lived quite comfortably.

"Besides," her eldest sister was bound to continue, "marriage to a man one both respects and loves is an exceedingly pleasant union, to say nothing of the joy of children." Margaret was sure that was true, if one loved a gentleman, but she could not even imagine having such feelings for any man. As for children, she loved her nieces and nephews dearly – young Henry Ferrars, and the three little Brandons she so doted on – but she was quite happy to remain an aunt, forgoing motherhood in favour of the relief one felt when, exhausted, one handed a child back to his or her parents.

Marianne's advice would be something else entirely. "Oh, to be in love – truly in love – is wonderful, Margaret! And love, though I did not believe it once, can be learned – but it cannot be forced. You must follow your heart," she would say, "and be cautious of false trails which might tempt you from your destined partner. Forget all practical considerations, and pursue happiness wherever you find it, whether it be in the overtures of an earl or the arms of a stable boy." That was all very well, but her sister had wasted no opportunity to encourage Marianne to marry, and soon. How was she to find an epic love to last the ages when she did not even understand what made a man any more attractive than, for example, a well-arranged vase of flowers or a scenic country view? And, having observed Willoughby's attentions to her sister those six years ago, she could not help but think that a charming and handsome man, just as a scenic view, was best regarded from the top of a tree, or else a still greater distance.

Margaret's mother, of course, saw only calamity in any deviation from the plans she had made for herself and her family. She would share Marianne's romantic sentiments and use Elinor's more practical arguments to full advantage. "You simply must be married, dear child, though it will grieve me to have my youngest fly the nest – marriage is wonderful beyond words, Margaret, and surely you would not deprive me of the comfort, in my advancing years, of seeing you settled with a house and children of your own? Would you be an old maid, never feeling the true passion of being loved so deeply and eternally?" No doubt it would go on forever, if the subject were broached.

It was with a heavy heart, then, that she resolved to ask her family what they thought when next they all dined at Delaford together. Before the women separated from the men after dinner, however, Colonel Brandon surprised her by asking if she might assist him with some advice of her own when the parties rejoined. She agreed, and readily so, but his request so piqued her curiosity that she quite forgot to speak to her sisters about her own dilemma. On the gentlemen's arrival, she had only to wait for Colonel Brandon to exchange a few words with Marianne before he came to join her where she was sitting a little apart from the others.

"I do not think we have spoken of my ward," he began uncomfortably, "though perhaps Marianne has confided in you."

Margaret replied that she had heard only that he *had* a ward, a young woman – though in truth she also knew that whatever story had led to Colonel Brandon's acquiring said ward had increased Elinor's respect for him tenfold and had led Marianne to declare that he was a true hero, worthy of all accolades but forced by circumstance and his own sense of honour to go unsung. Margaret had to admit that the thought of being included in the secret sent a flurry of butterflies aflutter in her stomach; she had always loved adventure, and now it seemed she might be about to hear of a real one. Colonel Brandon, however, did not elaborate.

"Let me add, then, only that she is a young lady – perhaps two years your senior, at most – unmarried, and that she has a son of five years old. The circumstances of his birth I shall not relate, but as the boy has grown, the family with whom Eliza – for that is her name – has lodged all this time have become unable to continue to accommodate them. They are becoming elderly, and the child –"

"I imagine he wishes to climb trees, and track mud through the house." Margaret smiled knowingly, recalling fond memories of her own rather wild childhood. "A younger home, or else their own place, might suit them better, if it can be managed. But forgive me – on what subject did you want my advice?"

Colonel Brandon laughed, a short soft sound that seemed to startle him, as if he had not expected to find merriment in the conversation. "You have already touched upon the heart of it. Eliza is of an age to live independently, now, and since she is unlikely to marry I mean to settle her, with her son, in a cottage on my estate. It has stood vacant these two years, and is past due to be put to good use once more." He paused. "I trust Eliza, and she has grown in wisdom since the events which led to her downfall. Still, I would not see her exposed unduly to the temptation which comes with being alone. You are sensible, of course, but much of an age with my ward. Would *you* be offended if your guardian, having only kind intentions, insisted that you accept a female companion to guide you?"

Margaret considered the question for a few moments. She had spent much of her life without a ready companion of her own age, but even so she could imagine the frustration of being paired with somebody she might not much care for, whose sole purpose was to curtail her few freedoms and pleasures. In fact, she did not need to imagine: back at Norland, she had had a governess. She could think of nothing worse than having a governess well into adulthood.

"I think that it would depend on the woman involved, and perhaps upon the companion, but I cannot pretend I might not feel a little stifled, especially if the arrangement were put to me in just those terms. Perhaps if you suggested that you feared she would be lonely … But surely you could watch over her yourself, if she is to be so close by?"

Colonel Brandon nodded slowly. "Still," he confided, "I would rather she had somebody with her in the house. An unmarried woman alone, especially in Eliza's circumstances … People will not be kind – she is used to that, I'm afraid – and I fear that dishonourable men might presume upon her hospitality. I shall take your advice into consideration, and give the matter further thought. And if I can ever advise you, please do not hesitate to –"

"Do you think I should marry?"

Colonel Brandon raised an eyebrow. "Well, you certainly *don't* hesitate." She opened her mouth to beg his pardon, but he held up a hand to stop her. "No, don't apologise; I offered advice, and I meant it sincerely." With an anxious glance across the room towards his own wife, he continued. "Forgive me for not being fully apprised of the situation, but who might be your intended?"

It was Margaret's turn to surprise herself by laughing. "Oh, I don't have an intended. It's just that there are several people suggesting that I should endeavour to marry very soon, and to tell you the truth, I don't relish the prospect."

"And why should you, indeed," Colonel Brandon exclaimed, "when you have formed no such attachment? Marriage should not be rushed into out of a sense of obligation. Though I understand that there can be a lot of pressure on a young woman, I myself have no regrets in waiting until I found the perfect woman before *I* married, and I hope my wife would agree that it was for the best that I did. You have years ahead of you, Margaret, in which to decide whether to marry or not. If you truly want *my* advice –"

"I do," she assured him.

"Well, then I should advise you not to rush into such things. You deserve only the best."

She smiled at him, then, relieved beyond belief. "Thank you. I fear you have been far more helpful to me than I to you."

"Not at all. Now, I see that your mother has rather decisively won the card game. Perhaps we should rejoin for the next, or else persuade Marianne to play for us." This meeting with her agreement, they rejoined the party and the evening proceeded with much cheer and merriment. Margaret, for one, felt as if a weight had been lifted from her shoulders, and only hoped that she had offered her brother-in-law some measure of the same consolation.

The following day, her mother was invited to the Middletons' house for the third time that week. Mrs Jennings, Lady Middleton's mother, was beginning to feel her age and found the company of her fellow widow comforting. Mrs Dashwood seemed to enjoy these visits more than Margaret could ever have expected, and always answered such summons with great alacrity and enthusiasm. Margaret herself liked to take advantage of her mother's absence on these occasions by climbing her favourite tree with a good book and settling down to read, and so from her lofty roost she was able to observe her mother's demeanour long before she neared the gate on her return that afternoon. Margaret had not seen her look so thoughtful in a long time; she hardly even cast a disapproving look at Margaret's scuffed and grubby clothing as she greeted her.

"Is everything all right, Mama?"

Her mother nodded, then sighed. "Yes, but I can't help but feel I'm disappointing a very dear friend."

"Mrs Jennings? You haven't delayed visiting after even one of her notes. How could you possibly disappoint her?"

"It's only that … Well, Lady Middleton is always very busy, and Sir John too, and she can't get out and about as much as she used to – I fear she's quite lonely up there, poor soul. And she did ask if I would like to move in as a companion, but of course I can't do that."

"Do you want to?" Margaret was surprised; she had had no idea they were so close.

Her mother sighed dramatically. "I wasn't sure, the first time she asked. But we do understand one another, and it is good to have somebody who's had similar experiences to talk to. It might be nice."

Margaret nodded. "Then why … Oh. It's just you they've invited."

"And I don't intend to leave you on your own."

Margaret sighed; she could not really argue with that, and trying would be futile. "I'm sorry," she told her, and excused herself for a walk to clear her head.

It was during another such walk, two days later, that a brilliant thought occurred to Margaret – a thought so brilliant that she had turned towards the Delaford estate and was halfway there before she realised that she might be acting rashly, without even consulting her mother first. Well, she had come too far to turn around now. By the time she arrived at Marianne's house, she had forgotten her possible impropriety altogether, swept up in the excitement of a new adventure.

"Marianne," she asked when she had been shown through to her sister's drawing room and exchanged the necessary formalities, "is Colonel Brandon at home? I wanted to speak to him about something we discussed the other day." It had not really occurred to her that he might *not* be there until she had already said it. She was fortunate, however.

"About Eliza? He told me he'd asked your advice. He's in his study, reading to William, but I think he'd be glad of your perspective. He's worried about what's best for her. I'll come with you and get William; his father has been keeping him more than his fair share, of late." Marianne's besotted smile belied her words, but there was no denying that both mother and son seemed very happy to leave Margaret and the colonel together.

"He was getting restless, anyway," Colonel Brandon assured her when she apologised for her intrusion. "I suppose at four years old, it is rather a stretch to hope that *Songs of Innocence* would hold his attention for long. What can I do for you?"

"Have you raised the idea of a companion with your ward yet, Colonel?"

He sat back a little in his seat, looking almost embarrassed. "No. I mean to do so within the next few days, but I haven't yet worked out how best to broach the subject. I confess, I am rather afraid that if I wound her pride, she won't come at all."

Margaret did not pry into the reasons behind his expression, which spoke of real grief and fear; instead, she set about trying to relieve his anxiety. "Well, I think I know a way you can suggest it without causing any offence. As it happens, I might soon be in need of companionship myself; perhaps you would be so kind as to ask a young lady of your acquaintance if she might oblige, as a very great favour?"

"Well, that could hardly cause offence," the Colonel conceded, "but how could I then explain the substitution of another girl in your place?"

"Well, unless you think me unsuitable, I don't believe you would have to make any such substitution. I have not consulted with my mother yet, but I would be happy to act as companion to your ward if she agrees."

"Truly? You would do that?" He relaxed for a moment, relief clear on his face, before frowning suddenly. "But why would your mother give up her own companion for my ward, a perfect stranger? Surely she has need of you at home."

"I believe that, were she free to do so, she would like to accept Mrs

Jennings' request to keep her company up at Barton Park. We may ask, at least. Can your letter to your ward wait a couple of days?"

"Yes. Yes, I should think so. Thank you, Margaret."

"No, thank you. If this works out, it will be to the benefit of us all, I hope."

Margaret was about to stand and return to Marianne when the Colonel spoke again.

"Margaret, I care deeply about Eliza, but I also care a great deal about you. I don't want you to be … ignorant of the situation. Eliza is likely to attract a certain amount of talk, even if she claims to be a widow, which she prefers not to do. If there is one quality Eliza has in abundance, it is honesty. But her experiences in life are very different from your own, especially in recent years. Living alongside her may not be easy. Do you understand?"

"Of course. I'm sure Elinor would have similar words of caution for me if she were here. Or perhaps not – she is a vicar's wife now, and she was never much for gossip."

"A trait I have always admired. But Christian charity can only go so far."

"Well, let us try, if you will. Let me ask my mother how she feels about the scheme, and then write to Miss … ?" She trailed off; she did not know Eliza's surname.

"Miss Williams. Yes, very well. I should be most grateful."

"I think you may be able to move up to the big house after all, Mama," Marianne told her mother on her return later that afternoon – Marianne had sent her in the carriage, thank God – and proceeded to explain how it could be achieved.

"The ward of Colonel Brandon? Well, if she wants for a companion, then I suppose nothing could be more simple and convenient. Has she any family of note?"

"None, save her young son. Colonel Brandon is most keen that she should not be alone."

"Her son? A widow, then – I was sure Marianne had told me his ward had never married …"

Margaret braced herself for the moment realisation dawned. She did not have long to wait.

"Do you mean to say that you intend to live alongside some sort of fallen woman? Margaret, you can't. I absolutely forbid it! Who knows what manner of misdeeds she may be involved in!"

"With both a guardian and a respectable companion close by to watch over her, I imagine there will be very few misdeeds. Besides, Colonel Brandon trusts her, and I trust his judgement. Don't you?"

It took a great deal more discussion to convince Mrs Dashwood to agree to the plan, but Margaret triumphed eventually. A note was dispatched to Delaford, and another to Mrs Jennings, and soon everything was settled to the satisfaction of all parties.

"Since she is not such a wild girl as I had supposed," Mrs Dashwood murmured absently to herself one evening, and did not trouble herself to finish the thought.

For all Margaret's ardent defence of Miss Williams' character and honour, as the time approached for their meeting, she felt her certainty waning. Indeed, by the time she sat in the parlour of the little cottage, among the possessions she had had brought over earlier that day, she was half convinced that the sound of hooves she awaited would herald the arrival of some sort of wild animal, a changeling child, and a string of disreputable men to heap attention on both women. It was too late to change her mind now; she would rather share a cottage with a rabid dog than disappoint Colonel Brandon at this juncture. No, she would try to make it work, and if it were truly unbearable after a few weeks, she would simply ask him to find a new companion for his ward.

The anticipated hoofbeats, when they came, were accompanied by yapping, and for a fleeting moment Margaret feared that she might *actually* have to live with a rabid dog. She quickly pulled herself together, however, and made her way out into the dusk. Relief flooded through her as her eyes settled on a little black and white dog, who did not look rabid in the slightest despite the commotion he was causing. Looking up, she found that the creature was on a lead which disappeared behind a smartly-dressed young lady. Her clothing was not fashionable, Margaret suspected, but she did seem to be wearing the proper type and number of garments, at least. The way Mrs Dashwood had spoken, Margaret had half expected the girl to arrive in a state of undress.

Colonel Brandon was the first to notice Margaret's presence. "Ah! Miss

Dashwood, my apologies – we had hoped to arrive earlier. May I introduce my ward, Miss Eliza Williams? Eliza, Miss Margaret Dashwood, my sister-in-law." The two women curtseyed formally, though Miss Williams was encumbered by a small person clinging to the back of her skirts and a small dog trying to wind the lead around her legs. Margaret, intrigued by the little boy she could not see, decided to take the initiative.

"I'm very pleased to meet you, Miss Williams. Forgive me, but I was under the impression that you were to be accompanied by another gentleman?" That did not work at all as she had hoped; Miss Williams narrowed her eyes as if unsure whether or not she was being mocked.

Colonel Brandon, however, followed the line of her gaze and let out a short bark of laughter. "Good Lord, you're right! Eliza, we seem to have misplaced Christopher – perhaps he is riding to meet us from the last stop?"

The woman's eyes widened and she turned to look over her shoulder, staring blankly past her son. "Oh … no, we shall have to go back and fetch him – I was *sure* he was attached to the dog."

That, it seemed, was too much for the dignity of any five-year-old to bear.

"Mama! Shep is attached to *me*! Look!" He popped out from behind his mother and tugged at her sleeve until she looked at him … then scuttled back to hide behind her as she feigned surprise.

"Oh, thank goodness … Forgive us, Miss Dashwood – Christopher is a little shy around new people. As for the dog, I apologise for surprising you with him – a friend decided to give him to Christopher as a parting gift. Colonel Brandon assures me that he will gladly keep the dog at his house if you would rather not have him here."

At this, a pair of dark eyes appeared over the dog's head and little arms wrapped protectively around the creature.

"Well," Margaret pretended to think about it, "I never had a dog of my own as a child, so I think Shep can stay on the condition that I am allowed to scratch him behind the ears every now and then. What do you think, Master Williams? Do you think Shep will agree to those terms?"

"Oh, yes, he won't mind that at all! Thank you, Miss!" With that, shyness was forgotten, and Colonel Brandon suggested that they move inside, out of the chill of the evening, and let the footmen set about unloading the Williams' possessions.

Once they were all seated in the drawing room, where a warm fire crackled, Margaret had the opportunity to better observe her new acquaintances. Young Christopher, still a little ill at ease, was tucked close against his mother's body where they shared a chaise longue, and kept turning between Colonel Brandon and Shep with only the occasional glance towards Margaret. She was able to discern, however, that he seemed healthy, and that the shade of his hair was a lighter brown than she had previously suspected – the same as his mother's. Miss Williams, when she turned her face towards the fire, was a handsome woman with delicate features, the light reflecting in her eyes to give them a rich amber glow. In sunlight, Margaret was sure that they would be a glorious brown colour, lighter than Christopher's.

"Miss Dashwood, I would like to extend my thanks to you for allowing us to share your new home."

"Oh." Margaret snapped out of her thoughts about the proper way to describe the colour of Miss Williams' hair – like dark honey, perhaps, but that did not quite capture the browner tones that matched her son's – and shook her head. "Oh, no – on the contrary, I should be thanking you. It does not do to live alone. And please, since we are to live together, call me Margaret."

"Very well. Then of course you must call me Eliza, if you wish."

"And Christopher!" piped a little voice as the boy turned away from Colonel Brandon, who took the opportunity to stand.

"Forgive me, ladies, but if you can manage without me from here, I ought to return to my own family."

"Of course, Colonel, we'll be quite all right. Won't we, Christopher?" Eliza smiled encouragingly, and her son hesitated before turning to Colonel Brandon.

"You *will* come back?"

"Of course, my boy. And I'm sure you'll come to visit me before very long. Good night, ladies. I hope this will be the first of many very comfortable nights here." Then, after embracing Eliza and Christopher, he took his leave with a bow. The footmen followed.

The three remaining occupants of the cottage were then left alone – four, including Shep, who was now sniffing around every nook and cranny, lead trailing behind him – and it was not long before Christopher began to yawn.

"Tired? Well, let's see if we can find you something to eat, and then we'll find your bedroom."

"My mother's housekeeper sent some cold meats and other temptations for travellers at the end of a long day. There should be more than enough for all of us – Shep too."

"Are you quite certain? We would be very grateful, then. Please, lead the way."

When they reached the kitchen, Eliza sent Shep out into their little garden, where Margaret imagined more sniffing would ensue. Only when they had eaten as much as they wanted was Christopher permitted to let him in, and to feed him a meal of leftover meat which the puppy seemed to enjoy thoroughly. Margaret was then left to mind both the dog and the dying fire in the drawing room while Eliza got her son settled into his new bed upstairs.

Shep, as it transpired, was quite happy, after a cursory sniff around the room, to fall asleep at Margaret's feet, one hind leg splayed out awkwardly across the rug. From her new vantage point, slightly above the creature, Margaret could see a copper-brown colour nestled in a long streak along his sides, between the black fur of his back and the white fur of his stomach. It had seemed strange that a predominantly black and white animal should have red markings only on his face and legs; Margaret found, for no reason she could discern, a certain satisfaction in discovering that the splash of brighter colour extended elsewhere. By the time Eliza returned, some half an hour later, Shep had flopped onto his side, head resting on Margaret's feet, and was snoring softly.

"He certainly trusts you," Eliza commented from the doorway. "They say dogs show excellent judgement in these matters."

"I hope to be worthy of it," Margaret replied.

Eliza, though she seemed quite exhausted by the trials of a day on the road, sat down opposite Margaret and regarded her frankly. "I suppose you will wish to hear my story, sooner or later, and I would rather Christopher were not present. I hardly care, any more, what is said or known about me, but my son is an innocent child and I would spare him what I can."

"Your story?" Margaret thought about it for a moment. "By all means, I will listen to you and keep your confidences – but are you not rather tired tonight? There will be time enough to share our histories as we live together."

"Please, I know you will have questions. You will wish to know what manner of woman you have accepted into your house."

"It is your guardian's house, not mine, and I believe that I can learn your character in just the same way as I would learn that of any other person, through familiarity. Already I can tell that you are a devoted mother."

Eliza took a deep breath, then set her shoulders as if braced for battle. "You need not be polite; when I am introduced to new acquaintances, I am quite used to relating the circumstances of my shame."

"Not to me," Margaret told her firmly, "not unless *you* wish to. Although I do have one rather pressing question."

"Ah." Eliza sighed, as if to say that she had known it all along. "Simply ask it; I will hide nothing."

"Where is the dog to sleep? I think it might be wise for us all to go to bed early."

Eliza stared at her for a moment in stunned silence, and then she laughed, a musical sound. "I expect he can sleep in the kitchen, though he has been accustomed to sleeping at the foot of Christopher's bed while we travelled."

"Can he not do so tonight? It may be comforting to your son if his pet is there when he wakes for the first time in a strange place."

But after a moment's consideration, Eliza shook her head. "No – he will only want it to continue, and I'm sure you don't want a dog roaming the cottage all night. Come, Shep. Kitchen. At least you'll be warm." The dog did not follow immediately, perhaps too young to understand the command, but a gentle tug on the lead soon had him moving, tail wagging. Eliza closed the door behind him, having released him from the lead, and offered a candle to Margaret to light her way to bed.

"Thank you," Margaret said, and then, "I hope that you don't mind taking the room nearest to your son's?"

"Not at all. That's perfect. Thank you."

At the top of the stairs, on the narrow landing, they parted.

"Good night, Eliza."

"Good night, Margaret. I look forward to seeing you in daylight."

As Margaret slipped between the sheets, minutes later, she felt a strange warmth bloom in her chest. She looked forward to it, too.

The next day dawned bright and clear, and Margaret woke to a hesitant tap on her door. Wrapping a shawl around her shoulders, she opened it to find Eliza on the other side.

"I'm sorry to wake you," she said, "but I've just got up to make the house ready for the day and there are a couple of servants here that Colonel Brandon has engaged for us. I thought I should warn you, so that you are not startled as I was."

In truth, Margaret had not even considered that there *would not* be servants at least coming in once or twice a day, but it seemed that Eliza had been expecting to fend for herself. She thanked her for the warning, and Eliza smiled.

"I also wondered if you would like to come and see something very sweet, before the maid reaches the kitchen."

Intrigued, Margaret followed her downstairs and allowed herself to be led into the kitchen.

"Oh …"

The sight that met her eyes was very touching indeed: little Christopher Williams must have crept downstairs in the night and was now slumbering peacefully on the hard stone floor, curled around his beloved dog. Shep looked up at them with soulful eyes and thumped his tail softly in greeting.

"Well, I think the dog had better sleep upstairs, in future," Margaret whispered, to a nod of agreement from Eliza, and they both crept away to dress.

When Margaret returned, the outer door was open and, beyond it, Shep was chasing an early butterfly. Christopher was sitting up on the floor, looking a little confused by the maid now unpacking provisions onto the table.

"Good morning, Christopher," Margaret greeted him politely, and he frowned for a moment, rubbing his eyes, before he seemed to remember where he was.

"Good morning, Miss Margaret." His attention was caught by movement over her shoulder. "Good morning, Mama."

"Good morning, little one."

Margaret interrupted the morning greetings with a sudden exclamation.

"Oh! Eliza, is Shep hurt? His leg –"

Both of her new companions turned to look, then relaxed.

"Oh, no, don't worry," Eliza assured her. "That leg is the reason he's never

going to be a sheepdog. He walks well enough, but when he runs …"
Margaret nodded. Shep was lurching alarmingly from side to side as he
frolicked, but it did not seem to dampen his enjoyment of the chase at all.

"Was there some kind of accident?"

"No, he was just born wrong, like me."

"Christopher! You were not *born wrong*. You're perfect, just perfect.
Come here." Eliza gathered her son protectively against her skirts. "The only
people who did anything wrong to make you were your father and I, and I
cannot regret the results. There's nothing wrong with you, *nothing*. Do you
understand?" She did not let go until he nodded. "Good boy. Come, let's see
what can be found for breakfast."

The maid seemed surprised, but not unhappy, when Eliza told her they
would see to their own meals, and declared that she would stop in later that
day to see to the evening's tasks. She was gone, heading back to her duties
at the main house, before Margaret could protest that she did not know *how*
to cook.

Eliza, however, seemed unperturbed when she told her. "Well, I can
handle all that. I could teach you, if you'd like."

That sounded lovely, and Margaret said so. This agreed, Eliza set about
making breakfast while Margaret supervised Shep and Christopher's antics
in the garden. More accurately, Margaret stood in the doorway and kept half
an eye on the pair while most of her attention was focused on watching Eliza
bustle around the kitchen, moving fluidly from cupboard to cupboard with
surprising grace considering that she did not know where anything was kept.
It was not long at all before the three of them were comfortably seated
around the table, eating and exchanging trivial stories about their lives, and
getting to know one another.

"… And the cook looked away for a few minutes to make the pastry, and
by the time either of us turned back to look, *this* little imp had eaten half a
basket of blackberries and was sitting there as innocent as could be, covered
in purple juice."

Christopher grinned, unrepentant, but had clearly lost interest in the
conversation and soon ran off to chase Shep around their little garden,
exploring together.

Eliza turned to Margaret. "How about you? Do you have any wild tales
from your childhood to tell?"

Margaret could only oblige with tales of imaginary adventures, battling pirates on the high seas – or rather, the high lawns. "And you? Did you drive any governesses to distraction?"

"I'm afraid I was a terribly well-behaved child, so I have no such stories, until I met Christopher's father."

Margaret hesitated, but Eliza had now raised the difficult subject more than once, and she remembered Colonel Brandon telling her that honesty was Eliza's defining trait.

"Would you like to tell me *that* story?"

"Some of it, perhaps. But if Christopher returns –"

"Of course. I wouldn't want to pry, anyway."

Eliza frowned. "I believe you. Most people, in my experience, want to know everything before they risk becoming connected to me in any way. My guardian tells me you asked him very little. But you should know some things, at least. The gossips in the village certainly will." She took a deep breath and released it slowly before she began.

"He was charming, you know. He made me feel, for the first time in my life, that I belonged to someone. *With* someone. I was young, and foolish, and I didn't understand why my guardian had to keep his distance. I was *somebody's* natural daughter, and everyone knew it – they would have assumed I was his. But I didn't understand, then – I just felt abandoned, left with a family who couldn't quite – I mean to say that – They were very kind. But none of us ever forgot what I was … He came along and he didn't care about that. He treated me like a duchess, even a queen. He told me he loved me. And then, when I found out that Christopher was growing inside me … He left. I don't know if … I think he would have left me even if I hadn't been with child. Abandoned me, like everyone else. But this time, it was my own fault. I was foolish, I believed him when he said … Colonel Brandon tells me that there was someone else, but she never –"

Eliza stopped, turning to stare out at the garden, but her glazed expression suggested that she did not really see anything. Finally, her eyes settled on Christopher, still playing with the dog in blissful ignorance.

"But I have *him*. Because of what I did … I have him. And I will never let him feel the way I felt. I may be ashamed of my actions, but I will never be ashamed of him."

Margaret did not know what to say to that, so she poured them each another cup of tea, stalling for time. At last, she dared to look Eliza in the eyes. "Did you love him? Christopher's father?"

For a moment, it was as if she did not know how to answer. "… I thought I did."

"Then I don't see that there's anything to be ashamed of. I've never been in love, but my sisters … I've seen how hard it is to fight it."

Just then, Shep bounded in, Christopher in pursuit, and so all Eliza could do was offer a quiet "thank you" before the matter was closed.

Over the next few weeks, Margaret dined with Marianne and her family on several occasions, but Eliza had declined every such invitation, citing a lack of suitable attire and the need for somebody to stay at home with Christopher. Margaret had offered to look after him, but despite their growing friendship the two women were still almost strangers and so it was hardly surprising that she preferred to invite her guardian to their house instead. Eventually, however, both women were invited to dinner and asked to bring Christopher and Shep with them. Colonel Brandon warned his ward that short of grave illness, Marianne would brook no further excuse. They duly dressed for the occasion and made sure both boy and dog were presentable before climbing into the carriage that had been sent for them.

"Are you nervous?" Margaret asked her friend as they settled their skirts around them.

Eliza nodded. "A little. Colonel Brandon speaks so highly of your sisters."

"He speaks just as highly of you," Margaret assured her, but this did not seem to calm her at all.

"Then he is too kind – how can I ever hope to match up to his praise?"

Margaret reached out and took her hand, squeezing it gently. "Believe me, you match up."

Eliza blushed – and then they were off. When they arrived, Christopher leapt from the carriage and helped the ladies down like a proper little gentleman. Eliza had to let go of Margaret's hand in order to take her son's, and Margaret realised with a start that she had found their contact reassuring, too.

Distracted by Shep, whose lead she had somehow ended up holding, Margaret paid little attention to the introductions taking place until she heard her sister gasp. She looked up to see Marianne staring, chalk-white, into Christopher's eyes.

"*Willoughby –*" she breathed, and then abruptly shook her head. "Er – I mean, that is, er –"

Fortunately, the Colonel was on hand and cut in smoothly with, "I think what Mrs Brandon means, Christopher, is that Will – our son, William, he's just a little younger than you – will be waiting to meet you in the nursery. But first, perhaps Miss Dashwood would like to assist me in introducing you and Shep to the rest of the family? Mrs Dashwood has brought her friend, Mrs Jennings, and Mr and Mrs Ferrars are here."

Marianne was now speaking to Eliza in a low, urgent voice, standing very close to her, and Margaret agreed with Colonel Brandon that Christopher would be better off distracted. It was with great pleasure that she introduced the little boy to her family and friends, and when she glanced back at Eliza and Marianne she was just in time to see the two women share a slightly tearful embrace. Edward, bless his soul, managed to hold Christopher's attention while handkerchiefs were produced and put to use, and then it was Eliza's turn to meet everybody.

Margaret was relieved to see that her mother and Mrs Jennings seemed to be behaving themselves, though no doubt they would be full of gossip and speculation later. Elinor had made the effort to keep Eliza talking while the Colonel and his wife entertained the older women, and all seemed to be going well. Margaret was all but lost in her thoughts, watching the candlelight playing on Eliza's hair and face, when her attention was caught once more by Christopher.

"You're a vicar, aren't you, Mr Ferrars? Does that mean God listens to you?"

Edward seemed rather taken aback, but he smiled as he answered. "Well, I think the thing to remember is that He listens to everyone."

But Christopher would not be so easily satisfied. "Would you ask Him to please love Mama and me again?"

A stunned sort of silence rippled outward from Christopher, his question falling like a rock dropping in a pool and causing just as much disturbance.

Edward, unusually, was the first to recover. "I don't need to do that. God loves everybody, especially children."

"But the people at church said He couldn't love us. They said we were bad. I don't want to be bad."

"Ah," Edward asked him, with a knowing glint in his eye, "but were those people vicars?"

"One of them was."

"Oh." Edward looked mildly affronted, frowning thoughtfully. "Well, I'm afraid you must not have had a very good vicar. The most important thing you need to know about God, Christopher, is that He loves you. He loves everyone, even if they're bad. And I don't think you look like somebody who's bad. I can still pray for you, though, if you'd like. And for your mother."

Christopher nodded firmly. "Thank you, Mr Ferrars." He turned to Colonel Brandon. "Can I meet your son now?"

"Of course. My daughters and Henry Ferrars, too. Let's take your mother with us, shall we? I'm sure they'll all want to meet her. And Shep, of course."

With Eliza and Christopher gone, there was nothing to stop Margaret joining her sisters and trying to find out what had just happened.

"Marianne? Why did you – I mean, what's wrong?"

Elinor placed a hand on Marianne's arm, a caution. "I think it's up to Eliza to explain that, Margaret, if she chooses to."

"But you know."

"I do. I found out before we knew Eliza. You know her, and it should be her choice whether or not she explains this to you."

"But it's Marianne who –"

"Margaret, please. Let it go, for now."

Marianne nodded her agreement, and then called out for Eliza to sit with them as she returned to the room. Mrs Dashwood soon insisted that she and Colonel Brandon make up the numbers at cards, and it was not until they were all in the carriage on the way home that Margaret had a chance to speak to Eliza again. With Christopher sitting there, however, it did not seem right to broach the subject. Whatever had spooked Marianne, it seemed to be something to do with him – and Eliza was fiercely protective of him.

Later, when Christopher was safely tucked up in bed, Margaret ventured the question. "Are you all right?"

"I am. It was a nice evening." But Eliza seemed withdrawn, pensive somehow.

"Marianne didn't upset you, I hope?"

"No. No, I rather think I upset her, but she was very kind."

"May I ask what happened? She said *Willoughby*."

"I had no idea, I promise you, Margaret. I didn't know she was the other lady he pursued."

"You mean … Willoughby is – ?"

"Mr John Willoughby is Christopher's father, yes. Christopher doesn't know, and I'd rather you didn't tell him."

"Of course not. Good Lord, the two have nothing in common."

"No, thank God. Except his eyes. That's what startled your sister."

"I'm sorry."

"There's no need. If you don't mind, I'm very tired. I think I shall retire."

Margaret let her go, but not before she patted her arm and apologised again for prying.

"That's quite all right." Eliza smiled wearily at her. "You're a good friend; I don't mind you knowing my secrets. I know I can trust you. Good night, Margaret."

As the summer days grew longer, so Eliza and Margaret grew closer. They spent as much time as they could out of doors together, walking and taking the air, utterly untroubled by those who pointed out that their skin would turn darker than was fashionable. Christopher and Shep had become accustomed to having the run of the estate, and seemed to have made firm friends with the manual workers of the countryside.

"That's how he came to have Shep," Eliza confided, when Margaret mentioned it. "He used to spend a lot of time with one of the shepherds, watching the sheep and so forth. Old Zeke took him under his wing, rather, and then when Shep was born with a twisted leg … He didn't want anyone else to have him but Christopher."

"Well, Shep was clearly the best present a boy could ask for."

While boy and dog rushed ahead, the ladies would follow at their own pace – Christopher knew better than to stray too far – and they would talk of nothing and everything. Sometimes, they walked arm in arm. When one of them was upset, they walked hand in hand, close together. And gradually, as time wore on, they began to realise that no topic was out of bounds between them.

"May I ask you something rather improper?" It was Eliza who started the conversation; usually she was the more proper of the two, having rather more at stake. Today was different, it seemed.

"Of course, but I shan't promise to answer until I have heard it."

"Have you ever felt the slightest inclination towards loving any man?" That could have been a rather impertinent question, but coming from Eliza it did not feel like that at all.

"I can't say that I have. Perhaps one day I will, but until now …" She had not felt the faintest stirrings of romantic interest in a man. Honestly, Margaret fancied that she was closer to Eliza than she could ever be to anybody she might one day marry. How could a gentleman ever know or understand her as well as her dearest friend? "What's it like?"

"Exciting, I suppose. It carries you away, at first. But then … it all went wrong, for me. And there are some things I don't think I'd like to do again."

"What sort of – ? Oh." Margaret blushed as she caught up with her friend's thoughts.

"I'm sorry. I was just thinking aloud … people don't usually ask *me* about romance."

"Is … the … er, union … not pleasant?"

"Perhaps it is because it was a sin. I think it was enjoyable for John, but … perhaps it is because men aren't as soft. When you and I share a friendly embrace, there are no hard angles, no pain. A man who feels for you is … different. I think I prefer the softer touch of a woman." Eliza stopped short, flustered. "I mean, not in the same way, obviously."

"Of course," Margaret assured her. "I can imagine that a more gentle embrace would be preferable." Then, after a few moments, "Do you think the blackberry harvest will be good this year?"

"I hope so," Eliza replied with some relief, "for Christopher and I love to pick them as we walk, and this year you might join us."

"I should think you would have some difficulty if you tried to stop me," Margaret told her solemnly, and they continued to walk.

Margaret was taking tea with her mother and Mrs Jennings when the conversation abruptly turned to her companion.

"There's no denying that the boy is very sweet," Mrs Jennings acknowledged, "and it is very gentlemanly of him to bring flowers from your garden whenever he visits the main house at Delaford."

"Perhaps too gentlemanly," Mrs Dashwood interjected. "I do hope he isn't following in the footsteps of his father."

"He's a little young to be chasing Marianne, don't you think? No, the boy is a fine lad, no doubt due to the influence of Colonel Brandon and the family he entrusted his wards to. It's his mother who makes me uneasy."

"His mother?" Margaret protested. "Why on earth would you say that?"

"Well, besides her dubious moral character – though what can one expect, when by all accounts her mother was just as foolish – there is the way she carries herself so guardedly, as if all the world was out to attack her. I simply cannot trust a person who trusts nobody." Mrs Jennings nodded decisively, and Margaret had just long enough to think that she could not imagine *why* Eliza was guarded, given the current conversation, before her mother joined in.

"She doesn't guard her tongue, though. Elinor told me – in the strictest confidence, of course – that she had no compunction whatsoever about telling her story to anybody who showed an interest."

"If she told you in confidence," Margaret countered, "you ought not to mention it at all. I, for one, appreciate Eliza's honesty. It is a great comfort to know that there are still some people who will give their truthful opinion when one asks them, rather than saying what they think one wants to hear to one's face and saying something quite different behind one's back."

If either of the older women took her meaning, they gave no sign of it. It was not until a good half hour later that the real reason for Mrs Jennings' disapprobation became clear.

"The girl looks positively *faded*, as if she should have been a fine, respectable brunette, but the colour has worn out of her with too much use."

"Too much use is exactly the problem," Mrs Dashwood told her, "and I shouldn't be surprised if one's appearance alters to reflect one's soul. It seems only fair that respectable people should have some way of being forewarned."

"Well, I think she's beautiful," Margaret declared, rising without ceremony, "and since I cannot convince you of her virtues I intend to return home and appreciate them for myself. Goodbye, Mother. Mrs Jennings."

Then she turned and walked out of the house without a single thought for propriety or respect for one's elders. If Eliza did not mind what people thought of her, why should Margaret? It seemed much more freeing to speak as one felt, where it did no harm.

At least, Margaret had thought that Eliza did not mind what people thought. When she returned home, however, she found Christopher and Shep playing alone in the kitchen, getting under the maid's feet in a way that Eliza would never usually permit.

"Christopher, Susan is trying to stock our cupboards for us. Perhaps you and Shep could play in the drawing room instead?"

"Oh! Sorry, Miss Susan. Come on, Shep."

Margaret exchanged a fondly exasperated look with the maid before following the boy into the drawing room, where Susan had already stoked a fire and set the guard in front of the grate. "Where is your mother, Christopher?"

"She's in bed. She didn't feel well."

"Oh, well, that's no good, is it? Will you be very good and stay away from the fire while I see if I can fetch her anything?"

"I'll be good. I'll make sure Shep's good, too." Christopher leant in conspiratorially, which meant he ended up addressing her waist. "He's a bit scared of the fire, but he likes to sit near it and keep warm."

"Well, just you mind you don't get any closer than that rug there, and I'll be back as quickly as I can." Nonetheless, she asked Susan to listen out for trouble before she hurried upstairs in search of her friend.

A knock at the door raised no response, and Margaret felt she had better push the door open to make sure that Eliza was just sleeping peacefully and not altogether more unwell than expected. When she did, however, she found Eliza lying fully clothed atop the covers, face buried in the pillow, sobbing her heart out.

Afraid that Christopher would hear his mother's weeping, Margaret stepped inside and closed the door swiftly behind her. "Eliza? Whatever has happened?"

"Margaret!" Eliza sat up, brushing her hands across her eyes in an attempt to stem the flow of tears. "I – I didn't expect you back until later."

"Well, here I am. And it's just as well, isn't it? Please, tell me what's wrong."

"It's nothing, I'm just being silly –"

"Nonsense." Margaret crossed the room and took her hands, perching on the edge of the bed with her. "You're not silly, and I want to help. What's happened?"

"Nothing – I just, at church yesterday …"

Margaret stiffened; she had hoped that Eliza had not heard the gossips starting up again. There was little chance of that, however – they had taken no pains to keep their voices down, and it now seemed that if ever a so-called gentleman returned to his wife smelling of an unfamiliar perfume, Eliza was to be blamed.

"Everybody seems to think that I am having an affair with Mr Rowley, and last month I was supposedly receiving frequent visits from Mr Sedgewick." Eliza sighed. "Frankly, I wonder that they think I have the time, with Christopher to look after – to say nothing of the inclination."

"Would you like me to put them right? I spend all my time with you, and I have seen no such gentlemen around."

"No, no – that's quite all right. They would think you were simply lying to defend me, or else that those gentlemen callers had been here to see you as well. I won't have your honour questioned, especially since it would do no good to mine anyway."

They sat quietly for a few moments, until it seemed that Eliza could be silent no more.

"I'm tired of people talking about me," she burst out. "Nobody sees past what I did."

"The people who love you do. Colonel Brandon does. Marianne and Elinor, Edward ... I do."

"I'm afraid that Christopher will realise what they say about me. That he will despise me, when he learns what I am."

"What you are?" Margaret squeezed Eliza's hands gently in reassurance. "Let me tell you what you are, Eliza."

"I'm a silly girl who threw her virtue away."

"No. Listen. You are the bravest woman I know. You're kind, and a good mother, and you keep going no matter what people say about you. You make *me* brave. And on top of all that, you happen to be absolutely beautiful. You're my best friend. And nothing in your past changes any of those things."

Eliza stared at her for a moment. "You think I'm beautiful?"

"Well, yes." Margaret blushed, feeling suddenly awkward. "I have eyes. And brave, and kind. And Christopher would be lost without you."

Eliza let go of her hands with a smile that seemed to warm the room. "He would be. Oh, goodness, he's probably driving Susan to distraction.

Thank you for saying those kind things, Margaret. Now let's go and see if we can get my son out of trouble."

Margaret was not entirely convinced that her words had been believed, but she let it go. Christopher *was*, after all, likely to be driving the maid to distraction.

Margaret found, a few weeks after that fateful day she had found Eliza crying, that she had rather an awful headache.

"I'm quite well within myself," she told her friend, "but I think it best that I stay indoors for today and rest. You and Christopher must go on your walk without me, I'm afraid."

"Are you quite certain that you're all right?"

"It's only a minor headache. It will soon pass, and we cannot keep Christopher cooped up all day."

"No," Eliza conceded, "he is in rather a frolicsome mood. Better that you have some peace to aid your recovery. Come along, Christopher."

"Make sure you tell me all about your adventures when you come back!"

Christopher shouted back from the door that he would, and then they were gone, Shep bounding along in front.

Margaret settled with a cup of tea by her bedroom window and closed her eyes, trying to rest as well as she could without moving away from the pleasant breeze drifting in. She must have fallen asleep, because when she opened her eyes again the last dregs of her tea were cold, the shadows falling in the room were longer than they had been and pointing in a different direction, and Christopher's voice could be heard in the hallway.

"Shh, remember that Margaret has a headache. Quietly. Go into the garden and see if you can get all of that grass out of Shep's fur while I see if she's all right." The noise died down into 'shhh' sounds and footsteps, and then there was a tap at the door. "May I come in, Margaret?"

"Of course, Eliza."

Her friend came in as quietly as a mouse, and closed the door silently behind her before holding out a bunch of purple flowers.

"Violets. I thought you might like them."

"I do, thank you. They're lovely."

Eliza beamed. "I'm glad." She pushed aside some of the larger leaves to reveal more purple blooms underneath. "We added some lavender from the garden, to help relax you a little. I always find the scent so soothing, especially when my head aches."

"That's very thoughtful of you." Margaret took the flowers and set them down on her dresser, intending to find a vase for them later. "Thank you. Please, sit with me awhile."

The bedchamber was small, and so the only reasonable place for them both to alight together was on Margaret's bed. They sat, side by side on the edge, and Margaret could not help but notice how close they were sitting to one another. Where her arm almost touched Eliza's, there seemed to be a sort of heat, far more than the usual warmth of a body, and it spread through her own body as they stayed close.

"Eliza?" She took a deep breath. "I've only ever really lived with my mother. So I don't know much about the world. But ... you know more, don't you?"

Eliza hummed softly to herself, as if in thought. "Of some things, perhaps."

"If I ask you something, will you promise not to judge me?" She took Eliza's answering hum as agreement and stumbled on before she could change her mind. "Are there any ... are there women who prefer ... other women, the way most women prefer men?"

"I ... I think so."

"Are you one of them?"

Eliza began stuttering a denial, but Margaret cut her off.

"Because – I think I might be. And, well, you mean a lot to me. More than you should. I look at you, and I understand what Marianne has been talking about all these years."

Eliza stared at her blankly for a few long, painful moments, and Margaret felt as though she was watching their friendship disintegrate.

"So ... you find me a temptation? Or a bad influence? You'd like Christopher and me to leave?"

"No! No. You must stay, of course. I wouldn't have you anywhere else. But ... well, I understand. It's not right, and I didn't expect you to –"

Eliza reached out and covered Margaret's hand with her own. "I am. One of those women. But nobody ... even Christopher ... nobody can ever know."

Margaret smiled sadly. "What is there to know? Surely just having feelings can't get us into too much trouble."

"Perhaps. Perhaps not." Eliza sighed. "But this might." Then she leant in, very slowly, and pressed their lips together in Margaret Dashwood's very first kiss.

Eleanor Musgrove

Eleanor Musgrove is a graduate of the University of Kent, and a one-woman word machine at least one month out of the year. She is currently working towards publishing her first novel, and has many more tales to tell.

eamusgrove.wordpress.com

The Wind over Pemberley

Fae Mcloughlin

The First Tuesday

Freshly carved into the wood, the neat letters declared, *This bench is dedicated to Harold, the place he spent his last day.* Last day? Did that mean he jumped off Pemberley cliff? Is my arse on the same spot on the bench where Harold's arse was before he leapt to his doom? I stood, took a few hesitant steps towards the edge, and leant forward to spy any possible remains of poor Harold. There were none.

The cliff was a notorious suicide spot. I never understood why, as the sea cliff, with its hair-whipping wind and stomach-churning sheer side, was my favourite place to be.

Pushing my overgrown fringe out of my eyes and then shielding them from the sea glare, I stared across the water. In the distance, the turbine farm whirled and above it, a mackerel sky. My grandma used to say, 'Change is afoot,' whenever she saw the distinctive cloud pattern. A seagull plummeted past me and disappeared; all that was left were its cries.

I turned back to Harold's bench. The faded council-green paint contrasted with the two curling black iron serpents whose tails held the wooden slatted backrest; their bodies formed the armrests, and heads shaped the supports. I called them Wickham, the scoundrel from Jane Austen's *Pride and Prejudice*, and Crawford, the womaniser from *Mansfield Park*. I spent all my spare time with Wickham and Crawford while I seized my books from the wind's grasp and daydreamed about becoming a famous writer.

Sitting with a sigh, I picked up *Mansfield Park*, flicked to the bookmarked page, and read, *Life seems but a quick succession of busy nothings.* Jane's words resonated with me; my life since the redundancy was pointless, dull, and invisible.

A burst of colour caught my eye; I turned in its direction. Jiggling too close to the edge of Pemberley, the colour came closer and morphed into human form. The runner had a dreadful outfit decorating his gangly frame.

Leggings that had had an unfortunate mishap in a paint factory and an orange t-shirt with a white handprint emblazoned across the chest, all topped with a luminous yellow headband trapping a mop of dancing hair. Overall, he looked as if he'd run from the pages of an eighties fitness magazine. The cosmic blur jogged past the bench, raised a finger in greeting, and then ran off. I watched it go until it was no more than a dot of colour between the line of green cliff and blue sky. Then it stopped and sprinted back.

The runner rested his hands on his knees and panted, "You read Austen?"

Do I reply to the cosmic weirdo, pretend to watch the turbines, or be polite? I was English so I politely replied, "Yes, um ... do you?"

Sitting next to me, he brought the smell of sweat and warmth off his rosy skin. His shaggy hair was varying shades of blond, red and brown, and as his leggings had obviously had an accident, so must've his hair. The runner's face lit, or maybe it was a reflection from the orange t-shirt, as he said, "I'm crazy about Jane Austen, I have all her books, and I'm a member of the Janeites."

I laid an arm on Crawford's metal body. "Oh, so am I! I'm an English teacher with a passion for Austen – or was. I was recently made redundant."

"Oh, I'm sorry. That must have been a dream job."

"It was."

He held out his hand. "I'm Lint."

I took it. "Lint? That's an unusual name."

"Yeah, my parents said I was always picking up bits of fluff so they nicknamed me Lint."

"Fluff?"

"Boys."

I laughed. "What's your real name?"

"Simon."

"Think I prefer Lint."

"Me too." Lint smiled.

"I'm Darcy."

"Darcy? That's an unusual name," Lint echoed.

"Yeah. My parents were old romantics."

"And Austen fans."

"Literature fans. I spent many a summer at the Hay Festival."

"You're lucky. I spent my summers in a tipi on the edge of the New Forest. Bloody freezing it was, even in July."

Tipi in the woods. Somehow, that didn't surprise me. I gathered my books to my chest, pushed hair out of my eyes, and considered a headband but certainly not as bright as Lint's, and I smiled before standing. "I'm afraid I have to go." Evelyn was expecting me for tea and, as a trainee chef, she used me as her guinea pig. Tonight was Aubergine Caponata with capers. I hated capers but forced them down. At some point, I'd tell her I was more a meat and two veg kind of guy.

Lint joined me. There was an attractive glow to him; it may have been the flush of exercise or ... something else. He was a good head taller than I was and round-shouldered, probably from avoiding low ceilings his whole life. For the first time I caught his eyes: one was pale blue while the other was hazel. I must have stared for far too long because he said, "Genetics."

My ears burnt as I stuttered, "Oh, yes, sorry, nice to meet you." With my head down against the wind, I strode away along the cliff edge towards the small car park where I'd left Betsy, my Morris Minor.

The Second Tuesday

On the blue-lined paper I wrote, *Tuesday*, and carefully underlined it. Then underneath, *Today I've decided to write a diary.* Then stopped. That was all I had. I could write, *Got up, brushed teeth, washed face, ate cornflakes, tripped over the cat, kicked Betsy for not starting, and drove to Pemberley.* After tapping the pen on my lips for a few seconds, I wrote that down. If I wanted to reinvent myself as a writer, I really needed to get a life.

"Darcy?"

I jumped and the pen leapt in the air. Nobody said my name on Pemberley cliff; in fact, not many people said my name full stop. Someone stood blocking the sun and all that remained was a silhouette, but I knew who it was from the height, long limbs, and hair.

"Lint. Nice to see you again." And it was.

He moved from the sun's grasp and I involuntarily drew a loud breath. He looked nothing like the eighties runner of two days ago. His pink checked shirt, opened to the chest, flapped in the breeze revealing downy hair, and his hands, shoved deep into the pockets of casual baggy pants, were probably keeping them from falling down. His hair danced in the gusts like Medusa's snakes.

He sat next to me. "We'll have to stop meeting like this."

Did he actually say that? "Yes." I murmured a laugh. "Not running today?"

"No, I only run on Tuesdays. I'm not that much of a runner really, just trying to lose a few pounds."

To me, he didn't need to lose anything, but I didn't comment, just smiled instead.

We sat in silence as the pages of my books fluttered, the seagulls called, and I could almost hear the turbines whine.

"You have an, um, fascinating running outfit." I'm a bloody English teacher who's crap at the art of conversation.

"Yes, I like to upset all the running snobs in their high performance gear."

I nodded as if I were fully aware of high performance running gear, then pointed to my left and blurted, "Lint, meet Wickham," then indicating right I said, "and Crawford." Fuck, now he was going to think I was a proper curio.

Lint dropped his head between his knees and said the serpents, "Pleased to meet you, I'm Lint."

I liked him. "So what do you do when you're not upsetting the performance runners?"

"Drive a forklift at the paper factory on Spur Point." He indicated towards the slither of land jutting into the ocean and the grim smoking mass that occupied the end. "But really I want to be a writer."

"Join the club," I sighed.

"Okay."

"Okay, what?"

"I'll join the club."

"No, no, it was a figure of speech."

Lint picked up my notebook, read my dreary post, and then one by one picked up *Mansfield Park*, *Pride and Prejudice*, and *Sense and Sensibility*. "Why not? We could share our passion for Austen. I'm free on Tuesdays."

I'd be very happy for a focus to my week so I said, "Okay. We could start right now," and went to take *Sense and Sensibility* from him but Lint, staring at my hand, held on to the book for a second.

"You're married," he blurted and his ears reddened.

Fiddling with the band of cheap silver on my ring finger, I said, "Yes."

"I, um."

I'd only known Lint for less than an hour but said, "I once tried to tell my parents I was gay." I paused and watched him relax back on the bench, slinging one long arm over the back. "But they cut into my words and said that their son wasn't gay and if he were he'd be disowned. Blah, blah, blah." I crossed my arms to ease the flutters in my chest and Lint shook his head. "I met Evelyn, my wife, at university and we were instantly soulmates. She was, and still is, a tearaway, and her mother had chucked her out. To cut a long story short, she needed somewhere to live and I needed my family off my back, so after graduation we married. Probably not the wisest of moves but we're happy with the situation and she even has a secret boyfriend, which we both find thrilling!"

Lint sat upright. "And do you have a secret boyfriend?"

It was clear from Lint's nickname that he'd had hundreds of bits of fluff, and I'd never had a boyfriend. If I told him, would he laugh or pity me? I knew the postman better than I knew the young man sat next to me. I shuffled and said, "I've never had a boyfriend."

"There's a first time for everything." He took *Sense and Sensibility* from me, flicked through the pages, and read, "*The more I know of the world, the more I am convinced that I shall never see a man whom I can really love.*" His eyes flicked up to mine and held them for an instant.

I looked away before saying, "Miss Austen was sharp you know, in mind and in wit."

"You can see echoes of Jane in her female characters," Lint replied.

"Yes, I've always thought that."

Lint bit his lip. "If I had to, you know, shag a woman. It'd be her."

I'd had a few fantasies about Jane Austen myself. "Oh, absolutely," I said and flushed.

Lint laughed. "This is a very improper conversation!"

"Well, with Miss Austen's unique view of the world, she might approve." I winked at him and immediately regretted it; I'd never winked at anybody in my life. Gathering my belongings, I got up to leave as more guinea-pig-tea was waiting. "Next Tuesday, then?" Somehow, next Tuesday was too far away.

"Next Tuesday." He slipped an arm around my shoulder and pulled me into a warm embrace. "This two person club of ours needs a name."

"What about the Bench Book Club?"

"The BBC it is." He kissed me lightly on the forehead and sauntered off too close to the edge of Pemberley, with hands in pockets and hair waving. I watched him go with the thrill of his kiss still tickling my skin.

The Third Tuesday

The council car park was not much to look at. The black and white metal height barrier had been bashed so many times it'd turned into an upside down V-shape, and around the edge huge misshapen boulders with iron rings on their heads bordered the parking area like discarded boat moorings. In the corner space was a small yellow car; it was always there, in the same spot, and maybe it never moved. I occasionally saw a young lad who looked like he needed a decent meal sat in the passenger side blowing smoke through the open window.

I guided Betsy into my usual parking space, yanked on her handbrake, and watched the usual movie through the windscreen – thin clouds drifting, sea waving, seagulls diving, turbines turning, and the horizon shimmering. Gathering my books, notebook, and bobble hat, I stepped out of the Morris.

The morning was clear and its light outlined every blade of grass and worn pebble that edged the single-track path to the bench.

Lint was there, waiting for me, smiling. On his head was a hat that looked like a curled up Persian cat with a tail wagging in the wind. Adorning his body was a black riding cape flapping around his arms like wings. He stood and hugged me. "Hello."

Yesterday I'd told Evelyn about Lint, casually bringing him up over a pan of boiling pasta. She'd squealed and went off at a tangent so far that she was deciding how best to tell my parents. I'd told her it was very early days to which she'd replied, "Tell Lint to shag you over the back of that fucking bench." I do love my Evelyn.

"So what's on the agenda, Mr BBC Chairman?"

I sat and pulled a seventies orange tartan flask out of my rucksack. "Drink?"

"Tea?"

"Nope."

"Coffee?"

"Nope, rum."

"Rum? Good one."

I passed him the black lid that doubled as the cup, filled with more than a drop.

"Are you trying to get me drunk, Mr Darcy?"

I laughed, as I often brought a cockle-warming flask of rum with me. But was I trying to get him tipsy? Would Pemberley, a tot of rum, Lint, and Austen be the perfect day? I poured myself a splash into a plastic beaker.

Delving into my bag again, I brought out two homemade jam tarts that Evelyn had made that morning, wrapped in a sheet of kitchen roll.

Lint joked, "Have you a blanket that matches your flask for our knees?"

Smiling I said, "No, sorry." I was rather old-fashioned, never needing to have the designer clothes, up to the minute mobile, or five-foot long telly. Instead, finding comfort in the familiar.

As we sipped rum and ate tarts I watched Lint. He'd settled back, cup aloft, crumbs down his front, and a faraway look. My gaze wandered down to where his cape had folded across his thighs. Lint's tight jeans left nothing to the imagination so my eyes flicked up a touch and settled on a swell in the denim.

"Do you like what you see, Mr Darcy?"

I jumped and stuttered, "No. Yes. Um. Fuck."

Lint laughed. "What is first on the BBC's agenda?"

Clearing my throat and straightening, I said, "We could discuss our thoughts on Jane's books in order, starting with *Sense and Sensibility*."

Lint opened his book and smoothed back a page. "Okay, I'll go. It was the first of Jane's books in which she used the pen name 'A Lady'."

"I never knew why that was."

"Apparently, back then it wasn't considered ladylike for a woman to publish work for money."

"That's stupid."

"Yeah, it is to our modern ears." Lint jammed his elbow against his book to stop it fluttering but was unsuccessful; the wind over Pemberley wanted his book and his book it would have.

I knew Jane's works backwards and I'm sure Lint did but in the spirit of the book club I asked the question, "So what is the novel about?"

He grinned at me. "The book is about two sisters, Elinor and Marianne, daughters of Mr Dashwood by his second wife. When their dad dies, the estate passes to the older brother, John, and the girls are left with nothing."

"You know, I wouldn't have wanted to be a girl back then."

"Not just back then. My aunt, who's fifty, says she's seen enormous changes towards women in just her lifetime," Lint said.

"Like what?"

"She's always saying that her daughter, Sarah, has the world at her feet, whereas she had a husband and children at hers."

I wasn't sure that Evelyn would agree that she had the world at her feet. "Please continue," I said, raised my rum beaker, and bowed dramatically.

Lint bowed back. "Yes, Mr Darcy."

I loved that he called me Mr Darcy; it made me come over all unnecessary and conjure up images of mischievous eyes and tight white trousers.

Lint continued. "It's a story of romance and heartbreak where the sisters eventually find love and happiness."

"With modern trappings, Jane's books could be sold today."

"That's it! We can rewrite Austen in a modern setting." Lint's face lit with excitement.

"Lint, it's been done a thousand times."

"Like what?"

"*Northanger Abbey* with vampires. *Pride and Prejudice* with time portals. *Sense and Sensibility* with iPods and Alfa Romeos."

"Oh." Lint's face fell.

Crap. I didn't want to make him feel bad. "You could always write one though. Who's to say it won't be a runaway success?"

He smiled, closed his book, and sat on it. "Why is it called *Sense and Sensibility*, do you think?"

"I've read that it's the balance the sisters find in life and love."

"Right." Lint downed his rum and held out the lid for another. "Actually it's not my favourite."

"Shock horror! Why not?" I poured him another tot.

"I think it's a bit, um, wobbly."

"Wobbly?"

"Yeah, I think Jane became unsure about a lady writing a novel and, compared to her other books, you can see that," Lint said.

"It may be the first book syndrome?"

"And that."

"It is funny, though."

"Yeah, Miss Austen certainly had humour." Lint picked a crumb off his jeans.

"I'd call it more satirical comedy. Her observations of life's shortcomings are brilliant."

"Oh I agree but I'm not sure it was noted at the time."

For a few minutes, we both gazed over the wide ocean. The sky was as grey as the water, and the line between them had disappeared. An old friend once said that you're comfortable with someone when you don't feel the need to fill silence with chatter. Lint put me at ease.

He stood. Suddenly.

"You're off?" Bloody 'ell, I said that far too quickly.

He shoved his stuff in his bag. "I said I'd do the late shift today and I'm, um, late."

"Okay. Yes. Of course." As I put the lid back on the flask Lint stepped between my feet, leaned in, and kissed my nose. He hung before me for a moment, which felt like an hour, before pulling away.

"See you next Tuesday." He slung the bag on his back, strolled away, and then stopped and called back. "Thanks for the rum."

"Um, yes, no problem," I said, and for some reason waved like the Queen.

He waved back and then took a long look at Spur Point as if he were considering something before sauntering away. I touched my nose where he'd kissed me and watched him go until the horizon swallowed him whole.

The Fourth Tuesday

"We never read any of *Sense and Sensibility* last time," Lint said.

"No, too much chatting." I caught a drip of ice cream before it threatened to puddle on my trousers.

"Yes." Lint licked his empty lolly stick far too slowly and I stared at him for far too long. He held the stick horizontally and read, "*One half of the world cannot understand the pleasures of the other.*"

"It doesn't say that!"

"It does. It's an Austen lolly."

"It isn't." I lunged for the stick but Lint pulled it away so I ended up sprawled across his lap with my ice cream held aloft.

Before I could freak out about the correct etiquette in such moments, Lint pushed me up. "I'll start," he said and cleared his throat. "*The family of Dashwood had long been settled in Sussex. Their estate was large, and their residence was at Norland Park, in the centre of their property, where, for many generations, they had lived in so respectable a manner, as to engage the general good opinion of their surrounding acquaint–*"

"Stop! Pass me the book."

"No! Why?"

"Impatience."

"For what?"

"For this." I took the book from him and flicked through until I reached chapter ten, second page – I really should go on *Mastermind* – and read, "*Willoughby was a young man of good abilities, quick imagination, lively spirits, and open, affectionate manners. He was exactly formed to engage Marianne's heart; for, with all this, he joined not only a captivating person, but a natural ardour of mind, which was now roused and increased by the example of her own, and which recommended him to her affection beyond everything else.*" I closed the book. "Willoughby, dashing, handsome, and rich, is the perfect lover for romantic Marianne. He fits into a Willoughby-shaped hole in her heart."

"Do you think everyone has a perfect-person-shaped hole in their heart?" Lint asked.

"Oh, absolutely."

"Okay, what shape is yours?"

"Man-shaped."

He laughed, nodded, and then said abruptly, "Will you ever tell your parents?"

"One day and it'll have to be soon." I half-smiled at him. "We're running out of ways of avoiding *the* baby conversation and if Evelyn refuses soft cheeses my mother eyes her eagerly."

"Mate." Lint stood. "You're gonna have to sort it out."

I heaved a sigh. "I know."

He took my hand, gazed at me from under his floppy fringe, and then kissed my fingers one by one as if they were precious jewels. I took a noisy breath and shuddered. "Chilly wind," I said to cover the blaring fact that he really started my engine.

Lint smiled. "Yes."

Don't go, don't go, my head chanted. "Next week?" my mouth said.

Lint pulled his cat hat around his ears. "I look forward to it."

I'd begun to live for the few precious hours on Pemberley cliff. When it wasn't Tuesday, I would daydream of Tuesday, and when it was Tuesday, I would arrive early just so I could watch Lint walk towards me.

The Fifth Tuesday

"*Pride and Prejudice*," Lint said as we strolled together along the cliff path. It was a hazy day but the breeze was warm and the sea twinkled.

"My favourite." I watched Lint's arms swing in time with his legs and tried to fall into step.

"Because it contains your namesake?"

"Yes, there is that, but I believe it's everyone's favourite and the most popular."

"Ah, Mr Darcy. He does it for everyone."

"I have played the 'lake scene' over and over and over. The pause button on my remote is worn out!"

Lint laughed. "I'm guessing on your own in a locked room?"

"Totally."

There was a seagull perched on Crawford. I shooed it off, plonked down, placed my hands behind my head and stretched out my legs.

Lint moved into the space between my thighs, placed a hand either side of my shoulders and leaned in. He hovered with a faint smell of patchouli, his breath on my cheek, and watching me carefully. My hands slid off my head. "No," he whispered, "leave them up." With my heart in my throat, I duly did so, knotting my fingers, and sensing the hairs rise on my nape.

At first Lint's lips barely touched mine, as if he were a figment of my imagination, a perfect fantasy. As I trembled, he kissed me, pressing my head back into Harold's bench. I've been kissed before but never like this, where the merest touch of skin on skin ignited every nerve. There was no other contact between us, just lips, and I felt utterly exposed and completely connected all at the same time, and it was the most erotic thing that had ever happened to me.

Lint pulled away and in doing so swept me into an embrace that made my stomach flip.

On the fifth Tuesday, there was no reading of passages, discussing sentence structure, or analysing social etiquette. There was no woo of the wind or call of the birds. There was only Lint, his lips on mine, his hand on my leg, his fingers twisting my hair, his warm breath on my cold cheek, and his soft murmurs in my ear. Tingles buzzed the pit of my stomach and fired to where his hand was moving slowly up my thigh. Good God, I wanted him. On me and in me.

We said goodbye twenty times, laughing more each time we said it. Lint walked away and then hurried back to cup my face and kiss me one more time. "Next Tuesday," he whispered and finally strolled away.

My feet shook on Betsy's pedals, my fingers wouldn't grip the steering wheel, and the aching grin on my face refused to subside.

The Sixth Tuesday

The sky darkened and creased like a grey wool blanket, the sea reared, sound left us as if sucked out to the horizon, and wind-whipped rain hit us from all directions. Gathering my things, I hunkered down against the storm and shouted, "Betsy." We ran the path splashing through the puddles and squealing like children. Nobody has ever died due to being wet, but being blown off the cliff was another matter.

Breathing hard I pushed the key into the lock of the car door, turned, yanked it open and fell onto the driver's seat. Reaching over, I opened the passenger door for Lint. He fell in a sodden heap. "Bloody hell, that was quick," he panted.

"The weather changes fast on Pemberley."

"You don't say."

The windows slowly misted and blotted out the storm, but Betsy's rocking and the wooing of the wind showed it was still there, and angry. Reaching onto the back seat, I grabbed a blanket. "Here. You better ... um, get out of those wet clothes."

Lint whipped off his jacket and shirt. "Did you order the storm so you could see me naked, Mr Darcy?" I blushed. Of course I hadn't, but I was glad of it. "And you as well." He reached for the picnic rug that had fallen onto the floor and threw it over my head.

Under Lint's gaze, I flung off my wet clothes and loosely wrapped the rug around my body.

He signalled with his thumb. "Back seat?"

They were two small words but gloriously full of promise. With no need to be asked twice, I scrabbled onto Betsy's back seat and watched Lint do the same. We sat so close a tenner couldn't have squeezed between us. Lint wound an arm around me, wandered a hand under my rug, and rested it on my knee. "Mr Darcy," he whispered. "If you want, I'll be your boyfriend and lover."

My heart leapt. Boyfriend? Lover? Fuck me. *Oh yes, yes*, my head screamed, but my mouth whispered, "Please." I was so English. And, it seems, hypnotised, losing all ability to move under his gaze. As Betsy swayed gently and the rain tapped on the window, Lint kissed me, and as my body stiffened, he walked chilly fingers up my thigh and stroked my stomach. I ached for him and rolled my hips closer.

"Yes?" he murmured.

"Yes," I whispered.

Lint wrapped his fingers around me one by one and so damn slowly and so damn tightly, I thought I might burst there and then on Betsy's back seat.

Moaning with contentment, I slid my fingers under his blanket and took him to hand. I couldn't see but, oh boy, I could feel, and my fist was satisfyingly full. I may not have had sex with a man but I was a self-professed expert when it came to these goings-on.

Lint purred, "Together."

I leant over and kissed him, using my tongue to part his lips and as he opened his mouth for me, I slid my fingers up. He growled and as the vibrations buzzed through me, he built an easy rhythm.

Betsy's suspension rocked with our movements and she creaked in complaint. It was a good job her windows were misted, as the OAP ramblers' club would've had heart attacks if they'd spied us, semi-naked with busy blanket-covered hands.

It didn't take me long. How could it have taken longer? I was naked in the back of Betsy with a handsome man. A man. And handsome. And an Austen lover. And paying me wonderfully intimate attention. I threw the rug off to watch, and the sight of Lint's wide hand on me was all too much. I came, shuddering and panting.

Lint murmured contented noises and sat back. Breathless, I sat back with him for a minute until I tugged off his blanket to expose him. Then I turned to face him, draped my leg over his lap, and moved my hand in time to a tune in my head.

"Oh. That. Feels. Good," Lint gasped.

"Beat it."

"Eh?"

"Michael Jackson."

For a long moment, the rain's tinkling, the wind's wooing, and Lint's moans were the only noise. Then he quietened before throwing his head back, raising his hips, and gripping the seat. He came in a fit of giggles. I stared at him disconcerted, until he threw his arms around me and kissed me all over my face and neck. Gathering the blankets around us, we sat in sticky entwinement for a moment and I silently thanked the emergency baby wipes in the glovebox.

"How utterly delicious," Lint said with a huge grin. "Mr Darcy has just pulled me off." He then drew a fist holding a somewhat dodgy-looking penis in the mist on the window. A permanent reminder every time my car misted up and I made a mental note to sit my mother in the front.

Sloppy kisses, jokes using the words gearstick, hardtop, and horn, and cheeky bottom holding, filled the parting of ways on the sixth Tuesday.

The Seventh Tuesday

I leapt out of Betsy, twirled on the spot, and skipped along the path. Today I would be able to tell Evelyn that Lint had indeed shagged me over the back of the bench. It was there in my mind's eye, naked bottom half, legs spread, wooden slats digging into my stomach, fingers gripping a serpent's body, the breeze prickling my skin, and Lint behind me, passionate and strong. Oh yes, today was the day.

The people around Harold's bench took me aback. Was it the OAP ramblers? Did they see us and were gathered to complain about indecency and exposure? I hoped that they didn't sit down as that would ruin all my plans. As I neared, I spied Lint's cat hat on the bench along with his books and a pen. I looked for him to complain that the old people were ruining my morning, but he was nowhere to be seen. Then I noticed that nobody was looking at me, or the bench; everyone was peering over the cliff.

Taking long strides to the closest bloke, I grasped his arm, turned him to face me, and asked, "What are you looking at?" I spoke the words but knew the answer, I knew why they were exchanging nervous chatter, why one woman was sat on the grass with her head in her hands, and I knew that I'd never come to Pemberley cliff again.

"Some chap fell over the edge quarter of an hour ago." The ruddy-faced man shouted above the wind. "Doris said she saw him standing far too close." He pointed to the woman on the ground.

"A jumper," Doris shook her head.

"Terribly blustery today," another woman added. "I think he was blown over."

Blown? I shook the man's arm. "What was he wearing? What? What?" I shouted.

He removed my hand, said, "I dunno, mate," and then turned to Doris. "Hey, what was the fella wearing?"

"A flappy cape thing."

Another bloke chuckled, "Perhaps he thought he was Batman?"

I don't remember running but my lungs were bursting as I tumbled onto Betsy's back seat, and I had no memory of gathering Lint's things, but there they were, clasped to my chest. Burying my head in the pile of blankets, I breathed him in and sobbed.

Should I have looked over the edge to make sure? No, it was Lint; he was always walking too close to the edge of Pemberley cliff. Do I need to ring anyone? I didn't have any numbers, not even Lint's, in fact I didn't even know where he lived and, come to think of it, I didn't know his surname or how old he was. We shared a passion for Jane Austen and each other and there had been no need for anything else.

Numb and hollowed out, I sat up. In the mist on Betsy's window Lint's drawing of a hand-job emerged. Despite myself, I smiled and opened his copy of *Pride and Prejudice*. Inside, biro-written words said, *For my Mr Darcy, you have bewitched me body and soul.* As I clasped it to my chest, and tears coursed my cheeks, I watched a large yellow helicopter buzz the sky. A man dangled below it swinging perilously in the wind and two other men dressed in fluorescent gear were running along the path flapping their arms as if they were fledglings learning to fly.

My eyes followed the cliff edge to Harold's bench. The ramblers had gone, the bench was alone. I was alone. And it was as if my life had rebooted – except not in the same way. Lint had come into my life for a few hours on six Tuesdays but he'd changed me forever. Tomorrow was the day to tell my parents about … everything.

Fae Mcloughlin

My passion is writing, but in my spare time, I like to photograph big skies and old ruins. You will also find me in museums, people watching in cafes, or standing on my garage roof taking pictures of the sunset.

twitter.com/FaeMcloughlin

Cross and Cast

Sam Evans

"He's nothing like Colin Firth, is he?"

Jonathan Darcy heard the words as clearly as he would have done if he'd been standing next to the three wardrobe assistants. Echoing through a closed door and along an empty corridor, they cut surprisingly deep.

He knew, of course, that they were right.

He was no Colin Firth and never would be. Firth was a powerhouse of an actor who would never lower himself to appear in a production as ludicrous as *Dance with Jane Austen*. But then Mr Firth wasn't (and nor would he ever be) an ex-soap-opera actor who had come runner-up to a retired Olympic swimmer in a dance contest.

No, quite simply, Jonathan Darcy, ex-soap-star bad boy, knew his place. He would never be a celebrated Oscar winner, and told himself regularly that he had no desire to be anyway, even if by a quirk of fate he had a tenuous link with someone who was.

It wasn't that Jonathan didn't like the actor – Firth was probably a thoroughly lovely guy. But he had been listening to the wardrobe assistants in the room next door discussing his un-Firth-like behaviour, the weather, and the latest sale at Marks and Spencer, for longer than he dared to admit, and it was beginning to grate on his nerves a little.

Of course it didn't help that he was currently wearing an actual pair of Firth's breeches from the original BBC production, which was the reason why he was drawing unfavourable comparisons with the man.

Did he know the Oscar winner had been a 'dream' to work with and that no one – not even a star from *Celebrity Dancing Through the Ages* – would ever compare to him?

Did he?

Much to his horror Jonathan felt his face flush beet red upon hearing that comment. Whether it was due to anger or embarrassment at the ridiculous situation he found himself in he would never know. All he could hope was that at some point Firth had also been made to drop a waist size so he could squeeze his arse cheeks into the said garment. How on earth the man had managed to swim in them was a mystery. In fact, the tightness Jonathan was experiencing in the crotch area already had him worried about the repetitive back to back, cast down, half-cocked hybrid dos-à-dos movements he was somehow expected to do that afternoon. It had come as no surprise to him that when the damn dance had been choreographed back in the seventeenth century (yes – he had done his homework) they'd made absolutely no concessions for a man wearing too tight breeches.

Ladies in their finery? Yes. Men? No.

Jonathan shook his head slowly and cast a glance down towards the stage area he had been shown on his arrival. Having only just seen the place for the first time – he'd been rehearsing prior to this in a warm dance studio just outside Prestwich – Jonathan wasn't sure he was impressed. The cavernous space had looked big and overwhelming as he walked through it. It was cold and had a harsh 'breeze' blowing through it like most Victorian-era theatres. He simply couldn't imagine it ever looking like it could host a live show, and a professional one at that …

This thing was as far removed from the stuff Jonathan had been auditioning for as it could be. A detective in a hard-hitting Netflix Original drama? Or a bit part as a surgeon in *Holby City*? No, *Dance with Jane Austen* was nothing like either of them. According to his agent, this 'thing' was going to be the making of him, though. If Jonathan could pull off a second-place win foxtrotting to a Rihanna song, learning the steps to the ridiculously titled 'Mr Beveridge's Maggot' dance surely wasn't going to be a problem, right?

Right?

'It'll be a piece of piss, Jonathan, think of it as Dancing Through the Ages *but with no spray tan, so go have fun, make friends,'* he had heard his bastard agent say with a laugh during one of their heated phone calls. Of course, the man was right; there wasn't any doubt in Jonathan's mind about the situation – if he could handle spray tan, he could handle anything – he was his father's son after all.

'Chin up, head down, Jonathan.' Richard James Darcy's words had been on repeat since Jonathan had set foot in the place.

Truthfully, though? Even as late as this morning while drinking an insipid cup of tea, the idea of doing another dancing gig had made Jonathan want to run back to the cobblestones and sign yet another contract to play his posh bad boy adulterer for a third time.

Except this time Jonathan knew he couldn't even do that, and didn't that fact hurt like a knife to the heart. It stung even more so when he thought about the sly stunt the new producers of the show had pulled on him. It was astounding to think they'd decided over a Starbucks coffee and a skinny blueberry muffin to kill off his character with a brick to the side of the head.

Instant death.

Cut to the credits.

Theme music.

Fin.

The only thing he felt he could be proud of was that the fall to the cobbles could be considered his best work, even if he did say so himself. Graceful yet hard-hitting (pun intended), it made the front page of at least three separate weekly television guides.

But whatever, Jonathan thought (and not for the first time), that was now in the past. Though there was nothing going to stop him from placing the blame firmly at the producers' door for having to pour himself into Colin Firth's too tight breeches.

A career high if there ever was one.

"You can go through to the main rehearsal room if you want," a voice suddenly said from Jonathan's left, making him jump. Lost in a cobble-filled world, he hadn't heard or seen anyone else in the corridor, so it was almost shocking to find a small woman sporting too much hair and holding a clipboard stood right next to him. Did he know her? More importantly, was he supposed to? Jonathan eyed the woman cautiously then frowned as his gaze landed on the bird's nest of curls perched precariously on her head.

"Jonathan Darcy, right?"

Jonathan wasn't sure if it was a question or a statement. He was (semi) used to being recognised (*TV Weekly*, for goodness' sake!), even if these days it was only for a sure-footed foxtrot. "Indeed," Jonathan murmured and watched as she smiled excitedly in return.

"This is so much fun," Bird's Nest said. She turned on her heel and began to make her way towards the stage area as she did so. "The dances are so beautiful and elegant; this place is so amazing. Do you know it once staged a Royal Variety Performance?" she asked. Jonathan hadn't but he nodded anyway. "In 1975 apparently. The Queen herself was here, sat in one of the boxes, she did. This, though, is going to be something else, so different, so original."

Jonathan hummed in response. "It's going to be something, that's for sure." A bloody mess if they didn't sort out the cold draught he had felt while standing on the stage earlier that day.

"You guys are going to be great, the choreographer is great. Everything is just great …"

Great.

Indeed.

Jonathan mentally switched her off and tutted under his breath. Didn't she realise how hard this dancing shit was? Was this her first gig? With her new clipboard and hipster hair she certainly looked like she was fresh meat.

As for the 'great' choreographer? Jonathan gritted his teeth at the thought of the man. Having been on the end of a severe tongue-lashing, Jonathan was going to – as he had been told to – stay away from him as much as possible.

"… he is so dreamy."

Of course he is.

"… and such a beautiful dancer."

Jonathan bit back a tut and half closed his eyes. If you were to ask him (and disappointingly nobody yet had), Elvin Benoît the great choreographer spent too much time fascinated with the ridiculous, as proven during his stint on the celebrity show. Sequins, tans, cha-cha-chas, and scathing opinions mostly directed in Jonathan's direction. The man was just … "Hmmm, yes," he replied vaguely, knowing it was probably the best answer he could offer under the circumstances.

"Do you not think so?"

Jonathan's thoughts immediately returned to his poorly executed attempt to open discourse with Benoît in the dressing room after the *Celebrity Dancing Through the Ages* grand final.

No.

Not now, he didn't.

Not after being laughed at.

"He's a professional," Jonathan said sternly. The language Benoît had used on that fateful evening had been far from professional, if Jonathan remembered rightly, but still …

"Wasn't he the … ?"

Dear God.

Jonathan took a deep breath at the question. Telling himself he needed a moment to compose himself before he answered, he drew to a halt a few metres from a second dressing room and the backstage area.

Before he could answer, though, his attention was caught by a loud howling noise echoing down the corridor. Was that the draught from the stage area causing that? Already?

God damn it.

"I'm pretty sure he was …"

"… the professional dancer who beat us by one point in the final?" Jonathan replied quickly, with a forced smile. "Yes. Damn unlucky. He deserved it though." *There you go,* Jonathan thought. Cold draught or not, if he had any chance of getting through this with his sanity intact, he was going to need to get the full story out now, and remind himself for the final time of the second place that going to haunt him. "Margo and I were obviously one of the favourites, but it wasn't to be," he said firmly. They should have won. He should have been the one to lift the Glitter Dance Shoe. He had smelt the victory in the quarter-finals and danced his socks off.

Jonathan bit his tongue in frustration at the memory.

When the other stuff had taken over …

No, Jonathan wasn't going there. What he had done was the right and proper thing to do. He was going to stand by his actions to the end. The fateful day he'd spent pleading (arguing) with Margo to choose the more rumbustious Lindy Hop for their final dance, still gave him sleepless nights. The look of worry that had fallen across Margo's face and their subsequent loss because of it would be etched on his memory forever.

If only he hadn't doubly ballsed it all up afterwards with Benoît hours later.

The answer Jonathan gave seemed to shut Bird's Nest up (he wished he'd asked for her name now), and he breathed a silent sigh of relief that he wasn't expected to explain it any further. It wasn't as if he was displeased with his second place (they should have won) but given the circumstances, and the fact that he had been raised a gentleman …

No, Jonathan attempted to shrug off the memory with a huff. He wasn't going there, not today, not when 'Benoît the Champion' was no doubt shimmying away to himself behind the closed doors Jonathan knew they were fast approaching.

Silently falling into step again Jonathan rounded the last corner and waited as Beatrice – as she finally announced herself to be – collected the last of the other 'celebrities from TV, stage and the sporting world' who had managed to bag the parts of Elizabeth, Bingley and Jane in the dance, and quickly shepherded them towards the rehearsal area.

"G'day, Jonathan," the man playing Bingley said with a twang as they were ushered onto the large empty stage. His deep Australian accent echoed around the room, shocking Jonathan a little. He didn't remember it being that strong, but then there was a distinct possibility (a certainty) that Jonathan might not have been paying much attention. "You ready for this? Did they say we needed to warm up?" the blond-haired guy asked.

It was a sensible enough question, Jonathan thought. Even for someone who had proven to himself these past few days that he had two left feet.

Jonathan couldn't remember anything being mentioned in the information pack about warming up, though. The limbering up Margo had made him religiously complete prior to the 'proper' dancing show had his legs stretched to the point of no return. There was no way he could imagine doing half those movements dressed like this.

Definitely not in breeches that fitted everywhere they touched.

Jonathan grunted at the thought.

Damn it.

Rather than answer, Jonathan distracted himself by turning his gaze to the centre of the room to where a small pod of people clad in the same period clothing as himself were loitering.

His eyes were not searching the faces for a familiar face.

He wasn't looking for the man.

There was a very distinct possibility Margo would be here. That was why he was looking. It would be good to see her, Jonathan told himself.

"They said nothing about warming up, although how I'm supposed to do anything in this ridiculous get-up is beyond me," Jonathan said suddenly. He pointed at the blue dress coat, ruffled shirt and white breeches he had been given to wear.

Luckily the tall, dark outline of Elvin Benoît was nowhere to be seen.

The Australian (Mark, was it?) answered with a chuckle. "Yeah, same here, mate."

"Apparently these are Firth's," Jonathan added conversationally. Out of nowhere his agent's insistence on getting the gig, that he at least try and make some friends outside of his front door, was ringing loudly in his ears. *'Jonathan, why do you think they killed you off?!'* Jonathan had snorted on hearing that. Utter poppycock. They killed him off because his bad-boy character Anthony Allan had served his purpose. It also didn't help that the script developers had had him work his way through enough of the show's female lead characters that there was no one else's on-screen marriage to break up.

"The costume?"

"Yes, apparently we're the same build; the BBC doesn't like to spend money. My agent says I now have a claim to fame – so to speak."

Mark chuckled again. "Your claim to fame is that you're wearing Colin Firth's tight pants?" The humour in the Australian's voice was evident.

Jonathan nodded sagely if not with a little embarrassment. His agent's suggestion that he ride on Firth's coat-tails was utterly ridiculous. Of course, Jonathan could not lie: he would have much preferred something made to measure, but then this *was* the BBC. It also didn't help that Mark the tennis player looked like an actual Adonis in his outfit. Younger, taller and fitter, with no grey hair; the man looked far more dashing in his tight breeches than Jonathan ever could have done.

Changing the subject quickly, Jonathan turned back towards the centre of the stage. Out of the corner of his eye he saw Mark do the same. "Have you managed to learn the steps yet?" Jonathan asked with a nod to the group. It was ridiculous, really. All the time they had been together as a group, 'bonding' and learning a few odd steps, they had yet to attempt a full dance.

"I watched a few videos after the final day of training yesterday – looks piss easy."

Jonathan was wide-eyed at the Australian's answer. Surely the man was joking? Dancing was the hardest thing Jonathan had ever done and at some point he had become weirdly protective of it. It didn't matter even if this was just a short showpiece; it was one that would be shown live in front of millions. "Well, it's easier than the foxtrot," Jonathan said with a sigh as he absent-mindedly scanned the stage a second time.

"Yeah, mate, like I said, piss easy."

This time Jonathan didn't reply (not yet anyway – Mark's 'piss easy' comment grated on him). Instead he left the three other dancers to casually make their way towards the centre of the stage while he circled the large space not looking for Benoît. He also wasn't thinking about the words they'd exchanged on the evening of the final, words which to this day stung hard inside Jonathan's chest – *'Not if you were the last man in the world.'* How he had managed to read Benoît so wrong was still a mystery. The signals the man had given off, their few conversations throughout the competition ... Jonathan cursed silently. Damn Margo and her –

"ALL DANCERS TO THE CENTRE PLEASE!"

The familiar voice caught Jonathan out, making him jump in surprise, but he recognised it immediately. Sharp, hard, with a hint of an accent Jonathan had never been able to decipher, it still sent shivers down his spine and had him scanning the large space for its point of origin.

He wanted to mentally kick himself at missing the man's entrance. If he had been paying attention and not –

"THAT INCLUDES YOU, DARCY!" the shouting continued, and Jonathan winced at the tone. Somehow it sounded even worse echoing around an empty auditorium. No, there was no doubt in his mind he'd ever be able to forget it.

"Good evening, Mr Benoît," Jonathan finally replied as his eyes fell on the man now stood front and centre. He was surprised to see Benoît's hair was a little longer and curling around his ears, but his waist was just as narrow as Jonathan remembered. Inadvertently shifting his gaze lower he couldn't help but note the Lycra pants that Benoît wore clung to his thighs gracefully. He was ... goodness ... the man would take his breath away if Jonathan allowed it.

But no, Jonathan stopped himself before his thoughts went any further. That wasn't going to happen.

Jonathan knew his place.

He had been told.

"Not quite the Blackpool Tower Ballroom, is it?" Jonathan commented. Civil.

That was the way forward.

Talk about something familiar.

The room, for example.

'Not if you were the last man in the world.'

"It's cold and damp, there is a draught from somewhere, and it's not at all suitable for a live show," Benoît replied with a huff.

At least they agreed on something. The building had no doubt been beautiful in its heyday, but now? "Less glitter too, Elvin," Jonathan added, earning him a little chuckle from the other dancers.

However if Elvin had heard Jonathan's comment he didn't acknowledge it. Instead Elvin stood front and centre stage and as rigid as a pole. It was like Jonathan wasn't even in the room.

"So, you've been practising, right?" Elvin finally said to the group, and a series of hmms, yeahs and nods replied immediately. "So, then …"

Rather than listen, Jonathan lost himself watching Elvin pace back and forwards as he continued to talk to the group. The broad dancer's shoulders, the strength in his arms that Elvin needed to lift the various dancers he performed with … all in all Jonathan thought it was …

"Well, good, this dance is fairly easy, but the timing and execution need to be perfect. Sometimes the simple stuff is the hardest." Elvin ended the sentence with a clap.

For the next few hours Jonathan found himself being positioned, pulled against and grappled with until his poor feet hurt in the ridiculous shoes he had been given to wear. After being told he could take a small break he joined the others offstage and took a swig from one of the bottles of water the production assistants had scattered about liberally. Just like the earlier breaks, Jonathan noticed Elvin didn't join them. Instead he stood near the curtain line and slowly began to walk through the steps alone. Jonathan watched as Elvin moved gracefully, placing one foot elegantly in front of the other, moving between the two imaginary rows of the dance. Jonathan saw him count out steps and note adjustments the dance might need, check timings, nod across to the sound engineers to repeat a section, and then call over individual dancers who he obviously thought were struggling, to dance a section with him.

And he did it all without taking a break.

Yet from the instant the rehearsals had started Elvin had not spoken a word to Jonathan. Not a word. Not one *'that's right'* or *'good form'*. Nothing. It was getting to the point that Jonathan wondered if Elvin even remembered he was there.

"No, Krissy," Jonathan heard Elvin say for the umpteenth time to the American actress playing Elizabeth Bennet. With every wrong move she made, the tone in Elvin's voice was shifting closer to the one he had used with Jonathan in the dressing room on that fateful evening. In fact it was obvious to anyone within a five-metre radius that Elvin's tolerance levels were falling with each minute that passed. "Have you even read the book or seen the film? Elizabeth would never search out Darcy. She thinks him aloof and –"

"Too proud!" Jonathan said loudly, causing the room to turn and face him. Out of habit he rocked back on his heels. He hadn't meant to shout, but … "He was proud and Elizabeth disliked him from their first meeting," he continued, ignoring the small shake that had appeared in his voice. Jonathan knew there was a chance he was talking out of turn, but surely it was obvious to everyone the nearest Krissy and Mark had ever got to Jane Austen were the advertisements appearing on the television and the front of the theatre. (It also turned out the man was even more of a disaster zone to dance next to than first expected. In Jonathan's opinion he might be an excellent tennis player but lacked the necessary coordination to go anywhere near a dance floor.)

Glancing across at Elvin, Jonathan looked for any sign of annoyance. He immediately saw a frown disappear as quickly as it had appeared.

God damn it.

He really needed to learn to keep his mouth closed.

"Maybe a little more focus next time, Krissy? And the same for you, Mark … ? Please? This dance is so simple and I love it. Shall we have a do over?" Elvin asked, calling the group back over. Polite and firm as always. If he had been bothered by Jonathan's interruption he wasn't letting it show.

"Erm, Elvin, I seem to have a good grasp of it. Maybe I could help with some of the steps and show everyone?" Jonathan said. "That's if you want me to, of course," he added quickly.

Silence filled the room and Jonathan pretty much heard his stomach drop to the floor. Had he lost his goddamn mind? Had Elvin's declaration of '*Not if you were the last man in the world*' not been final enough for Jonathan to hear?

Especially now.

Mid-rehearsal?

In public?

"Ignore me, I'm being ridiculous," Jonathan said with a wave of his hand. He took a ridiculously large step away from the group as he did so and kept on going at speed. Why he always spouted utter rubbish in front of members of the Benoît family was anyone's guess. Some people thought it was endearing.

Cute, even.

But Elvin was not one of those people.

In fact it wasn't until Jonathan saw the apron approaching that he realised he'd never reversed out of anywhere as fast in his life.

Even in his Jag.

That's better, Jonathan thought as his feet finally skimmed the edges of the wooden flooring. He was far more comfortable here; even the breeches felt looser with a quick bend of the knee. It was clear that this was where he should have stood right from the start and only gone to the head of the group when the dance called for it.

"Actually it's not ..." he heard Elvin say – and Jonathan cut him off with a wave of his hand, before the man could say any more. He would not be ridiculed again.

"Don't worry, it was a stupid idea, I'm a beginner as much as anyone here," Jonathan said, and he locked his arms firmly behind his back. He was going to ignore the murmur that rippled around the group.

"But you aren't, you beat the woman from *Antiques Roadshow*," someone said. Jonathan looked up to find out who it was only to see the whole group staring at him. Some looked confused, while others smiled, though most were eating their imaginary popcorn as their gaze shifted from Jonathan to Elvin and back again.

"That was only because she had an injury," he said quietly, but the sound echoed around the large space. The hint of a smile he added as an afterthought would hopefully draw the attention away from him. Surely embarrassing oneself in the privacy of a dressing room was enough for one lifetime? "Just ignore me; can we crack on instead? We only have a few weeks left!" He was practically begging them.

"Actually ... I think it's a good idea, Jonathan, you do have a very good grasp of the steps," a voice said abruptly.

Surely Benoît was just playing with him now?

"He's right, you do, mate."

"You're the best one of us all."

"You beat that Olympic boxer into third place!"

"Yeah, you did, and he was dead graceful for a big guy."

Jonathan made a shooing motion at the group. "Well, I'm not sure ... I mean, I can foxtrot well enough," he replied. "What about breaking for lunch first?"

The group didn't look like they were going to let this go, though. He could read the looks of unabashed hope on their faces even at this distance.

"Your foxtrot was beautiful."

"Yeah, dude, the way you held Margo was just ..."

Jonathan shook his head at the group's words. No, he couldn't. He hadn't meant to volunteer himself to dance with ... no. If Margo had been there he might have done, but given her current state it was a ridiculous of Jonathan to have hoped she'd be there in the first place.

"Shall I be the Elizabeth to your Darcy?" Elvin was closer to Jonathan now. As usual his voice sent a shiver down Jonathan's spine making his heart rate spike. "You know the steps well enough."

"Well, I ..."

"Just remember I'm not my sister. You can't throw me around like you did her."

Jonathan winced at Elvin's words. "I never threw your sister ... not once. Even during 'lifts' week." In fact when it had come down to the wire, Margo had been the perfect partner for ex-soap-star and actor Jonathan Darcy – even the press had said so. She'd ignored his rants about getting killed off from the soap. *'If you hadn't have died so dramatically you would have never met me,'* she told him more than once. She'd even listened to the rants about Elvin, and gone with Jonathan on a nostalgic return visit to the cobbled street for one of the video blogs the BBC had insisted they do.

In fact it was only when the whole thing had gone to shit –

"Darcy? Are you ready?"

Elvin's voice cut through Jonathan's ruminations like a knife, and he watched as the man circled the group like a cat, then positioned himself where Krissy had been standing.

"Please may I have this dance, Mr Darcy?"

Lord have mercy.

For the first time ever Elvin's voice was soft and smooth, making Jonathan flinch and force himself to push aside the feelings it churned up. Was Elvin actually expecting Jonathan to dance with him? Hadn't the man made it perfectly clear that they should stay out of each other's way?

Jonathan didn't usually swear much but *Holy Fuck.* He unfolded his arms from behind his back and took a deep breath. Could a man be any more resigned to his fate than he was at that moment? If it was a choice of hot coals or touching Benoît, he would choose the hot coals each time, even if the thought of doing it made his stomach lurch upwards.

Jonathan turned and looked at the group of celebrities, seeing the hopeful expressions on their faces. Were they really relying on him to get it right?

Jonathan felt his body sag inward leaving Firth's breeches feeling like they had shrunk again. He blew out a puff of air. If this was what he was going to do, he would do it well and the consequences would be on Benoît's head. "Yes … yes, you may," Jonathan replied.

Jonathan moved slowly (almost at a crawl) to his position. Exactly a metre away from Elvin he bowed his head lightly and as instructed.

Over the past year he'd danced far worse dances than this (the rumba sprang randomly into his head) but 'Mr Beveridge's Maggot' was, as everyone knew, the dance that Firth had performed in the BBC series. Hell, even if the audience didn't know it by its ridiculous name, they would recognise it from the iconic scene – it was pivotal to the whole story. Slow and steady, it required two rows of dancers (in this case male to female – although Jonathan thought that it mattered not a dot who performed the routine) to mirror each other's actions, cross each other and then cast down the line, repeat steps three and four, then repeat it all again with the next couple along the line.

It had to be timed perfectly.

The pace kept.

The dancers needed to know their positions.

Of course, it also needed for Jonathan not to make it look like it was the hardest thing he had ever danced. Especially since his new partner was now eyeballing him with the fiercest expression he had ever seen.

"Are you ready, Darcy?" Elvin asked, returning the bow. He then turned to the stage wings as he sought out two of his lead dancers. "Johan, Karen, will you be our number twos?" he asked as soon as he spotted the pair. Jonathan watched as the dancers nodded, then practically bounced to the centre of the stage.

"We would all do well to remember this is a sixteen-bar dance," Elvin announced directly to the group of four. "Series of four sets. I think we are all familiar with its set-up, yes? Duple minor longways?"

Duple minor longways?

Jonathan had to peel his eyes off the ceiling. What in God's name … ? "What on earth are you talking about … ?" Jonathan said before he could stop himself.

"The dance … two linear rows, man to the left of the woman, we each dance in our own setlet then move along … easy," Elvin replied with a *'don't you know that'* tone.

(Jonathan didn't know that. Or at least he wasn't sure if he knew. Elvin was suddenly describing the dance in such a way that it sounded completely different to the one they had been rehearsing.)

"Oh."

Jonathan could see Elvin wasn't finished dishing out the orders though. He recognised that stance well. His hands had moved back to his hips and he was standing his proverbial ground. Jonathan just hoped whatever he was going to say wasn't anything else technical. "Have you ever practised the full sequence?"

That Jonathan could answer. "If you include the two hours we have spent today? Yes."

"Before now?"

"No. Not really."

"How is that even …" but Elvin didn't finish the sentence. Jonathan wasn't entirely sure the man was still speaking to him. Instead Elvin wore a fixed expression and clenched his fists against his hips.

"It's been a tough few weeks, Elvin. Some of us –" Jonathan began, but Elvin cut him off with a swipe of his hand.

"It's been a tough year, Darcy."

Again Jonathan wasn't sure if Elvin was directing the words at him or not, even if he did use his name. "Elvin …"

Elvin looked like he had already tuned Jonathan out. "So?" he said, the impatience screaming from his body. "Are we ready? Darcy, we are the first

148

couple."

Jonathan nodded. He didn't feel ready, not right at that moment anyway. Not when Elvin looked like he was going to explode into tiny pieces and splatter the back curtain.

When the music that accompanied the dance kicked in, Jonathan bit back any protest he was going to make. All he could do now was mentally run through the steps he'd read in the instruction sheet and hope it looked like he knew what he was doing.

With one hand braced behind his back, Jonathan repeated his bow from earlier and turned to face Elvin.

First couple cross facing partners and dos-à-dos with neighbours.

Disappointment hit Jonathan square in the chest when Elvin couldn't even bring himself to look at him as they passed.

First couple turn single up and towards each other. Turn neighbour with right hand. Half turn partner then back to place.

Again nothing. Not even when Jonathan turned Elvin back into place.

First couple cross and cast down, dos-à-dos across dance floor.

"We need to speak," Jonathan finally said as they met and crossed over for a third time. He kept his voice a low whisper and hoped Elvin would do the same.

"What about? We've already discussed the room, Darcy."

Second couple take hands and pass up and cast the ends of the line of four across the dance floor.

"You made it perfectly clear I wasn't to come anywhere near you, Elvin, and then you do this?"

"This?"

"Dance with me."

"I think you will find, Jonathan …"

Four dancers move up three steps.

"… hmmmm?"

First couple cross and cast …

"… that we have found ourselves in a position where it is difficult *not* to dance with one another. Margo taught you well."

It was the first compliment Jonathan had ever heard out of the man. The mention of Margo, though. "Margo, is she …"

"She is doing well. I wondered when she would come up."

"I was going to ask at some point. I mean …"

… as second couple move and meet up.

"But that's all down to you, of course, her being okay."

And repeat.

"It is?"

"Of course, Darcy. Apparently you are some sort of hero and not just in Margo's opinion either."

"Pardon?"

"Later."

"Wait … what? Was that … ? What do you mean?"

"We're in a room full of people, Darcy. Get a grip."

Oh. Right.

Jonathan wasn't sure how he managed it, but somehow he'd stopped dancing the exact moment the music ended. Drawing a breath he briefly closed his eyes and counted to five. What exactly had just happened? Was Benoît apologising? Had Jonathan heard him right?

"Well done," Elvin said as he turned to face Jonathan and the two other dancers. Frustratingly Jonathan watched him hold his hand out so Karen could grab it, before turning turn back towards their audience. "Shall we give them a round of applause then break for lunch? Maybe food would help us get through the afternoon session."

Jonathan was past listening though. He didn't need food to get him through the next session. What he needed was time alone in a locked dressing room. With one hand clenched into a fist he found himself leaping down into the auditorium (the breeches did stretch) and running towards the door which he knew led him backstage.

"Mr Darcy? Are you okay?" someone shouted, but Jonathan ignored it and shook his head. He didn't care if they thought it rude of him to simply walk out. Elvin had called lunch; Jonathan could do what he liked and he just needed to get out of there.

The corridors were quiet as Jonathan finally gathered his bearings and found the door to his dressing room. He turned the handle, pushed the door open as quickly as he could then closed it.

"Good lord," Jonathan whispered. His hand was now shaking against the handle as he attempted to let go. Elvin had implied … ? Well, what had he implied? Jonathan rolled the words around in his brain in an attempt to get a handle on them: *'but that's down to you of course'*.

Yes, Elvin had definitely said that.

But that would mean …

Jonathan finally loosened his grasp on the handle and turned towards the centre of the dressing room. Thankfully the chair was exactly where he had left it and Jonathan plonked his body onto the crushed velvet with a thud.

The day Jonathan had argued with Margo about their final three dances had been playing on his mind for nearly a year. Over the few months they had spent together Margo's single-mindedness and impulsiveness had almost done him in. One minute she had been open and honest, the next closed and guarded. There had been times when Jonathan had enquired into her well-being, family and health but Margo had shut him down. Couple that with a blatant disregard for her own self-preservation, and Jonathan had decided very early on that Margo's decision making and life choices tended to leave a lot to be desired.

In fact it came as no surprise to anyone that they had argued more than once. Finding her lip-locked with last year's champion in the rehearsal room at the start of their journey was almost too much to take in but for some reason Jonathan had been a gentleman about it. Keeping her secret to himself. One was surely allowed the odd indiscretion. Of course, the secret hadn't been his to tell anyway.

It was only when she declared a week before the final that she was eight weeks pregnant, and suffering such terrible morning sickness, that Jonathan had broken down and the news had finally sunk in. They couldn't perform the Lindy Hop, or the Jive; she could hardly make it through the dress rehearsals. But Jonathan was angry, still angry.

So they threw it. Both of them.

The final.

They had had it locked down, their hands almost on the Glitter Dance Shoe.

And then nothing.

Jonathan still felt stupid that he hadn't seen on the horizon the confrontation with her brother. They had danced around each other for so long, throughout the group rehearsals, the press work; Jonathan remembered it all. The snipes, the backhanded comments. Benoît could be quick-witted and lethal all at the same time and yet somehow Jonathan had liked it. Not at first … but then later, afterwards, closer to the final, when he thought he could make his move on the man …

Jonathan huffed at the memory and turned to look at himself in the mirror. Had he really been so stupid?

Benoît was Margo's brother; it was obvious he would defend her. Benoît had heard them arguing and afterwards walked into Jonathan's dressing room, verbal guns blazing. Jonathan remembered it well because Elvin was still covered in shiny pieces of gold glitter cannon foil. At the time Jonathan thought it almost made Elvin look beautiful but then –

"Go away," Jonathan said as he heard the door open. He knew who it was without even looking. He always would do. The lightly padding footsteps that crossed the room could only belong to one person. "I'd like to be alone, Elvin."

"I wish you wouldn't call me that, you know it's not my real name."

Jonathan snorted in annoyance. Of course it wasn't.

"You know the story, I know she must have told you. Five kids – Margaret, Eric, Malcolm, Rupert and Linda Bennett. Our dad named us; but mum had 'ideas above her station' when it came to dancing. Wanted us to sound, I don't know … more … *exotic?* I'm not posh, not even close. A Yorkshireman actually, born in Cleckheaton."

Jonathan tapped the dressing table with his fingers. "And the reason why you are telling me all this?" he asked calmly. "Shall we compare? Although likewise, I'm damn sure you already know. Darcy, Jonathan Richard, thirty-six, eldest son of Lord and Lady Darcy of Calderhouse Manor, Derbyshire. Gentleman, dancer, half-cocked bad-boy actor, and son. As of yet I have produced no heir of my own."

Jonathan felt embarrassed to say it all out loud. Hearing his father's and eventually his own grand-sounding title still unnerved him terribly.

"That's … I'd heard, I mean I knew, Margo talked about you, but said you keep it close to your chest and all that, and I can see why, like. Wow. Does that mean you … ? No …" Elvin paused and Jonathan heard him take a deep breath as if he was steadying himself. "She thinks the world of you, you know," Elvin said finally, his Yorkshire accent finally showing itself. Jonathan thought it sounded rather beautiful. "Apparently I am a right bastard though."

That made Jonathan chuckle. "It's a fine club to be in," he replied.

However, Elvin wasn't finished. "The night of the final, I saw red. I knew damn well you were a better dancer than that. I put two and two together and came up with forty-six."

Jonathan slowly looked up to the mirror to find Elvin staring back at him, head cocked to one side. "You thought I'd messed up her chances, right?"

Elvin nodded.

"You thought it was me who ruined the dances." It wasn't a question; Jonathan was merely stating a fact. He wasn't in the least bit surprised though; it was as he had thought all along. The anger, the things Elvin had said to him and the sleepless nights that had followed. It still didn't make Jonathan feel any better about it all. In fact his behaviour with Elvin that night justified his own actions to help out Margo.

"I did. A little bit of simple mathematics says differently though."

"She has four weeks left." Or so the app on Jonathan's phone told him. "Does she see him? The father?" Jonathan was still worried that the man would track her down even now.

Elvin shook his head in reply. "No. The cottage and village you found for her to hide out in does its job well. She needed to hide and you gave her that in spades. All that makes sense to me now. I take it your father owns it? The village of Calderhouse?"

"Technically I do. The cottage anyway," Jonathan replied, letting out a humourless laugh. He hadn't been there for years, not since getting the acting job in Manchester. Jonathan had made sure, however, that Margo wanted for nothing. In fact, she was apparently a regular up at the big house on a Sunday.

"It's your own stately pile?"

This time Jonathan did laugh. *Stately pile.* "No. Well, maybe, I inherited it. I actually own a converted barn on the Pennine moors. It's functional, I get snowed in and it's windswept, but in the end it's mine."

"I still don't know how you managed to get her up there to hide away. She likes the warmth, does our Margo."

Jonathan laughed. "Margo never really put up with my shit, I'm pretty sure at one point she gave me the beginnings of a hernia. She's a tough cookie though, a bit like you but with less sass. Her head is up in the clouds. Well, it was six months ago." He suspected it still was.

Elvin shook his head and pressed his lips together. He then paused for what felt like forever. "The things I said that evening. I was angry. I judged you. You're a good man, Jonathan Darcy," he said as he motioned towards their reflection. "I knew what you were asking on that evening, about us, but for some reason it annoyed me because you were so fucking polite about it. I was so quick to decline your invitation to dinner and all you could do was apologise. Which ended up annoying me even more."

Jonathan took a deep breath at Elvin's words.

"I need to know if we're good, Darcy? Is this over?"

Christ, what a question, thought Jonathan. Had it even started?

"I know it wasn't your fault Margo wasn't on the winning team. Anger was my first go-to, I was so pumped up from winning, but you were bloody pompous, all that *I'm an actor* shite. It was like someone had stuck a selfie stick up your arse."

Jonathan smiled. "What can I say? I'm a legacy of my own upbringing." There was still something that was unnerving, Jonathan thought. He'd never admitted it to anyone, but he had lost sleep over Elvin's rejection. Had his clumsy advances been read the wrong way? There had been no physical contact between the two of them; in fact Jonathan had, he felt, acted like a complete gentleman. Yet he could still remember waking up every hour for weeks after, terrified about the repercussions of it. "So was that why you turned me down?"

Elvin didn't answer; instead Jonathan felt a hand squeeze his shoulder.

"Of course it's totally understandable that you did. I was arrogant to think …" Jonathan stammered. "Now I realise what a fool I was. I read the signals all wrong. I've never been very good at this." The last few words he said in a whisper and Jonathan felt the hand on his shoulder tighten. In the mirror, Elvin looked embarrassed, shy almost. Jonathan was surprised to see him shuffling on the spot.

Jonathan needed to get it all out, though. Ignoring the tightening grip Elvin had on him, he spoke as clearly as he could. "I'm nothing like Anthony Allan, the TV character they killed off. He was written in a way that made him so confident with the ladies – which probably says more than I would like it to," Jonathan admitted. "Maybe it was easier for me to pretend rather than do the damn thing for real. Your words? They hurt though … all that last man in the world stuff. That hurt."

"I'm so sorry."

"No, I understand. You were protecting Margo, whereas I was asking too much, considering. Dinner at the Savoy, a night together in one of the rooms, a bit of romance, it was all rather silly."

Elvin huffed. His lips formed a small pout before he spoke. "Part of me was petrified of you. Not that night … from the first day I met you, to be honest. Remember the first day we met and they were filming us? You strode into the room and I literally felt my knees go weak. Then you opened your mouth and …"

Jonathan remembered the day clearly. It had been a blur of press releases, make-up head shots, career backstories, admissions of dancing experience. It all flooded back to him. "In all honesty I didn't want the celebrity dancing gig," he said. "I hated all of you on sight, didn't want to compete; I believed I was too good for it. In fact if I remember rightly the only person who was remotely tolerable was your sister and even she pushed my limits. I'd even go as far as to say I don't want this gig either. I can dance, I enjoy it to a certain extent, but much to my parents' displeasure I'm an actor. It's what I want to do."

Elvin sighed. "Maybe I was a little star-struck when I met you. I think I was supposed to bow and curtsey and I couldn't – I still can't, it's not my way."

If there had been any doubt about Elvin's feeling towards him, this pretty much confirmed it. Elvin had quite rightly turned down Jonathan's advances when he had made a fool of himself letting his ego get the better of him. Yet for some reason Jonathan felt like he needed that confirming again. He was a TV actor wearing an Oscar winner's breeches for pity's sake. "I take it your feelings haven't changed then," he asked quietly, all hope gone.

Jonathan felt the grip on his shoulder tighten.

"They … I."

Before Jonathan could reply the grip on his shoulder disappeared and he found himself with a lap full of dancer. "What the … ?" he said as his reflection in the mirror was blocked by the body of Elvin Benoît.

"Oh Darcy … my feelings are …"

Good lord. This was – Without thinking Jonathan pulled him close and gave Elvin's lips a quick tender kiss. Now he definitely knew he had lost his damn mind. "I'm sorry, I'm not sure I … ?" Jonathan was so confused. Should he go for it? The way in which Elvin had dropped himself onto

Jonathan's lap had stolen his breath away. "Maybe we should wait, talk, not be in a dressing room?"

With both hands Elvin gripped Jonathan shoulders and shook his head. "No. I don't want to. This," he said, indicating the two of them, "is what I've wanted for a while."

Really? Jonathan almost couldn't believe it. But the way Elvin's lips parted and how he shifted his body on his lap? Jonathan finally nodded his head and slipped a hand around the back of Elvin's neck. If this was going to be his only opportunity to get the man, he was taking it.

The kiss was gentle at first, quickly turning into something more as Jonathan pressed Elvin's lips open further and slipped his tongue inside.

"We should probably wait, however," he said with a pant. Another kiss followed quickly. "I can't possibly do anything too strenuous in this costume, however much I'd like to."

Elvin pulled back at Jonathan's words and smiled. "I thought they looked a bit tight," Elvin said brushing his lips against Jonathan's.

They met again a third, fourth and fifth time and Jonathan felt the resulting lightning bolts reach his toes. "You know Jane Austen did say *'to be fond of dancing was a certain step …'*" Jonathan began, but Elvin stopped him with another kiss before he could finish.

Maybe wearing Firth's breeches wasn't so bad after all.

Author's Notes

Although I haven't mentioned the name of the piece of music that accompanies the dance in this story I have based all my research on work published by John Playford and his successors from 1696 onwards as part of his Dancing Master manual. 'Mr Beveridge's Maggot' is the dance you will see in most TV and film adaptions of *Pride and Prejudice* and *Emma*. However, neither it nor the music would have been used in Jane Austen's day. During my research I also found many different interpretations of the dance. For the purpose of this story I have combined them slightly and kept it as close to the original as I could.

Sam Evans

I live just outside Manchester in an ex-coal mining town, semi-famous for its Rugby League. I've been writing for what seems like ever but only found the MM genre after discovering a paranormal shifter series. I have short stories published in anthologies for both Manifold Press and Dreamspinner Press. I'm currently working on a contemporary series set in Manchester and the world of Rugby League, as well as other short stories.

samevans1975.wordpress.com
twitter.com/samjevansstuff

Know Your Own Happiness

Narrelle M. Harris

"Know your own happiness. You want nothing but patience – or give it a more fascinating name, call it hope."

Jane Austen
Sense and Sensibility

A suitcase, stuffed full and zips straining, stood before the front door like a barrier made of polyester and defeat. A surprise to come home to after his day at work, but not exactly a shock.

Cooper knew the suitcase was his and not Ruby's by the tag on the handle. *Cooper West.* His address was printed neatly below the name. The place where bag and man could be reunited in the event the bag went missing. His home address.

The address that was now, apparently, no longer his home.

The front door opened and Ruby stood there, arms folded, giving him a pitying look.

"You know you want this, Coop."

Her assurance hurt because it was true, and he didn't like being that transparent. It wasn't as if he hadn't tried. It wasn't as if he hadn't wanted to love her more than he actually loved her.

Fucking Archer Flynn.

That hurt more, because it wasn't Archer's fault, any more than it was Ruby's fault. It might have been Noah's fault.

But no. This whole awful mess was Cooper's own fault for having been young and scared, once, and listening to his stupid brother Noah. Four years ago, only nineteen, he'd made a stupid choice; he'd let panic guide his heart instead of love; and now he was getting mercifully turfed out of his latest failed relationship before it went completely sour and began to include the breaking of things.

Things other than Ruby's heart.

"I'm sorry, Ruby."

"I know you are," she said, though she sounded more exasperated than kind or even heartbroken. "Kate's coming to get you. I'll send the rest of your things on later."

Cooper nodded. Swallowed. He picked up his suitcase and took it to the kerb to wait for Kate to collect him.

Such a meek little thing he was, just leaving without a fight. *Again*. He hated that about himself. He wanted to rage and rail against a decision made for him. He wanted to stand up and shout and say it wasn't over. He *did* love her, and if she gave him time he'd learn to love *her* more and the memory of Archer Flynn *less*. He'd grow the fuck up and be a good friend. A good lover. Hell, a good husband and father, if she wanted that.

But he didn't fight. Because Ruby was right. He wanted this – the not being with her any more. He wanted to stop trying to love her more than he could, because it was exhausting and unfair on everyone.

As Kate's car came into view at the end of the street, Cooper took up his suitcase.

"Coop?"

He turned, surprised. He hadn't realised Ruby was still there. Maybe she'd been there the whole time. Watching him not fight to stay.

"You'll find someone," she said. "Some nice girl who suits you."

"Or a nice boy," he said.

Ruby frowned. Cooper could see the thought hovering in her mouth and wished she would say it, because then it wouldn't make it *his* fault he was leaving.

You don't like boys, Cooper West. That was just a phase. You like women.

*I like **both**,* was his silent reply. *Monogamy doesn't make me not bi. And I loved Archer Flynn and I let him go because I let Noah persuade me it was just a phase, because of all the girls I'd dated. And I listened because I didn't want to lose my family.*

Kate's car pulled up behind him. He heard the passenger door open and turned to see his cousin, her expression rueful and without judgement.

"Hey, Coop. I could use a flatmate for a bit, just to help with the bills for a few months. How about it?" Typical of her, to make this sound like a favour from him to her and not her rescuing him again.

I lost my family anyway. And I lost Archer, and I lost myself.

Cooper glanced back towards the house, but Ruby had disappeared inside and shut the door. Probably a metaphor for something, he thought wearily, if only he could feel enough to work it out.

"Sure, Kate. Back to my old room then, eh?"

"I've even vacuumed," Kate promised him as she took him away.

"Come to my book group with me on Thursday, Coop," Kate told her melancholy new flatmate.

Cooper sighed and shook his head, resisting the inevitable.

"C'mon," she wheedled. "You've been lying around the flat like a depressed slug for eight weeks. So it didn't work out with Ruby."

Cooper grunted.

"Or with Shen, or that boy with the mohawk," she added, "or ... Helena wasn't it, before that, and Mandy? They were about the same time, anyway, and before that Isla, Poppy ..."

He grunted again. More of a snarl, really.

"Okay, so you've had a run of miserable luck. Shake it off. Read a book, eat something with vitamins in it, have a fucking bath, spritz up your sad hair and come out with me on Thursday. We're reading Jane Austen this month."

Cooper made a noise like it was the end of the world, and the end-times smelled like cheap dog food. "Aren't you meant to make this sound appealing?"

"What's not appealing about Austen, you cretin?"

"It's all fucking bonnets and county balls."

"Shows what you know," Kate sneered back. "It's all sass and snark, though I will admit there are bonnets. And you like *balls*, don't you? As well as boobies?"

"Ha fucking ha."

"No, really, Coop. You smell like a school bathroom. Scrub up, pull on your glad rags and come to book club. You could meet a lovely girl. Or a lovely boy. With or without bonnets. Besides, if you don't, I won't have anyone to be my wingman at the club after. And I need a wingman."

"You said I had a face like a wet week and to stay the hell away from you when you were on the pull."

"That was last week. This week I need a wingman. So get up you lazy, mopey sod, and read this." She tossed a pre-loved paperback at him, "And gird your loins for Captain Wentworth. He's hot. Imagine Hugh Jackman in tight breeches."

Cooper took up the copy of *Persuasion* and leafed through the first few pages. "All right," he said, unenthusiastically, "I'll come to your book group. I'll even wash."

"That's the spirit," said Kate, with a little air punch. She grinned, then sobered at Cooper's frown. "Really, Coop," she said, "it'll be good."

Cooper smiled at her, giving her some crumb of effort in exchange for hers.

His cousin patted his shoulder and it made him want to weep.

"Are you ever going to tell me what happened? I mean ... you came back with one bloody suitcase, and Ruby sent four boxes over, and that was it. Most of your stuff was still here in your room. My spare room." She shook her head. "*Your* room. You never really moved in with her, did you? That was the problem."

Cooper looked at his feet. "It was a manifestation of the problem."

"Want to talk about it?"

"No."

"Is it about what happened when you came out to your mum and dad?" Which was why Cooper now lived in Kate's spare room on such a regular basis.

"Before then. But. I don't want to talk about it. I messed up. I ran away because I was scared of losing everything, and lost it anyway when I stopped pretending I wasn't bi. So." He shrugged. "I'll get over it."

Kate stooped to kiss his forehead. "You're a good guy, Coop. You've got a good heart, and a good brain. It'll get better."

He nodded and smiled, more successfully than last time.

He was better than he'd been after abandoning Archer. He was better than he'd been after his family abandoned him. It would get better again. Not as good as it had been with Archer, but better.

It *would*.

"Coop, what's taking so long? It's not a date night!"

Cooper sighed at his reflection. A date night would not have been a problem. He knew how to dress for date night. Skinny jeans to emphasise his long legs and make his arse look good. Dark brown hair gelled to look artfully messy, and so ambient light would catch the chestnut highlights. T-shirt for bands or a plain button-up for a dinner, both of which drew attention to how his shoulders had broadened and chest filled out just that elegant little since he was a teen. He'd stopped looking thirteen about the time he graduated with his social work degree last year. Sometimes, depending on the person of interest, a dusting of eyeshadow above his dark brown eyes and sparkles across his elegant cheekbones if he wanted to look especially ethereal, as opposed to just slender and intense. Maybe polish on one or more of the nails of his ridiculously large hands.

But what the hell should he wear to a book club? To gel or not to gel? Band tee or that one Kate had given him, with Oscar Wilde on it? Or was that try-hard?

Dear god, he was worried that *book club nerds* would find him pretentious.

Be yourself, Cooper West. You fought hard for the right.

He went for the jeans, the Wilde shirt because he liked it, and the gel because he needed a haircut and it was that or a beanie.

Cooper and Kate trammed it to Prahran, that perfect Melbourne intersection of grunge, hip, diverse and up-and-coming posh. The venue was a cute, red brick, mid-Victorian terrace house trimmed with iron lace and a sticker in the window reading 'Practise random acts of kindness and senseless beauty'.

The Wilde shirt was definitely not try-hard. Three others were wearing book-related T-shirts. A fourth joked she'd come dressed as Neil Gaiman, being in black clothes from head to foot and with a halo of dark curly hair around her head that defied gravity. The couple hosting the meeting made Cooper feel welcome in their house, the walls of which were festooned with posters of book quotes and classic covers. The husband's right foot was encased in a black velcroed splint and he joked about being Long John Silver, only short and Indian and he didn't have a parrot.

Offered tea, cola or booze, Cooper opted for a glass of Prosecco. He claimed a kitchen chair in the corner of the living room, where he could observe the proceedings. Kate flumped down on the overstuffed armchair next to him.

"See, nobody bites. Well, Brody might, he's a bit of a fartmuffin, but he's not here yet."

"Fartmuffin." Cooper raised his eyebrows at her. "Where the hell do you come up with these things?"

"My last girlfriend's little sister has a notebook full of 'em. Whenever she thought of a new one, she'd write it down. I admired her brain immensely."

Cooper laughed. As he recalled it, Kate admiring her ex-girlfriend's twenty-year-old sister's brain immensely was what had led to the ex in front of girlfriend.

The eight of them – hosts, book-shirt-trio, lady Gaiman (real name Corrie), Kate and Cooper – found their seats, leaving spares for the latecomer.

"I suppose I'll get the ball rolling," said Alice, Host #1. "I have to say I loved the Crofts. They felt like a really modern couple to me, her going off to sea with him, and he even helped around the house."

"She's highlighted passages in our print copy and sent it to her dad," joked Jayesh, Host #2.

"What's she highlighted for *you*?" asked Corrie cheekily.

"How skylarking around on the steps can be bad for your health," Jayesh confessed ruefully, waggling his splinted foot.

Conversation rolled back and forth, with concurrence and disagreement both. It was actually kind of fun, Cooper allowed, especially when it got to the question of whether Captain Wentworth and Dick Musgrove, who the Captain had nursed back to health for half a year, had actually been More Than Just Good Friends.

"But he's in love with Anne!" protested Alice.

"That doesn't mean he didn't have a little Dick on the side," countered Tseen, who wore a Jane Austen T-shirt. "The book's full of sly references to *naval matters*. And anyway, he and Anne weren't together then. No reason he can't be bisexual."

Cooper chewed on the inside of his lip and said nothing.

Conversation turned to exactly how awful Anne's vain father was ("Oh, John Sessions should totally play him in a film!") and still Cooper said nothing.

He began to feel that he really ought to have read the damned book; watched the film at least. Surely there was a film? But he'd only had four days to read it, and he'd found his mood incompatible with getting into the rhythm of the language. He'd got as far as the fact that Anne was plain, her sisters were silly and her father a snob, and gone to read snarky deconstructions of comic book film trailers on Tumblr instead. He'd mostly come to keep Kate company, anyway.

While discussion turned to whether Captain Wentworth had ever really had the hots for Louisa, Cooper excused himself and went to the bathroom. After flushing, he washed his hands and stared in the mirror.

That was not the face of a man who was sad he'd been dumped by his girlfriend. It was the face of a man who'd come to a book group because he really needed to get out more, and thought it would be a quiet way to start interacting with strangers again, only to find out that they talked *a lot*.

Mind you, nobody had actually asked his opinion yet. Maybe it wasn't all as mildly terrifying as he'd started to find it.

Chill, Coop.

He returned to the living room, ready to chill, only to have Alice say, "We're just talking about whether Anne was a totally spineless ninny to have let herself be persuaded against Captain Wentworth by Lady Russell, or if her argument about family duty holds any water at all. Oh, and this is Brody, he got here late, and his friend, another club newbie like you, Ar …"

Cooper didn't hear the rest over the roaring in his ears.

Archer.

Fuck.

Fuck.

Fuck.

Archer Flynn. His Archer, dark hair longer than the close crop he once had, and his beautiful face solemn instead of lit up with the impish, illuminating smile of old. Sitting right there on a straight-backed kitchen chair, staring at him, dumbstruck, and then with the most expressionless of faces. Like Cooper didn't mean a thing in the world to him.

Well, he didn't, did he? Not any more.

"She was a spineless idiot," Cooper heard Tseen declare when he began to function again.

Corrie protested this as harsh. "She was young, and this is Regency, remember. Duty was important in those times, and she's a model of decorum. Not like the rest of her lot."

"She regrets it though," pointed out Theo in the *Fuck off, I'm reading* T-shirt. "She spent eight years pining for the guy. She's just too good a soul to be pissed off at Lady Russell for talking her out of it just because Wentworth wasn't a rich toff."

"So you're with me," said Corrie. "She's not at fault."

"I didn't say she wasn't at fault," countered Theo.

The argument continued. Cooper's hands were clasped hard against each other, an anxious habit of his. He stared at the floor and wished he could dissolve into it. He was already turned to wood, if not to stone, and if the parquet would just absorb him into the grains now, that would be terrific, thanks.

He really, *really* should have read the book.

So, plain Anne Elliot of *Persuasion* had been persuaded away from the love of her life. Christ. If he'd known that, he'd never have come to talk about it. Bloody Kate. Though he couldn't blame Kate. She didn't know about Archer.

Cooper didn't dare look at Archer. Had he read the damned book too? Had he seen him and Cooper in it, reflected in the idiot Anne and maybe-bi Captain Wentworth? Would he have come if he had? Would he have come if he'd known Cooper would be here?

Of course not. Archer wasn't an arsehole. That was Cooper's job. Archer was ...

Cooper risked a glance. Archer was sitting in his straight-backed chair, staring at the bookshelf beyond Jayesh's right shoulder. Unreadable, but not obviously tense. Checking out the library.

An old conversation intruded into Cooper's memory.

"I always take a stickybeak at someone's library, given half a chance. You can tell a lot about someone from their shelves."

"What does my library tell you, Archer?"

"That you're smart, you're open to new ideas, and you have a thing for Foggy Nelson."

"Not Daredevil?"

"Nah. He's too obsessive. Foggy for you, Defender of the People. He's why you're studying social work."

Cooper clenched his hands harder together.

The guy Archer had come with, Brody (a *fartmuffin*, Kate had called him; Archer was dating a *fartmuffin*) had hustled his chair close to Archer's. Now he was resting a forearm on Archer's shoulder. He looked comfortable, like using Archer as a warm bit of furniture was a thing they did, so at ease with each other they could just use each other as props.

Oh, fuckety fuck times a billion.

And Archer looked so calm. Nodding along with the conversation, even if he didn't have anything to add while he browsed the book spines from a distance. Brody made a few references to "the eroticisation of illness" and Anne's evolution from passive to active player in the drama. He sounded to Cooper like he'd been cribbing for the book club so he could impress everyone with his command of queer theory and the Hero's Journey of the Regency Heroine.

When being turned into nicely polished parquet blocks was clearly not an option, Cooper considered bolting.

He didn't, though. He stayed and raised his head and listened, even to Brody. Because Archer was here. Untouched by and uncaring of Cooper's presence, but he was *here*, and just seeing him again soothed an ache in Cooper's heart that had been hurting for four years.

Cooper had been nineteen and in his first year of social work studies when he met Archer at a launch party for a mutual acquaintance's reggae-punk album.

The night Cooper fell in love with him.

It didn't happen the moment their eyes met. They danced first, and laughed about how they didn't really like the music, so they snuck out for coffee. Over espresso and biscotti, Cooper and Archer found a common passion for Oscar Wilde. Further connection points were made: cabaret at the Butterfly Club, the hot chocolate at Hash Café, Daredevil comics, and Helen Mirren in anything.

Love didn't happen at one in the morning either, when Cooper and Archer were sitting on a brick wall overlooking the Yarra River, and Archer pointed out a water rat diving into the dark water that flowed fast and silent under the bridge towards the bay. Cooper leaned over to see and nearly slid off the wall, but Archer wrapped his arms around Cooper's waist and steadied him.

"Don't go getting washed out to sea," Archer laughed, "I've only just met you." He left his arms around Cooper's waist.

Cooper, heart racing, in the circle of Archer's arms, stared into Archer's blue eyes, and blurted: "I've only dated girls before. But I like boys, too."

It was the first time he'd ever let the thought outside his own head.

"I know you like boys." Archer smiled at him and his eyes were warm and kind but also mischievous. "Don't think I don't know it. I know you like *me*."

Cooper's mouth pulled tight in a frown. "No. I mean yeah. I mean. I've been attracted to guys before, but I like girls, too. But I haven't. Been with a guy. Before."

Archer drew Cooper closer in. "Okay," he said. "I've got it. Guys and girls. You do like me though, eh?"

"Yes."

"Good. I really like you, too."

"Oh. Good."

"I'd really like to kiss you. Please. Can I kiss you, Cooper?"

Cooper leaned in and Archer held him close and they kissed. For Cooper it was nothing like kissing a girl. More bristles, for a start. Archer smelled of faint aftershave. His mouth was firmer, lips less full than Cooper's previous girlfriend.

Archer was a much better kisser than Cooper's previous girlfriend, too.

They kissed for a long time, almost stopping but then seeking each other again. They angled themselves on that brick wall to slot more comfortably together, and went straight back to kissing. Eventually, Archer pulled reluctantly away, in stages, returning over and over for brief touches of their lips, like Cooper was an addiction Archer couldn't quite wean himself off.

"Cooper."

"Hmmmm?" Cooper was kiss-dazed, languid in Archer's arms.

A nudging little kiss again, and then, "I think you've missed the last tram home."

That woke Cooper from his serotonin-sodden stupor. "Oh, shit."

Archer's eyes crinkled and his mouth pursed in a grin that Cooper later associated with Archer thinking his tall, fey boyfriend was being adorable. "I've got a flat in the city. It's only small."

"Ah …"

"You can have the couch. No funny business, I promise."

At the flat, Archer looked at his two-seater couch, and at Cooper, head-to-foot at least two-and-three-quarter-seats' worth of loveliness, and said, "You take the bed, I'll take the couch."

"I can't throw you out of your own bed, Archer."

"You're not throwing, I'm offering. If you try to sleep on that, you'll get bent and crinkled in all your important places. I'm not going to be responsible for breaking a flawless lanky elf spirit like you."

Flawless. Cooper flushed, but still protested. "You're nearly as tall as me." Archer was shorter, but stockier. If Cooper was an elf, Archer was a hardy woodsman, broad-chested and slender hipped. A prince who'd been enchanted to forget his princely origins.

"Yeah, but I'm more used to it. I'll live."

"I don't want your important places getting bent and crinkled either."

In the end, Cooper slept beside Archer on Archer's bed. Archer wore pyjamas; Cooper borrowed a pair of track pants.

The moment that Cooper fell in love with Archer – when, at least, that seed was planted – was when he woke up briefly, feeling content, to find that he'd snuggled up to Archer in the night. Not really waking, Archer's lips brushed against Cooper's forehead. Archer sighed, a happy sound, and fell back to sleep.

Cooper didn't know why Archer holding him as they slept made him feel whole. They were nearly strangers, when he looked at it squarely. But there it was. For years Cooper had felt awkward and uncertain about his attractions to people, and he'd just blurted out to Archer about the liking guys as well as girls thing. Instead of the scorn he'd expected, there'd just been acceptance.

"I've got it. Guys and girls. You do like me though, eh?"

With Archer's body radiating warmth, his sleep-soft breath gentle on Cooper's skin, the promise made and kept of no pressure, Cooper knew it for a fact.

I like you. I think maybe I love you a bit already.

Their courtship – Cooper felt quite strongly that it was a *courtship* – was wonderful. Archer was everything Cooper ever dreamed of – patient, funny, stimulating, loving and attentive. They'd been absolutely besotted with each other. Archer, a graphic artist with his uni days behind him, helped Cooper write papers and study for exams. He reinforced learning with rewards on a sliding scale, from kisses to blow jobs. They didn't live together – Cooper was still at home with his parents and older brother – but spent so much time together they might as well have done.

I love you, thought Cooper often, but he didn't say it. Archer didn't say it either. Cooper didn't know if Archer loved him, but knowing only his own heart was enough for now.

Cooper loved Archer with every beat of his heart, and he held the secret close inside, something beautiful to treasure and not let out. If he said anything, maybe it would be tarnished by not being loved back as much, or by the grubbiness of his brother's rough prejudices. None of Cooper's old friends were here, and his new ones – second-year students with the world-weary, wise cynicism of those who had discovered the complicated world beyond high school – would have laughed at his starry-eyed adoration.

And he adored Archer. Adored him and loved him and worshipped him so much, it was sometimes terrifying. It was like being in love with the sun.

Nearly seven months it lasted.

Then Archer met Noah.

Cooper didn't realise Noah was even behind them at the café, until he spoke.

"You're not a chick."

Archer raised an eyebrow at the stupendously evident observation.

Cooper turned in a panic. "Noah, what the hell are you doing on campus?"

"I'm doing coffee with a hot bird I met at the bar last night. She said to meet her here."

Cooper swallowed convulsively and wouldn't look at Archer.

"You *are* Archer, aren't you?" Noah said to Archer, who was looking from Cooper to Noah, trying to work out the connection, "I heard Coop call you Archer a second ago."

"Yes, I'm Archer," said Archer carefully. "Who the hell are you?"

"Noah. Coop's brother. He told us he's been dating someone. We've been waiting to meet her. Only she's not a she, she's you. Unless this is even more revolting than it looks."

Archer tilted his head and frowned. "You told me your brother was an ass," he said conversationally to Cooper. "You didn't tell me he was a complete one."

"You and me have to have a talk, little bro."

"Let's not do this," Cooper said, already on the verge of hyperventilation.

"Yes, we'd fucking *better*."

Noah stalked off, forgetting his rendezvous. Archer tried to hold Cooper's hand but Cooper had drawn in on himself. His hands clenched together, holding on as though there were no one else to hold his hand for him.

"You told your family I was your *girlfriend?*"

"I didn't tell them anything except your name. They don't know I like guys."

Archer stared at Cooper, then he pushed back from the table. "Fine. Fine. Whatever."

He walked away and Cooper let him. Cooper ran after Noah instead.

And what a talk it was: about how Mum and Dad would freak out: disown him. Or maybe they'd forgive him, because uni could be a weird place. Mum always said she worried about Cooper here, and this Archer dude – *Cooper, man, a fucking **dude?*** – was older and taking advantage, and it was probably just a phase, and did Cooper really want to get thrown out of the house, because that's what would happen.

"I could just go live with Archer," Cooper had protested, but his voice had wobbled because … could he? A penniless student, a nineteen-year-old kid, thrown out by his parents onto the streets? Would Archer really take that on?

Because Cooper had seen what happened to some of the queer kids kicked out. And even if he hadn't, Noah spent the drive back to the family home telling him about the kids bashed up and dropping out of school and all the bad things that happened. Noah said that his boyfriend – *seriously gross, Coop, a fucking **dude**, fucking my little brother, I can't even!* – was just messing with him, getting his hands on a *twink*, a soft-hearted little *twink* like him.

"You're a soft touch, Coop, you always were. He's messed with your head. You always dated girls before. You've fucked girls before this. This is just a phase. Don't worry about it. I won't tell Mum and Dad. I'll look after you. Don't you worry."

"But, Archer …"

"He'll find some other kid to move on to. He doesn't need you. I'll cover for you with Mum and Dad. Tell 'em you broke up with your girlfriend. You're just a kid, how the hell do you know what you want? No such thing as bi anyway. You're either straight or gay, and you've had girlfriends, so you're fucking straight, you hear me? And even if you are bi, you can just stick to girls. Easier, yeah? Easier for everyone."

By the time they were home, Cooper was cowed, in tears, and terrified.

Cooper tried calling Archer later, to try to explain why he'd just left. To say he'd changed his mind. To say sorry. He left message after message. Archer never called back.

Noah offered to go get the things Cooper had left behind at Archer's place. Cooper didn't have the courage to go himself. When Noah returned, it was with a box of meaningless junk, a handful of study notes and Noah's bristling brotherly compassion about the fact that Archer didn't want Cooper ringing him any more.

By the time Cooper had the courage to go by Archer's old flat, Archer didn't live there any more. Archer didn't even know Cooper's home address, either. Cooper, scared of the consequences of Archer showing up unannounced, had never given it to him.

Cooper had no idea whether he'd broken Archer's heart, but he knew he had broken his own.

Two years after that, sick of the self-loathing and feeling like an alien in his own skin, Cooper came out to his parents. He did it by emerging from his room in eyeshadow and nail polish and telling Noah and his mum and dad, "This is me. This is who I really am. I'm Cooper West, bisexual."

"No such thing," his father declared. "Anyway. You date girls."

"I like guys, too, Dad."

"You date girls."

"I have a boyfriend." He did. Nothing serious. "Nico. He's in one of my cl-"

"The *fuck* you're a faggot."

"Bisexual," Cooper insisted.

"You're just confused," said his mother.

"For fuck's sake, Mum ..."

A lot of shouting followed. Noah claimed he knew nothing about Cooper's sudden announcement. Half an hour later, Kate met Cooper at the mall to collect him. He had a rucksack and a suitcase of clothes and university books, and a fading red mark on his cheek where his mother had slapped him for swearing at her.

He got a part-time job. He paid board to Kate. He studied and he bloody well graduated and got a job and grew the fuck up and tried to fall in love again. Came close a couple of times, with men and with women.

Never close enough.

Kate, sitting next to Cooper, nudged his knee. "You okay?" she whispered. "I mean, obviously you're not. Want to go?"

Corrie and Theo had taken Mrs Clay's part in an argument over whether she was a gold-digger or just a woman of her time trying to survive. T'seen and the other T-shirt guy – Cooper couldn't find the energy to remember his name at all – claimed she got what she deserved when she ran off with the scheming Mr Elliot. Brody weighed in on Clay's side, and the hosts were split.

Archer had gone to the sideboard for a drink. He was taking a long time about it.

"It's okay," said Cooper, watching Archer loiter by the glasses. "Maybe in a minute."

Brody cast Cooper an acid look, then rose to stand beside Archer. He placed a hand on Archer's hip. "One for me, Arch?"

He doesn't like to be called Arch.

Archer poured Brody a drink, then poured one for himself. White wine.

You don't like white wine.

Archer sipped the wine, grimaced, and put the glass down.

"What do you think – Cooper, isn't it?"

Cooper looked up to find Brody smiling at him. It wasn't a friendly smile. "Pardon?"

"What do you think of Penelope Clay? You haven't said much. Did you even read the book?"

"I. Ah. No. Kate only asked me to come a few days ago. I didn't have time."

"Bit rude, coming for the plonk and not having anything to contribute."

Cooper felt the warmth rising in his cheeks.

"Oh we don't mind, do we, hon?" said Alice chirpily to Jayesh.

"Did you catch a film version?" Jayesh offered.

"No. Busy. Sorry."

"He really only came to keep me company," Kate said.

"I should go," said Cooper, rising.

"Aren't you Ruby Bishop's ex-boyfriend?" asked Brody pointedly.

Archer's head jerked up at that, and he looked straight at Cooper.

"Yeah," said Cooper, clenching his jaw, glaring at Brody and refusing to meet Archer's accusing expression.

Brody smiled, that not-friendly smile again. "Must be rough, getting kicked out like that."

"Brody," said Jayesh warningly, "don't be an arse. This is a book group, not Fight Club."

"Sorry." He didn't sound sorry. "Sorry, Cooper. No harm meant, *mate*."

Cooper excused himself to push past Brody into the kitchen. He ran a glass of water and sipped it.

What the hell am I doing here? Haven't even read the fucking book. Time to get out.

He heard someone behind him, and thinking it was Kate, he turned.

It was Brody.

"Fuck off out of here," said Brody in a low, angry voice. "Arch keeps fucking looking at you, and you're messing up my plans to get a leg over."

He keeps looking at me? When? How?

"Isn't he your boyfriend, then?" Cooper asked.

Brody snorted. "I don't do *boyfriends*. This isn't *High School Musical*. I do *fucking*. And he's fuckable as anything. So piss off out of it."

That's not what Archer's like. He likes to cuddle.

Actually, Cooper remembered too well the way Archer's body and his would move together, hot and urgent, grunting with pleasure and holding each other while they kissed and sucked and fondled and *loved* each other. Sweaty-hard-fast; slow-languid-sweet. Cooper's body ached with missing how Archer touched him.

"Ruby told me all about you."

"What?"

"Gay-curious, she said."

"Bi," said Cooper through gritted teeth, "and monogamous."

"God, you bastards, you want it all. Fucking gay *tourist*. Or are you after a threesome? You, Archer and Kate, eh?"

"Jesus, Brody, what the hell is wrong with you?" came a deep, angry voice.

Brody and Cooper both whirled at the sudden intrusion, to see Archer standing at the kitchen door, glaring at them both.

"Nothing," said Brody, fixing on a thousand-watt grin for Archer. "Hey, want to piss off and go clubbing? Stupid book this month. Shouldn't have let Tseen pick it. She's got shit taste. I wanted the latest Lee Child."

"No, I don't want to go clubbing with you," said Archer icily. "Turns out you're a prick."

"You're the one who can't keep his eyes off the have-it-all-ways twink when you're meant to be out with me."

"You invited me to join your book club, you –" Archer's mouth twitched in an acid smile. "*Fartmuffin*. That's what she called you a second ago, wasn't it? Kate?"

Brody bristled, his shoulders set aggressively.

He's going to hit Archer.

Cooper stepped forward, thinking to grab Brody's elbow and check the blow. Brody, sensing him, deliberately jerked his elbow back hard. The high jab caught Cooper in the diaphragm and the breath whooshed out of him. He stumbled back, hit the sink, wobbled and sagged to the floor.

Cooper wasn't entirely sure what happened next because he was busy trying to inhale, but he was aware of Brody being tugged fiercely out of view. The next thing, Archer was crouched in front of him, warm palm pressed to the middle of Cooper's chest.

"Breathe, Cooper. Breathe, that's it. You'll be okay."

Cooper blinked at him rapidly, not because of the pain, which was easing, but because he couldn't see. His eyes were stinging. His face was wet.

"Don't cry," said Archer gently. "It'll stop hurting in a minute."

Cooper's face crumpled. "Why are you being kind?"

Archer stared at him stupidly. "Because that arsehole just elbowed you and took off in a snit."

"You shouldn't be kind to me."

"Well, that's just stupid."

"No, it isn't. Why would you be kind to me? I was such an idiot. I left and I didn't say goodbye."

"Yeah," said Archer drily, "I remember."

"I didn't explain."

"Yeah, well, Noah did. So ..." he shrugged. "It was made very clear to me that I wasn't to try to get in touch with you. He said he'd tell your parents if

I tried to call. I'd have written, but you never gave me your home address. Keeping me secret from your parents, I suppose."

Cooper started to cry in earnest.

"I'm sorry," he said, his voice choked with misery. "I'm sorry. I'm sorry. I'm sorry. I'm sorry. I'm sorry."

"Hey," said Archer, concerned. "Hey, it's okay. Shh, now."

"It's not okay." A sobbing breath, and another, and then it all poured out. "I'm sorry I hurt you. I'm sorry I left. I'm sorry. I'm sorry, Archer. I'm so sorry. I'm sorry I listened to Noah. I'm sorry I lied about you to my parents. I'm sorry I wasn't brave. I thought if they knew, they'd kick me out. And I was so scared, because I loved you so much and I thought, how could you love me the same way I loved you? And if Noah and my parents threw me out, I'd be all alone if you didn't love me, too."

Archer's expression was the weirdest combination of angry and lost. "I didn't think you loved me that much."

"I love you so much I can't breathe, sometimes. But you never said you loved me."

"Neither did you."

"I was so scared," was all Cooper could say.

Archer put a hand on Cooper's cheek, brushing tears away with his thumb. "Shh, now," he said softly. "Breathe. You know you make yourself sick when you get upset like this."

Cooper was soggy and snotty and just a wreck. He drew a hiccupping breath and tried to be calm. Archer's warm palm on his face made that hard. Or … not. Maybe Archer's skin on his, and the kindness in his voice, made it easier.

Cooper drew a deep breath and exhaled slowly.

"Sorry."

"You don't have to keep saying that."

"I do. I was such a coward. I let fear take you away from me. I messed up, and you don't like me any more. That's okay. But can I tell you? Can I tell you I've changed? I've grown up. I stopped hiding who I was. They threw me out, but the world didn't end. I graduated and I work with at-risk kids now, like I said I wanted to."

"Always knew you'd be great at that," said Archer with a fond smile.

"And I'm on my own feet now. Mostly. Well, apart from Kate. She's my cousin. She's great. I broke up with Ruby, like Brody said. Commitment issues, I guess. It's a bit of a problem for me. I've met people but they're not you. You still live in so much of my heart and they can't push you out."

Cooper shrugged sheepishly at the way Archer stared at him, amazed.

"Sorry, Archer. I'm sorry. I'll stop bothering you. I know I fucked it up. It's okay. Thanks for helping just now." He tried to rise.

Archer's hand was back in the centre of Cooper's chest, gentle but firm, holding him in place. "You still love me?"

Cooper's mouth twisted dolefully. "I've always loved you, Archer. I was just too much of a coward to stay with you."

Archer, who had always been endlessly kind and patient, said, "I'm sorry about your family."

"It's okay. There are worse things than being rejected by your family for being queer. Spending your whole life trying to pretend you're not, trying to kill the parts of you they won't accept, that's right up there with the worst."

Archer nodded. "I was thinking when I saw you there – well, after I got over the shock of seeing you there – that you looked …" He laughed. "I was going to say taller, but I think I mean less confined. You used to try to tuck all that height down, except when we were alone. Anyway. You look good. I'm glad we bumped into each other."

"Yeah. It's been good. Well, no, it's been largely awful, I guess. But you look good. You look well, I mean. And, you know, don't worry about all the stuff I said. About still being in lo- ah, anyway. It's not your job or anything to –" Cooper scrubbed a hand through his hair and tugged on it, as though trying to derail his thoughts, or start some new ones.

"I want you to be happy," Cooper continued at last, "I know it's not my place, but you know, with Brody? You can do better. You deserve better. You deserve everything beautiful and perfect, and unless there's a secret Brody hiding inside the Brody I'm seeing, he doesn't treat you right." Another hair-tug. "Sorry. Sorry. Not my business. Be happy though, yeah?"

"Working on it," said Archer. He glanced over his shoulder. "Here comes Kate. I'll say goodnight, then. See you, Cooper. You be happy, too."

Cooper nodded. He'd try. This sense he suddenly had now that he'd seen Archer again – and said all the things he should have said four years ago – that maybe everything would one day be okay, was new. A gift from Archer.

He saw Archer exchange a few words with Kate. Then Kate offered

Cooper her hand and heaved him off the floor.

"Let's blow clubbing," she said. "I'm not in the mood for hooking up. Austen makes me go all demure. Let's go home."

Cooper went to work Friday morning. Despite the night he'd had, he found he looked forward to it. It meant something, to work with those teenagers struggling with their gender identity and sexuality, trying to help them understand that it *would* get better, even when they couldn't be brave all the time.

He felt pretty good, really, when he got to Kate's at the end of the day, throwing the door open with a theatrical flourish. "Good evening, Miss Cox! Play something for me on the harpsichord and I shall do needlepoint!"

A deep, masculine laugh greeted the announcement. "You really have picked up some new skills in the last few years, Cooper."

Cooper almost tripped over his own feet at Archer's warm voice teasing him from the lounge.

Cooper stared at Archer. Blinked. Yep. Archer was still there.

Kate plucked her jacket up from the coat rack and pulled it on, grinning. "Right. I have to take the dog for a walk, Cooper. You two talk."

"You don't have a dog," said Cooper.

"Fine. I have to go *buy* a dog. You two talk."

She swept out, leaving Cooper and Archer staring at each other.

Archer smiled crookedly at Cooper.

"Nobody measures up to you, either," he said. "I thought maybe we could give it another try?"

Cooper couldn't speak. So he nodded. And kept on nodding. Like a demented nodding toy, that couldn't breathe.

When Archer cupped Cooper's face in his hands, Cooper could see through his own salt-stinging eyes that Archer's lashes were wet, too.

And then they were kissing, and Cooper could breathe again, and he used his breath and his mouth and his arms around Archer's shoulders to communicate his speechless wonder at this second chance.

They didn't mean to move so quickly, but two months later, Archer's lease was up. He and Cooper found a new place and moved in together. This time, not a single one of Cooper's things was left in Kate's spare bedroom. This time, he was fully committed.

Surrounded by unpacked boxes, Cooper and Archer stretched out on their bed, on this first night in their new home.

"I've always loved your hands," said Archer with languid contentment as those big hands caressed his spine and down to the curve of his backside.

"I always liked your hair short," said Cooper, and brushed his cheek against the newly-cropped soft fuzz on Archer's scalp.

Archer moved suddenly, pushing Cooper onto his back so that he could rub his fuzzy pate all over Cooper's chest and belly, tickling him until they were both giggling like idiots. The giggling stopped abruptly when Archer's fuzzy hair brushed soft between Cooper's legs.

"Oh!" gasped Cooper and then, laughing, "You keep doing that, you're going to get sticky hair."

"You can wash me later, then. With your big manly hands." He carefully moved his scalp to make Cooper moan again, then kissed his thighs.

Cooper gazed down at Archer's pale blue eyes, crinkled in impish merriment.

"I love you," said Cooper. "I thought you should know." As though he didn't say it daily.

"I love you, too. In case you didn't realise." As though he didn't leave it on post-it notes and in whispered words every single day.

Cooper reached for Archer and drew him up to kiss him.

And nothing could ever dim their sunshine again.

Author's Notes

I often 'cast' characters in a romance to help me write their descriptions. In this case, Cooper was modelled on Dylan O'Brien, and Archer on Wentworth Miller. In my favourite ever coincidence, I learned after the fact that Wentworth Miller is named after his father, who is named after *his* father – who was named for Austen's Captain Wentworth. How perfect is that?

Narrelle M Harris

Narrelle M Harris is a Melbourne-based writer of crime, horror, fantasy, romance, erotica and non-fiction. Her books include *Fly By Night* (nominated for a Ned Kelly Award for First Crime Novel), fantasies *Witch Honour* and *Witch Faith* (both short-listed for the George Turner Prize) and vampire book, *The Opposite of Life*, set in Melbourne.

In March 2012, her short story collection, *Showtime*, became the fifth of the 12 Planets series (released by World Fantasy Award winning Twelfth Planet Press). *Walking Shadows*, the sequel to *The Opposite of Life*, was released by Clan Destine Press in June 2012, and was nominated for the Chronos Awards for SF and fantasy, and shortlisted for the Davitt Awards for crime writing.

In 2013, Narrelle also began writing erotic romance with Encounters (Clan Destine Press) and Escape Publishing. Six short stories have been published to date. Her first full-length romance, *The Adventure of the Colonial Boy* – a Holmes/Watson crime/romance set in Australia in 1893 – was published by Improbable Press in 2016. A queer paranormal romance and more short stories are in the pipelines with Clan Destine and Improbable Press.

narrellemharris.com
mortalwords.com.au
twitter.com/daggyvamp

Thirteen Hours in Austen

Fae Mcloughlin

My mother slid the gold-edged teacup towards me. "Try this one, it's called Dong Ding."

This was tea number three; my mother's intentions were to work through as many of the seventeen varieties on offer as she could. She needed to get a life.

"Nothing is called Dong Ding, Mother." My chair faced a large painting of Mr Darcy that hung above our table in the Regency Tea Room, first floor of the Austen museum. He looked like Colin Firth from *Bridget Jones's Diary* and his eyes followed me as I took the tiny handle between thumb and forefinger and lifted the bright green liquid to my lips. Tea number three tasted like cabbage; I clattered the cup back onto its saucer.

"Ashley, would I lie to you?" My mother's little finger pointed towards me as she sipped the cabbage.

I sighed and glanced around the room. On the next table, three girls dressed as Elizabeth Bennet – as my mother informed me – nibbled white triangular sandwiches, and giggled about how Peter's new haircut made him look like Hugh Grant. The round table in the bay window held four tourists drowning in a mass of cameras, umbrellas, and plastic bags that screamed 'Jacks of Bath' in big black letters.

The light blue walls did nothing to help the fact that the room was hot. Sunlight streaming through a window was burning the back of my neck, and on the sideboard, tea urns wheezed clouds of steam. Plus, the constant clink of china and high-pitched chatter was giving me one of my heads.

"Ashley, please be cheerful, we seldom spend quality time together." My mother always saw through me as if I were invisible, which these days I felt I was.

"I'm going for a cig, and then I'm off." The chair rasped across the wooden floor as I stood.

"I don't like you smoking, Ashley."

"Mother, I'm nineteen years old. And it's not smoking, not really."

Pulling the slim pink e-cig from my pocket, I fled the tea room and my mother before she could argue.

It was quiet and cool in the shadows around the back of the museum. A breeze toyed with a stack of cardboard boxes, and piles of broken furniture reminded me of an art installation by a famous sculptor whose name escaped me. On the brick wall next to me, a sign read 'Loading Area'. I looked at my feet to see yellow painted cross-hatches. The museum's soundtrack of annoying classical music was still audible and as a sweet smell of baking drifted from the window above, I was reminded that I'd had no lunch, only cabbage tea. I inhaled the chemical vapour, my shoulders slumped, and I stared at my trainers.

My mates think it's so cool to be a runner in my dad's film company. They're deluded. It's all fetch me a coffee, photocopy this, pick up my dry-cleaning, fetch my belt which I left in the hotel which is a cab ride away, and smile. The talent never acknowledge my presence and nobody ever uses my name, I'm just 'boy'. But the sleazy leading man in my father's current film has acknowledged my arse. He keeps pestering me for 'sleepovers' in his trailer, which I politely decline and remind myself to be careful what I wish for. By the end of the day, my legs are screaming for relief, my stomach is growling, and my head is riding a merry-go-round.

"Visitors are not allowed into the cast areas." A young guy appeared at my side dressed in full military garb, including red jacket and leave-nothing-to-the-imagination white trousers.

"Cast?" I said with my eyes still on his nether regions.

"Yes, we're all actors in the big Austen performance. I am Mr Wickham from *Pride and Prejudice*, at your service." He bowed before gesturing towards the open fire door I had slipped out of five minutes earlier. "Now you need to leave."

"Boy, you guys take it seriously, don't you?"

The boy swung his sword like a propeller, whacked the green recycle bin, and sheathed it with a red face. "Miss Jane Austen is to be taken seriously."

I leaned in. "In my opinion she writes literary crap and all Janeites need to get laid." Bloody 'ell, I'm in a bad mood today. It's halfway through the month and my pittance of a pay has run out meaning it's beans-on-toast in my cold flat or cap-in-hand to my folks. My mother gives me the money but always whispers, "Don't tell your father."

The boy straightened. "I'm a Janeite!"

"And do you need to get laid?" I lifted my head and blew a cloud of sweet-smelling vapour into the air.

He opened his mouth with a pop and then shut it again whilst fiddling with a shiny brass button.

"Who did you say you were?"

"Mr Wickham."

"Did this Wickham guy have ginger hair?"

"No." The boy kicked a pebble at his feet. Why the fuck did I say that? Just because I had a crap-pay-no-future life, this boy didn't need to take my unhappiness.

He flounced in front of me like a drunken ballerina, all arms and out-of-control legs, forcing me to retreat against the brickwork. "But, like Mr Wickham I'm charming, an excellent conversationalist, and possess a gift for making friends. Unlike him, I'm not wicked, although sometimes it might be fun to be so," he said and winked.

I smiled. There was something appealing about the nineteenth-century soldier amongst rubbish of the twenty-first. I held out my hand. "Ashley, Ash."

"Hello Ashleyash, I'm Mr Wickham." He clicked his heels and shook my hand with a surprisingly firm handshake.

"No, you're not."

"Okay, I'm Noah and you're still out of bounds."

I took one last draw on the e-cig then said, "Don't worry, I'm off."

"What is that?" Noah pointed towards the vaporiser.

"Um, an electronic cigarette. Have you not seen one before?"

"No. Why do you smoke that and not a real cigarette?"

Did he live under a rock? "Erm, for health reasons." I turned to leave.

He caught my arm and there was urgency to the grip. "Did you dress up today? It's the museum's most popular activity."

I pulled away. "Nope. I'd rather stick pins in my eyes."

"Oh, you're out of luck, the wardrobe department has run out of pins."

"Ha-ha." I turned towards the door.

A red jacket filled my vision and blocked the way. "Why are you here if you hate Austen so much?" Noah asked.

"My mother dragged me along on some kind of parent/child bonding thing."

Noah leaned in; he smelt of mints and brass polish, and his breathing was quick and low. "I bet you a week's wage I can make you fall in love with Austen before the night's out," he murmured.

"My week's wage wouldn't buy a novelty eraser from your shop."

"If they are your thing then my week's wage would buy you a thousand." He waited, his eyes round, and his lips parted.

The only people who spend a night at the museum are boffins and Ben Stiller. It was lunacy, but I said, "What the hell. Nothing to lose –"

"– and a lot to gain." Noah took my hand.

In the large entrance hall of the museum, I sat on the floor behind a skirted mannequin, which smelt of mothballs, with my back jammed into a corner and my knees to my chest. Flapping the dark blue skirt material, I coughed at the dust and said, "And who is this?"

The ginger Mr Wickham, who had removed his red jacket but not his pleasingly tight white trousers, was hiding behind another row of women. "That is Lydia, youngest daughter of Mr and Mrs Bennet from *Pride and Prejudice*. Unfortunately, she had an unhappy marriage with Mr Wickham."

"Oh, Mr Wickham, did you not keep your wife satisfied in the bedroom?"

"Shut up. I'll have you know that Mr Wickham was very … manly."

"With the ladies?"

"Of course with the ladies." Noah blushed.

"No 'soldier mate' on the side?" I teased.

"No!"

I laughed and shuffled my backside to get a more comfortable position. "Remind me again why I'm here?"

"You need the money." Noah looked at his watch. "The museum closes at five. Hold tight."

"Why can't we hide in the loos? That's what they do on the telly. I've seen them stand on the rim and hold their breath."

"We are not running from a drug cartel and there's only one cubicle, which John checks before leaving."

Then I spied my mother. She was in deep conversation with the museum's curator and waving her long hands in front of her face.

"I think she's the last person to leave," Noah whispered.

That figured, she'd never had a sense of timing.

The man, dressed in top hat and tails, smiled and showed my mother the large wooden double doors. He locked them with two definite clicks that echoed around the large room. My heart leapt at the sound. At what point is hiding behind a frozen Lydia Bennet with her husband, Mr Wickham, a good idea? Stretching my fingers, I consoled myself with the thought that as long as Noah wasn't an axe-murderer all would be okay.

The curator turned off the lights as he left the hall. Now the remaining light was the dimming sun through a ceiling window. I tried to untangle my legs but only moved my ankles. "Noah, you might lose your job for this."

"Absolutely."

"Then why the fuck are you doing it?"

He twisted onto all fours and faced me. "A little mischief feeds the soul."

"Are you quoting Miss Austen?"

"*My sore throats are always worse than anyone's.*"

"Eh?"

"That's quoting Jane Austen."

"You're nuts. I'm in a dark out-of-time museum with a madman."

Noah laughed. "Come on, let's go. John will have left by the back door by now so the coast will be clear." He stood, grabbed my hands, and heaved me to my feet.

"What now? Food?" I asked, dropping off the raised display platform onto the polished wooden floor.

"Dancing."

"Dancing?"

"Yes. I'm going to teach you the art of dance. In Austen's novels, a ball was the ultimate occasion for flirting."

"Flirting?" I repeated.

"Yes. It was a rare chance to mix with the opposite sex, to be in close proximity, touch, and talk. A ball was erotica in front of a hundred pairs of eyes." He blushed.

I was all for a bit of erotica but my stomach was shouting louder. "I'm hungry."

To our left was an impressive flight of stairs, like the ones you see in stately homes but narrower. Noah kicked off his knee-length boots and padded towards it. "I'll feed you later," he called over his shoulder.

I scowled and didn't make a move to follow. "Where are you going?"

Noah stopped, turned, and considered me. "The museum's ballroom," he said as if I should've known.

"Can't we do something … else?" My mother once told me that nobody truly hated anything. That wasn't true, I hated dancing.

Noah sock-slid across the wooden floor, into my space, and levelled his face with mine. In the darkening hallway, the whites of his wide eyes were like slivers of porcelain. For a long moment, he said nothing and then leaned in and whispered, "Ashley, dancing was a chance for a release of passion." He giggled and slid off.

Was he hitting on me? I replayed the hitching breath, the softness of his voice and the flash of eye. Good God, well at least it made a change from overpaid screwed-up actors wanting a quick arse shuffle on the pull-out in their trailer.

"Take your shoes off." Noah interjected my thoughts.

"What?"

"Shoes. Off."

I obliged and took off my size elevens to expose fluffy winter socks, totally wrong for summer but they were the last ones in the drawer. My feet stunk and if Noah wanted the socks removing also, he was in for a shock.

He circled me, placed both hands on my lower back, revved his feet like roadrunner, and then propelled me snake-like across the hall floor. The urge to shout *wheeee* was strong, but I resisted and instead leaned into Noah's hands, flung my arms sideways and pretended to be a plane. It had been a long time since I'd acted the fool.

Approaching the grand stairs, Noah played chicken with the bottom step, aiming me towards it, and then veering off at the last moment so I did a banking turn with pleasing accuracy. Noah panted at my back; at nearly two metres and eighty kilos at the last check, it was a miracle he'd pushed me to the stairs never mind circled the room. We approached the staircase for a second time and with one almighty effort, he drove me into it. I landed, sprawled across steps one, two and three, with stubbed toes and grazed elbows. "Fucking hell, Noah, you could've warned me." Rearranging my limbs, I rubbed my arms, and examined my toes.

Noah collapsed in a heap next to me laughing and puffing. "And where's the fun in that?"

The boy was mad enough to eat nails, but I liked him. However, forever the gloomy Gus I said, "Well, fun that sock-sliding in a dark museum is, how does that teach me about Austen?"

"It doesn't." Noah grabbed my hand and tugged me up the stairs.

The vast first floor was all shadows and unidentified shapes, with a low ceiling and a definite chill in the air. Something rustled behind me; I turned to see nothing but emptiness. To my left, another row of blank-faced mannequins lined my way. Half-lit in streetlight coming from a nearby window, they reminded me of *Doctor Who*'s Autons, life-sized plastic dummies controlled by an evil consciousness. I shuddered and realised that Noah still had hold of my hand. The feel of the smooth skin, the lump of knuckles sticking into mine, and the cool of his surprisingly strong grasp was enjoyable. A full-blown image of his fingers gripping lower on my body darted into my vision and hung for a tantalising moment. I shook it away, readjusted my stance, and concentrated on whether I should let go of Noah's hand first or wait for him to – like a telephone call between two lovers when neither one will replace the receiver.

Noah didn't seem to notice as I untangled our fingers, instead he loped towards a shady doorway and disappeared through its frame. Holding my hands in front of me like Frankenstein's creature, I tiptoed after him. "Noah …" Something pointy connected with my shoeless toe. "Ow. Fucking hell! Noah!"

He appeared from the gloom and into my space. Again. The amber streetlight backlit him so with his features faded and his hair glowing, he looked saint-like. I stared at him for far too long.

"Dancing," Noah said, breaking the moment, and then, "Candles." He brought his hands under my face to reveal two fat church candles. Rummaging round in his pocket, he produced a box of matches, and then like the cat that got the cream he grinned at me, lit one candle, and passed it over. Lighting the other, he placed it close to his chin so his face lit spookily, flapped his spare arm, and woo'd like a ghost. I smiled at him, moved my candle in front of my nose and woo'd back.

"So, dancing?" I said with the flame burning my nostrils.

"Yes." Noah pointed towards the shadowy doorway. "The ballroom hides a dark secret. When this building was a private residence, the housemaid caught the butler with his trousers round his ankles and his face the colour of a sunburnt pig."

"What was he doing?"

"It's not what he was doing, it's what the footman kneeling in front of him was doing. The butler turned, saw the maid, smiled at her, knotted his fingers into the footman's hair and grunted with release. The housemaid fainted and it took a whole bottle of smelling salts to revive her."

Moving closer to Noah, I whispered as if the mannequins would hear and disapprove, "What happened then?"

"The lord of the house, one Mr Grant, employed the butler as his personal valet instead and it's rumoured they spent so much time getting dressed of an evening, that the footman was required to help." Noah winked. "Mr Grant sandwich springs to mind."

Taking a dramatic step away I declared, "Mr Wickham, you are disgusting!"

He laughed, reached for my hand, and led me into the den of iniquity.

Considering the size of the museum, the footman-suck-butler ballroom was larger than I'd imagined. Two central wooden columns sullied with age stood sentry-like in the centre. Below blood-red walls, a row of dark wood panelling framed the room and there was a smell of old leather. Suspended from the white ornate ceiling were two pink lights, globes with round black fittings, that looked for all the world like breasts.

A chill made my skin prickle as Noah placed his candle on a small side table and showed that I should do the same. Flame patterns dancing on the bloody walls gave a sense of being in Hell and I didn't know whether to enjoy the feeling or realise that what I was doing was weird, and run. Before I could decide, Noah skipped to the centre of the room and held his hands out to me.

"What?" I knew what.

"Dance with me."

"I don't dance. In fact I would go as far as saying I hate dancing."

"Let me show you."

"Nope." I crossed my arms and resisted the urge to pout.

Noah stepped towards me, dressed as Wickham, fingers come-hither, and half-lit in the candlelight. I felt as if I'd stepped back in time and it was fucking irresistible.

My feet walked towards him before my brain could argue. He took my hands in his, said, "*To be fond of dancing was a certain step towards falling in love*," and led me to the middle of the room and slipped one hand around my waist. I straightened to his touch. "The main dance in Jane's books was the La Boulangere – a simple circle dance for groups of couples."

"Isn't that French for bakery?"

"No, Ashley, it's a country waltz."

"How the hell do you know how to waltz?"

"I spend a lot of time watching people."

"Noah, that's creepy."

"Put your hand on my shoulder."

I duly did so.

With his hand gripping mine, he lifted them as if we were playing a game of *I'm a Little Teapot*, applied pressure to my back and then before I knew what was happening he'd spun me in a circle. My legs crossed and uncrossed like two knitting needles.

"One could tell where a person was on the social scale by their understanding of the ballroom rules." He twirled me again and I stamped on his foot. Twice.

"Rules?"

"Codes of behaviour. For example if a woman turns down one dance she must turn down all others." Noah tugged me upright, dragged me a few steps to the left and round we went again. "Understanding the codes were part of the courtship." He kicked my twisted legs apart.

Pulling away from him, I muttered, "Noah, this is not showing. It's assault."

"Ashley, on the count of three we'll take two steps to the right."

Noah pushed me to arm's length, counted to three, dragged me to the right, and looped me around.

"Noah, mate, can we cease with the circle-thing?" I puffed and wiped my brow on my sleeve. The room had warmed and I wasn't sure if that was the spinning or being in Noah's arms.

Ignoring me he said, "Did you know a dance could last fifteen minutes and in a room lit only by candles the heat could reach fainting level."

"Like *Amnesia*?"

"What?"

"Ibiza … ?"

He shook his head and pulled me into the teapot-embrace. His body ran the length of mine and his breath grazed my cheek as he whispered, "To dance was to be sexually alive. Couples felt each other's heat and each other's breath, and all that whilst being watched. It was terribly arousing."

I readjusted my stance, swallowed hard, and stuttered, "So. If. You're Wickham. Who am I?"

"Lydia Bennet."

"Who?"

"She was Elizabeth Bennet's sister and Wickham's wife."

"I don't want to be the girl," I moaned.

"Oh, who doesn't want to be pretend to be a girl?"

"Um. Me." Once, when I was young, I'd put on my sister's dress and twirled around my bedroom enjoying the draught on my legs. My father caught me, turned purple, and tore off the dress. I never came out to my parents; I left them to guess. My mother thought it was cool to have a gay son and would bring it up whenever she could at her weekly bridge meets. My father tried to understand for my mother's benefit, but it never sat well with him. "However," I said, "if I were a girl I would've had my eyes on the Darcy prize."

"I absolutely agree – mysterious, noble, wealthy, and a nice arse."

"Noah, they're not real, you know."

He huffed and spun away from me to perform pirouettes like a pro. I liked the boy in tight trousers spinning in a dark museum. There was an ease to him, a devil-may-care attitude, a like-it-or-lump-it outlook and I envied that. I'd always found it difficult being myself: I'd change my accent depending on who I was talking to – our Scottish receptionist was often greeted with an och-aye-the-noo, which doesn't even mean hello. My conversations with the Australian producer were peppered with bewdy, and worst of all I'd turn Liverpudlian with the make-up boy from Newcastle, which was embarrassing because I fancied him.

I called, "Now where?"

Noah retrieved the candles. "Now? The archive."

"I never saw an archive on my mother-trip around the museum."

"It's not open to the public, only special people." He flashed a toothy grin and in the half-light, he looked like the evil Count from *Sesame Street*. I fully expected him to say, 'One, hahaha, two, hahaha,' but he didn't; he muttered something about *Pride and Prejudice* instead.

The corridor that led towards the secret archive was small, grey and cold, smelt musty, and reminded me of a World War Two bunker, not that I'd ever been in one. We'd descended three flights of creepy stairs before we even got to the start.

"Why is the archive so inaccessible?" I whispered.

Noah held an old oil lamp out in front of him. It swung cheerily from his fingers. God knows where he'd picked it up but the lamp threw out more light than the candles. "Why are you whispering?" he asked.

"It's like a fucking underground tomb down here. I thought I might wake the dead."

"They're already awake."

I shuffled in front of him. "What did you say?"

"Joke. Come on. The archive houses a lot of precious first editions, that's why it's in the basement."

"And they allow a nitwit like you access?"

"No." Noah stopped. "I nicked the entry card off John."

"Noah!"

"You need to feel the book that Jane Austen felt, to read her beautifully crafted words, to hold history in your hands, and to breathe in the lives that those pages have seen." Noah slid in front of me and the corridor felt hot, and the air thick. There was something about him, like an old soul in a young body, or the past in his eyes.

"So am I special people?" My words echoed in the stillness.

"You are the boy who said yes to a night in a museum with Mr Wickham." Noah placed the lamp onto the floor. "Of course you are special," he breathed. And that's how we stayed, staring at each other, for an eternity, until I herded him into the breeze blocks, placed a hand either side of his shoulders and waited for my heart to stop beating in my throat and for my brain to register what I was doing.

Today, Noah was exactly what I needed – a welcome distraction from my dead-end job and beans-on-toast life. I could easily lose myself in the amicable, strangely attractive Mr Wickham.

Noah looked like a rabbit caught in the headlights with his eyes round and glassy. Had he kissed anyone before? Was I the first? I leaned in as if I were doing press-ups and he was my bench. He nodded his head, it was the tiniest movement, but it was all I needed.

His lips were smooth, cold, and clumsy. I'd prepared for passion, but his lips flapped on mine as if I was kissing a fish. I pulled back, but only a little. "First time?"

Noah examined his fingers. "Sorry. No. Second. The first was with a boy round the back of the cricket pavilion who bit my lip. I was hoping the, um, inexperience didn't show." He ducked under my arms and stooped towards the lamp.

"Here." Catching his hand, I wound him in my arms, and bumped him against the wall. I was no Casanova but hoped I had more skill than a lip-biter behind a hut. Wrapping one arm around his slender waist, I drew him in until his body ran the length of mine. He was ice-cold. "You're fucking freezing."

"Maybe I need … warming up?"

I laughed. "If you think I'm warming you up in this death bunker you're sadly mistaken."

"Kiss me, then."

Sweeping stray hair from Noah's face I gently placed my lips on his, applying more pressure until his head rubbed up the cold wall. One hand roamed the material covering his neat backside, as the other plucked the shirt away from the trousers and searched the goosebumped skin under his navel. Noah whimpered and his lips trembled on mine, zipping a shudder down my spine and into my groin. Then he copied me hand for hand with one grazing the denim on my backside and the other pulling at my shirt.

Standing on my tiptoes, I thrust him into the wall so hard he groaned. Was I so desperate? There was something irresistible about Noah, he made my mouth water, and every nerve ending pulsate. I felt as if I'd known him forever, not a few hours, and as if it weren't the first or second kiss but the one-thousandth. In that moment, I wanted to make Noah love me more than he loved Jane Austen.

"Ca-n't bre-athe," Noah gasped.

"Shit, sorry." I moved away but for only as much that allowed him to suck in air.

Noah laughed and kissed me, this time so softly it was as if I was kissing air. Then he hummed a tune that sounded like canned lift music.

"Er?" I questioned.

"I always hum when I'm happy."

"O-kay." I was sure that Noah would be quite happy being the only bottle of orange in a crate full of milk.

My hand settled into his back pocket with my fingers hugging the delightful curve between cheek and thigh, and Noah's fingers pleasingly tucked into the waistband of my trousers. And there we hung, entangled, humming, and cold.

It had been a while since I'd been with anyone. The quick hand shuffles and knee scraping with the new runner, Jude, behind the sound trailer didn't count. Well, apart from Calum Monterey: he promised me yachts, exotic places, fine clothes, and I believed him until I caught him red-faced and breathless behind a sheepish Jude.

"Let's find somewhere more comfortable and bloody warmer." There must be beds in the museum – the four-poster variety with barriers around them so kids didn't jump on them.

"No!" Noah untangled us and bounced away. "I have to show you the archive and I promised you'd be in love with Austen before the night was out."

"Urgh." I slumped. "Fuck the archive." My desire for the lanky weirdo took me a-back – I went for drummers, bass players, wearers of leather, the ones that left you dangling and panting for more.

Noah's fingers knitted with mine and pulled. "Come on."

I planted my feet and resisted like a sulky schoolboy.

He yanked me by his side. "Plenty of time for … warming."

"What time is it?"

"Seven."

"What time does the museum open?"

"The tea room people are in at six."

"Eleven hours. What are we gonna do for the rest of the night?"

"We have a bet, remember? You are going to love Austen before the night's over or you win a week's wage."

I didn't care about the bet; my interest lay with the odd boy with the cold lips but I sighed and said, "Come on, then."

The so-called archive was little more than a long thin room with white walls, low violet lighting that made us appeared bruised, and one of those concrete ceilings that you see in multi-storey car parks. Every available space was crammed with shelves, and on them in neat rows were books of every size and colour. Larger ones were on the bottom with smaller ones on the top. There was a clinical feel to the room as if the books were waiting for autopsy, and a nasty whiff of bleach. A loud drone buzzed like a fat bee, and by the chill in the room, I guessed it was air-conditioning,

"You bring me to the nicest places," I grumbled.

"I do! Here." Noah threw a colourful cushion at me. Embroidered with a giraffe set against a bright red savanna it looked strange against the stark background.

"Where the hell did this come from?"

"John's chair." Noah nodded towards a sparse table and swivel chair in a corner behind us. "Right, if memory serves me correctly it's in row four and on shelf twenty-one."

Tucking the out-of-place cushion under my arm I asked, "What is?" Could he mean a secret handle to an underground laboratory, or the lost orb of Andalucía, or possibly a sandwich? I was starving.

"One of the first editions."

"Noah, mate, I need more info than that."

"Of *Pride and Prejudice* which was first published in 1813. That's two hundred years ago!" He turned his palms to the ceiling as if I was an idiot.

"I can count." The cushion and I trudged behind Noah as he marched along row four swinging his head left and right looking for shelf twenty-one.

He stopped with an abruptness that made me lurch. "It's here," he said in awe, and reached out long fingers towards a row of books. With the chosen book in his hand, he said, "Ashley, this is the most expensive piece in the museum, along with the other four, starting with *Northanger Abbey*, then –"

I held up my hand. "I don't need that much info." Personally, I wouldn't have shouted from the rooftops about the book in Noah's hands. It was about the size of my iPad; the spine was dark green with gold decorations and the front and back resembled blue-grey marble. Overall, the most expensive piece in the museum was doing a good impression of an accounts ledger that my dad used.

Noah opened the cover and held the book under my nose and an image of the dusty, cobwebbed, wine cellar my Uncle Bob hid from my Aunt Sheila appeared. The first page was soft cream colour with the faintest remnants of the words, *Pride and Prejudice: A Novel*, printed at the top. It didn't even state 'Jane Austen', only *from the author of Sense and Sensibility*, whatever that was.

I jabbed my finger at the page. "What's the point of writing a book and not telling anybody you wrote it?"

"Jane didn't put her name on her novels, they would only ever say *by a lady*. Now, sit."

"Sit? Where?"

"On your cushion. I'm going to tell you a story."

I scanned the stark concrete floor and it didn't look inviting. Noah plonked down, leaned against shelf twenty-one, and smiled at me.

"Can't you read a few words while I'm standing?" The last thing I wanted was for this to become a boring reading of words from a long dead woman. My friend, Sam, is a writer, he'd read me chapters of his book whenever and wherever he was able – in the corridor, in the car park, over the phone, over a burger. It's annoying, I'm not into fantasy and once you've heard one ogre-killing spell you've heard them all. I looked at Noah's bright face, and realised there was no way I was going to get away with it, so I threw the cushion next to him and sat on the giraffe's face. "Fire away."

Noah cleared his throat. "It's a simple story about a boy who's rude to a girl, so the girl dislikes the boy, then the boy proposes to the girl and she refuses, until she discovers the magnificent Pemberley."

"And then they fuck like rabbits."

"Ashley!"

"How rich was he?"

"In today's money – it's around twelve million a year."

"Bloody hell! Miss Bennet landed on her feet."

"Can I continue please?"

"Sure."

Noah ran his finger under the first line of the book, and said, *"It is a truth universally acknowledged that a single man in possession of a good fortune must be in want of a wife. However little kn-"*

Holding up my hand, I said, "Stop, stop. That's how it begins?"

"Beautiful, isn't it?"

"No!"

"Okay." Noah carefully leafed through the book. "This is funny." He took a breath then giggled before saying, *"But no such happy marriage could now teach the admiring multitude what connubial felicity really was."*

"What the fuck does 'connubial felicity' mean?"

"Happy marriage. It's funny. Okay." Noah skimmed the thin pages. *"Mr Darcy had at first scarcely allowed her to be pretty; he had looked at her without admiration at the ball; and when they next met, he looked at her only to criticise. But no sooner had he made it clear to himself and his friends that she had hardly a good feature in her face, than he began to find it was rendered uncommonly intelligent by the beautiful expression of her dark eyes."*

"Noah. It's hollow la-di-da."

Noah leapt up, hugging the book to his chest. "Oh! How can you call Jane Austen's beautiful literature 'la-di-da'? That's uneducated."

I pushed up to join him. "Uneducated? It's my opinion, that's all."

Noah harrumphed and carefully slid the book into a slot between two other account ledgers.

"I've offended you, haven't I?" Now I was never gonna get a shag in a cordoned-off four-poster.

He spoke to his socks. "I was going to be polite and say no, but damn it, yes, you have."

Taking his hand in mine, I stroked his fingers with long light caresses. "I'm sorry. Allow me to make it up to you."

Without lifting his eyes from our hands, Noah said, "Ashleyash, is your mind always in your trousers?"

I laughed. "No, tonight it's in yours."

"Okay."

"Okay, what?"

"You can make it up to me."

"Lovely," I breathed.

"After cake."

"Cake?"

"You said you were hungry."

"I am … but for something other than cake."

Ignoring the reply, he pulled me along row four, out of the war bunker archive, back up the creepy stairs, along a corridor lined with pictures of portly men with cherubs by their sides, and into the comforting surroundings of the Regency Tea Room.

The street light outside the museum threw amber squares through the leaded bay window giving more than enough light to see, and the room smelt of a wet forest floor, which would be the seventeen varieties of tea on offer. Noah had never let go of my hand and I'd enjoyed his touch, and the hard pull of his lead was commanding and arousing, but his hand was fucking freezing.

"Noah, seriously mate, you need warming up."

His eyes smiled before he skipped towards the food counter, and grabbed a plate. "What do you want?" he called. "Soggy cake? Stale sandwiches? Weird gluten-free stuff?"

"Um, Noah, you're not selling it to me." I joined him, peered through the windows of the sandwich display, and then lifted the lids on the glass cake stands releasing a sugary whiff.

He clamped a piece of jam sponge in the jaws of some silver tongs and dropped it onto a plate. It landed sideways with a squelch. Then using the same sticky tongs he picked up an egg and cress sandwich, which succumbed to the same fate.

"Mate, don't ever work in the tea room."

Noah grinned, handed me the plate, and turned on his heels.

"What are you having?"

"I'm not hungry," he said and plonked on the floor in front of the sideboard with the now silent urns.

I dropped next to him, leant against the cool wood, and whilst picking out jam from my egg sandwich, considered my bizarre situation. When I was a kid, my mother had given me her precious collection of twenty-one *Famous Five* books with strict instructions not to lose them. I lost three – one on the school bus, one on a camping trip to Wales and one on a wall near the post office. This night was as if I was in one of their adventures but without the blonde one, the girl who wanted to be a boy, and the dog. Like *Two Go to the Museum and Piss About*, or something like that, and instead of finding a treasure chest I had to find Austen. So far, all I'd found was I had a penchant for tight white trousers.

"So. Do you do this with all the visitors?" I asked through mouthfuls of sandwich.

"What?"

"You know. Spend the night. In the museum. With a stranger."

"Oh yes, all the time. I mark on my headboard the number of lays I manage. Now it's hovering around fifty. However, one night a chap punched me; totally my fault, I read him wrong."

I choked.

Noah laughed.

"You're joking?"

"Of course."

With my curiosity piqued about the boy who dressed as a fictional character, I asked, "Did you have to go to college to get a job here? Did you do English or History or Austenology?"

Ignoring me, Noah got to his feet, wandered to the large portrait of Mr Darcy, and knitted his fingers behind his back, which reminded me of my grandad. "It was such a wonderful era – genteel, mannerly, and romantic," he said to the painting.

"Um, don't you mean an era that was oppressive to women and with a colossal rich-poor divide?"

"Party pooper."

"Starry-eyed."

"Absolutely." Noah glanced at my empty plate then at the clock that read 8:26 and said, "Okay. Now we can dress up."

"Dress up? You're kidding?"

"It'll be fun, I promise."

I wasn't so sure. Six years old and a sheep in the nativity was the last time I'd dressed up. I slipped the e-cig from my pocket, stood, pressed the button, placed it between my lips, and began a long drag until Noah whipped it out of my mouth.

"Nasty," he said simply.

"Give me it back."

"No."

"Noah."

"Yes, Ashley?"

I held out my hand. "Now."

Noah spun, waved the e-cig above his head, and pelted out of the tea room as if his arse was on fire. He ran like a fucking hare – all blurry legs and sharp movements. Fuelled by jammy egg, I sprinted after him, skidding on the wooden floor in my winter socks. He was hard to follow in the dark museum and I occasionally lost sight of him, but the sound of his giggling and a flash of white trousers laid a trail through the half-lit displays and dim corridors.

I chased Noah into a large room, skidded to a panting halt behind him, and placed my hands on my knees to catch my breath. Lined with dark wood panelling and a ceiling painted grey, the room was oppressive. At one end was a wide mirror that leant against the wall at a drunken angle, and at the other was a window so narrow that if there were a fire there'd be no way you'd get though – even with my skinny hips. I always thought tiny windows were pointless but maybe in the olden days they didn't think about health and safety. Dominating the room and the reason for the draught round my ankles was a huge stone fireplace. If they desired, ten people would be able to stand in its mouth and if it desired, it could swallow them whole. It gave me the creeps.

"It still works," Noah puffed and pointed with my e-cig towards the toothless monster.

"What? Is it animated?"

"No silly. I could light a fire." He nodded towards log basket, coal scuttle, and irons that sat on the hearth.

"How romantic."

After building and lighting a fire with surprising skill, and with the room softer, cheerier, and – romantic, Noah tugged me towards a huge wooden box that lurked in a shadowy corner, lifted the lid, which creaked loudly, and asked, "Who do you want to be?"

"A housemaid. The ones with short skirts, frilly aprons, and possibly no knickers."

"Oh! I see. That's your thing." Noah put his head in the box.

I sighed. "Joke. I'll be Mr Darcy."

"I was hoping you'd say that."

"Why? Because you've always wanted to fuck Darcy?"

Noah blushed. "Well, um, possibly."

"I'd say definitely."

"Okay. Yes. Who doesn't want those smouldering eyes piercing your soul while his wide hands search your … creases?"

"Er, um, me," I said and then, "Mr Darcy, I presume?" as a tailcoat flew past my nose, then a top hat, trousers, a large shirt, a black cravat, a waistcoat, and boots.

Noah materialised in front of me, so close our socks touched. He stared at me for a minute and said, "Take your clothes off."

Innuendo loaded his command as his faraway eyes never left mine and his mouth never cracked a smile. It was masterful and stirred grumblings in my groin. Tonight, Austen could take a fucking leap. I'd learnt that a boy in soldier cosplay can make me tremble; being told to strip by firelight makes my hips twitch; tight trousers rule; and not to combine jam and egg.

My mouth opened to speak but all that came out was a crackled croak. What the hell? I laughed ... for far too long.

"I can help," Noah offered.

Clearing my throat, I said, "Yes, help, yes, um, thanks."

Noah whipped my shirt off before I could blink and left me with my hands hanging above my head and slightly dazed. Then his fingers were working the button on my jeans and tugging at the zip – there was no denying, this was where he wanted to be. He skimmed the front of my boxers, gathering the material, parting the fly, and letting the air in to play. I quivered with each touch, and as he let his fingers hover for a teasing moment, his breath quickened. Then those fingers hooked my denims and dragged them down so fast I had to grasp his shoulders for balance.

I regained my stability and said, "Um, thanks," then swept the deflated Mr Darcy off the floor and placed him on the box. "So do you think Darcy and Wickham ever shagged?"

"Only in your head, Ashley. They didn't see eye to eye after Wickham did the dirty on Darcy's sister."

"They could've had angry sex?"

"No, Ashley, I'm sure they didn't."

"Isn't Wickham supposed to be naughty and randy?"

"Yes, I guess he was Jane's bad boy."

"Then he'll have gone after the handsome and wealthy Mr Darcy – even if it was to play a game of Butler and Footman shuffle." I winked at Noah.

"Ashley! Jane Austen would turn in her grave."

I laughed at him, slipped on the puffy white shirt, and buttoned it up. Noah, with eyes gleaming, helped me into the waistcoat and fastened it, slid the tailcoat onto my back, then fussed with the cravat, tying it a bit too tight. I reached for the trousers but Noah batted them away.

"No," he said.

"What?"

He shuffled on the spot. "No trousers – and no boxers." Then whilst fiddling with the hem of his shirt, he whispered, "Please."

"Noah! A fantasy of yours?"

"You mean a young good-looking chap dressed as Mr Darcy but with his bottom half exposed? Absolutely."

Sliding out of my boxers, I swept the shirt and tailcoat aside, and posed, top-half Darcy and bottom-half wanting Ashley. I felt wide-open, vulnerable and, even though the fire was roaring, I was chilled to the bone, but it was one of the most sensuous things I'd ever done.

Noah's eyes were round and his mouth slack as he scanned me. All his fantasies rolled into one were stood in front of him and his luck was in, ready and waiting. "You look absolutely amazing," he croaked.

My gaze dropped to Noah's tight white trousers, which outlined his excitement in perfect detail. It appeared I was the lucky one. "So do you, Noah, so do you."

Reaching for his shirt, I grabbed the material and heaved him towards me. As quick as my fingers would move, I opened a flap and undid five fiddly buttons. As I finally removed the object of my attentions and slid the material around his hips, I breathed, "No underwear."

Noah said nothing, simply wriggled the trousers off, kicked them away for the shadows to eat, and froze. Wanting to savour the sight, the moment, the suspense, so did I.

We remained, lit by firelight, surrounded by discarded clothes, half-dressed as fictional characters, and hungry for each other until Noah took my hand, placed it in the small of his back, and stepped towards me until his skin contacted mine. He leaned in and whispered in my ear, "I've never … *you know.*"

"'S okay," I said to his smooth neck, "we don't have to. We'll keep *you know* for another time."

He muttered something and dotted my ear with kisses, which made my stomach flip and my breath catch. Another time? Yes, that suited me. I wanted lots of other times with Noah: countless secret meetings, whispers in the dark, and oodles of sex.

Taking his arm, I dragged him onto the floor but he leapt up, ran to the box, and threw two large cloaks at me. "Bedding."

I laughed, arranged the cloaks into a rough bed shape, and said, "Come here," before reaching for his hand and yanking him to me.

We lay side by side with the fire silhouetting Noah's form. I gathered his shirt and slid my hand onto his chest. A scar, about the length and width of a pencil, lay below his ribs. "What did you do?" I asked as my fingers traced it.

"Something silly." Noah shifted in and I glided my hand onto his backside, which satisfyingly filled my hand as I drew him towards me. He lifted one leg, dropped it over my hips, and shimmied closer. His heel dug into the small of my back, and his excitement poked below my navel. We fitted together like a Regency porn jigsaw and as he mirrored me with his hand on my arse, we lay for a long moment breathing each other's air and shifting our hips to produce a delicious friction that shot little prickles up my spine.

"I need to tell you something," Noah breathed.

Placing my lips on his, I hummed, "Um?"

He pressed me onto my back, shifted onto my chest, and kissed a trail down my neck before saying, "It'll wait."

Twisting my head to the side to allow Noah more access, I caught his white arse, a knot of our bare legs, and four searching hands, reflected in the mirror. Gripped, I watched our parallel selves as we shifted. It was a reflection of two halves – as if Darcy and Wickham were scrapping and Noah and Ashley were – having a fucking great time.

Pushing Noah back onto his side, I undid the stifling cravat and slithered it off. A kink of mine is bondage and it was probably too soon to ask Noah but I chanced it. I waved the tie in front of his face. "Trust me?" To my delight, he understood my intent and nodded. "Raise your hands above your head." He lifted his arms and I tied his wrists tightly with the fabric. To drive home the point that, for now, he was mine, I held them tightly in place whilst I kissed him. He tasted of fresh air – as if he were spanking new.

One wonderful weekend not so long ago, a now ex-boyfriend, on discovering my large hands, taught me how best to use them. With this new skill, I forced a leg between Noah's thighs and walked fingers down his body. The other hand remained firm on Noah's bound wrists as I wiggled my hips into his and wrapped us together, as one, in my wide palm. The difference between us was clear and when the *another time* came I was a very lucky boy indeed.

Noah sucked in a long breath and held it as his knees locked, arms stiffened, and fingers splayed. I covered his mouth with mine, longing to absorb his passion, and keen to breathe in my name as he came.

"Let's go," I breathed and worked my God-given hand slowly at first and then I increased the pace and swayed my hips. As Noah was captive, he had no choice but to fall into the same rocking rhythm.

The room, the fire, the mirror, all faded away. My dead-end job and my beans-on-toast life evaporated. All that remained in the empty space was tied Noah, skin on skin, my busy hand, the nervy tingles, and the pulsing of my heart. I wanted to stay in that glorious void. Forever.

Noah squirmed against his binding, his whines became bleats, and then there was a change, a growing, a faltering in the pace, and a pull of breath. His eyes disappeared into creases, his back arched, he cried out "Ashley" and the word echoed around my skull with utter satisfaction. Then I got my prize as the throb of release pulsed in my hand. All the while, I'd continued to slide my hand and before the tension had quit Noah's body, I came in a shock that tore from my toes and compelled my body to stiffen and unleash a strangled cry. Then the rush freed itself into the sticky narrow gap between our bodies.

We lay in the moment, breathless, spent, bedraggled and messy, until I undid the cravat and rubbed Noah's wrists. "Okay?" I asked in a statement that I hoped would cover possible sore wrists, fucking a stranger, and the fact that the costumes definitely needed a wash.

"I'm more than okay, Ashley." Noah sighed and warmth pooled in my chest as I gazed at the half-naked, sticky, grinning boy in front of me.

After an amount of time that I judged as mannerly – I was Darcy after all – I said, "Can we wash?"

Noah pushed up, chucked another log on the fire, and stripped off Mr Wickham. I swear he was so pale he was almost see-through. "Do you not like the sun?" I asked in jest.

Noah glanced at his body, "Oh. Too busy working." He held out a hand, I took it and he pulled me to my feet. I stripped off and threw Darcy onto the same pile as Wickham. Noah passed me one of the cloaks. "Come on."

I wrapped the material around my shoulders and, like two naked highwaymen, we crept out of the room and along the corridor towards the bathroom.

Blue paper towels are not flannels and each swipe of our stomachs resulted in torn wet bits drifting to the floor of the bathroom.

"'S not working," I stated to the tiles.

"No." Noah was staring into the mirror that ran the length of the four porcelain washbasins with his fingers gripping the edge of a sink and his mouth slack.

"What is it?"

"Again."

"Again?"

He nodded and swept his cloak aside.

Ah. Again. I stood behind him and rested my head on his shoulder. Watching my mirror image, I snaked my arms around his waist and took him to hand, both hands, one wrapped on top of the other.

"What about you?" Noah's reflection whispered.

"Just you," I mumbled into his ear, more than happy to see him crumble in my hands.

Noah's knuckles whitened as he spread his legs and leant into me. In the mirror, I stared with fascination. I didn't want him to come, I wanted to watch the sliding of my hands and the bewitching reflection of the cloaked boy.

Come he did though, all too soon, shuddering and moaning. I could have gazed at him forever. There'd been a lot of forevers this night and a lot of firsts. I'd never shagged a boy in cosplay or pulled off someone in a dim bathroom in a spooky museum.

Wrapping Noah's cloak around him, I spun him into my arms. "Can I offer you an inadequate blue towel," I muttered before kissing him.

In the panelled costume room, I lay in front of the fire whilst Noah chucked various items of clothing on top of me, including a tiny corset, a pink petticoat, a voluminous green satin ballgown, beige jodhpurs, a blue military jacket, a long white nightie, a feather boa, and a pair of woollen socks.

"Great, I'm sleeping in a Regency jumble sale," I complained and sent the itchy wool socks pirouetting across the floor like ice skaters.

Noah pushed aside a large green skirt and wriggled in next to me. I smiled at him as tiredness swept from my toes. In the firelit wooden room, with my head on a nightie, Noah's hand in mine, and his breath gently fanning my fringe, I let sleep take me.

I awoke to a jarring brightness and a long dead fire. Rocking the slumbering boy by my side I said, "Noah? Noah? Fuck. What time is it?"

"Er, um." With his eyes half-shut, he fumbled for his old-fashioned watch. "Fifteen minutes to the hour."

"What hour?"

"Six."

"Shit." I scrambled out of the crumpled cloak. "I better move."

In the sock-sliding hallway, I turned to Noah. "I have work for the next few days but I'll come back to see you."

He took my face in his hands and dropped his forehead onto mine. "Remember me, Ashleyash."

"Remember you? Don't be a ninny. What's your number? I'll text you."

Noah, with a cloak wrapped tightly around his naked form, took a step away. "I don't have a mobile phone."

Smiling at my odd soldier, I ran a hand down his arm, and kissed his nose. "Oh, right. I'll see you soon. I promise."

I snuck out of the museum, past the milkman, and a drunk with no shoes on. I'd never found Jane Austen, I'd never fallen in love with her, and I was certainly not interested in joining the Janeites. But I had found Noah, I might have fallen in love, and I was definitely interested in joining him … with me.

Two days later, I hammered on the large front door of the museum. The grating of the heavy bolts echoed through and the door opened slowly, creaking like old bones. First John's head poked round, followed by his body. He was dressed as Darcy and I hoped it wasn't the same costume that led to – I chuckled inwardly. If only he knew.

"Good morning," he said.

With an urge to spread my joy, I smiled the smile that's normally reserved for Keith the Butcher who always gives me an extra sausage, and repeated, "Good morning."

"The museum doesn't open until nine." John sank back inside.

"Yes, I know. I've come to see Noah."

"Noah?"

"Yes, the guy who dresses as Mr Wickham. I'm sorry it's early. I, um, couldn't wait."

John emerged onto the doorstep. "Mr Wickham, you say?"

"Yes! He wears a red jacket, tight white trousers, and –" I cleared my throat at the memory, "carries a sword."

"Noah? Erm, nope." John frowned and hesitated before saying, "Maybe you're thinking about the Civil War Museum three streets away."

Fucking hell, this man was irritating. I invaded his space and growled, "No. No. No. It's *this* museum."

John inched back through the doorway as if I were a lunatic. "Like I said, there's no one here with the name Noah. Good day." He made to close the door.

He was a bloody fool with no idea who was on his staff. "Please. John. There is. I only saw him a few days ago."

John paused then his face brightened. "Ah! Yes. I wondered why the name rang a bell. There was a lad called Noah."

"Was?"

His shoulders shuddered. "Yes. But that was one hundred years ago."

"Well, that's clearly not *my* Noah as I saw him two days ago."

"It's the only Noah I know. He died in a terrible accident."

A woman, dressed as a cook or a maid or something, joined John at the door. "Is everything okay?" she asked.

"This chap is asking if there's a Noah here. The only Noah I can think of is the lad that died here a hundred plus years ago when the museum was a family home."

"Yes, John's right, love. No Noah here." Her smile backed up John's belief that I was the village idiot.

"Died?" I repeated.

The woman patted my arm. "He fell down the stairs and landed on his sword, terrible shame. But some say he died of a broken heart."

"Also folk say he haunts the upper floors," John added with a wobble in his voice.

"Haunts," I repeated as the wind ceased, John and the woman seemed to slow down, the air rushed from my lungs, and my heart parted company with my body. Noah's lips and hands were cold, his movements were ethereal, fluid, and he didn't eat. But most of all was the look in his eyes – faraway, transparent, unfocused.

Despite the alarming thoughts, I said, "No. He *was* real. He *was* alive. And he *was* breathing for fuck's sake." Then I looked at my feet and apologised for swearing.

"There's a sketch of the boy in one of our archived newspapers. Was he a skinny lad with a shock of hair, big grin, and a military style uniform?"

"Er, yes."

"That's the boy who died. I'm sorry, lad, you must be thinking of someone else."

"I'm NOT thinking of someone else! That costume you have on, I was wearing one like that the other night – when we – and it *was* real and he was so *very very* real."

As John hastily closed the door, I looked at my feet, my stomach fluttered and I couldn't breathe. And why was it so fucking hot? Run. I had to run.

As I darted away from the museum, I glanced over my shoulder, and saw something that made me skid to a halt. In the bay window was a red and white shape. It hung for a moment, then in a heartbeat it vanished. Was it a reflection of a bus, my imagination, a desperate wish, or Noah? Then a breeze played with my fringe and brought with it a low hum that sounded for the entire world like *Ashleyash*. I turned and sprinted, not towards home and my dead-end job, but towards … who knew.

Fae Mcloughlin

My passion is writing, but in my spare time, I like to photograph big skies and old ruins. You will also find me in museums, people watching in cafes, or standing on my garage roof taking pictures of the sunset.

twitter.com/FaeMcloughlin

Man of War

Sandra Lindsey

HM Sloop *Thrush* was exactly the type of vessel William Price had long wished for a posting aboard. He fancied that his luck could not have been greater than in receiving his first commission aboard a lively sloop likely to become involved in daring exploits. Letters to his dear sister Fanny continued the enthusiasm they had shared in many conversations since the news of his posting arrived.

In truth, though he avoided dwelling on such things, he was keenly aware that having spent all seven of his years at sea aboard a larger ship, there were gaps in his practical knowledge of handling a sloop compared to a ship of the line like the *Antwerp*. He bent his effort to plugging those gaps, learning the best trim and set of the *Thrush*'s sails, feeling her creaks and groans while under way and understanding how to get the best performance he could from her.

Mortimer, the first lieutenant, had served aboard the *Thrush* for a year already, and seemed a pleasant fellow happy to share his knowledge of the ship. William was happier than he had thought he would be to find the first lieutenant such a congenial gentleman. Far from the wild imaginings of glory he had indulged in with his sister, he soon came to hope that Mortimer and he would find their next step on the ladder of success together, by some shared adventure and glory. In his letters to Fanny, he contented himself by summarising that "the first lieutenant, Mortimer, is a very pleasant fellow, and I find in him much to be admired. He seems entirely lacking in the jealousy I have observed elsewhere between brother officers."

Mortimer could not always be on hand to check and correct William's small misjudgements in the early days of the voyage. For the main part, they served on different watches as directed by their captain. Instead, William found an unexpected assistant among the crew.

The first time Robert Oakes dared suggest to his second lieutenant that a slight change of trim would benefit them, William inwardly dismissed him as impertinent while making a mental note to check his disciplinary record.

After an hour, with the wind unchanged and progress not quite as swift as William had expected, he ordered the change of trim suggested by Oakes and was pleased to note an improvement in their speed.

After making his discreet enquiries and learning that Mr Oakes was as far from a troublemaker as an ordinary sailor could be, William wondered what had made the man speak up in such a fashion. Whenever he could, he watched Oakes at his work, and found himself impressed by the young man's persuasiveness when working with his less willing crew-mates, as well as his knowledge of his ship and profession. He noted also that Oakes behaved correctly with the midshipmen, a task which did not always come easily to experienced able seamen. Polite and deferential, as he should be, Oakes also guided and taught the young gentlemen, honing their knowledge of sea-craft in a manner which seemed quite in advance of Oakes's seemingly young age.

On a sloop such as the *Thrush*, it was easier to see and to know the men as individuals than it had been on the *Antwerp*. Over the course of his first fortnight aboard, William observed that it was this ability to discern and know one man from another that enabled their captain to maintain such good discipline. Far from the tales spread in fearful whispers of ships lorded over by a rule of iron, aboard the *Thrush* he saw about him the Navy's ideal of every man working together from a sense of comradeship with his crew-mates and respect for his officers.

As they progressed throughout the Mediterranean carrying dispatches and news from one station to another, William grew into his place within the *Thrush*. Confident in command, he yet wished to contribute something particular beyond his standard duties. An idea of what this might be began to form after a further few conversations with the ordinary sailors, especially young Mr Robert Oakes.

Standing near the helm one morning, he was immersed in contemplation of these thoughts when he was startled by the captain diverting from his morning routine of pacing the tiny quarterdeck.

"How are you finding our sloop, Mr Price?"

William suppressed his immediate reaction. Being easily surprised was not reckoned to be an admirable quality in an officer. "Very well, sir. I am honoured to serve aboard her."

"Good, good," the captain gave a brief smile, "and how do you find our men?"

"Well-drilled and attentive to their duties, sir. Just as every officer wishes to find his crew, sir."

"Good." The captain lapsed into silence but remained at William's side.

"I have wondered, sir," William hesitated. Some captains appeared agreeable but did not like their lieutenants to have ideas. He had been on the *Thrush* too short a time to know his captain's personal preference but a slight nod encouraged him to continue, "Do you encourage the men to seek promotion?"

"Not often if it would mean their moving to other ships, but … are you thinking of anyone in particular?"

"I cannot claim to have assessed all the men, sir, but young Mr Oakes has impressed me with his knowledge and demeanour. He seems no less intelligent or capable than any midshipman I have served with these past seven years …"

The captain smiled again. "I had been wondering if I was the only person who thought so, Mr Price. You have my permission to enquire of him if he has ambitions towards command. I believe he has already served several years, so at least he will not have as much to learn as most young gentlemen." He broke off to pass a reprimand down to the waist of the ship where one of the younger midshipmen was leading a group of men in a drill, then turned and resumed his customary pacing, leaving William to his duty as officer of the watch.

William waited a day before taking up the captain's suggestion. After considering different approaches, he decided to be as simple and straightforward as he could and requested that Mr Oakes attend him at the end of his watch.

Oakes knocked on the wardroom door as William was eating his dinner. He continued to eat as the man entered and stood, cap doffed, between two beams supporting the deck above and at the opposite edge of the narrow table.

"Have you eaten?" asked William, barely glancing up from his plate.

"Not yet, sir."

"Jones!" William called the wardroom serving man. "Fetch Mr Oakes's dinner, then you may leave us. Oakes, sit down."

A wooden dish of stew was placed before Oakes. William instructed him to eat up, then ignored his presence until his own meal was finished.

"How do you see your career in the Navy, Oakes?" William asked after he pushed his empty plate out of his way.

Oakes looked up, wariness in his eyes, and swallowed the food he had been chewing. "By the grace of God, sir, a long and happy one."

"I mean, have you thought of advancement?"

"I would like to, sir. Did you have something in mind?" The wariness had not left his voice, but the directness with which he returned William's gaze spoke of a strong character.

"You seem of an age that, if you had patronage, you could advance beyond your position as an ordinary seaman, with the chance of a commission if you applied yourself to your studies."

Oakes's surprise showed on his face, though he hastily hid it again, "I … Do you truly think I could, sir? That I might one day have a place on the quarterdeck?"

William shrugged as it mattered not one way or the other to him what Oakes chose to do with his life. "You seem skilled enough at your work, and bright enough to gain an officer's understanding of navigation and suchlike. Plenty of men do rise from the lower deck. Would you object if I put your name forward to the captain as a man who would like to better himself in this way?"

"I … Your offer is kind, sir, Lieutenant Price, but," he seemed to shrink in on himself, "I have seen the young gentlemen at their studies, sir, and the Master and his Mates at their work. I would not be able to join them."

"Why not?" William felt his voice rise and brought his emotions back under control while he waited for an answer.

"I cannot read nor write, sir." Oakes hid his face, staring at the wooden tabletop.

"Are you willing to learn?"

His head shot up like a firework, emotion making his face seem to glow. "If someone can teach me? Of course, sir! Who wouldn't be willing to learn?"

William laughed at the young man's enthusiasm. "You would be surprised, Mr Oakes, at the number of people willing to live in ignorance and reliance on other people's knowledge of letters. I'll speak to the captain about it, Oakes. You'd better get along now. Take your dish with you."

Over the next few weeks, as HMS *Thrush* dashed about the Mediterranean on one errand or another, Mortimer grew as accustomed as William to the sight of Oakes bent over his books at the wardroom table. Oakes had been given the duties of wardroom servant, releasing the other sailor, as this allowed him more time to study and the other man to return to his mates in the main body of the crew. To the lieutenants' delight, the young sailor proved to be as eager a student of cuisine as he was keen to master his letters, and on a provisioning trip ashore to one of the larger towns, Mortimer brought back a volume of cooking receipts for Oakes to study in an attempt to vary their cuisine.

After the first intensive week when William drilled Oakes on his alphabet, simple words, and well known texts from the prayer book and hymnal, he had given the sailor free access to his small library of books on navigation and other seafaring lore. Each day, after his evening meal, William questioned the young man on what he had read, and between them they discussed and dissected the passage with reference to other theoretical texts as well as their practical knowledge. At times when the two lieutenants dined together, Mortimer joined in these discussions with an air of aloof amusement at William's project. From comments made by the captain whenever the subject of Oakes arose between him and William, it was clear that Mortimer had been tasked with independently overseeing the young sailor's conduct and reporting to the captain on his progress.

Six weeks after they had sailed through the Straits of Gibraltar, trouble arrived over a flat blue horizon.

"Sail-ho!" called the lookout from above. The breeze was light; they were already sailing as close to the wind as the sloop would bear, and barely making way. William waited for further information from the old sailor on the foremast. Bates had only one eye after Copenhagen, but he had the sharpest memory of any sailor and a reputation for recognising any British ship by the set of her sails. "Not ours!" came the cry from above, and William sent a young midshipman scuttling up the ratlines, glass slung over his back, to join Bates in his eyrie. Dispatching his second midshipman to inform the captain, William stood calm, awaiting further information or instruction from the cabin below.

An hour later, the captain emerged and joined William on the quarterdeck.

"Larger ship than us, sir," William reported all he had learned from the lookouts above, "not British, approaching, and making better way than us in these light airs."

"Taller masts. Could be stronger winds higher up. Anything else?"

"Bates doesn't recognise her, sir. Showing no flag that he or Mr Morgan can see, but thinks she might be a French frigate."

"Blockade runner?"

"Or newly launched."

"Could be. Well, clear the decks, Lieutenant. Battle-ready, but keep the guns inboard, and do it steadily. We'll have at least another hour, if not more, before we're within signalling distance. Call me if there are any developments."

William tipped his hat as the captain returned to his cabin, then passed the orders and watched the men's movements about the decks become more focused, their demeanour stiffen as if arming themselves before the possibility of battle. Quietly, methodically, the men below dismantled cabin walls, stowed chests against the wooden walls, and carried bundled hammocks above deck to hang in the rigging. Flimsy protection compared to stone-walled fortresses which land armies beat themselves against, but every action, every stowage place aboard a warship had at least two purposes. Boys sanded the deck, and young Mr Morgan, summoned back from the heights, slid down the backstay like an old hand for all that he had only been at sea a few months.

"Signal flags, Mr Morgan," William told the pink-cheeked lad, "and then let the captain know we're ready."

"Aye, sir." Morgan tipped his hat to William just as William had tipped his to the captain.

The ship's bell sounded the next half hour before the captain returned to the quarterdeck. By that time William could see from the deck the topgallants of the unknown frigate. Mortimer had joined him a few minutes earlier, and they exchanged a tight smile.

"Still an hour before we know their intentions," the captain said after examining the log and observing the other ship. "Tell cook to distribute food and the purser to issue a tot per man."

"Aye, sir." William, being still the officer of the watch, passed the order down to the lower deck, then joined Mortimer and the captain who were discussing which signal flags to run up and when.

When the unknown ship drew close enough for signals, their preparation proved unnecessary. The frigate hoisted a French flag, Morgan hoisted the *Thrush*'s ensign, and both ships ran out their guns.

"Fire as you bear," the captain ordered. In the light airs, and against a larger enemy, there was no reason to hold back for a full broadside. Better to let the crew fire as many rounds as they could while the two ships drifted past each other.

William felt suddenly, hopelessly, ill-prepared for his first action in the sloop. In the *Antwerp* he had rarely been on the quarterdeck during action, instead being posted to the lower gun deck, relaying orders from above, dealing only with the noise and stench of battle rather than watching, anticipating, and seeing the inevitability of the first encounter. He had known it would be different, exposed on the deck rather than hidden deep in the belly of the ship, but he had not expected to feel so vulnerable. If anything, he had thought that seeing the other ship would be easier than just waiting for another man's voice in the dark.

"Starboard quarter," murmured Mortimer, bending his tall frame to speak directly in the captain's ear. William saw rather than heard the words, and was glad of the excuse to turn his head from the first impact of the Frenchman's chain shot in their rigging. Expecting to see another ship, he saw instead a darkening of the sky and disturbance in the water.

"Well spotted, Mortimer," praised the captain, followed by a louder cry of, "Good shot there!" as one of their forward gun crews hit the enemy's gun port straight-on. "Bear away a little after this pass, make as if we're coming round for more." He nodded to William, including him in the orders. "We may need to give them another show of strength, but get the crew ready to haul her around as soon as that breeze hits."

"Aye, sir."

"Good. Pass the message yourself, Lieutenant, and make sure they're getting the injured down to Mr Campbell."

"Aye, sir." William tipped his hat and called the midshipmen to follow him. In a drawn-out action on a small ship like this, the most useful thing the young gentlemen could do was help clear the injured from the deck.

The stern of the French frigate passed their quarterdeck, and, turning in his walk along the deck, William read her name. *Jeanne de Mer*. He saw their own helmsmen leaning as hard as they dared, sharpening the angle between the two ships, then the telltale puffs of smoke at the frigate's stern, followed by the crack of shot leaving a barrel.

"Heads down!" he called instinctively, knowing the men would obey even as he forced himself to remain upright as expected of an officer. "Goddamn froggy stern-chasers!" Then his attention returned to his task and he called off certain men, leaving enough to man the guns when the *Jeanne de Mer* completed the turn she was now engaged in and gave chase once more, but ensuring those he called away knew their task, were aware of its importance, and, most of all, that they understood the need for hiding their purpose in moving from the guns when the moment came.

The *Jeanne de Mer* had turned through the wind and now lay on the same tack as the *Thrush*, bearing down on them from astern to pass their lee side. With her taller masts, and topgallants which reached the higher, stronger airs than the *Thrush*'s topsails, her captain had no fear of being caught in the *Thrush*'s shadow. William, returning to his captain's side, saw a gleam in the other man's eye.

"He should have taken our windward side," observed Mortimer.

"She's a new ship," ventured William. "*Jeanne de Mer* – I've not heard of her before."

"Likely a new commander too," observed the captain, "since we've got all their best ones holed up behind our blockade. Seems I was right so far to count on his over-confidence. The battle's not won yet though, gentlemen."

At a soft-spoken command to the helmsmen the *Thrush* wore away a little more, a point closer to the wind, away from the *Jeanne de Mer*. The Frenchman followed, and the silent British sailors heard jeers tumbling down the frigate's hull and across the barely-moving sea towards them. The gun captains looked to the quarterdeck for their order, and the sailors William had selected moved into position as inconspicuously as possible, tidying the stacks of shot, smoothing the sand against the deck, fiddling with minor repairs to the rigging within their reach.

The frigate drew closer, her bowsprit within spitting distance of the *Thrush*'s gilded stern, and William felt the faintest livening of the air against his cheek.

"Fire as you bear!" called the captain, his gaze fixed on the masthead pennant, but it was an empty command. The *Thrush*'s guns were a long way from bearing on the *Jeanne de Mer* at this angle in the light airs.

Again the innocent-looking puffs of smoke, the crack of doom-laden shot, and dull thuds as the frigate's forecastle guns unloaded into the bundle of hammocks above the *Thrush*'s quarterdeck.

The air stirred again. Once, twice, and holding.

"Two points to starboard!" cried the captain. "Loose the main course! Stow the guns!" and in moments the *Thrush* was flying across waves arrived as suddenly as if conjured by Poseidon himself.

Yells and curses faded behind them as the Frenchmen, surprised by their quarry's abandonment of the fight, struggled to loose their sails, and in their lesser speed, lost the advantage they had held all day.

The *Thrush*'s captain held her as close to the wind as he safely could until their enemy dropped far enough below the horizon that not even Bates in his eyrie could spy her sails on the horizon.

"Five more minutes, and if the *Jeanne de Mer* is not seen again, change to the other tack," ordered the captain. "Keep as much speed as possible. The ship is yours, Lieutenant Mortimer. Price, get the deck cleared and ship put back to rights. Use the young gentlemen as you see fit to speed the task."

Less than an hour later, the ship was back to rights as far as possible and William's watch had been stood down. Morale and common Christian duty to his fellow man required that he visit the sickbay where Mr Campbell worked, but first he needed to eat. Experience told him that retching brought on by the stench of blood or worse in the sickbay was slightly more tolerable with a meal in his stomach than if his belly were empty. Oakes was ready in the wardroom as William settled into one of the chairs recently returned from the hold.

"I can bring you cheese and biscuit, sir, or if you fancy something warmer I found some eggs earlier?"

"Yes to all of it, Oakes. Cheese and biscuit now, and eggs as soon as they're ready."

"Very good, sir."

William chuckled to himself as the young man disappeared into the wardroom stores. Found some eggs indeed! No doubt the youth had pilfered them in the bustling ordered chaos of breaking and rebuilding the ship's interior, but at least he was wise enough to share them with his lieutenant.

In the cramped space of the orlop deck after his meal, William found one of the sloop's midshipmen hovering by the sailcloth-curtained entrance to the sickbay. At the sight of his lieutenant, the young Mr Morgan drew himself as straight as he could and tipped his hat.

"Lieutenant Price, sir. Lieutenant Mortimer said I was to come down and help Mr Campbell with the injured."

William waited, hands clasped behind his back.

"… but Mr Campbell's too busy to instruct me, sir," Morgan added, eyes fixed on the deck.

"Well, there's a good many men here who have already been treated by Mr Campbell. Make sure they've all had a drink of water, Mr Morgan, and then report back to me if Mr Campbell's still busy."

He nodded and dashed from the stink of blood.

A short scream came from behind a second sailcloth curtain. William stepped through and nodded to the blood-spattered surgeon. "Bad?"

"Known worse, Lieutenant."

"Haven't we all?"

"Aye," Mr Campbell paused to wipe his hands dry as the patient on his operating table was replaced with the next by sailors acting as orderlies. "At least it was a short scrap. The captain did well to get us away when he did. The last volley came close to taking my medical supplies."

William followed his gaze and saw the unevenness in the wooden wall which belied a carpenter's hasty repair. "There's mending to be done in the rigging as well," he said, "but if this wind holds in our favour we'll be in port within the week."

"Good. I'll need to replenish some of my supplies. Have you done something with the young gentleman, by the way?"

"I set him to watering the men out there."

"Thanks." Campbell smiled briefly. "I know why Lieutenant Mortimer sends them down, but at this stage I'm a mite too busy to be issuing commands. Speaking of …"

"I'll make myself scarce too. Just wanted to check how things are."

"Thank you, Lieutenant. We've lost a few good men, but fewer than I feared we might when I heard a French frigate had set her sights on us."

William ducked back through to the main sickbay area and made his way over to the young midshipman crouched helping an injured sailor drink from a wooden cup. "A word outside when you're done there, Mr Morgan," he ordered, then continued past the curtain into the ordinary gloom of the orlop deck.

"Lieutenant Price, sir?" Morgan was at his elbow within a minute.

"Do you know why the first lieutenant sent you down here, Mr Morgan?"

"No, sir, I was …" his head fell, "I was talking about the battle, sir, while I went about my duties. Lieutenant Mortimer heard and ordered me to come down and assist Mr Campbell."

William nodded, seeing from the young man's expression that he had learned the intended lesson. "Make sure every injured man in there has had a drink of water, and if any have died, get a couple of men to see to the bodies. Call on the experienced hands, they know what needs doing."

"Yes, sir."

"Then report back to Lieutenant Mortimer. I'm sure he has other duties for you. And, Morgan?" The lad had tipped his hat and half turned away, but turned back at being addressed once more. William smiled, recalling the innocence of his own now-distant youth. "That wasn't a battle, it was barely a skirmish. You'll see, in time." He turned and left then, feeling the lad's gaze on him as he hurried back to the cleaner air of the wardroom.

The wind which had enabled their escape died away with the evening light during the course of William's next watch. No further signs of enemy shipping were seen, and after handing the helm back to Mortimer, William gladly tumbled directly into his cot. Next morning, Oakes was ready with his breakfast as always, but moving oddly. William chose to ignore it, but when the man's awkwardness was more pronounced in the afternoon, he ordered him to wait at the table while William finished his meal.

"You injured, Oakes?"

"Yes, sir." Oakes's tone showed he knew where the conversation would lead.

"I've not seen you down in sickbay, nor your name in Mr Campbell's records."

"No, sir."

William wiped his mouth and threw his napkin down on the table in irritation. "Been fighting, have you?"

"No, sir!" Oakes's head shot up from its bowed position and his gaze locked with William's. "It was in the action with the French ship."

"Then why have you not been to Mr Campbell?"

"I didn't want to bother him, sir. It was only a minor scrape …"

"But it hurts worse now than it did at the time?"

Oakes nodded.

"You need to get it seen to, lad. Infections are a nasty business. Go see Mr Campbell. I assure you he will not see your visit as an inconvenience if it means he can prevent us losing another good man."

Oakes remained where he stood. Even when William waved his hand in dismissal, the young man stood firm.

"Please, sir, don't make me," he begged. "I know Mr Campbell is better than most sawbones, sir, but …"

William cut him off with a wave of his hand, concerned from the young man's wavering tone that he might break down. Fear of medical treatment was common enough, especially in a lad of Oakes's class, and the general reputation of naval 'sawbones' did not help to encourage the men to seek treatment in time for proper treatment. "Show me the wound," he offered instead, "it may just be you've not cleaned it properly."

"I …" Oakes wavered still, but William hardened his expression, making it clear the offer was also an order. With obvious reluctance the young sailor untucked his shirt and pulled it over his head.

"Holy –" William cursed, shocked out of his usual manners at the sight of Oakes's chest. "Pull your shirt back down, girl."

"Please!" Oakes fell to his – her – knees at William's side. "Please, sir, don't … You see I can't show Mr Campbell, I'll be ruined!"

"Don't what, Oakes? Don't tell the truth now I know it? Don't treat you as I ought to? Don't do as I ought, which is everything in my power to ensure your safety?"

"My safety?" Oakes broke in with a tone he – *she* should never have used in front of an officer. "Sir, I have served in the Royal Navy for six years now and I have never felt safer than when enclosed in wooden walls with my fellow men. Sir, please, I beg of you … Please, sir, I know it seems strange but I never felt completely myself until I put on a sailor's clothes and signed aboard ship. If I lose this, if you tell my secret, I will have nothing."

"Sit," ordered William, pointing to a chair. "I can't think straight with you kneeling there."

Oakes obeyed in her usual prompt fashion, but kept her eyes beseechingly on William rather than dropping them to the floor as had been her previous habit. William sat avoiding meeting the sailor's gaze. His thoughts whirled, the assumptions on which he judged his fellow man turned upside down by the revelation that the young man he had been tutoring was a woman in disguise. His belief in the rightness of naval law was shaken by the individual before him, and his understanding of the female sex stood at odds with Oakes's pleading belief in the life of a sailor being better than any she could find as a woman.

Irritated by his inability to swiftly resolve the issue even in his own mind, William delayed the inevitable. "Come here," he said. "Lift your shirt enough to show me the wound."

"Thank you, sir," Oakes whispered as William untied the bandage covering the wound across the centre of Oakes's ribcage.

"It doesn't look like a deep wound. Were you caught by something in the air?"

"Yes, sir. I think it was a splinter, sir. There was a bit of wood I pulled out of it yesterday."

"Nasty things, splinters. It is to be hoped that you got it all out. Do you mind if I have a closer look?"

"I'd be very grateful, sir."

"Fetch a bowl of seawater and some clean cloths, Oakes. Oh, and Oakes?" The sailor had dropped her shirt and turned to go, but turned back to listen respectfully to the remainder of William's words. "This doesn't mean I'll keep your secret. I find I need a little time."

"I understand, sir." Oakes's voice was soft and her inflection seemed more feminine than before. William wondered if he only thought that because he knew Oakes would never speak with a man's deep voice. Had there been any difference to normal? Had William always ignored or simply not seen any feminine traits when he had believed the sailor to be a boy?

He shook his head, tried to clear it of his thoughts so that when Oakes returned he could focus on checking the sailor's wound. He would leave weighing up the dangers of hiding Oakes's secret until later.

William could not recall the last time that sleep had eluded him when an opportunity arose to rest. The problem of Oakes nagged at his mind. Naval law was clear on the matter, and it happened just often enough that he could be assured no harm would befall a girl discovered to have disguised herself among the crew of a warship, but the sailor's pleas had baffled him. He thought about his sisters: Fanny, living in their uncle's large house, and Susan, helping their mother at home. Would either of them ever think to prefer a life aboard ship, disguised as a man, living within the strictures and harsh conditions demanded by the world of naval warfare? He could not picture either of them doing so, even in the better conditions of an officer's cabin, but he sorely wished he could call on Fanny's attentive ear no matter how shocked she might be to learn the truth about Oakes.

Shifting position in his cot, he tried to come at the problem another way, imagining Oakes living as a woman ashore, as she would necessarily have to do once he gave up her secret to the captain. No matter how hard he tried, the images would not form. Nimble, quick-witted, light-footed Oakes, who scrambled through the rigging like one born in a nest of rope, just would not fit into the mould of any woman William had ever met. What use would be Oakes's skills, his knowledge, his eagerness to learn and swiftness of understanding everything William had tutored him in so far, in a life bound to home and family? Even considering those women of business William had met when accompanying his sisters around the shops, there seemed no place that Oakes might fit into a woman's role.

And then, he sighed inwardly, there was that damned thing Oakes had said about never feeling completely himself until he clothed himself as a boy and signed aboard His Majesty's Navy. William knew all too well how that felt. Even the joy of seeing Fanny after so long apart had not fully numbed the feeling of wrongness he had felt in being ashore and away from his wooden world.

As he drifted to sleep at last, William realised the answer lay in the midst of his tangle of thoughts. Despite seeing the evidence to the contrary, he continued to think of Oakes as 'he' and 'him', and so, therefore, he must be. No mere habit of thought would persist if he truly believed Oakes should be in a different position to the one he had chosen for himself.

"We should make port by this evening," Lieutenant Mortimer announced, joining William in the wardroom when he came in off the dawn watch. "The captain says we'll take one day for resupply and repairs, and be off again the day after tomorrow." He nodded thanks to Oakes for the hurriedly assembled plate of breakfast and began to eat.

William used the last of his morning's bacon to wipe his plate clean. "We could do with some more provisions for our stores. Would the captain allow me ashore to acquire them, or will we be reliant on bumboats?"

"Oh, I shouldn't think there'd be any problem with you going ashore here, Price. The quartermaster will probably hog all the bumboat supplies anyway, there are never many here. Not that there will be a lot more in town either, I'll warn you. You might pick up some meat and fruit, but damned if I've ever found a decent pot of mustard here!"

"Oh, I've plenty of mustard and that sort of thing," William assured his fellow lieutenant. "I thought a bit of fresh bread might be nice for our evening meal if we've a chance, and just a general stocking up to keep us going."

Mortimer smiled at William's mention of fresh bread. "I'll get Oakes to check through what we've got and we'll work out tonight what you might be likely to find."

"My thanks, sir. I'd best get out on deck. The captain asked me to keep an eye on the repairs to the foremast during this watch."

Mortimer laughed and waved him goodbye.

Overseeing the men working at the repairs necessary after their skirmish, in addition to his normal duties, called on so much of William's time that it was not until after they had anchored in the safety of the natural harbour that he was able to sit down to another meal. Taking advantage of Mortimer being out on deck, William ordered Oakes to remain in the wardroom while he ate.

"How is the wound?" William asked between mouthfuls.

"Still sore, sir."

"Tender?"

"Yes, sir."

"Hmm." William attacked the dried meat on his plate, slathering the piece he had cut in mustard and swallowing it before he continued, "That could be bad news, Oakes. It's a damned shame that sending you to Mr Campbell would cause unwelcome complications. However, I've permission to go ashore tomorrow. You will accompany me to carry anything necessary, and while we're ashore we will find an apothecary."

"Thank you, sir. And, sir? Thank you, for … the other thing."

"Well, it'd be a damned shame to lose a good sailor, Oakes. Tell me what you've learned from my books today."

Breakfasting late after a meeting with the captain, William was concerned to observe a deterioration in Oakes's condition. The sailor's face was flushed, and his attention wandered in a manner entirely abnormal for him. William ate quickly and hastily reviewed the list of items Mortimer and he had agreed were required for their stores. Hearing a call out on deck for the longboat to be swung out, William abandoned his plate and ordered Oakes to accompany him ashore.

As they passed from one shopkeeper to another in the small town, Oakes made discreet enquiries for a trustworthy apothecary, and after wending their way through the few grocers in the lower part of town, they set off up the narrow cobbled street indicated to him by several of the shopkeepers. Oakes's attention and steadiness had deteriorated further, and after checking for troublemaking observers, William slipped an arm around the sailor's waist to support him up the steepening climb. Oakes's skin felt warm to the touch and, this close to, William could see beads of sweat in greater number than would be accounted for by the warmth of the morning sun. William urged as fast a pace as he felt possible, and felt relief as they found around the next corner a shop window filled with jars and bottles of potions. A bell tinkled as he opened the door and manhandled Oakes across the threshold.

"Have you a seat?" he barked at the proprietor, who rushed over with a wooden chair.

"This sailor has a wound which I suspect has some infection. How much to clean it, provide us with any items necessary to his recovery, and keep your mouth shut about the matter?"

"I will need to see the wound first, but to keep quiet will be expensive. It would be very costly to me if your marines come to investigate whatever trouble this is."

"How much to keep quiet?" William responded. "We can negotiate payment for treatment after you've inspected the wound; the other does not depend on the amount of treatment required."

The apothecary named a price. It would take the majority of the coins William had left after the morning's purchases, but looking around the quantity of stock the man had on display in his shop, it seemed a fair price for the risk the man could be taking, so William nodded and turned his back to give Oakes as much privacy as he could. He heard the apothecary speak quietly with Oakes, and the hesitation in the sailor's reply. A whisper of linen on skin followed, and then the apothecary spoke again to William rather than Oakes.

"I can see why you need the secrecy, sir." The inflection of the 'sir' indicated the man's full displeasure in being involved in William's business.

"Just treat the damned wound!"

The apothecary muttered something in his native tongue, but soon enough William heard sounds of the bandage being unwound from Oakes's chest, and then footsteps crossing the wooden floor and more mutterings in the foreign tongue, so he relaxed slightly in this assurance of the man's commitment to treating the sick and wounded.

After half an hour, the apothecary summoned William over to the small counter at the rear of the shop. Oakes had re-dressed, and sat more upright on the chair, but avoided William's eyes as he passed.

"The wound will need to be cleaned and checked daily, and some of this paste applied," the apothecary pushed a small wooden pot across the counter to William. "She is also showing signs of wound-fever and will need more rest than normal."

"Anything else?"

"Pray." The apothecary's expression of distaste showed he counted William a sinner, and probably had since his first mention of the need for secrecy.

"How much?" William demanded and, as the man named a price not much higher than the price he had given for secrecy alone, William counted out the coins as swiftly as possible then turned and left the shop, ordering

Oakes to follow him.

"Thank you, sir." Oakes sounded out of breath simply from catching up with him three strides down the street, so William slackened his pace and shortened his stride, reminding himself that his anger was over the apothecary's assumptions, and should not be directed at the wounded sailor. "I will pay you back, sir, I promise."

"Pay me back by recovering and then proving I was correct to recommend you for promotion, Oakes."

"Thank you, sir."

"We're not in clear water yet, Oakes, but let us return to mundane matters. We need to collect the provisions we ordered earlier and get them stowed away aboard ship."

Oakes's recovery after treatment by the apothecary was smoother than William had feared. The fever passed after another day. Within a week the wound itself had healed to the point where Oakes no longer needed assistance with the bandages, and William felt the burden of secretive behaviour lift. His mind felt clearer than it had for days. Though he would never have said anything to make Oakes feel more uncomfortable than the situation already had, he was relieved no longer to be confronted with the sight of Oakes's unclothed chest. Whilst he did his best to dismiss it as a gentlemanly dislike of the situation, and the unnaturalness of an officer tending so intimately to his subordinate's wounds, he knew his feelings went deeper than social niceties and concern for the authority of rank. His relief at Oakes's recovery was therefore in part due to William no longer being forced to confront his own feelings or to question assumptions about his own nature.

"A word in my cabin when you've finished your watch, Lieutenant?"

Though phrased as a request, the captain's word was a command and William answered, "Yes, sir," and did his best over the next hour not to wonder what the captain wanted from him. The captain's tone had not revealed whether William should be concerned or celebrating over the summons.

On entering the aft cabin, William found the captain sat at his desk, and Lieutenant Mortimer seated at his right. William took the seat before the desk, relieved not to have been left to stoop beneath the low ceiling.

"I am sorry to question you about this, Lieutenant," the captain began, "but it has been brought to our attention that a dangerous rumour has begun circulating within the ship."

William sat and waited, unsure what the rumour could be as he had heard no whispers himself.

"It concerns, Lieutenant, your relationship with the young sailor Oakes." The captain paused, distaste clear on his face. "The rumour is that Oakes has been spending far longer in your cabin than his duties or studies would suggest necessary. According to the rumour, you and Oakes have been observed entering and leaving your cabin together at times when you would expect to be unobserved. Of course, Lieutenant, I have no idea why someone would set himself up to observe you so closely, but I do not wish rumour or speculation to spread dissent among the crew. I am therefore duty-bound to investigate the matter, and in the first instance ask you if there is any truth in these rumours, and if so, could you provide either an explanation or a confession?"

"I am sorry to hear of the rumours, sir," William began, understanding the underlying insinuation and the threat it posed to him, "and I must confess that the points on which the rumours are said to be based are true. Oakes has recently spent more time than usual in my quarters, and we have been alone in my cabin. The truth is, sir, that he sustained an injury, and for one reason and another – first a fear of medical men, then a fear of punishment for not having gone to Mr Campbell in the first instance – he was reluctant to seek the proper help. While we were in port gathering provisions for the wardroom, I realised he was not himself, and on his confession of stupidly not seeking the help he should have, I marched him to an apothecary in the town to get the wound treated. I'm sorry, sir, I should have informed you of the incident on our return. I was just so damned glad when the apothecary said we'd caught the infection in time ..." He paused, swallowing hard before continuing, "The treatment prescribed by the apothecary included a paste which was required to be applied once a day and then the bandage retying, and as Oakes struggled to do this on his own, I assisted him with it. I should have insisted that he find a crew-mate to do that, and then there would have been no basis for anyone to suggest – or even think – that I might violate the Articles of War and the laws of nature and common decency in any manner. I apologise, sir, most heartily, for letting the sympathy developed during my tutoring of the young man blind me to the possibilities of misinterpretation."

The captain nodded, and looked to Lieutenant Mortimer, who also nodded though with a grim smile.

"An injury and infection would fit with my own observation of the sailor's recent behaviour."

"Thank you, Lieutenant." The captain turned his attention back to William. "I will deal with the matter of rumours being spread amongst the crew. You, Lieutenant Price, must take this incident as a warning and not leave yourself open to such suggestion in the future. Moreover, do not let your sympathy for any one man sway you from insisting the man do what is right and proper."

"Yes, sir."

The captain dismissed him and William hurried, hollow-hearted, to his own quarters. The warning, and the situation he had narrowly escaped, were dire indeed. Although he knew the Navy never condemned a man without witness accounts to the acts of which he was accused, a rumour could be enough to bring about a court martial, and that would be the death of his career.

"Are you all right, sir?"

William started from his grim contemplation and realised he'd been pushing the same piece of meat around his plate for several minutes. "Yes, Oakes, thank you, I am well. How have your studies been today?"

Oakes smiled and began to describe the passage he had read that day from *The Young Sea Officer's Sheet Anchor*, but William's attention wandered again, and after Oakes had had to prompt him twice during their discussion, the sailor frowned and challenged him.

"You're not all right, sir, so don't try to pretend."

"It's not … It's all sorted, Oakes. Don't bother me about it," he replied in irritation. "Just finish telling me about your studies and then you'd better get back to your crew-mates. You have kept away from them too much recently."

"Sir! I …" Oakes seemed to recall himself, his expression turned from one of protest to that of pleading and he knelt beside William's chair. "Please, sir, if I have done something wrong, please tell me?"

William sat back in his chair, letting his hand fall to Oakes's shoulder. "No. It is – was – I forgot how others might interpret things. I have just been informed that rumours were circulating about … us. About … our relationship, and whether it is proper." He sighed and curled his fingers into Oakes's boyishly cut hair. "I explained about your wound, Oakes, without revealing your secret. Our captain is a good man, and I am to take this as a warning against fraternising too openly with the lower deck. So you see, Oakes, you really ought to go and spend some time with your crew-mates."

"Oh, sir, I …" Oakes looked up at William, his eyes wide and pupil-dark in the thin candlelight. "Please, sir, please swear to me that you will never again risk your reputation for me! Sir, if anyone … I would rather be called a harlot than have such things said of you."

"And if I had revealed your secret, and that I had kept it from the captain?"

"Then you would have received a reprimand, I would have been paid off, and the ballad-writers would have another pretty tale to tell! Sir, please, I beg of you!"

William sat, unspeaking, looking down into Oakes's face. Oakes tentatively raised his hand and slipped it into William's that lay listlessly in his lap.

"Sir," he whispered, "I truly beg of you, don't risk the yardarm."

"But, Oakes," William replied in the same tone, "I know you are a man in every way which matters, I cannot think of you as anything other than a man, no matter how hard I try or what I have seen of you. And yet, I care for you more deeply than for any person, save my dear sister Fanny. Do you see, Oakes? I may not have committed the crime of which someone sought to accuse me, but I see now the truth of my own nature."

"Sir, I …" Oakes, often as eloquent as any gentleman, stumbled over his thoughts. "You are the most generous, kind-hearted and understanding of men. It is an honour to be well-thought of and cared for by you. Your feelings, I assure you, are reciprocated so strongly I might even venture to call them 'love'. I can only imagine how poor my life will feel when fate separates us, as no doubt will come to pass. If I may speak so bold, sir, I desire you. Knowing what I do of myself, and of the Bible, I have tried to deny these feelings lurking in my heart, but I cannot. I would that I felt comfortable enough in my body to live as a woman, for then I might have hope of a life with you."

Smiling at Oakes's confession, William lowered his head and brushed a kiss against Oakes's upturned cheek. Drawing the young man into his lap, he then gently kissed him on the lips before resting his head against Oakes's shoulder.

"Sir?" asked Oakes after a few moments while they listened to the noise of the ship, both alert to any sound of approaching footsteps. "May I know your given name?"

"Of course, Robert." William smiled and kissed him again before giving his answer and adding a caution that they not get in the habit of using anything other than the standard address.

Oakes sighed and kissed William's brow. "Would that such a little thing did not seem so great a luxury. Though we are more fortunate than other men like ourselves, we dare not forget the danger."

"Indeed. You belong here, Oakes, in the Navy. I want you to succeed because it is your world as much as mine, and I'll be damned if I let anyone take that from you due to the contents of your trousers." He released his hold on Oakes and the young man slid from his lap to stand before him once more. "And that is why you need to get back to your duties now that you have recovered."

"Yes, sir," Oakes replied with a smile, "but not before you finish your meal, sir, so that I may clean up and finish my duties here."

"Sly devil," smiled William, and suddenly the confessional atmosphere of a few moments before fell away, and he unleashed a barrage of questions on the subject Oakes had said he had studied that day, releasing him to go about his duties only after they had argued the points to and fro a dozen times, and half a dozen more with Lieutenant Mortimer after he entered the wardroom.

"Well done," Mortimer told William after they had sent Oakes away until morning, "he's made excellent progress thanks to your tutoring. Once we rejoin the fleet, the captain will recommend the lad for the next available position as Master's Mate. He may well be off the ship within the week, and we can bid farewell to the ugly whispers."

"You think they will be dealt with that swiftly? I feared ..." William took a swig of claret and left his fears unvoiced.

Mortimer nodded in understanding, but then smiled brightly. "I may not have known you long, Price, but I flatter myself that I have come to know you as well as I may. You have a respect for your position, and a natural air of trustworthiness about you. I say that because you are a complete contrast to another man I knew, back when I was a wide-eyed youthful midshipman ..." Mortimer laughed, stretched out his legs and fell into relating a long and convoluted tale to William, after which William felt obliged to respond in kind, and soon they found they had passed a full hour exchanging tales about youthful adventures before they gained their commissions.

Relaxed and reassured by this friendly gesture from his senior lieutenant, and with experience gained from years of dismissing battle-fear, William put aside concerns over his feelings for Robert Oakes. A resolution to his unexpected situation would arise in time, and time would also tell if his attachment to the younger man was a fleeting thing or his true heart's desire.

Author's Notes

There is always a balance in historical fiction between telling a story true to its era, and phrasing events and dialogue so that they are not hurtful to a modern reader. I hope that I have struck a correct balance here. Unfortunately, it is almost impossible to know how people like Robert Oakes viewed themselves; the few accounts left to us which venture beyond the bare facts of a seaman being dismissed on grounds of biology are biographies edited by male publishers. If you are interested in reading more than fiction, I highly recommend Suzanne Stark's *Female Tars* and the account of William Chandler.

Sandra Lindsey

Sandra lives in the mountains of Mid-Wales with her husband. Their garden is full of fruit and veg plants as well as home to a small flock of rare breed chickens, and she is a servant to two cats.

Sandra loves indulging in stories because she gets to spend her time with imaginary friends, and the research and observation required to write fiction open her eyes to a myriad different ways of seeing the world. Find her on Twitter - or curled up out of the way reading a good book!

twitter.com/SLindseyWales
sandralindsey.wales

Elinor and Ada

Julie Bozza

I

"It is enough," said Mrs Dashwood. "To say that Ada is unlike Fanny is enough. It implies everything amiable. I love her already."

Elinor smiled at her mother's warm response, so typical of her enthusiasms. "I think you will like Ada, when you know more of her."

"*You* love her, Elinor," said Marianne. Her look expressed her full meaning more fervently than her tone. "*You* love Ada already."

Elinor glanced at Marianne to acknowledge the truth that the sisters had never shared with their mother, but she responded honestly when she said, "I cannot deny that I greatly esteem her."

Mrs Dashwood cried, "I have never yet known what it was to separate esteem and love."

"It takes time," Elinor argued, "to become so well acquainted with someone that liking and esteem become love."

Marianne rolled her eyes in impatience, while Mrs Dashwood settled for patting Elinor's hand. For a while the small parlour was quiet again, as Mrs Dashwood returned to her embroidery, Marianne her book, and Elinor her mending.

The three women often retreated to this room in the evenings after they had settled the youngest sister Margaret for the night. The parlour, while adjacent to Mrs Dashwood's bedroom, was narrow, dark and inconvenient – but it was private. Almost as soon as Mr Henry Dashwood had died, his son from his first marriage, and John's wife Fanny, had come to live at Norland Park. They were entitled to, of course, for it belonged to them now – but the widow and her three daughters were reduced to guests in what had been their own beloved home, and guests who were often made to feel they had outstayed their welcome, too. As soon as a new home could be found that would suit them and their very modest income, they would move.

"John will never help us," Marianne said, breaking the silence. "We can never expect help from John and Fanny, when Fanny's mother won't help

Ada. Mrs Ferrars is rich beyond our imaginings, isn't she? And yet Ada must earn her living as a governess!"

"It is true, my dear," Mrs Dashwood said with resignation.

"From what Fanny was saying, even her brother Robert is kept tied to his mother's purse strings. What a selfish family they are … And John grows more like them every day! You'd think he'd have changed his name to Ferrars when he married."

"Marianne," Elinor chided – but Mrs Dashwood often let Marianne say what she liked, when they were alone, and so she continued.

"You'd think Mrs Ferrars would be too proud to have a niece in employment. There's no excuse for it! Ada is a gentleman's daughter, just as we are. It's unconscionable."

Elinor reassured her. "We will have enough to live on, Marianne. If we are careful. There is no need to fear the same fate." For a few moments, Elinor's hands were idle as she thought back over the weeks. "In any case, Ada does not seem to mind very much," she eventually asserted. "Do you remember that first morning she came here? I've never seen a lady who so perfectly combined self-possession and an empathy for others. Such confidence, and yet with no presumption, and no immodesty. I was quite struck by her!"

Marianne laughed fondly. "*How* much time does it take for liking to become love, Elinor? A year, a month – or a minute!"

Mrs Dashwood was amused as well. "First impressions are so telling, my dear!"

Elinor shot Marianne a quelling glance, though it was no use, of course, and as the mirth continued even Elinor could not help but smile.

Marianne's genius was musical, while Elinor's talents lay in drawing and in painting with watercolours. Elinor had been so busy, however, with the tasks relating to the significant change in her family's circumstances, that it had been several weeks since she had taken her sketchbook out into the countryside. On this day, with the fine weather looking set to continue, Marianne implored Elinor to have a few hours away from more mundane demands, and Mrs Dashwood insisted.

"May I join you, Miss Dashwood?" Ada asked over breakfast, when Elinor's intentions were made clear. "Or – no, I am sure you would prefer solitude."

"I would be happy for your company, Miss Ferrars," Elinor steadily replied, ignoring Marianne's playful smile.

"Can I come, too?" Margaret demanded. "Are you going to climb the Beacon? It's been *months* since we last went up there. We could take a picnic. Oh, I know: I'll bring my kite!"

Elinor faltered for a reply. At any other time, she would have happily indulged Margaret, but the thought of a carefree day alone with her sketchbook and Ada Ferrars could make even Elinor Dashwood forget her duties.

Mrs Dashwood apparently agreed. "No, spend the day with me, Margaret. Let Miss Ferrars and Elinor take a holiday. We shall entertain ourselves. I seem to remember that your kite needed a new tail."

"Oh yes!" Margaret's eyes shone. "Can it be red? Or red and white! I think red and white would make a *fine* tail."

Elinor and Ada shared a quiet smile. "When can you be ready?" Elinor asked.

"Within quarter of an hour, if I may have time to find my own sketchbook."

"You may indeed."

They took the old grey mare Galathe with them, with provisions and gear in her saddlebags. The three of them walked together quietly through the park to the foot of the Downs, and then struck out onto the pathway that would lead them up to the Beacon.

"This is such beautiful countryside," Ada remarked as the path turned the shoulder of a hill to reveal a view along the line of the Downs, with fields and woods undulating below.

"It is beautiful, yes," Elinor agreed.

She must have sounded more wistful than she intended, for Ada turned to her with an apology. Then Ada carefully asked, "Do I understand you may soon be moving to Devonshire?"

"I believe so. A cousin of my mother's has offered us a new home on his property there, in the parish of Barton. Do you know it? It is a little north of Exeter."

"I am sure you'll find Devonshire has its own beauties. You will not want for landscapes to draw or paint."

Elinor nodded an acknowledgement. "You have been living there yourself, have you not?"

Ada's expression was briefly stormy, but then she gathered herself. "I was some years in the house of a Mr Pratt, in Longstaple, as governess to his daughters and nieces. Longstaple is near Plymouth, to the south and west of Exeter. The countryside can be … wilder than this, and perhaps not as gentle – but just as beautiful in its own way, I promise you."

"You reassure me; thank you."

They were both silent again, having each troubled the other without intending it. Eventually they reached the Beacon, and turned off the path to where a level area provided a natural place to settle, with the summit sheltering them from behind and the view spread out below. Ada and Elinor looked out across the gently rolling green farmland for a while. Galathe cropped the grass.

"Shall we have a drink," Elinor suggested, "and then make a start on a sketch?"

"I am hoping to learn from you," Ada said across Galathe's back as they both divested the mare of her burdens.

"Learn from me … ? I'm afraid you'll be disappointed."

"Miss Margaret gave me a very thorough tour of all your pictures hanging at Norland Park. I cannot imagine I'll be disappointed at all."

Elinor felt a blush warm her cheeks. "Miss Ferrars, you have taught drawing to your own charges, I am sure – and when we have spoken of art, it is obvious that you have a fine natural taste. I would imagine that I have much to learn from you."

Ada flung out the blanket across the turf, and the two women settled with their sketchbooks and pencils. "I understand perspective, and yet my drawings always seem flat, as if they are all on one plane. *Your* drawings, Miss Dashwood, have depth to them."

Elinor saw that Ada had not yet opened her sketchbook, but was holding it firmly closed in both hands. "Will you show me one or two? I might be able to help." And, indeed, the problem was soon apparent. "I believe a little attention to how the light falls on objects would soon provide your solution."

"Will you show me, Miss Dashwood?"

"Yes," said Elinor. "Yes, I will."

"Will you be returning to Plymouth?" Elinor asked as she watched Ada neatly quarter and core an apple. "You'll be very welcome to visit us at Barton."

"No," Ada said, with a slight shiver. "No, I won't be returning."

"Oh." Elinor was unable to deny her disappointment. "I did understand you wouldn't be going to Longstaple, but I wondered if …"

Ada passed her a quarter of the apple. "I don't have many choices, Miss Dashwood, but I wouldn't choose to renew my engagement there, nor indeed seek any other in that county."

Elinor did not want to pry, but she wondered how very few people Ada could really confide in. Certainly Elinor could not imagine Fanny providing a sympathetic reception. She gave herself licence to pursue the matter. "Where will you go, then? When you leave Fanny and John."

Ada took a breath. "I am expected by my aunt – Mrs Ferrars – in London, for a while." Elinor very carefully did not react, but a brief exchange of glances was enough. "I know," Ada agreed with a sigh, "but I seem to have … more doubts than certainties at present. My aunt will allow me time to regain my confidence. Or perhaps … stiffen my resolve."

Elinor murmured regretfully, "I only wish we were in a position to engage you for Margaret's sake."

"You are too kind," Ada replied with a truly lovely smile, "but I am sure that you and your mother, and Miss Marianne, manage her education splendidly."

Elinor shook her head, but did not take the risk of replying. The smile had lightened Ada's expression so much that Elinor appreciated for the first time just how troubled Ada had been feeling since she arrived at Norland. Elinor feared that any misjudged words would cast a shadow across that momentary happiness.

Quietly Elinor turned a page in her sketchbook, and began drawing her companion. Not that she could capture the rich brown of Ada's hair with her pencil, or the perfection of her complexion, or the beautiful blue of her eyes, but Elinor could perhaps do some justice to her neat figure, upright posture, and air of self-possession. She might even be able to catch a glimpse of that smile and commit it to paper.

Ada had set her sketchbook aside and seemed to have forgotten the half-eaten apple. She was sitting with her hands idle, cupped together in her lap, gazing across the green countryside. After long moments, she looked down at her hands and murmured, "If *you* are to live in Devonshire, Miss Dashwood, I might –"

But in that moment, Ada glanced around, saw the subject of Elinor's drawing, and her words faltered into a laugh.

"I'm sorry," said Elinor, "I should have asked. Do you mind *very* much?"

Ada laughed beautifully, like a joyous peal of bells. "No, but here is all of Sussex at your feet, and you choose to draw *me*."

Elinor was smiling, too, and blushing a little. Perhaps she could attribute that to the breeze or the sunlight, soft though they were. "The subjects are equally as lovely," she argued, "equally as gentle."

"You have a talent for sweet flattery, Miss Dashwood!"

Elinor laughed, and did not risk a reply – for the full compliment was only half paid, when the truth was that she thought Ada Ferrars *twice* as lovely as the Sussex countryside, and more.

There were moments in which Elinor dared to hope that Ada Ferrars had feelings and inclinations that accorded with her own. Moments in which Ada smiled at her, or watched her, or sought her conversation. When Ada announced that she would leave Norland for London on the very day that Mrs Dashwood and her daughters would leave for Devonshire, Elinor was tempted to feel that as a compliment to herself. Her mother, at least, recognised their friendship, and Mrs Dashwood's invitation to Ada to visit them at Barton Cottage was much more affectionate than her invitation to John and Fanny.

"I would be very happy, I thank you, ma'am," Ada replied, though she sounded a little hesitant, as if confused. "I did not envisage returning to Devonshire, but the prospect seems rather brighter now."

Mrs Dashwood inclined her head in gratitude, and smiled at Elinor, knowing whence the brightness came.

"May I write to you?" Elinor asked quietly as the others' conversation turned away from her and Ada. "I would like to know how you get on in London – and when there is news about your engagement as governess with another family, I should like to hear it."

Ada was silent, and seemed to be frowning down at her hands, cupped together in her lap.

"Perhaps, if there is no engagement in the next few months, you could come to us when you leave Mrs Ferrars."

"Perhaps," Ada finally agreed. "But no letters, Elinor. I beseech you, no letters."

Elinor was startled, and then disheartened. After long moments, she suggested, "Notes, then. The briefest of notes, if we may … for I should like to know where you are and how you do."

Ada lifted her gaze to Elinor's, though she seemed distracted by troubling thoughts. Eventually, however, the clouds passed, and the sun shone again, though weakly. "Yes, I thank you, Elinor. Forgive me, yes. We shall write."

Elinor lay awake that night, curled around an aching sensation of love and grief, pity and … curiosity.

II

Their new home, Barton Cottage, was pleasant and comfortable. In comparison with Norland, it was poor and small indeed, but the Dashwoods first saw it on a fine September day, and each for the sake of the others resolved to be happy.

Their landlord and his lady were their nearest neighbours. Sir John Middleton was a hearty and good-humoured man, while Lady Middleton's manners had all the elegance which her husband's wanted – but she lacked his frankness and warmth, and had very little conversation. The only thing that animated Lady Middleton was her four noisy children. Whenever they appeared, they put an end to anything that did not relate to them. Elinor would not have minded, she reflected, if it were possible that Ada might be engaged as governess for the two girls when they were older.

The Middletons currently had two visitors. One was Mrs Jennings, Lady Middleton's mother. She was a merry woman, who talked a great deal and could be disconcertingly vulgar. Within an hour of the Dashwoods meeting her, she had said many witty things on the subject of lovers and husbands, and pretended to see the young women blush whether they did or not.

The Middletons' other visitor was Colonel Brandon, a friend of Sir John's

– though they were very different in temperament, the Colonel being quiet and serious. His appearance, however, was not unpleasing, despite him being on the wrong side of thirty-five, and his manner was particularly gentlemanlike.

When Marianne was discovered to be musical, she was invited to play the pianoforte at Barton Park as often as she liked. She sang very well, and her performances were always highly applauded. It was only Colonel Brandon of that party, however, who paid her the compliment of sincere attention, and so Marianne came to feel a respect for him and his pleasure in music, despite him being neither lively nor young.

Soon Mrs Jennings was convinced that Colonel Brandon was very much in love with Marianne Dashwood. She thought it would be an excellent match, and so Mrs Jennings found frequent cause to praise the Colonel's estate in Delaford and speculate on his wealth. Marianne, however, disobliged her schemes by promptly falling in love with Mr John Willoughby, a young man visiting his relation nearby. Willoughby's manly beauty and gracefulness were admired by everyone – and Marianne thought he surpassed the heroes of all her favourite tales.

Colonel Brandon's partiality for Marianne gradually became clear to Elinor – when it ceased to have any hope at all. But Elinor was happy for Marianne to have found a kindred soul in Willoughby, even if in this heady flush of first love they tended to encourage each other's faults and everyone else's gossip.

After a few weeks, though, it began to trouble Elinor that they did not put their engagement on a more formal footing. For an engagement their friends must consider it, in every way – except that neither had yet spoken to Mrs Dashwood nor sought her permission to marry. Elinor could not fathom what they were waiting for.

Eventually Elinor received a brief note from Ada, advising that she was settled now at Mrs Ferrars' house in London, and would probably remain there for two months. Elinor replied rather more promptly, and a little less briefly, describing Barton Cottage and the beauties of the surrounding countryside in terms as inviting as she could make them.

She was still awaiting a reply when Colonel Brandon received a note from London likewise, though with a more dramatic outcome. Despite his friends and acquaintances being gathered at Barton Park for an outing under his direction, Brandon immediately called for his horse – and he would be off, with no explanation, despite all that anyone could argue for him remaining overnight or even for a few hours.

Another departure soon occurred which was more disturbing still. Willoughby also left Devonshire, without explaining himself let alone declaring himself. Marianne was distraught. For a week, Marianne did little but cry, and play again all her and Willoughby's favourite music, read again all their favourite poems, and she walked alone. But eventually she sank into a calmer melancholy. She did not seem to expect Willoughby to write, for she did not watch for the post as Elinor did …

Elinor found it all very puzzling, but Mrs Dashwood would not be pushed into forcing a confidence from her daughter.

The four Dashwoods were occupied with mending and embroidering one morning, when the post arrived. Elinor saw that she had finally received another note from Ada. Again, it was brief, and reserved in tone. Elinor would have felt crushed, if she had allowed herself to have expectations. Instead she felt uneasy about Ada's low spirits. Elinor sat quietly amidst her family, remembering the few smiles Ada had bestowed upon her, the few glances exchanged in which all seemed known, or at least possible.

This unnatural idleness could not remain unremarked for long. "What are you thinking of, Elinor?" Mrs Dashwood asked. "I hope you have not received sad news."

"No, it is a note from Miss Ferrars. Ada. She is in London. I'm afraid she doesn't sound very happy."

Marianne cast Elinor a compassionate look, but spoke tartly. "Who could be, staying with Mrs Ferrars?"

"We've never even met Mrs Ferrars," Elinor felt bound to remind her.

"And long may we so continue!"

Mrs Dashwood glanced at Marianne with a scolding expression undermined by much affection. "I cannot think she is a warm-hearted woman. Does Ada mention a place with a new family? She will be happier with work to engage her time, and responsibilities to interest her. Better a governess with children to teach and care for, than the only companion of someone so unamiable."

"No, she doesn't mention it." Elinor sighed. "I suspect you are right, Mama, but there were times at Norland when Ada seemed almost reluctant to apply for a new position."

"And who could blame her?"

"She has little more to live on than any of us, Marianne, and no family to share the costs with, as we do. I'm sure you wouldn't want her relying on the hospitality of the Ferrars for any longer than necessary."

"She should come here," Marianne countered in a low voice.

"I wish she would," Elinor said in the same tones.

III

Two new visitors arrived at Barton Park from Plymouth: Miss Anne Steele and her sister, Miss Lucy, who were relations of Mrs Jennings. They were not very elegant, but Lady Middleton was soon won over by their doting attentions to the four Middleton children, and Sir John declared them the sweetest girls in the world.

He hurried down to the Cottage to ask the Miss Dashwoods to visit the Park that very day and be introduced to the Miss Steeles. "Do come now," he cried. "You can't think how you will like them – and they both long to see you, for they have heard you are the most beautiful creatures in the world, and I have told them it is all very true. You will be delighted with them, I'm sure."

Despite a natural curiosity about where the Miss Steeles had heard such a thing, the Miss Dashwoods only promised to call the next day. Sir John was amazed at their indifference.

And indifferent Elinor and Marianne remained once the introductions had taken place. Miss Steele was not a sensible person, though Miss Lucy had a smartness about her which gave distinction if not refinement. Unfortunately, their ingratiating tactic of admiring and playing with the Middleton children meant that their conversation was forever interrupted. Not that the situation was vastly improved when Lady Middleton eventually left the room with the children in tow.

Miss Steele broke the momentary peace by asking rather abruptly, "How do you like Devonshire, Miss Dashwood? I suppose you were very sorry to leave Sussex."

Elinor was surprised at the familiarity of this question, but replied that she had been sorry indeed.

"Norland is a prodigious beautiful place, is not it?" added Miss Steele.

"We have heard Sir John admire it excessively," Lucy offered in explanation.

Elinor did not have the chance to reply before Miss Steele continued, "Had you a great many beaux there? You must be sad to leave them behind. I'm afraid you might find it very dull here. However," she simpered, "I heard that Miss Marianne has already begun conquering hearts in Devonshire."

How did one respond to such impertinence? Elinor turned the talk to the weather.

Marianne could never tolerate vulgarity, and her spirits were still low, so she treated the Miss Steeles as coldly as she might without offending the Middleton family. The Miss Steeles were therefore friendlier towards Elinor than she could be comfortable about. In particular, Lucy missed no opportunity of engaging her in conversation and of being, on occasion, appallingly frank.

Lucy was naturally clever, and well read, and her remarks were often just and amusing. As a companion for half an hour Elinor often found her agreeable. However, Lucy lacked delicacy and integrity of mind, and her flatteries at the Park betrayed a thorough insincerity. Elinor could not like her, and did not value Lucy's attentions to herself. And yet Lucy persisted.

"You will think my question an odd one, I dare say," Lucy said to Elinor one day as they were walking together from the Park to the Cottage, "but are you personally acquainted with your brother's mother-in-law, Mrs Ferrars?"

Elinor did think the question a very odd one, but answered pleasantly enough that she had never seen Mrs Ferrars.

"I wondered if you might have seen her at Norland sometimes. But perhaps you cannot tell me what sort of a woman she is?"

"No," replied Elinor, "I know nothing of her."

"Oh," said Lucy in disappointed tones. They walked on in silence for a short while, before Lucy continued, "I am sure you think me very strange for enquiring about her, but I know I can trust you."

"I hope you can," Elinor said in some confusion.

"Thank you – I should be very glad of your advice – but if you do not know Mrs Ferrars –"

"I am sorry if I cannot help, but I didn't know you were at all connected with that family, so I don't understand – ?"

The two of them walked on. Lucy was very agitated, and stared down at her clasped hands, but she spoke quite loudly. "If only I dared tell you all! Mrs Ferrars is nothing to me at present – but the time may come when we may be closely connected – and my life may depend entirely upon her generosity."

"Good heavens!" cried Elinor. "What do you mean? Are you acquainted with Mr Robert Ferrars? Can you be – ?" And she did not feel delighted by the idea of such a sister-in-law.

"No," replied Lucy, "not with Mr Robert Ferrars, for I have never once met him – but," fixing her eyes upon Elinor, "with his cousin Ada."

Elinor was astonished – and her feelings would have been very painful indeed if she thought this assertion meant to Lucy what it would have meant to Elinor. She turned towards Lucy and, though she blushed, she asked firmly enough, "You are acquainted with Miss Ferrars?"

"Yes. Ada was governess for myself and Anne and my cousins Pratt at Longstaple, near Plymouth. Perhaps she spoke of it?"

"Longstaple, yes," Elinor confirmed faintly. "I believe she mentioned Mr Pratt."

"My uncle, yes," Lucy said. The two of them had halted in their walk, but now Lucy led them off again in a circuitous route to the Cottage.

"But what has this to do with Mrs Ferrars – ?"

"It was always meant to be a great secret, and no one knows but Anne – but Ada will not mind that I have trusted you. She has the highest opinion in the world of you and your family."

Elinor knew herself afraid, but at length she said as calmly as she might, "I do beg your pardon, Miss Steele, but I remain confused. Will you tell me something of the nature of this secret?"

"Why, I should have thought you would understand, Miss Dashwood! Ada and I are … particular friends. *Very* particular. We have been so these four years."

"Four years!"

"Yes. Have you not noticed, Miss Dashwood, that I always wear yellow, or have something of yellow about me?"

Elinor stared at Lucy in surprise. She *had* noticed, as she always noticed colours and forms, but she had never ascribed any importance to the matter.

Lucy laughed. "I always wear it for *her* sake. Did you not know that yellow is Ada's favourite colour?"

"No, I didn't," she was forced to concede. And then Elinor persisted in seeking the truth, though she felt greatly shocked. "And you asked about Mrs Ferrars because … ?"

"Ada and I wish to set up house together, you see, to live together – like the two ladies who live in Llangollen. I am sure Mrs Ferrars won't approve of it, or not at first – but we must rely upon Mrs Ferrars settling some money on Ada. *I* shall have no fortune, and of course Ada could not work as a governess and maintain a home of her own." Lucy sighed, and glanced at Elinor. "I believe, however, that Mrs Ferrars is an exceeding proud woman."

Elinor nodded a little, as if agreeing with this last statement. Eventually she managed, "Your secret is safe with me, of course – but I do wonder why you told me."

"I was afraid you'd think I was taking a great liberty, but I have heard so much about you and your family, and as soon as I saw you I felt as if we were old acquaintances. I am so unfortunate, and have no one whose advice I can ask. You must have seen … Anne has no judgement at all. Miss Dashwood, I have suffered so much for Ada's sake these last four years. Everything is in such suspense and uncertainty – and now with my youngest cousin turned eighteen, Ada is released from her engagement with the family, and I cannot see her. I do not know how my heart is not broke."

Here Lucy took out her handkerchief, but Elinor did not feel very compassionate.

"Sometimes," continued Lucy, after dabbing at her eyes, "I wonder if it wouldn't be better for us both to break off the matter entirely." As she said this, she looked directly at her companion. "But I know even the mention of it would make Ada so miserable – and so dear as she is to me, I just don't think I could." Another pause and another direct look. "What would you advise me to do, Miss Dashwood? What would you do yourself?"

"Pardon me," replied Elinor, startled by the question. "I can give you no advice under such circumstances. Your own judgement must guide you."

After a short silence, Lucy said, "Poor Ada is so cast down about the situation! If you could read her letters to me! They are so dreadful low-spirited. I am afraid she will become quite ill." Lucy took a letter from her pocket and carelessly showed the direction to Elinor. "Perhaps you know her hand, and a charming one it is, but that is not written so well as usual. She was tired, I dare say, for she had just filled the sheet to me as full as possible."

Elinor saw that it was Ada's hand, and any last doubts she had had were done away with.

"Did not you think her sadly out of spirits when she stayed with you at Norland?" asked Lucy.

"Miss Ferrars did seem so," Elinor agreed, with a composure of voice under which was concealed an emotion and distress beyond anything she had ever felt before.

Fortunately for Elinor they had now reached the Cottage, and the conversation could be continued no further. After sitting with them a few minutes, Lucy returned to the Park, and Elinor was then free to think and be wretched.

Elinor had not dared to rely on the thought that Ada felt for her what she felt for Ada, but she had glimpsed the possibilities of a rare accord. She might never again meet a woman so well suited to Elinor's ideas of happiness. Now she learned that Ada might well have felt the same – but was unable to pursue the matter due to a prior commitment. It was all the harder to bear when Elinor suspected that Lucy Steele was not the person who could make a woman of integrity happy in the long-term. However this had begun, years before, when Lucy was younger, more innocent and eager to learn, Elinor could not think it would end well. Lucy's cleverness was now conniving, her sincerity had become artifice, and Ada's heart and mind must be hurt every day by such a companion. Elinor wept more for Ada than for herself.

The necessity of concealing from her mother and Marianne, what had been entrusted in confidence to herself, obliged Elinor to constant effort. But it was also a relief to be spared the communication of what would upset Mrs Dashwood and afflict Marianne, and to be saved likewise from hearing any condemnation of Ada. Elinor was stronger alone. Despite her poignant regrets, her own good sense so well supported her, that her firmness was as unshaken and her appearance of cheerfulness as invariable, as it was possible for them to be.

It soon occurred to Elinor that Lucy must be jealous of her, for how else could Lucy have learned so much about Norland Park and the Dashwood family – and Elinor in particular – if not in letters from Ada? What other reason for the disclosure of the relationship could there be, but that Elinor might be informed of Lucy's superior claims on Ada, and learn to avoid her in future? Elinor had little difficulty in understanding this much of her rival's intentions, and she was firmly resolved to act as every principle of honour directed, to combat her own affection for Ada and to see her as little as possible. Elinor could not deny herself the comfort, however, of pretending to Lucy that her heart was unwounded.

Lucy treated Elinor from now on as the closest of friends, and unburdened herself during any moments in which the two women found themselves alone. She also continued to make clear her own claims on Ada's loyalties. "I am rather of a jealous temper," Lucy said one day at Barton Park, while Marianne's passionate piano-playing enabled quietly spoken confidences. "I would find out the truth in an instant, if there was the slightest alteration in her behaviour to me, or any lowness of spirits I could not account for, or if she had talked more of one lady than another. In such a case I am sure I could not be deceived."

"But what are your plans?" Elinor asked. "You must be waiting every day to hear good news from Miss Ferrars. Indeed, I am rather surprised you have not heard already."

"Heard what?" Lucy's sharp little eyes turned towards her in suspicion.

"Surely Miss Ferrars will explain the situation to her aunt while she is staying with her in London? I cannot think there will be a better opportunity."

Lucy faltered for a moment. "Ada must approach the subject carefully, of course."

"The suspense must be quite tedious, after all these years of waiting."

"Mrs Ferrars is a very headstrong, proud woman. In her first fit of anger upon hearing it, she may secure everything to Robert, and leave nothing for Ada – or for your sister Fanny. You could not want Ada to act hastily, Miss Dashwood."

"I am sure Fanny is already well taken care of," Elinor commented rather tartly. "You need not fear for her."

"But for Ada's sake, and mine," Lucy persisted.

"Yes, indeed," Elinor agreed.

IV

As January approached, Mrs Jennings' thoughts turned to her own home on Berkeley Street in London – and unexpectedly one day she asked the elder Miss Dashwoods to accompany her there for the winter.

Elinor was far from happy about the scheme, but Mrs Jennings was not an easy woman to refuse. Marianne soon made it obvious that she very much wanted to go. Elinor realised how eager her sister was to be with Willoughby again, and she pitied Marianne, but felt uneasy when she remembered the uncertain, informal state of Marianne's relationship with Willoughby.

Of course Elinor had her own reasons for wanting to avoid London – for Ada would still be there. Not that the Dashwoods would be at all likely to visit Mrs Ferrars, especially while under Mrs Jennings' protection, but once John and Fanny were in town, that would throw them into the same circles.

Mrs Dashwood was delighted with the invitation, however, and insisted on their both accepting it directly. Mrs Jennings was overjoyed, Marianne was exhilarated – and Elinor soon learned to feel less reluctant.

"When you see Miss Ferrars –" said Miss Lucy Steele to Elinor.

"I am not sure that we shall," Elinor replied.

"When you do," Lucy complacently continued, "pray give her my regards. And say to her – that I have her letters."

"If I do –"

"Just that," said Lucy, with a smile that did not reach her sharp eyes. "I have her letters."

"Yes, of course," Elinor finally agreed. Her reluctance for the whole London scheme returned in full measure.

As soon as they arrived in London and were shown to their room in Mrs Jennings' house, Marianne wrote a note that Elinor saw was addressed to Willoughby. Marianne received no reply that evening or in the following days, and grew restless and pale with anxiety. Colonel Brandon came to visit them almost every morning, and was often invited to dinner, but of course his company was more comfort to Elinor than to the woman he so obviously cared for. Marianne wrote again to Willoughby, but still he did not reply, and it was soon clear that he was in London and deliberately avoiding them.

Eventually Elinor and Marianne saw Willoughby at a party to which they had accompanied Lady Middleton – and he acknowledged them only once a gentleman could not have ignored them any longer. He was embarrassed, and obviously conscious of wrongdoing. As soon as he could, he escaped the Dashwoods to return to the side of a fashionable young woman.

It was clear that any understanding that had existed between Marianne and him was over for ever – and the next day brought a letter from him confirming that he was engaged to another.

Marianne was so miserable and wretched, so choked by grief. She lay stretched on the bed with Willoughby's letter in her hand. Elinor sat near her, took her hand, kissed her affectionately several times – and then gave way to a burst of tears, which at first was scarcely less violent than Marianne's.

Eventually, however, Elinor regained enough presence of mind to be calm, and called on Marianne to endeavour to restrain her torrent of grief. "Think of your mother's misery while you suffer," she pleaded. "For her sake you must exert yourself."

"I cannot, I cannot," cried Marianne. "Do not torture me. Oh! How easy for those who have no sorrow of their own to talk of exertion!"

"Do you think me happy, Marianne? Ah, if you knew! And how could I be happy when I see you so wretched?"

"Forgive me, forgive me." Marianne threw her arms around her sister's neck. "I know you feel for me; I know what a heart you have. But you must be happy; Ada loves you. Oh! What can do away such happiness as that?"

"Many, many circumstances," said Elinor quietly. But Marianne was too distraught to pay this any mind.

Willoughby was married early in February, to a Miss Grey, whose main appeal seemed to be her fifty thousand pounds. Colonel Brandon had, in the meantime, confided to Elinor the story of how Willoughby had seduced and abandoned Brandon's ward, Miss Eliza Williams, who had since borne a child. Elinor was authorised to tell this story to Marianne – and as a result Marianne was less shockingly grief-stricken, but she sank into a gloomy dejection, she barely ate, and she refused to leave Mrs Jennings' house.

Elinor was glad to hear that Willoughby and his new wife had left town immediately after their wedding – but was less pleased to find that the two Miss Steeles had since arrived, and were staying with a cousin in Holborn. Soon also, John and Fanny Dashwood came to town, to a house they had taken in Harley Street. All the necessary visits and introductions were made.

Lucy very shortly claimed Elinor's compassion on being unable to see Ada, for apparently Mrs Ferrars considered Bartlett's Buildings in Holborn too undesirable an address for Ada to visit alone, and Ada had not yet secured an invitation for Lucy to visit Mrs Ferrars. Though Lucy and Ada's mutual impatience to meet was not to be told, they could do nothing at present but write.

It seemed that Ada was permitted to visit in Berkeley Street, however. Twice her card was found on the table, when Mrs Jennings and Miss Dashwood returned from their morning's engagements. Elinor was pleased that Ada had called, and still more pleased that she had missed her.

She was less lucky in missing Lucy, however, who called regularly in order to fret and triumph in equal measure. That Lucy might have had another motive for her attentions only occurred to Elinor one morning when the two women were alone – and the door was thrown open, the servant announced Miss Ferrars, and Ada walked in.

It was a very awkward moment, and they were all exceedingly discomfited. Ada seemed almost inclined to walk directly out again. She stayed, however, and the three of them bobbed a curtsey at each other.

Elinor forced herself, after a moment, to welcome their visitor in a manner that was almost natural. She would not allow the presence of Lucy, nor the consciousness of her own loss, to deter her from saying that she was happy to see Ada, and that she had regretted being from home when she called before in Berkeley Street. Elinor would not be frightened from paying Ada those attentions which, as a friend and a relation, were her due – despite knowing Lucy was narrowly watching her.

Elinor's relative composure gave some reassurance to Ada, who sat down when invited. Lucy, with a demure and settled air, seemed determined to make no contribution to the comfort of the others, and barely said a word. Elinor made all the proper enquiries about Mrs Ferrars' well-being and Ada's stay in town, and prompted Ada's own halting enquiries about Mrs

Dashwood's health.

Elinor's heroic exertions did not stop here, for she decided to fetch Marianne, and thereby leave the others by themselves for a while. She even loitered away several minutes on the stairs, with the most high-minded fortitude, before she went to her sister.

When that was done, however, Marianne's joy hurried her into the drawing-room immediately. She met Ada with a hand that would be taken, and a voice that expressed the affection of a sister. "Dear Ada!" she cried. "This is a moment of great happiness! This almost makes amends for everything!"

"Oh, Marianne," Ada replied, obviously startled by Marianne's pale looks. "I'm afraid you haven't been well. Does London not suit you?"

"Not at all. I expected much pleasure in it, but I have found none. The sight of *you*, Ada, is the only comfort it has afforded."

"You are very kind," Ada murmured.

They all fell silent again, to Marianne's evident surprise. After a moment she continued, "But don't think of *my* health, dear Ada. Elinor is well, you see. That must be enough for us both."

This remark did not make Ada or Elinor feel any less awkward, and Lucy cast the oblivious Marianne a rather malicious look. And so the conversation stuttered on for another five minutes, until Ada at last stood and said her farewells. Lucy left not long afterwards.

"What can bring Lucy Steele here so often!" cried Marianne as soon as she and Elinor were alone again. "Could she not see that we wanted her gone?"

"Miss Ferrars has known Miss Steele longer than either of us," Elinor replied as calmly as she could. "Why should they not take the chance to enjoy each other's company?"

Marianne looked unimpressed. "Elinor, you know very well that I am the *last* person to oblige if you only hope to have your assertions contradicted."

And Elinor must remain silent, for she was still bound by her promise of secrecy to Lucy. All she could hope was that there would not be many meetings in the future that could cause her such pain as this one had.

Elinor's wish was not granted, as Ada called again on the very next morning – and the two of them were alone, as Mrs Jennings was at her daughter's, and Elinor chose not to fetch Marianne this time. Instead Elinor led Ada into the smaller parlour at the back of the house, where it would be understood that they chose not to be disturbed.

As soon as they sat down, Elinor opened the conversation in a way which would avoid any misunderstandings. "You might have been surprised to see Miss Lucy Steele here yesterday, Miss Ferrars. Perhaps you were not aware that she and her sister had been visiting Barton Park for some weeks before we came to town."

"I was not – unaware," Ada said falteringly. She gestured, as if searching for the right words with which to continue.

Elinor, however, did not wait. "Indeed, Miss Steele's last request to me before I left Barton was to remember her to you, and – and to reassure you that she has your letters."

"Letters," Ada repeated faintly. Her complexion lost all colour, and for a moment she looked as distraught as ever Marianne had. "Then you know everything, Miss Dashwood. That is the worst of it, for me. You know how very foolish I have been."

Elinor watched her friend with heartfelt regret, as the story came tumbling out.

"Oh, she was as fresh as a daffodil when first I knew her. The spring of our friendship was nothing but sunlight. Then slowly it all began to go wrong. It is the secrets, I think. Secrets such as she and I must keep. They make everything … unwholesome."

"I am very sorry," Elinor said in a low voice. After a moment, she asked, "Have your letters, since you came away from Mr Pratt's, been … perhaps a little too unguarded?"

Ada shook her head, looking miserable.

"You must have trusted Miss Steele, of course. It is only natural to trust – those we love."

"No, there has been nothing in my own letters that could be seen as anything more than an affectionate friendship." Ada took a breath. "The foolishness occurred while I was still living in Longstaple. She and I had this notion that we would write an epistolary novel, in the style of Mrs Radcliffe. It was Lucy's idea that we use our own names, and write the letters back and forth. We used to exchange the latest letter in secret, in the hot-house." Ada groaned quietly. "I should have known better. It grew – beyond what was decorous – so quickly. Before I was properly aware. Like a plant forced to flower out of season."

Ada fell quiet again, and Elinor tried to calm her own dismay enough to consider the matter carefully. She and Ada might have all too few opportunities to talk in private, and Elinor knew she must make the most of that morning.

Eventually Elinor asked, "What can Miss Steele intend to do with the letters? If she shows them to anyone, she will also be implicated."

"Yes, a little. Perhaps. She would endeavour to be seen as young, and too easily misled in her innocence. But the fact of the matter is that *I* was responsible, Miss Dashwood. I'm the one who'll be ruined, and I'll deserve it. No one will want to engage me to care for their daughters."

"And so –"

"And so I must do as she wishes. She and I used to talk about – living together –"

"Like the two ladies of Llangollen," Elinor supplied.

Ada smiled faintly. "Yes. She will keep me to my promises, made so long ago. Even though so much has changed since then."

After a moment, Elinor said, "Your sense of honour does you great credit, Miss Ferrars."

"Thank you, Miss Dashwood," Ada said in a whisper. And then she rose and she silently took her leave.

Three or four days later, Mrs Jennings returned from her morning visits, and burst into the drawing-room, where Elinor was sitting alone. "Lord! My dear Miss Dashwood, have you heard the news?"

"No, ma'am. What is it?"

"Something so strange! Your cousin Miss Ada Ferrars is to set up home together with my cousin Lucy! They have been planning it all this while, and not a creature knew of it except Anne! Could you have believed such a thing possible? It was all kept a great secret, as of course Mrs Ferrars is a fearsomely proud woman, and even now she talks of marrying Miss Ada off to some lord or other, I forget who. Well! I say that if the two girls are so set against marriage and a regular establishment, then let them be friends together, and have done with it. They wouldn't be the first and they won't be the last. But can you imagine the uproar! I heard tell that poor Anne was on her knees and crying bitterly, for she thought your brother and his wife had taken such a shine to Lucy, and so out it all popped. Lucy walks in, little dreaming what is going on – and is so furiously scolded that she quite faints away – and then Mrs Dashwood falls into hysterics."

Mrs Jennings paused for breath, and Elinor asked with some concern, "Has anyone taken seriously ill, ma'am, do you know?"

"Lord bless you! I heard tell that Mr Donavan was called to attend to Mrs Dashwood and Mrs Ferrars – and my two cousins are young, with good constitutions. You needn't fear for them, my dear, but I have no pity for your sister-in-law and her mother, making such a to-do about money and greatness. Miss Ada and Lucy would be so snug and respectable together in a little cottage such as yours – and I could help them to a housemaid, for my Betty has a sister out of place who would suit them exactly."

Elinor had had time enough to compose herself. "It is too soon to know, I suppose, how things will be settled."

"Oh! My poor Lucy has next to nothing, and Miss Ada has only two thousand of her own. They will need more than that to live on, and you would think Mrs Ferrars' great pride would not want her own family to be so poor, with all the world to see it."

"Then Mrs Ferrars is determined to do nothing for her niece?"

Mrs Jennings shook her head. "That is what they say, Miss Dashwood, though I could scarce believe it of anyone."

As Mrs Jennings could talk of nothing else, Elinor soon realised she must break the news to Marianne. This was a painful duty. Elinor knew that Marianne's chief consolation was her faith in Elinor and Ada's understanding – and now Elinor was not only going to ruin Marianne's good opinion of Ada, but also renew Marianne's own disappointment by knowing her sister had suffered a similar loss.

Marianne had barely heard the first particulars before she burst out, "How long have you known this, Elinor?"

"Four months. Since Lucy came to Barton Park last November."

"Four months!" cried Marianne. "Yet you've been so calm! So cheerful!"

"I understand you," Elinor replied. "You do not suppose that I have ever felt much. But for four months, Marianne, I have had all this hanging on my mind, without being at liberty to speak of it to a single creature. It was told me – it was *forced* on me by the very person whose prior understanding ruined all my hopes. And told me with triumph! She suspected me, so I had to appear indifferent, while I had to listen to her exultation again and again. I knew I had lost Ada for ever, but I heard nothing to make me think less of her – or to make me think her indifferent to me. And as you know only too well, this has not been my only unhappiness. If you can think me capable of real feeling – surely you must see that I have suffered. Marianne, I have been *very* unhappy."

"Oh, my dear Elinor …" Marianne reached for Elinor, and the sisters held each other tenderly, as each other's only comfort.

When John Dashwood next visited Berkeley Street, he passed on the news that Mrs Ferrars had settled another thousand on Ada – and, to make matters clear, had at the same time settled an estate in Norfolk on her son Robert. Mrs Ferrars had also declared that she would have nothing more to do with Ada. Indeed, Ada had been expelled from the house, and the Dashwoods felt unable to take her in, so Ada had taken a room at Bartlett's Buildings.

"Three thousand!" said Mrs Jennings. "That isn't much for the young women to live on – but of course they mustn't expect the kind of establishment that a married couple would want, and Lucy knows well enough how to make the most of everything."

John remained unconvinced. "As well she might, but Ada was not born for such poverty. She might have had ten times that, if only she would marry Lord Morton. But our arguments were useless. All that Mrs Ferrars could say to make her put an end to the arrangement was of no avail. Duty, affection, everything was disregarded. I never thought Ada so stubborn, so unfeeling, before. She said she would keep her promise, no matter what it cost."

"Then," cried Mrs Jennings, with blunt sincerity, "she has acted honestly! I would think her a rascal if she abandoned Lucy now, and left her exposed to the world's malice and gossip."

"Well," John concluded, "Ada has drawn her own lot, and I fear it will be a bad one."

Marianne sighed in agreement, and Elinor's heart wrung for Ada, who was suffering so much in securing such unhappy prospects. At last John went away again – leaving the three ladies unanimous in their sentiments, at least in regard to Mrs Ferrars' conduct and Ada's. Marianne's indignation burst forth as soon as they were alone – and as her vehemence made reserve impossible in Elinor, and unnecessary in Mrs Jennings, they all joined in a very spirited critique upon the situation.

"I have heard," said Colonel Brandon to Elinor one morning, while Mrs Jennings and Marianne were otherwise occupied, "that your friend Miss Ferrars has been cast off by her family for persevering in her friendship with a deserving young woman. Is this true?"

"Yes, it is."

"I have seen Miss Ferrars two or three times in Harley Street, and am much pleased with her. That she is well read and well informed is obvious from her conversation. That she will not break a promise to a friend is proof enough of her character – if proof I needed, knowing she is a friend of yours."

"Miss Ferrars is all this, and more," Elinor quietly agreed.

Colonel Brandon hesitated for a moment before continuing. "The village at Delaford is in need of a schoolteacher. I hope she will not feel offended by such an offer, having been a governess before now. The income is modest, but I understand she has some means of her own, and the schoolroom is attached to a pleasant cottage and garden, which I believe two young women would find quite suitable. Will you be so good as to tell her that the place is hers if she wishes it?"

Elinor was astonished to receive such a commission, and her gratitude to the Colonel for his thoughtful benevolence was strongly felt. It certainly seemed a very eligible situation, and Elinor's pleasure and relief for Ada's sake was only slightly soured by feelings less pure. She had feared a far more humble outcome for Ada and Lucy than this.

"It is all to my own advantage," the Colonel insisted when Elinor began to thank him again. "I am securing two very respectable and agreeable neighbours – and I trust," he added with a slight bow to Elinor, "they will often be visited by their most amiable friends."

She smiled softly. "We shall always be very much obliged to you."

Ada was stunned by the news that Elinor passed on in the small parlour at the back of Mrs Jennings' house. "Colonel Brandon!" was all she managed to say in response.

"Yes. He means it as proof of his high esteem for your character. He particularly admires your honest behaviour in these trying circumstances."

"Colonel Brandon! Can it be possible? I have only met him a very few times."

"Do not fear," Elinor said gently. "He is a good man. He thinks only of helping you. You should have received such kindness from your family, but instead you must accept it from your friends."

Ada leant forward a little to say earnestly, "I owe this to *your* kindness, Miss Dashwood, I know it well."

"You are very much mistaken, Miss Ferrars. You owe it entirely to your own merit, which Colonel Brandon discerned for himself."

They were silent for a few moments, until at last Ada said, "Please, will you tell me Colonel Brandon's address? I must write to him, to thank him. I must try to find the words – to convey – such very unexpected fortune –"

"Such excellent and well-deserved fortune," Elinor agreed.

Ada shot her such a beseeching look that Elinor found it wise to busy herself in writing down the Colonel's address. And then, after a stumbling, heartfelt exchange of good wishes, they parted.

Elinor sat by herself for a while afterwards, reflecting that the next time they met, Ada would belong fully to Lucy.

V

At last Elinor and Marianne were to return home to Barton, travelling with Mrs Jennings to visit her other daughter at Cleveland in Somersetshire, and accompanied by Colonel Brandon. From Cleveland they planned to send for their mother's servant, Thomas, who would escort them for the last day of their journey.

But while walking at twilight in the gardens at Cleveland – in the wildest place, where the trees were the oldest, and the grass was the longest and wettest – Marianne caught a chill which soon became a violent cold. She was still weak and low in spirits following her recent disappointments, and so what should have been a short illness descended into a feverish delirium.

Elinor spent long days and nights caring for Marianne, only leaving her side and seeking rest when Mrs Jennings insisted. Indeed, Mrs Jennings' unstinting usefulness in this crisis, and her constant kindness of heart, at last made Elinor really love her.

Colonel Brandon must necessarily have less to do, but whatever tasks he was given, he performed promptly and diligently. Finally, late one night when Elinor really began to fear the worst, she asked the Colonel to fetch her mother from Barton. Whatever despair he might feel in hearing her fears, he acted with all the firmness of a collected mind. Every necessary arrangement was made, and soon he was gone.

Around noon the next day, however, Elinor began to sense an improvement in Marianne's condition. She watched carefully, hardly daring to hope. But her sister's pulse, her breath, her complexion, all grew less hectic and more tranquil. At last Marianne opened her eyes and fixed them on Elinor with a rational though languid gaze.

Marianne would be well again.

VI

How comfortable and welcoming was Barton Cottage! It was true that Marianne seemed pensive at first when considering certain places and objects she associated with the memory of Willoughby. But the soothing company of her mother, and the delightful spirits of Margaret, soon banished any gloom, and they all quietly settled into their beloved home.

After a while, despite her own hopes being resigned, Elinor began to wish for news of Ada. She had heard nothing of her since the Dashwoods left London, not from Ada herself or Lucy, nor from John and Fanny or Colonel Brandon.

A few days passed, bringing no letters, no tidings. One morning, however, the sound of a carriage approaching drew Elinor to the window. Recognising the chaise as belonging to the Colonel, Elinor was pleased to think that he would be able to appease her curiosity. As the carriage drew up to their gate, however, Elinor realised that a figure sat beside him – the figure of a woman – and as Elinor watched Brandon hand her down, she recognised the woman as Ada Ferrars.

Elinor took a breath, moved to the nearest chair, and sat down.

Marianne must have noticed the identities of their visitors as well, for she turned pale and cast Elinor a look of distress and concern. Mrs Dashwood, meanwhile, rejoiced in the sight of Colonel Brandon, for she had decided that he would make the perfect husband for Marianne – and Marianne's change in colour implied to her partial mother that Marianne was perhaps beginning to feel the same.

Luckily Margaret was not aware of all these complications, so her honest happiness in seeing two of her favourite people was of great assistance to Mrs Dashwood in greeting their visitors. Elinor was too agitated and Marianne too concerned to be of much help.

Soon, however, the initial flurry was over, and the usual enquiries had been made about the guests' journey and everyone's health. A silence ensued. At last Colonel Brandon cleared his throat, and asked in a rather strained voice whether the Dashwoods had had much news from town.

"No, none at all," Mrs Dashwood replied. "Not since we returned from Cleveland. Elinor? You have more acquaintance in London."

Elinor managed a smile, and echoed, "None at all."

Colonel Brandon acknowledged this, and then looked at Ada, who nodded – and then the Colonel turned towards Elinor. "Miss Dashwood, would you do me the kindest favour? I fear Miss Ferrars didn't find the chaise very comfortable. Perhaps you would take her for a stroll in the fresh air? It is a lovely day, and such a very lovely garden. I'm sure it would restore her."

"Yes," said Elinor as calmly as she could. "Yes, of course."

Ada had already stood, and now said, "Thank you, Miss Dashwood," without lifting her gaze from the floor. Elinor collected a parasol and led her outside.

For a little while they walked in silence by the flowerbeds. Elinor was aware when the conversation began again inside the Cottage, and was prompted to make a similar effort. "I trust that Miss Steele is well."

Ada glanced at her, and answered, "Yes, I believe so."

"You left her at Delaford? Is the cottage as pleasant as I've heard?"

"You mean … I think you mean to enquire after Mrs Ferrars."

"Oh!" Elinor took a breath. "Yes, of course. How is your aunt? Neither John nor Fanny has written in some while."

Ada was considering Elinor very carefully by now. "Can you really not have heard?"

There were cries of surprise from within the Cottage, and then everyone seemed to be talking at once, but Elinor could not make out anything that was said. She turned a confused look upon her companion.

"Come and sit down," Ada said, leading Elinor towards the wooden bench from which one could enjoy the roses. Once they were settled next together, Ada gently continued, "I think you were enquiring after Mrs Robert Ferrars. I think you have not heard that my cousin Robert is lately married to – the younger – to Miss Lucy Steele."

Elinor stared at Ada, too astonished to really comprehend this news.

"They were married last week," Ada said, "and are now at Brighton."

Ada was free.

Elinor tried to speak but could not – she reached a hand towards her friend, and Ada took it firmly in hers. A moment later Elinor burst into tears of joy. Ada drew closer, and let go her hand – but only so that she could draw Elinor snugly into her arms.

"But how can this be?" was the natural question that arose once Elinor had regained her voice. "I wasn't aware that Robert and Lucy knew each other at all."

"Somehow they met after I went down to Delaford to prepare the school," said Ada. "Perhaps he thought he could persuade her to give up her connection with me. I knew nothing of it until she wrote to me on the very day they were married. She told me that they had burned our novel – reading the letters one by one as they were consigned to the flames. I wonder if she didn't inspire and provoke him, in the ways that she used to inspire and provoke me."

"So the letters are gone, Lucy is gone ..."

Ada smiled at her. "And I am free once more to make my own choices. I intend to choose far more wisely this time."

Elinor could feel her own smile matching the warmth of Ada's. "What do you intend to do with your freedom, then?"

"Why, to immediately curtail it, and ask if you would consent to be the companion of a village schoolteacher in Delaford."

"I do so consent," said Elinor. "With all my heart, I do."

Julie Bozza

Julie Bozza is an English-Australian hybrid who is fuelled by espresso, calmed by knitting, unreasonably excited by photography, and madly in love with John Keats.

juliebozza.com
twitter.com/juliebozza
goodreads.com/juliebozza

Father Doesn't Dance

Eleanor Musgrove

"My dear ladies," Mr George Darcy began, having settled his family in his study, "I have important matters to discuss with you."

This was already evident; even Lady Anne Darcy was rarely admitted to her husband's inner sanctum, to say nothing of his daughters. Georgiana, not quite eleven years old, might not have realised the significance of the location, but Lavinia, a little over ten years her senior, saw it all and knew that what was being discussed must be of grave import indeed. Grave, as it turned out, was far too apt a word.

"And so you see, my dears, I must leave you sooner rather than later, and though my solicitor has had, as yet, no success in finding the man who will inherit Pemberley, the entail must be obeyed. There is nothing I can offer you, save a small amount of income, in order to ease your grief upon my passing."

"No fortune could offer such consolation," Lady Anne sniffed, "but I have known that you were ill this past twelvemonth. Is there more that you must tell me?"

"The girls, however, did not know," Mr Darcy pointed out, and reached out his arm for Georgiana. "Come, my love, it is not so bad. I have lived a full and luxurious life. All I hope is that you will now find a way to do the same." But Georgiana clung to him, sobbing into his shoulder, until her mother stood and took her hand.

"Help me find some fresh flowers for your father's bedside," she told her gently, "to cheer his days. You have the best instinct of all of us for a pleasing bloom." Georgiana wiped her eyes roughly and, with one last embrace for her father, followed her mother out.

Lavinia stayed where she was, perched on the edge of the chair as if it were the only thing solid in all the world. That was what it felt like; the room seemed to spin for a moment, and when she regained her bearings her father was gazing at her with tender concern.

"How long … ?" It was all she could manage, and she felt the impropriety of it immediately. "I'm sorry –"

"No, no, you have the right to know. Mr Swinton, my doctor, thinks that it will not now be beyond a few weeks' suffering, though I will become quite weak very quickly now. I have endeavoured to keep going until the last, but I can go on no further as I was."

"Oh, Father – !" It was Lavinia's turn to cross the room and lay a hand on her father's arm. "Is there something I can do to make you comfortable?"

"No, no, dear child, I want for nothing. Except … well, there is one thing I would ask of you."

"You need only name it."

"Please … in any way you can … look after your sister. I do not know what will become of any of you, but it is important that you all take care of one another. Your mother's family gives her an income, and so you should be supported, but an entail is a hard thing, and will leave you in rather poorer circumstances than I could wish."

"Of course we shall take care of her, Father – Mother and I both."

"And I do hope that you will hold friends with Mr Wickham and his son. Fine, upstanding men."

"Indeed, Mr Wickham has never been anything but kind to me." Her father seemed satisfied with her answer, and they turned talk to other things: to sickrooms and flowers, and to the unknown man who would take over Pemberley.

"I only wish that, whoever he is, he should let you and your mother guide him in the first months of his tenure. He may never have had a grand house, and certainly none so prestigious as Pemberley."

As the weeks went by, Lavinia could only watch as her father became more frail and his expression became more worried. She could hardly blame him for his preoccupation; she imagined that losing one's health so quickly was quite difficult enough without having to contend with the knowledge of an entail that would leave one's family, if not destitute, considerably less comfortable than one would wish. Lavinia hated to see her father so disconsolate, and so she began to rack her brain for some brilliant scheme that might make him happy. When at last the idea occurred, it was such a preposterous notion that she discarded it immediately, but the thought would not leave her. At last, she knocked on the door of her father's study, where she was increasingly likely to find both parents closeted together.

"I've been thinking," she told them once the door was closed behind her, "about the entail."

"You needn't worry yourself about that, Lavinia. There's nothing to be done," her mother began in a soothing tone, but Lavinia turned her head to address her father.

"Has Mr Lowick found the heir yet?"

"No. No, he hasn't." Perhaps he noticed the glint in her eye, because he raised an eyebrow as he continued. "If I had a son, it would be quite a different matter. Nothing could be simpler. But with so few men left in my family ... well, it's a little harder to trace the line of succession."

Lavinia took a deep breath. "What if you *did* have a son?"

"Lavinia!" The reprimand seemed to escape Lady Anne in a rush of air. "I hope you're not suggesting that your father –"

"No! No, nothing like – It's only that, well, for Georgiana's sake, and – and with my figure, I could easily be mistaken – perhaps a little older than me, three-and-twenty or so, but nobody would know him, so maybe it wouldn't –"

Mr Darcy interrupted with a heavy sigh. "Dear me, Lavinia. Spare an old man these mental exertions, and explain what you mean, I beg of you."

"I could be your son." A terrible silence hung in the air for a moment, and Lavinia felt her cheeks begin to burn. "I mean, I could pretend ... so that we'd be looked after. *I* could inherit for us."

Her parents stared at her, as well they might; the whole idea was ludicrous, and yet ...

"Your father and I have no son," Lady Anne pointed out, "how would we ever explain it?"

"Perhaps I can answer that." Her father's voice startled her. "Perhaps he was sent away, or else went travelling. Some excuse might be contrived. Lavinia has plenty of me in her looks ... I don't see how anybody could question the parentage of a son with her face."

"George, surely you aren't entertaining the notion? Can it even be done?"

"In all our trying, we have found no other solution. With our support – Well, nobody would expect us to do such a thing. It might be believed."

"Perhaps ... I could write to my sister – not Catherine, Lavinia, you needn't look so scared – no, I shall write to your uncle's wife, Mary. If this is foolish, or sinful, she is far enough removed to see it, and we may say no more about it. I believe, however, that she would go to great pains for us, and may be able to offer us some manner of help." Lady Anne paused for a moment, before continuing with a worried frown, "But what would become of *you*, Lavinia? How would we explain your absence? How could you ever return?"

"I do not know, Mother. I don't know how, but … I feel I could live forever as a man if only it would safeguard Georgiana, and the children she will one day have. I would do anything to protect her."

"That, I believe," her father said after a thoughtful pause, "but we must not rush into anything foolish – and this could be very foolish indeed."

"Yes, Father." Lavinia turned to leave, but Mr Darcy's voice stopped her in her tracks.

"It may be foolish," he repeated, "but all I ask is that you think very carefully about what you are offering to do, and how you plan to achieve it. Your mother and I will do the same. If you are still decided upon this course in one week, come to me again and, if we all agree that it seems possible, we shall set to work."

A week later, the three adults of the Darcy family met once more in George's study. It had been difficult, for the first time in her life, for Lavinia to keep something so important from Georgiana, but time had not weakened her resolve.

"I'm afraid I haven't thought better of … the matter we discussed, but I will bow to your counsel. Please, tell me what I can do."

Her parents exchanged wary glances before her mother spoke, her voice gentle.

"You are certain, Lavinia? To live as a man? Never to marry, or bear children – you would choose that life?"

She nodded. "I care for but one child in all England, Mother, and I have met no man to tempt me. I would choose this life to keep Georgiana here in her home – in my home, too, and yours. Father?"

"I would much rather think of you living here, and not a stranger. I will help you, if you are sure of your course. I can inform Mr Lowick of my son and heir."

"But how are we to explain his absence?"

"I have written to Aunt Mary, as I said I would," her mother offered, "though I did not tell her your part in it, lest you feel pressured. She was shocked, but her letter arrived yesterday and she says she will help. She will even claim that the boy – you – lodged with her as a child, and that he then ventured overseas to explore as a young man might."

"Will people not remember that she had no such ward?"

"My brother the earl spent a great deal of time in town, or at court." Lady Anne gave a disapproving sigh. "His eldest son, your cousin Edward, went with him, so your younger cousin Richard needed company, and your aunt took in a great many children during that time, for short periods and long. I should not think that any person could state with certainty that no such boy was there."

"Then we should make haste, should we not? The earlier my brother arrives, the more convincing –"

"No." Her father spoke firmly. "No, I want my daughters with me when I … It's important to me, Lavinia. I want *you* there, not a son I've never known."

"Father, it would still be me. But I understand. We can wait."

"Thank you, dear one. However, I will make an appointment with Mr Lowick, to tell him of my son and alter my will accordingly. It will be easier if the ground is prepared for you now."

Lavinia nodded slowly. "And Lavinia Darcy? What of your daughter? How is she to disappear?" She hoped that she would not have to pretend a death; the idea made her feel quite unwell.

"Mary can help us there, too. She will take you into her home – just as she did your brother, I suppose – in an attempt to dissuade you from traveling to a remote convent and taking vows there. Should anything change your mind, you can return and your brother will simply have an accident on his journey home, never to be seen again. But if you are truly committed to this course … well, she will not be as persuasive as she had hoped, and poor Fitzwilliam will never again see his father or his sister."

"Fitzwilliam? Is that … to be my name?"

"Forgive me, Lavinia. Of course you should have your choice. It is only that your father and I were talking, and it seemed a fitting name – it is more than likely the name we would have given you if you had been born a boy."

"It would help to establish you as the legitimate child of us both, too," her father added, "since you favour my looks."

"Fitzwilliam. I do not dislike it." She tested the name again on her tongue, then smiled. "Besides, you named me once. It is right and proper that you should do so again."

"Well, then." Her father nodded. "That is that settled. I shall speak to Lowick with all haste."

The next few weeks passed swiftly, and Mr Darcy's health declined rapidly. The sickness which he had kept hidden for so long now ravaged his body without mercy, and at last he called his family to his bedside, along with the parish vicar, to say his farewells. The Wickhams, elder and younger, left the room as the family entered, with many soft condolences, and Mr Darcy saw his eldest daughter's gaze follow them.

"I wished to say goodbye to them, and to give them what comfort I can by way of fortune. I have left instructions with my solicitor, that young Mr Wickham should be appointed to the living currently filled by Dr Allen, and I hope that you will add your recommendation to mine, vicar." Dr Allen agreed that of course he would, and retreated to a respectful distance while the family crowded around the bed.

"Georgiana, my dear, don't cry for me. I go to my Father's house in Heaven, after all. Do you remember your lessons?"

"I do. But … but I wish you could stay in *our* house in Derbyshire!"

"As do I, little lamb, but it cannot be helped. Be strong for me, and be good to your mother and sister. Lavinia, you too must look after your family."

"I will, Father," she promised, "in any way I can." A look of understanding passed between them, and Mr Darcy nodded slightly in approval.

"Good girl. Thank you. Then leave me now, my daughters, and know that I love you."

"We love you, too!" Georgiana threw her arms around his neck and kissed him, weeping openly; Lavinia blinked back her own tears as she pressed a more gentle kiss to his cheek. Then she took her younger sister's hand and led her out, leaving her parents to exchange their own farewells with one another.

Not half an hour later, the vicar emerged, and, shortly afterwards, their mother.

"Lady Anne," Dr Allen began softly, "Miss Darcy, Miss Georgiana. Please allow me to offer my most sincere sympathies at this terrible time."

"Thank you, vicar," she responded with tightly-controlled grace, and the girls echoed her words through their tears. "You have done all you can here, and we will keep you no longer." The vicar nodded and took his leave, and Lady Anne swept through the nearest set of doors into a vacant bedchamber. Her daughters, waiting outside for somebody to tell them what they should do, pretended that they did not hear her cry of anguish and the broken sobs that followed. It came as a shock, to hear their usually composed mother falling apart, but not as a surprise. She had truly loved their father, after all.

Hours passed, and then days, days of trying to find their way around the gaps left by their father's absence. The ladies of the house sat vigil – relieved, on occasion, by old Mr Wickham or his son – and saw off the funeral procession, which was woefully bereft of relatives and consisted of only the Wickhams and some hired mourners when it first set off. Other gentlemen, those the late Mr Darcy had known from business, would meet the procession as it travelled, but Lavinia was assured that their late attendance stemmed from respect – her father kept his family separate from his working life, and they enjoyed the isolation of Pemberley with only the occasional appearance in town. Georgiana would not be introduced to society for some years yet, Lavinia had attended only three balls herself, and her father had kept his affection for his family strictly confined to his private time, just as he did not bother her mother with the details of his business. It was no wonder, really, that the men he had worked alongside did not feel they should intrude.

Weeks passed, and at last Lavinia felt she could approach Lady Anne to remind her of her father's dying wish – she only hoped that her mother had not changed her mind.

"Mother? I think it might be time Fitzwilliam came home."

"Oh, Lavinia … You are quite right, I agree. That is, if you are sure you wish to do this?"

"I promised Father that I would take care of Georgiana, and I meant it. I find I'm rather looking forward to the challenge, actually."

"Well, then, I think we had better arrange for you to visit your Aunt Mary. And see about bringing Fitzwilliam home."

"It is a pity that my brother did not receive news of Father's sickness until after his passing. And now, with my hitherto unsuspected desire to take my sacred vows, he stands to miss me, too. The poor man has no luck at all."

"Indeed." Her mother smiled fondly. "You always were talented in the polite falsehood. Who could have thought that it might have uses beyond telling Aunt Catherine her sense of fashion was exquisite?"

"While we are on the subject of telling people things … I hoped that you might be willing to help me break the news to Georgiana."

"Of course I will. I only hope she takes it well, for we will need her cooperation."

"She loves Pemberley. I'm sure she will keep our secret if it means that our family stays safely here."

Georgiana was slow to understand.

"But you are my sister – how can you become a brother?"

"It will all be an act, my dear, but a very important one. Nobody can ever know of the game," Lady Anne explained, "or we shall all be in a great deal of trouble. We are rather taking liberties with the law of the land, but not I think with the laws of God."

"*A good man leaves an inheritance to his children's children,*" Lavinia quoted softly, "so it says in Proverbs."

"*But the sinner's wealth is laid up for the righteous,*" Georgiana finished the verse, "and Father was a good man. I cannot believe that God would disagree."

"Quite so," their mother agreed, "though I suggest that we do not speak openly of any of this."

"And Father knew?" It was clear, by the troubled expression on her face, that this was of some concern to her.

"He knew." Lavinia patted her sister's hand in affectionate reassurance. "He helped us to bring it about, in fact."

"Tell me how it will work, again," Georgiana asked, brightening considerably, and when they had finished, she only said, "Our cousin is still living with his mother, is he not?"

"Rather, she lives with him, in legal terms – what little they have is all his. Still, Mary believes that Richard can be trusted with the secret, and I must trust her judgement. He has a great deal of respect for you, Lavinia, though he is four years your senior – and he doted upon you when he visited as a child. I believe he will help you more than Mary alone ever could."

Barely two months after her father's death, Lavinia Darcy stood in her mourning gown and bid farewell to her mother and sister.

"Be safe, Sister," Georgiana whispered as they embraced.

"God speed, Lavinia. I have every faith in you, no matter what you choose to do from here." Lady Anne spoke more loudly, knowing that old Mr Wickham – waiting to drive her the day's journey to her aunt's home – would hear it and think she referred to the religious ambitions Lavinia was supposed to be experiencing.

"Thank you, Mother. I put my trust in our Lord; he will guide my steps." At any rate, she hoped that her cousin Richard Fitzwilliam would help to guide her steps. The Lord would have to approve or disapprove as he might; Lavinia's concern was her family.

"Indeed. Travel safely."

There were those, no doubt, who would have questioned the propriety of Mr Wickham accompanying her on such lonely roads, with no chaperone, but he was a trusted friend of the family – a second father, almost, as far as Lavinia was concerned. It was comforting to have him with her, one last remnant of Pemberley, as she set off on this most important journey into the unknown. He left her at her aunt's door, as it opened, and turned the carriage straight around to spend the night at the nearest inn.

"If you change your mind about your visit, or … the church, well, you send somebody to call at the King's Arms tonight and I'll take you straight home."

"Thank you, Mr Wickham, but I'm sure I'll soon settle in." She followed the servant inside, and her aunt held out her arms in welcome.

"Lavinia! My, you've grown quite tall – it must have been too long since I last saw you at Pemberley. Come in, sit down, and make yourself comfortable. Richard should be home very shortly – it is almost time for dinner, after all, and he never misses a meal." Lavinia settled in the comfort of the drawing room, tried to steady her nerves, and listened gratefully to her aunt's easy flow of news from the village.

When Richard arrived home, they exchanged the usual pleasantries before he cleared his throat awkwardly.

"Now, Cousin, Mother tells me you have an interesting scheme in mind to keep Pemberley safely in your family's hands. If I can help in any way at all, I will – I have no wish to see you turned out of your home, especially in favour of a distant relative of your father's. But are you quite sure …" He lowered his voice with a glance towards window and door. "Are you quite sure that you can live as a man for the rest of your life?"

"I mean to try. For Georgiana, Richard, you know I would do anything."

"As would I. Your parents appointed me her guardian, in the event of their passing – an office I would, of course, share with you as her, er, brother. Well, then, we must move fast to make you a gentleman before your father's solicitor finds another heir."

"Father visited him before he died, to make the case for my brother's inheritance. I expect that he will declare me the heir, as long as he truly believes that I am a man. Please, teach me your ways, Richard – there is no man in the world I wish more to emulate."

"I am flattered – and of course I will teach you. First, however, there are logistical changes to be made. Come with me and we shall have a look at my wardrobe. Excuse us, Mother."

They spent a good few hours going through Richard's collection of garments.

"Never mind that one; that is my father's uniform, which I have kept in his memory. I hope you have no intention to turn soldier."

"None at all. Have you?"

"I intend to enlist very shortly, but not until I have seen you and Georgiana settled and safe. Now, these might fit you," he pulled out a pair of breeches, "but can you describe the circumstances in which you would wear them?"

At last, with a little of her cousin's rather embarrassed help with the outer garments, she stood in men's borrowed garments, looking down at herself rather dubiously.

"What do you think, Richard? Will I pass?"

"You look a little more feminine … in shape … than most gentlemen of my acquaintance. I … er, I don't know about such … is there something you could do about that?" She glanced down at the slight curve at the front of her shirt and sighed. Perhaps, with a few attempts, she could find some way of binding herself to a more masculine figure.

"I fear I cannot eliminate the problem entirely, but with all these layers … yes, I believe I can reduce the issue."

"Then I think you might actually stand a chance. Tie your hair back as gentlemen do, and let us see the effect."

A little later, Lavinia trailed her cousin down the stairs and back into the drawing room, where he made a polite little bow and nudged Lavinia to do the same. She mimicked the movement as closely as she could, and he nodded approvingly.

"Madam, may I present to you my cousin, La- oh, no. That won't do." He turned to Lavinia. "Do you know what you mean to be called?"

She took a deep breath and stepped forward, offering a hand to her aunt.

"Fitzwilliam Darcy, madam. It is an honour to make your acquaintance."

"Goodness," her aunt began, "I hardly recognised you. If you mean to see this through, however, we shall have to cut your hair to a more masculine style."

"I do mean to see it through. Do you really think it will work?"

"Perhaps some work on your voice," Richard suggested, "and we must work on your proper manners – ladies are quite different in that respect – but you'll do. And nobody could ever doubt your parentage: you have so much of your father in you."

"And so much of Anne, too," her aunt continued. "What does she think of your being named Fitzwilliam?"

"My parents named me, as is right. It was a most inspired idea of my mother's."

"Indeed it was, and it suits you. Now, we must sort you out with a full wardrobe, and you cannot have only Richard's cast-offs. It has been a while since I sewed for any purpose beside embroidery, but I was fascinated by the seamstress in my youth, and I remember what I learned from her. Richard can go into town with your measurements, and we can alter your clothing here at home. You shall have no valet, of course, but for a while that can be explained by your looking after yourself while you were travelling. Yes, I believe this might work – if you are truly committed to the plan. Please, Lavinia, tell me now if you have the slightest shadow of doubt."

"Not for a moment, if becoming a man will save my family from the loss of our home and our security."

"Then we must hope your mother carries her part well. Dress for dinner, now, as Lavinia, and we shall continue our work in the morning."

Weeks passed, Lavinia – no, *Fitzwilliam* – spending her mornings with Richard, learning to ride like a man, speak like a man, and behave like a man, then joining her aunt after lunch to alter the new wardrobe she was slowly accumulating, paid for out of her mother's private income. Finally, some seventeen days into her stay, her aunt and her cousin exchanged secret glances and nodded.

"Lavinia … are you ready to go off to the convent and return as Fitzwilliam?"

She took a deep breath and nodded. "I believe so. How are we to accomplish this?"

"Richard will take the carriage out into the countryside, then stop by to visit your mother before he returns. We will claim to have put you – the *old* you, Lavinia – onto a stagecoach to get you to the convent, though we will not specify where. Of course, it will be assumed that you have gone to Ireland, and perhaps that you have joined the Roman church, but –"

"I do not mind that; I need not worry about Lavinia Darcy's reputation any more, unless I am discovered – and then my faith will be the least of it."

"Well spoken," Richard said, "and now to Fitzwilliam."

"You will stay here for a few days, perhaps a week, and you will not be seen. My most trusted maid will cut your hair – she was long responsible for Richard's, and she is very trustworthy when it comes to both secrets and style. Then, towards the latter end of that week, Richard will go and buy a horse, making no secret of the fact that he means to meet his cousin from the port and escort him directly to Pemberley. Once he has returned here, you can set out together for home."

"No doubt you are missing your family," Richard told her, "since you have been overseas for so long. I am sorry you did not return sooner."

"As am I," Fitzwilliam Darcy intoned gravely, in his deep tones, "for now I learn I have lost a sister as well as a father."

The plan went as well as could be hoped, and it seemed as if no time had passed at all before Fitzwilliam Darcy was bowing to his aunt and preparing to mount his new horse.

"One last hug," Mary told him sternly, and bestowed that very gift upon him. "Good luck," she whispered, "my brave nie- nephew."

"Thank you for everything, Aunt Mary. I hope to see you soon at Pemberley." Then he swung himself into the saddle, shook out his reins, and set off at a trot beside his cousin. They continued at a sedate pace until they were quite out of sight of the house – then Richard turned to Fitzwilliam with a smile that meant mischief.

"Now, I think it's time you took advantage of some of your new freedoms. How do you feel about a race?" He spurred his horse and, after a moment's stunned hesitation, Fitzwilliam laughed as he followed.

They reined in at last, breathless and happy, with Richard a good horse's length ahead. Well, he had no doubt had a lot more practice than Fitzwilliam, who was still trying to process the sheer level of liberation he now felt.

"I must be honest," Richard admitted when he regained the power of audible speech, "that was not particularly respectable, but we are young men, and no man can begrudge us a little entertainment on the long road. We must be more sedate when we approach Pemberley, however: you are mourning."

"I am." He hung his head, suddenly ashamed. "I *am*. How could I laugh like that, with Father gone?"

"You must keep living, Fitzwilliam. It took me a long time to accept that, after my father died. But a little joy in a harmless ride, the wind rushing past you and the thunder of hooves below ... that is no crime, nor a sin."

"Well ... let us just hasten home, Richard. I would like to see my sister's smile again."

When they arrived at Pemberley, they left the horses – the grooms had been briefed, it seemed, for they muttered a welcome to 'young Mr Darcy', obviously reluctant to acknowledge any newcomer with the title formerly held by their late master – and strode straight into the house, Richard waving off the servants with a declaration that Mr Darcy wanted to see his family with all haste.

"I'll see him through, thank you – they are expecting us, and there is no need for you all to bear witness to what may be an emotional reunion for the ladies. I fear my aunt would be terribly embarrassed." This having had the desired effect, they found their way to the drawing room, where the ladies were waiting for them.

"Mother," Fitzwilliam began formally, but they were soon interrupted by Georgiana.

"Lavinia! You look so – I mean, er, you must be my brother, Fitzwilliam. I don't believe we've ever actually met." She corrected herself with the air of one who had rehearsed her speech for some time.

"I have not had the honour," Fitzwilliam told her gravely, "but we shall not be overheard here."

"You *sound* so –"

"Georgiana, you must remember –" Richard's protests were cut off by Lady Anne's quiet authority.

"No, no. Let her have her moment of surprise, so that she will not be tempted again. I must say, Lavinia, the transformation is quite extraordinary."

"Thank you, Mother. We have Aunt Mary and cousin Richard to thank for that. Did Father's solicitor say what he thought?"

"He was surprised, but he accepted that we found our son very hard to speak of when he was so far away, and that we preferred to keep our family out of the public eye as much as possible besides. He is withholding judgement until he can meet with you, but he has faith in my word."

"Then we shall see. I will not meet with him for a few days, at least, until we have all adjusted somewhat." He turned to his sister with a smile. "Georgiana, I see you shaking with the effort of holding back your questions. What would you like to ask?"

Many, many breathless questions later – "Who cut your hair? Does it tickle? How do you make your voice sound so deep? Is it very strange to be a man?" – Georgiana finally ran out of energy and settled for just throwing her arms around her new brother. Richard had dropped into a chair, speaking quietly to Lady Anne, and Fitzwilliam finally managed to manoeuvre Georgiana so that they could sit down together as well. Her mother turned to him with a cautious expression.

"Are you still very certain of your course, L- Fitzwilliam? It is not too late."

"I have never been more certain of anything, Mother. Besides, what brother would not do all this and more to keep his family safe at home?"

"I don't know that I could become a woman," Richard teased, "even for my mother's sake."

"Well, you would never have to," Fitzwilliam pointed out, "for a son is infinitely better placed to assist his family."

"That is true. Still, I doff my hat to you, Darcy. It's a bold venture."

"We must only hope that it pays off. The servants may recognise me before it goes any further."

The servants, however, did not recognise him – or if they did, they made no sign – and when the Wickhams came to pay their respects to the Darcys' newly-returned son, they showed no hint of suspicion either. Old Mr Wickham, however, sent his son home ahead of him, and stayed behind for a moment.

"Begging your pardon, Mr Darcy, but I just wanted to say what a terrible pity it is that you missed your sister, Lavinia. You have something much alike in your looks." The glint in his eye became more apparent. "Of course, nobody else on the estate was here all those years ago, when you were born. I remember it well. Such a shame that your cousin so badly needed a companion." Fitzwilliam recoiled – he had been discovered, and so easily – but Mr Wickham had not yet finished. "I will be sure to tell anyone who asks exactly that, Mr Darcy, but I do not think you need to worry yourself. My son has known you since childhood, and does not know you now. This is a very brave thing you are doing."

"So people keep telling me, but I do wonder if it is folly. Your support means a great deal, Mr Wickham."

"Well, your family's success means a great deal to me. In truth, I have worked long and hard at maintaining this estate, and I would be very sorry to see it go to a stranger instead of the family who so richly deserve it. I am sure your father would have wanted the same thing, if you will pardon my presumption."

"No pardon needed, for indeed he did. Thank you – you have set my mind at rest."

Wickham, true to his word, even drove Fitzwilliam and his mother to the solicitor's office later that week, and cheerfully addressed them each by name in a loud, strong voice as he assured them that he would wait for them for as long as he was wanted. Fitzwilliam glanced back over his shoulder as they reached the door, and saw that curious passers-by were already congregating around him, no doubt keen to get all the gossip while it was still fresh.

"I fear I may have created a scandal, Mother," he told her quietly, and she laughed.

"Oh, my dear Fitzwilliam. Perhaps in France or Spain, that would constitute a scandal, but here in Derbyshire it is nothing but a little curiosity making itself known. They will see you in church on Sunday, and then they will have something different to talk about by the Friday."

"Very true," the solicitor told them, arriving from a back room to greet them. "Lady Anne, a pleasure as always."

"Thank you, Mr Lowick. May I introduce my son, Fitzwilliam Darcy?"

"You may indeed. Mr Darcy, I am sorry for your loss."

"I am sorrier still, to have come too late," Fitzwilliam responded with a sigh. "By the time I heard that my father was in danger ..."

"It can be so difficult to receive one's letters in a timely fashion when one is abroad, and travelling," Lowick sympathised, "and your father was young. There was no reason for you to suspect ..."

"All the same, I feel a certain measure of guilt," he said, truthfully – though the guilt was not due to any absence, but rather the deception he was now undertaking.

"You have nothing to feel guilty about," Lady Anne told him firmly, perhaps sensing his true meaning, "and a lot of responsibility to take on, if Mr Lowick is satisfied that you are the heir."

Lowick looked at him shrewdly for a moment, and Fitzwilliam was sure that he would be exposed for the fraud he was.

"You have the look of your father," Lowick concluded after a moment, "nobody could doubt you were his son, if they were to see you stood before them. Please, come through, sit down, and we can begin to set this process into motion."

"I must say, I am glad to find that the search for your father's heir is over," Lowick commented as he walked them to the door, their business concluded for the time being. "So many records were lost in the flood, including the baptism records of your eldest children and no doubt a great many distant cousins. Had I known of Mr Fitzwilliam Darcy …"

"You understand, of course, that my late husband did not wish to complicate matters unduly," Lady Anne pointed out. "Our son had long been far from Derbyshire, and we could not be sure that he would return."

"Of course I would," Fitzwilliam told her softly, "I never meant to be so long away, but the years ran away from me."

"Of course, I quite understand, Lady Anne. I only meant to say that I am glad that he did tell me in the end, and that the issue has been resolved in a satisfactory manner. Leave this matter with me, and I shall have everything put into place very shortly." They made their farewells and left the office to find Mr Wickham valiantly fielding questions from onlookers, who retreated to a safe distance at the sight of Lady Anne and her son, then watched intently as they drove away.

"Well, you'll be popular at church, I think, Mr Darcy." Wickham was as cheerful as ever.

"I fear I will," he replied anxiously, "I fear I will."

Dr Allen fought a losing battle, that Sunday, to hold anyone's attention on the sermon. Fitzwilliam kept his eyes fixed on a point straight ahead of him, trying to focus on the words the vicar was saying rather than the whispers and stares of those around him. *Could they see through him? Did they still see Lavinia Darcy, sitting bolt upright beside her mother and sister in the Darcy family pew?* He had to wait until after the service to find out if anyone would speak out to expose him, and every moment was agony, until at last the congregation began to file out and gather outside the church for a little friendly conversation. The Darcy family hung back – Lady Anne was still besieged by well-wishers and sympathetic comments every time she left the house, though it was only to attend church, and it was beginning to wear a little thin – until they were the last to leave.

"Dr Allen, I don't believe you've met my son. He is a little older than my elder daughter, and you were not yet in this parish when they were baptised."

"I haven't had the honour, Lady Anne. Mr Darcy, it is a pleasure, though I'm sorry we could not have met in happier circumstances. Such a shame you were unable to reach home before your father's passing."

"I regret that very deeply, Dr Allen." Then they were stepping out into the sunshine, only to be swarmed by their fellow parishioners.

"Mr Darcy! So wonderful to have you back in Derbyshire."

"Welcome back, Mr Darcy."

"You don't remember me, do you?"

Fitzwilliam was a little startled by the question, until he realised it came from one of the more elderly ladies of the village, who was known to be a little vague. Still, if she claimed to remember him … "I'm afraid I do not, madam."

"Oh, not to worry, you were only a babe in arms at the time –"

"You know, I think *I* remember you, come to think of it – though of course I was just a slip of a girl myself back then." That was Mrs Dunn, who was forty-eight if she was a day and had already been married by the time Fitzwilliam would have been born.

"I apologise for being unable to return the favour." This curt reply was all he could offer, nerves overcoming him as he bowed stiffly and turned away, striding through the churchyard before he could be accosted by anybody else. The ladies made their excuses and followed, until at last they were all safely ensconced in the peace of the carriage.

Fitzwilliam had never felt more relieved – or more anxious – than he did on the day he received the news that Pemberley was legally his. Georgiana squealed and grabbed his hands, forcing him to dance awkwardly in a circle with her, and his mother smiled the warmest, most genuine smile he had seen on her face since his father had died.

"Thank you, Fitzwilliam. And well done."

"You're very welcome, Mother. And, of course, let it be said aloud that Georgiana and yourself may always call Pemberley home."

"Even when I'm married?" Georgiana asked curiously, and Fitzwilliam looked down into those wide, innocent eyes with a sort of cold dread for the future. Yes, Georgiana would marry and leave him one day, and the man she accepted had better hope that he was worthy of her, or he would have Fitzwilliam to answer to.

"Even when you're married, Georgiana. You and yours will always be welcome here."

"Very good. Georgiana, let go of your brother before you entirely crush the wind out of him." Lady Anne laughed to herself, a soft, surprised sound.

"Your brother – it comes so naturally. You play the part so well, Fitzwilliam, and are so unlike your former self that even I often forget who you are."

"I shall endeavour to take that as a compliment, Mother …"

"Do! For so it was meant."

Months passed, and young George Wickham began to pay the same sort of attentions to the new master of Pemberley that he had to the former Mr Darcy, who had been his godfather and had quite doted on him. The new Mr Darcy, however, preferred to keep him at arm's length, not only because he might recognise his former friend with prolonged exposure, but also because their friendship had become strange and stilted long before his father's death. George had become different, as he grew older – sullen and resentful when he thought nobody was looking, and all flattery when Lavinia *was*. Fitzwilliam refused to fall prey to his charms. He much preferred the company of the older Mr Wickham, who was a sincere and friendly sort, and kept the estate blooming, to boot. He seemed quite happy to teach Fitzwilliam the basics of running the house and estate, along with the various other investments he had inherited. They took to spending long hours poring over documents and figures together, until Fitzwilliam was quite certain of his business.

Perhaps that was why it was such a shock when, with no warning at all, Mr Wickham died. One day he was there, laughing and joking and showing Fitzwilliam the inner workings of the home he had enjoyed without effort for so long – the next he was lying, still and pale, in a coffin in the sitting room that now belonged to George. As a mark of the great respect they had for their late steward, Lady Anne, Georgiana, and even Fitzwilliam himself offered to take turns in sitting vigil with the body, and George accepted with good grace. That was how Fitzwilliam found himself, aged four-and-twenty, walking with his first ever funeral procession, and standing with the small cluster of men at an interment. When he returned, pale and shaken, he accompanied George to his home for a much-needed drink, then retired to Pemberley after dark to rest.

Early the following afternoon, George arrived to speak to Fitzwilliam, and Fitzwilliam agreed to see him.

"Your father promised me Dr Allen's living, before he died."

"I am aware of it; however, Dr Allen is still very much alive and continues to occupy the parsonage."

"I had noticed. However, with my father's death ... I have no further wish to enter the church, and haven't for some time. I intend, instead, to study law, but to do so I will require funding. I believe your father would have considered it right to pay my way to a good start in the legal profession, as a means of discharging his promise under these circumstances."

"Indeed?" Fitzwilliam considered it for a moment. "This must be on the understanding that if I give you your inheritance by way of fortune now, you forfeit all claim to the living currently possessed by Dr Allen. Do you agree?"

"Of course. I shall ask nothing more of you for the rest of my life."

"Very well, then you shall have what you need."

He picked up his pen, intending to write instructions to that effect, but paused when he realised George had not left. "Was there something else?"

"Your sister. Lavinia."

Fitzwilliam drew in a breath sharply, then turned it into a cough. "Yes?"

"It must be terribly embarrassing, to have her shut herself away with Irish nuns. Ghastly. No doubt you would like to see her home."

"On the contrary: Lavinia must do as she feels is right. Though, of course, I am sorry to have missed my chance of seeing her again."

"Well, exactly! You must take her in hand, bring her home – quash all this religious nonsense by seeing her swiftly married."

"Religious nonsense?" Fitzwilliam raised an eyebrow. "Strong words, for a man who until recently wanted nothing more than to be ordained in the church himself."

"Yes, as a *vicar* – I never had any intention of becoming a *monk*," George countered. "There is something quite unnatural about that way of life, in my opinion – quite wrong for Lavinia. And you could be sure that your sister would be well cared for – would never have to leave you for a distant home – if you married her to somebody she knows, somebody local –"

"Somebody like you, I suppose?" If Fitzwilliam had ever been amused by this conversation, he certainly was not now – and George was not yet finished.

"Well, since you mention it ... I didn't like to mention it before, given that the household was so very recently bereaved, but Lavinia and I had formed rather an attachment before she left. It was the grief of your father's passing that drove her to the church, away from me, and I am sure that she is even now waiting for some summons that may bring her home –"

"You presume too far, Wickham. Take your money, pursue your career in the law, and leave my sister to follow her own conscience." He was all formality now, stomach turned by Wickham's lies.

"But –"

"And, when you speak of her, you will refer to her as *Miss Darcy*. Am I understood?"

Wickham gaped at him for a moment, then recovered his composure and nodded. "Forgive me. It must have been my own grief speaking."

"Indeed. Perhaps some rest and quiet will serve you best."

Thankfully, the man took the dismissal for what it was and left him in peace.

That evening, Fitzwilliam lay in bed and stared disconsolately up at the ceiling. He might not have been particularly fond of George Wickham during recent years, but he had certainly never imagined that Wickham would try to manipulate his old friend into marriage in such a way. Fitzwilliam had not even thought that he felt that way about Lavinia … He spoke to his mother about it the next morning, and she sighed.

"Young Mr Wickham seems to have nothing but his own fortune on his mind of late – you mustn't take it personally, or you shall never get on in life."

"He has just lost his father – perhaps he is simply lonely," Georgiana countered, but Fitzwilliam privately felt that his mother had the true measure of Wickham. He was very pleased when the man left for town to study his precious law.

As time passed, Fitzwilliam began to relax into his new life. At first, people were very curious about him whenever he left his own house, but he soon found that being as curt as he could without being impolite – and being a little *more* curt if pressed – caused people to stop asking questions and go away. The going away was something of an unfortunate side effect at first – he had always been interested in talking to people. At length, however, he began to find the solitude comforting; he did not need to choose every word so carefully when he was among the few people who knew who he was. As for being a gentleman, once he had adapted to the new ways of behaving and adjusted to his new freedoms and responsibilities, he was finding that it suited him better than being a young lady ever had. Richard visited quite frequently – he was Georgiana's co-guardian, after all, Lady Anne notwithstanding – and he brought his mother with him whenever he could pull her away from her good works, expanding the Pemberley social circle a little more.

Fitzwilliam walked into the stables one day at precisely the wrong moment, just as one of the footmen was taking rather a physical interest in one of the grooms. The poor men thought they were fired for certain, and no doubt feared still worse fates, but their employer laughed and offered to promote the footman immediately.

"I am in need of a valet who can be discreet," he confided, "and who has no interest in the temptations of the female body. I hope that you will fit my requirements perfectly."

Sure enough, a promise of secrecy was soon obtained, the secret shared with one more person – and then, unexpectedly, with another, as the new valet's sister became Fitzwilliam's personal laundress, able to deal discreetly with the more feminine aspects of the task. The risk of discovery reduced, and the humiliation of washing his own underclothes secretly in the dead of night removed entirely, Fitzwilliam began to feel as though he could breathe for the first time in months.

With Wickham gone, a new steward was engaged, and though it felt very strange to see him taking over old Mr Wickham's duties, Fitzwilliam soon found that they could work very well together. He was quite equal to the task of managing the estate with his new employee's help, and as time went on he began to risk attending more social functions, though without encouraging close friendships. He felt he was keeping people at a comfortable arm's distance rather well, until he realised that one of the young gentlemen of his acquaintance did not seem to be taking the hint.

"Mr Darcy, I was wondering if you might like to visit the country house I currently hold and give me your opinion on its suitability for permanent residence. I should be very much obliged to you, and there is plenty of opportunity for sport on the grounds."

"*My* opinion? Why on earth should you want *my* opinion?"

"Well, I respect your taste and judgement, and your home is well known for being the very best in the country. My sister, especially, often speaks of how she hopes I will choose a home as grand as Pemberley, though she has never had the pleasure of seeing the place for herself. I would value your opinion almost as much as I would your friendship."

Fitzwilliam narrowed his eyes at him, but he seemed sincere – all smiles and charm.

"Truly? Then I hardly feel I can refuse."

The visit went off without mishap – Charles Bingley proved himself to be most amiable, and very forgiving of Fitzwilliam's emotional distance, and his sisters Louisa and Caroline were very kind to him also. Caroline, in particular, was attentive to the point of intrusion, and he had to be rather on his guard around her – but even that was easier with his own little travelling household in attendance. In fact, Fitzwilliam took to spending a lot of time with Charles and his family; none of them seemed to suspect anything, and it was wonderful to have some friends around his own age to consort with for once. Charles always had a room for him at his London town house, and they often travelled together in search of a house Charles could truly call his own. None of the houses he rented were quite what Charles ought to have, however – Fitzwilliam or Caroline always raised an objection of some sort to sway Charles's opinion, and he always listened – so they continued to move around during the sporting season.

Being friends with Charles Bingley, a ludicrously personable man who made friends as easily as smiling, also meant that Fitzwilliam began to be included in invitations from the wealthy and titled, just as he had been before he earned his reputation for being unnervingly curt. The only thing he would not do was dance, with the exception of obliging his companions now and again. His father had never danced, he was certain of it, and the Darcy family had a reputation to uphold. And, if his father had owed some of his reticence at even private balls to an ankle weakened by a riding accident, well, Fitzwilliam had an excuse, too. The last thing he needed was for some nice young lady to become attracted to him.

For a couple of years, things went well, until Lady Anne quietly succumbed to the last throes of the severe measles epidemic that had swept the country. Fitzwilliam had visited her only a few months earlier, and she had seemed to be in good health, fully enjoying the society of London for the first time since his father had died. As if from nowhere, he was summoned to say goodbye, but by the time he arrived there was nothing left to do but take her body back to Pemberley, to rest beside her husband in the parish churchyard as she would have wanted.

Georgiana was distraught, spending hours at the piano playing all her mother's favourite songs over and over again, and Fitzwilliam sat silently beside her and waited until she flung herself into his arms and sobbed.

"She's gone, Lavinia! She's gone."

He did not even correct her; he just sat with her, stroking her hair by way of comfort and hoping she would not notice the tears rolling down his own cheeks. He was not sure, even now, if a gentleman was supposed to cry at times such as these.

Several weeks passed before he felt equal to leaving Pemberley, and he promised Georgiana that he would visit more frequently. Further, he would be sure to arrange some sort of expedition for her, away from Derbyshire. She was a young woman now, and ought to see something of the world. Perhaps in a year or so, he would make arrangements. For now, her co-guardian, their cousin Richard, would keep a close eye on her whenever he came home on leave from his adventures with the army.

Four years after his father died, Fitzwilliam found himself telling a rather optimistic George Wickham that he certainly could not have any more money – nor could he have Dr Allen's former living, which was now in the hands of another capable young vicar. Wickham resisted this decision, but was eventually forced to return to town empty-handed, which was the literal state of affairs as far as Fitzwilliam could make out. He could not fathom how Wickham had burned through his money so fast, but it seemed he had. No matter. It was none of his concern.

Fitzwilliam was more concerned, in fact, with his young sister, recently turned fifteen and living with a governess in London. Her last few letters had seemed to suggest something amiss. He could not quite pinpoint the reason – was it her tone, or the way she leapt from subject to subject, or a certain hint of anxious deliberation in the formation of her familiar cursive?

– but he felt a sudden need to check up on his sister, and soon. They were returning to town, he and the remaining Bingleys, after celebrating Louisa's marriage to a singularly unremarkable man by the name of Hurst. Georgiana's governess, Mrs Younge, had taken her down to Ramsgate to enjoy some healthy sea air, and Fitzwilliam rather thought it would be fun to surprise her before rejoining his party in London.

He arrived without warning, and was fortunate enough to find Georgiana all but alone in the house. When he was shown into the drawing room, he found her staring out of the window at the sea, a pensive expression clouding her features.

"Georgiana, are you well?"

"Fitzwilliam!" She almost fell over in her haste to greet him, but even the way she embraced him seemed awkward, somehow. Distant.

"I came to surprise you," he confessed, "but I fear I may have alarmed you instead."

"Oh, no, it's lovely to see you – it's just that I didn't think I would – oh, now I don't know what to do."

"Well, why don't you start by telling me all your news?"

"That's just it – I wanted to tell you, truly, but dear George insisted –"

"George?" Now Fitzwilliam was worried. "Who is George?"

"George Wickham, of course. He said I mustn't tell you, but I wanted to, and now here you are. So I must, mustn't I?"

"I don't think George Wickham should be forbidding you to tell me anything, and so I'm afraid you must."

"Oh – well, that's best, isn't it? Then you can come to the wedding, and you ought to be there."

An icy dread settled in Fitzwilliam's stomach. "Wedding? Whose wedding do you mean?"

"Why, mine, of course. George and I are going to elope."

By the time Fitzwilliam had finished with him, George Wickham was a cowering wreck of a man, helpless in the face of his fury. Wickham had said terrible things – about Fitzwilliam, about Georgiana, about how all the world was to blame but himself – and then he had surrendered under the weight of Fitzwilliam's verbal onslaught. Mrs Younge, who had tried to make a case in Wickham's defence, and who had apparently helped to orchestrate the whole sorry affair, was dismissed with no hope of a favourable reference. And Georgiana, his sweet little sister, was sitting silently beside him in a carriage on the way home to Pemberley, tears rolling down her cheeks as she refused even to look at him.

"Georgiana," he began, "it's for –"

"He – the things he said – I thought he loved me."

"George Wickham doesn't know how to love, Georgiana. I wouldn't give him money, so he came for your thirty thousand. I'm sure spiting me was part of the bargain."

"I'm so foolish – I should have known he wouldn't –"

"Georgiana Darcy, that man was not worthy of your time, and never could be."

"I didn't tell him," she started abruptly, "about you. And however … even though I'm angry with you, for stopping me from marrying m- Wickham … I wouldn't tell anyone. You do know that, don't you?"

"I do," Fitzwilliam said, though he had had his fears until that very moment, "and I'm very grateful. Tell me, how do you feel about some company when we arrive at Pemberley? It would do you good to have the society of friends until I can engage a new governess to take care of you in London."

"Not Ramsgate?" He shook his head. "Good. I can hardly stand to think of the place. We had such dreams, Fitzwilliam, and now – tell me, am I ruined?"

"No. No, I think not. Let me introduce you to my friends. They may be able to impart some wisdom, even – dare I say it – Caroline."

"Then invite them to stay, with all haste, please. I feel sorely in need of wisdom just now."

They travelled in silence after that, until at last they passed through the gates of Pemberley.

"I'll always look after you, Georgiana. Whether you're wise or not."

"Thank goodness I have my big brother to protect me." She rested her head on his shoulder as the carriage rumbled up the driveway. "I don't know what I'd do without you."

"Well, I don't think there can ever be another woman in my life, so I'm afraid you have my undivided attention."

"As it should be," she told him with a tired smile. He opened the carriage door for her and helped her out. "But I think I can share you with your friends."

Fitzwilliam was glad to hear it. It was time for Charles and Caroline to visit Pemberley.

Furthermore, Fitzwilliam decided – and, to his astonishment, Georgiana agreed – that it was best for everyone if the Bingleys became both Darcys' primary connection with society, at least for a while. Georgiana would have a new governess, of course, back in London where he could supervise more closely – and their cousin Richard would continue to watch over her on her stays in Derbyshire – but besides her existing female friends in London, Georgiana was going to have to live a more lonely lifestyle, and therefore so was Fitzwilliam. He could hardly condemn her to isolation and continue to go off on hunting trips to far-flung estates: that was not fair at all. But for now, while she came to terms with what had happened between her and Wickham, it might be best to keep her away from the world. He could not trust the gentlemen of England with his precious, innocent little sister, not until they learned some manners. He would not have her heart broken again, and neither of them had any stomach for her marriage after what had just transpired.

Yes, it was time for the Darcy siblings to try for a somewhat quieter life, brother and sister standing together against a cold, uncaring world until it lost interest in their private trials and deepest secrets.

Author's Notes

I'd just like to make it clear that while I consider this particular version of Fitzwilliam Darcy to be transgender, being transgender does not in any way mean pretending to be the gender you identify with. Rather, in this case, adopting the persona and living as a man was the catalyst allowing Fitzwilliam to discover and embrace his true gender identity. I apologise if the way he reached this conclusion offends anyone – but I'd also like to add that there was probably a reason this particular plan sprung to the eldest Darcy's mind in the first place!

Eleanor Musgrove

Eleanor Musgrove is a graduate of the University of Kent, and a one-woman word machine at least one month out of the year. She is currently working towards publishing her first novel, and has many more tales to tell.

eamusgrove.wordpress.com

A Particular Friend

JL Merrow

It was undoubtedly a fault, Mary reflected, to have retained at the staid old age of nine-and-twenty that playfulness, that lack of regard for consequences, which men found so captivating in a girl of nineteen. And yet, she could not help herself, nor indeed would she, if she could. Let others wait for old age to excuse their eccentricities; she would have what fun she might while still young enough to enjoy it.

And was it so *very* bad a sin, merely to introduce oneself to a young lady whose handsome face and tall figure had caught one's eye across the pump-room?

By no means, were it not that Mary needed no introduction to tell her this young lady's name – and was, moreover, quite aware that the young lady's family would not wish for the acquaintance. Mary felt her spirits lift with the prospect of mischief as she crossed the room with unhurried tread.

"Excuse me," she said, directing her most charming smile at her fair quarry, who was presently engaged in fetching a glass of water. "But are you not Miss Susan Price, of Mansfield Park?"

Miss Price smiled back, an uncertain smile, but not a hesitant one. "I am indeed. But forgive me …"

"Ah! No forgiveness is needed, I assure you. And how are you enjoying the waters?" Mary asked, inclining her head in the direction of the glass held by Miss Price. Amusement bubbled within her, but it would not do to let it show. "Or as I should rather say, how are you enjoying Bath? For I am quite sure nobody enjoys the waters."

"I like Bath very well, thank you, and although I dare say you are correct about the waters, this glass is for my aunt." Miss Price's eyes showed her confusion, but she forged bravely on, Mary was delighted to see. "You are acquainted with my aunt, Lady Bertram?"

"Oh, yes, indeed. At least, I was formerly so. I regret to say we have not been greatly in contact, these past ten years. Tell me, how does your sister, Mrs Bertram?"

"Fanny? Oh, Fanny is very well." A flush of colour suffused Miss Price's cheek as she spoke with enthusiasm of her sister. "She is lately delivered of their second child, a fine, healthy boy. They have named him William, after his uncle."

It was not often Mary surprised herself, but to her astonishment she found her pleasure at this news entirely untainted by jealousy. "I am so pleased to hear that. You will perhaps not know this, but at one time dear Fanny and I were quite intimate. I wonder if she still wears the gold chain I gave her?"

Miss Price took a breath, and appeared to straighten her back, although indeed her posture needed no correction. "Perhaps you would be so good as to tell me your name, so that when I write, I may remember you to her?"

"Oh, have I neglected to mention it? How very careless of me. But of course. I am Mrs Lynd – now widowed, alas. But formerly I was Mary Crawford, of Mansfield Parsonage."

Miss Susan Price, it seemed, was made of sterner stuff than her elder sister. Her jaw did not drop; she did not swoon; her eyes widened but a fraction and her gasp was barely audible.

Nonetheless, as Mary inclined her head and glided away, she found herself entirely pleased with the consternation she had caused.

Susan's feelings, as she returned to her aunt, were such that she strove in vain to entirely repress them. So *that* was the scandalous Mary Crawford – sister to the yet more scandalous Henry, who had seduced her married cousin Maria into an elopement, all while professing his love for her sister Fanny?

It had not, of course, been easy for Susan, who had then been barely more than a child, to discover the true facts of the matter. Fanny had been most adamant that maids should not be encouraged to gossip – and naturally, within the family, the dreadful story was not to be alluded to in even the most oblique way. Maria's name was never mentioned at Mansfield Park; to speak of the author of her disgrace would be unthinkable. Susan had, at last, to seek a tête-à-tête with her sister and *demand* to know the truth, lest she embarrass herself or cause unwitting pain to her uncle and aunt.

Fanny had relented, at last, and had told all. Susan had been unable to repress a shudder at her sister's narrow escape from marriage to a man capable of such monstrous behaviour – for she had asked, had been unable to keep herself from asking, *what if* the elopement had not taken place, and cousin Edmund had married Miss Crawford? Would not Fanny, then, have succumbed to the pressure from her family, and the importuning of the man himself, and married Mr Crawford? To which Fanny had only, and with visible reluctance, replied that she did not know.

Yet, while the behaviour of Mr Crawford was clearly reprehensible – indeed, Susan could only wonder that Fanny had, so soon afterwards, found it in her to accept an offer from her cousin Edmund – Susan had always found it harder to understand Fanny's censure of his sister. All Susan could discover was that she had been slow to condemn his actions as evil. But was it not her duty to love and defend her brother? Susan could not conceive of any action by her own brother William that might cause her to abjure him – although in fairness, neither could she imagine him ever testing her love very severely.

Nevertheless, Susan could not be sorry for whatever had caused Edmund to break with the then Miss Crawford. Whether she understood the matter aright or no, clearly Edmund made Fanny happy, for which Susan could only rejoice.

Although now, having met the lady in question, she marvelled all the more – for even after all these years, Mrs Lynd was excessively pretty …

Susan was recalled to her present surroundings by her aunt's voice. "Susan? My dear, are you quite well? I have been speaking to you these last five minutes, although I forget now, of what. Would you be so kind as to fetch my wrap?"

"Of course, Aunt Bertram," Susan replied. "I am so sorry to have neglected you."

She went to fetch her aunt's wrap without delay. Poor aunt Bertram, her health had sadly declined in recent years. Susan had heard it blamed upon the trials her children had brought – Maria's disgrace, Julia's imprudent marriage, and Tom's broken health and consequent failure to marry – but Susan herself felt rather that the cause must be physical. Certainly, her aunt's disposition was placid enough to weather any emotional storm to which Susan had yet seen it subjected. Her delight in her grandchildren seemed genuine, and her regret at being unequal to long periods in the tumult of their company, sincere.

As she returned, Susan caught sight of Mrs Lynd once more, now talking animatedly with a tall gentleman who stooped low to catch his fair companion's *bon mots*. Their laughter carried even above the general chatter, and rang out carefree and light.

For a foolish moment, Susan yearned to be a part of that conversation, to have those arch smiles, that musical laughter, directed at *her* – then she shook her head firmly, and carried on her way to tend to her aunt's needs.

"Mrs Lynd?"

Mary turned from her languid appreciation of the dancers, and was astonished to find herself addressed by none other than Miss Susan Price. Not, of course, that she allowed her countenance to display anything other than the unabashed pleasure she truly felt. "Miss Price. How delightful to see you again. How do you do?"

"Very well, thank you." Miss Price hesitated, and glanced around. "You are not with your tall friend this evening?"

Mary cocked her head, which she had been told she did rather prettily. "My tall friend? I'm afraid I don't know whom you mean. In fact, I should think that in all Bath, *you* are the only person who might be described thus."

"Oh –" Miss Price took a deep breath. "I meant the gentleman you were conversing with the last time we met."

"Was I? I'm afraid I can tell you nothing of him. I make it quite a rule these days never to remember gentlemen." Mary allowed herself a wicked smile, and was rewarded with a heightening of her companion's colour. Then she relented, and continued with commonplace politeness: "Are you here with your aunt Bertram?"

It seemed unlikely, for this was the Assembly Rooms, and the crush within was entirely unsuitable for an invalid. However, not more so than for an unchaperoned young lady.

Miss Price appeared quite aware of this, for there was a sardonic tilt to her eyebrow as she answered. "My aunt, as you may recall, does not care for the heat and the noise of such places even when in the best of health. However, she has been kind enough to insist that I should enjoy an evening's entertainment. I am here with the Slocombes, a family of her acquaintance." She paused. "Do you wish me to introduce you to them?"

As it was evident that Miss Price did *not* wish this, Mary declined. "Thank you, but I must return to my sister, Mrs Grant. Formerly of

Mansfield Parsonage," she added in a spirit of mischief.

"Oh – is Mrs Grant well? My sister has spoken of her." Miss Price seemed embarrassed.

"She is not, I am afraid, but she still loves to attend these evenings." Mary could not but concur with her sister's oft-expressed sentiment on the matter: *"If ever I become too ill to enjoy myself, Mary dear, you may as well shuffle me off this mortal coil and have done with it."* She fixed Miss Price with a quizzical eye. "If you are not averse, I believe she would be glad to meet you."

The crush within the Upper Room was, indeed, unsuitable for someone in Louisa's state of health, but Mary had found her a comfortable seat away from draughts, where she might sit and watch the goings-on, or chat to the similarly infirm and aged – for Louisa would not countenance that Mary remain by her side all night. The heat, at least, was nothing to her; she had remarked only the previous evening that she never felt truly warm these days. Mary could not help a sigh, in private; it seemed she was destined soon to be deprived once more of one whose company she valued greatly.

But to counterfeit a smile as she approached her ailing sister was no great task for Mary. "Louisa, dearest, can you guess who this young lady is?"

Louisa brightened, animation easing the lines that pain had marked cruelly upon a once-beautiful face. "I confess I cannot, although there is something familiar about her."

"This, my dear, is Miss Susan Price, of Mansfield Park. Miss Price, my sister, Mrs Grant."

"Miss Price! Well now, Mary, you have astonished me. It's a good long while since I last heard that name mentioned. How do you do, Miss Price, and how is your dear elder sister? Still well, I trust? You must excuse me from rising, I fear."

"Please do not trouble yourself. My sister is quite well, thank you." Miss Price's eyes, Mary was touched to see, were filled with compassion for Louisa's sad state.

"And how does she like living in the Parsonage?" Louisa continued. "I trust she finds it comfortable. Tell me, does the apricot still thrive?"

Poor Miss Price looked quite confused, and as if she wondered whether Louisa's illness had affected her brain.

"Louisa, dear, you must not tease her so. The apricot," Mary explained, turning to Miss Price, "is something of a family joke. It was planted by my sister's predecessor in the parsonage, your aunt Norris, and was I believe rather in the nature of a favourite child. Pray, is your aunt Norris still hale?"

"I … That is to say, I believe so. She resides with my cousin Maria."

That, Mary had not been aware of. Poor Maria. "Ah. Perhaps we should not speak of such things."

"Should we not?" Miss Price returned with a fearlessness that delighted Mary. "For it seems to me that we all know of them, and I do not believe there are any here who would be injured by their discussion. That is," she added hastily, with a guilty look at Mary, "if you do not object, Mrs Lynd?"

"By no means. Shall we sit down?"

They sat, and chatted. Miss Price enquired after their brother, whom they owned to be now living in respectably married misery with a wife who saw his faults only too clearly and delighted in sharing them with him, and four children. A lucky query from Louisa induced Miss Price to speak of her own brother, William. Mary found the greatest pleasure in watching the animation of her face as she spoke with touching enthusiasm of his glowing naval career.

As someone who had once found Fanny Price *almost* enchanting, Mary was amazed how much more she liked her younger sister, who was so very unlike her. Mary was about to suggest some joint excursion, preferably for the very next fine day, when her sister interrupted her.

"I think your friends are seeking you, Miss Price, and we must give up your company for now. Perhaps I might invite you to call upon us one morning, however?"

Mary glanced around, and indeed, a young lady, newly out if Mary was any judge, was making for them with an air of mixed determination and anxiety. Arrangements were made, therefore, for Miss Price to call upon them at her leisure, and they relinquished her company with good nature on Louisa's part and, Mary was quite aware, *bad* nature on hers.

"She has something of the air of her sister about her, does she not?" Louisa said when their young companion had departed. "Although she is far less timid. I believe you like her, Mary dear."

Mary smiled. "I believe I do."

"Ah, but does she like you too?"

"Why, Louisa dearest, I believe she does." Mary flicked open her fan, yet its shade was insufficient to conceal her laughter.

Louisa laughed too, but then her expression took a sombre cast. "And do you not worry that her aunt may discover you? For I cannot think she would welcome a renewal of the connection between our families. All the more," she added severely, "should she ever suspect its true nature."

"Remember, dear sister," Mary said with determined lightness, "I know Lady Bertram of old. She has not the liveliness of imagination to discover us."

"Really? I seem to recall you being much mistaken in regard to a son of hers, once upon a time."

"That was many years ago," Mary said, fanning herself. Really, these rooms were deplorably hot. "Indeed, I do not recall it at all, and neither should you."

Susan's visit to Mrs Lynd and Mrs Grant the following morning was not made without some trepidation. If truth were told, she had been less than honest with her aunt Bertram as to the identity of her new acquaintances, describing them merely as a Mrs Lynd and her ailing sister. Yet how could she have told the whole truth without injuring her aunt's peace of mind? Without raking up old sorrows to no present effect? Moreover, what evil could there be in a visit to two highly respectable widowed ladies?

Fanny's voice in her head threatened to read her chapter and verse upon the matter. Fortunately, however, having grown up in a tumultuous house, Susan was quite equal to the task of ignoring a sister, particularly one with so soft a voice as Fanny.

She knocked upon the door of a genteel residence in a quiet, well-kept street, and was shown into the drawing room, where Mrs Lynd was presently writing letters.

Mrs Lynd jumped up from her chair with a flattering appearance of eagerness to greet her guest. "My dear Miss Price, you have saved me."

"I have?" was all Susan could think of to reply, distracted by the liveliness in her hostess's manner.

"Why, certainly. I was engaged in writing a very dull letter."

Susan gave her a direct look. "I find that hard to believe of you."

"Oh, but I was. To my late husband's widowed sister, who is an exceedingly dull woman who can stand to hear only of exceedingly dull things. I almost fear I must dose myself with laudanum before I commence writing, so that I may achieve the necessary torpor. Now, I have shocked you, have I not?"

"A little," Susan said with a sardonic tone that appeared to delight Mrs Lynd. "Is Mrs Grant in good health today?"

Mrs Lynd sighed. "My poor Louisa is rarely well enough to receive visitors the day after an evening excursion, I am afraid, so you shall have to be satisfied with my company, mean and lacking though it may be."

"You know," Susan said thoughtfully, "I think you belittle yourself merely to be gainsaid."

"But will you not oblige me nonetheless? Ah, you are quite right to refuse me. How else will I ever be swayed from my self-serving ways?"

"I doubt anyone has ever managed to sway you from a course, once you have set your heart upon it." It was a quality Susan could not but admire.

"Oh, but you are mistaken there. I was once firmly of the opinion that I should marry only a young man of good fortune, but I found myself thoroughly swayed by Mr Lynd. I have much to thank my late husband for," Mrs Lynd added, seeming for a moment lost in memory.

Susan wished it might be proper to ask in precisely what way Mr Lynd had deviated from his wife's ideals. And it seemed Susan's curiosity was to be indulged, for the next thing Mrs Lynd said was: "I have a miniature of him – would you like to see it?" She smiled. "Now, I know full well there is only one answer you can possibly make to that, but I confess I should like to show you. Do not fear, it will take but a moment to fetch it."

"By all means, I should like to see it." Susan kept her tone calm, and measured. Too keen an interest would not be at all well-mannered.

Mrs Lynd hastened to the bureau and opened a drawer. "Here, Miss Price. My dear, late Robert Lynd."

Susan examined the portrait eagerly, but was sadly at a loss to discover from it just what excited the tender tone in her hostess's voice. The miniature showed a stern-looking man in his sixties or thereabouts. With whiskers. She found herself more thankful than ever for her aunt's assurances that she need never worry about marriage, "for of course I shall always want you with me, and when I am gone, you will be well provided for."

Realising politeness demanded that she say something complimentary, Susan took a deep breath. "He seems very … distinguished," was all she could manage at such short notice.

Mrs Lynd's laugh, when it came, was musical in its delight. "In fact in many ways he was a dreadful old roué. Have I shocked you again? But he was a gentleman where it counted. By which I mean, of course, that he always behaved in a gentleman-like manner towards *me*. And he was very fond of our children."

"Your children?" Susan flushed, aware she had failed to keep the surprise from showing in her voice.

"Certainly. I have two: my Robert is a fine young man of four years old, and Sophia is but two. They are with their nurse, but I should very much like you to meet them upon another occasion. Why, did you think I should have none? I assure you, for all his years, my husband was a virile man." There was laughter in Mrs Lynd's tone.

Not knowing quite what to say, Susan merely bowed her head, and marvelled at her friend's fortitude.

"Come now, admit it. You think me a victim of our dreadful marriage mart, sold into servitude to a man of advanced years and repulsive habits? I assure you it was not so. Our marriage was one of shared tastes and true affection." Mrs Lynd's face turned unwontedly sombre and for a moment, she looked her true age – or at least, what Susan imagined it must be, for after all, was not Fanny now approaching thirty? "Indeed, it grieves me only that I have so far been unable to fulfil his dying wish for me: that I should find another to make me as happy as I was with him."

Then she smiled, suddenly young and carefree once more. "But enough of me! Tell me of yourself, Miss Price. Do you have a suitor? Several suitors? I cannot imagine such a pretty face and determined manner to have escaped admiration, even in the depths of Northamptonshire."

Susan frowned. Determined manner, yes: she would own to that. But a pretty face – no. She was not pretty. Not as Mrs Lynd was, with her fine features, her small yet womanly figure, her quick smile and her lively, dark eyes. Susan was too tall, too angular, too slow to mirth, and her movements lacked grace. She knew this to be true, and she felt it a little unkind of Mrs Lynd to mock her. "I have no suitors," she said, and looked Mrs Lynd straight in the eye, daring her to continue in her jest.

Mrs Lynd's face softened. "Then the young men of Northamptonshire must be a dull company, indeed. I take it there is none of them that has caught your eye?"

"I am content to remain with my aunt."

"That is not what I asked."

"Then, no." Susan found it hard to stay out of countenance with Mrs Lynd for long. "I regret that my life is so disappointingly free of romance and intrigue," she said dryly.

"Ah – but one can have too much of either, as both our families well know. Well then, my poor opinion of the young men of Northamptonshire is confirmed."

Susan hesitated – but she was not one to shy from a question some might find indelicate, particularly when she doubted Mrs Lynd would be of that number. "You would not marry again, though, would you?"

She was *almost* confident of the answer she would receive. For who would wish to lose the independent position of a wealthy widow? But the fact remained – although it astonished her – that wealthy widows *did* marry, and frequently unwisely.

Mrs Lynd regarded her, an almost pitying look in her eye. "If I loved again, and the person I loved was free to marry me, then yes, I would. But I see you do not understand me. Very well, I shall be plain: I do not intend to marry again. Is that better?"

Susan felt that it *was* better, without quite understanding why it should be so.

When she returned, with some reluctance, to their lodgings, Susan found her aunt upon the sofa. Lady Bertram smiled to see her. "Susan, dear. Is your friend well? You have been with your friend Mrs Lynd, have you not?"

"I have. She is in very good health."

"And you are looking well too, my dear. I'm so glad to see you with a little colour in your cheeks. It seems Mrs Lynd's society agrees with you."

Susan bowed her head in some confusion, and knew herself to be uncharacteristically quiet for the rest of the morning.

Mary was not one to leave her next meeting with Miss Price to the vagaries of chance. She called upon her one morning when she knew full well both Miss Price and her aunt had dined out the night before.

As Mary had expected, when she was shown into the drawing room, only Miss Price was present. She rose at once, a very becoming flush upon her cheek, and stepped forward to take Mary by the hand.

"Mrs Lynd, how good to see you."

"And you. I would enquire after your health, but your looks are more than adequate reassurance on that count." Mary cocked her head. "Now you must tell me if last night you found yourself a beau. I should be most put out not to hear it from you, if that were the case."

Miss Price laughed. "Do *you* look for a beau every time you are abroad?"

"No, but I have been married. Perhaps your case is different."

"I assure you, Mrs Lynd, it is not." She drew a deep breath. "Indeed, I believe I may honestly promise you I shall *never* look for a beau. Female companionship is all I require."

Mary's heart, which she had once been used to think of as a merely practical organ, gave a leap. "I too. I would not have you think I did not love my husband, for I did. But I have no desire to find another. I have come, I believe, to value female friendship above all else."

"I am glad of it. Men are all very well" – Mary did *not* laugh at Miss Price's naive dismissal of the whole of the more vigorous sex – "but I believe it is only within the feminine that a woman can find true kinship."

Miss Price, Mary reflected, had an extraordinary changeability about her. Unmoved, she was handsome, a well-made statue; but animated, she was beautiful. Mary was unused to considering the beauty of a soul, but she could not help but believe it was Miss Price's *animus* she so admired. "Oh, my dear, will not you call me Mary? I confess I should like to call you Susan. *Miss Price* always puts me in mind of your sister – and will you be very angry with me if I tell you I prefer to think only of you?"

"Mary, then," Susan said, with a shy smile that, for a moment, genuinely *did* make Mary think of Fanny.

She covered her unwonted confusion by taking her companion by both hands. "There. Is not that better, my dear Susan?"

"Indeed it is." This time, Susan's tone was most delightfully resolute.

She really was extraordinarily beautiful. Mary could only be thankful that she had not known Susan in her younger, more impulsive days. And yet …

"May I kiss you? For friendship's sake?" Mary asked, proving she could be every bit as impulsive now as in her youth.

Susan blinked. "For friendship," she breathed, and pressed her lips to Mary's.

Perhaps the kiss was begun in friendship, on Susan's part at least. Mary knew it had not been on hers. Certainly, it ended in more – much more. Her bosom pressed against her friend's, Mary was in heaven – until the very last thing she had counted upon occurred. The door opened, and Lady Bertram stepped into the room.

The two sprang apart, Susan's face flushing a guilty crimson as she stammered a greeting to her aunt. "Oh! A-aunt Bertram, this is my friend, Mrs Lynd. Mrs Lynd, this is my aunt, Lady Bertram."

Mary curtseyed with little grace, her own face uncomfortably heated. Really, she thought, quite out of temper with herself, they could not have looked less innocent had they studied for it. Had she learned *nothing* in all her twenty-nine years?

Her heart fluttered in her breast – would she be banished from the house?

But Lady Bertram merely nodded graciously to her, and sank down upon the sofa. "So pleased to make the acquaintance of my niece's dear friend. Caring for an invalid can be such a tiresome task. From what I hear, you have given her welcome respite. Susan, dearest, would you be so kind as to fetch me a glass of wine?" Her eyes closed.

"Of course, Aunt Bertram," Susan replied, hastening to the sideboard.

As she returned, she sent Mary a wide-eyed glance.

Her spirits skipping, Mary returned it.

Their secret, it seemed, was safe.

It was clear, as Mary took her leave, that she did so with an unburdened heart, secure in the belief they were undiscovered. Susan only wished she could share in such optimism. Her aunt had seen them in close embrace; of that she was certain. She felt hot and uncomfortable as she returned to Lady Bertram's side.

"Are you well, Aunt Bertram? I did not expect you to come downstairs this morning."

"I dare say you did not," said her aunt placidly. "But I found myself in want of company. A handsome woman, is she not, your Mrs Lynd?"

"Indeed, she is the handsomest woman I know," Susan said warmly, at once regretting her unguarded tongue.

"She puts me in mind of someone I was once acquainted with," Lady Bertram continued.

Had she thought the room hot? Susan felt now rather as if ice-water ran through her veins. "Indeed?"

"Ah – I have it. A girl I knew in my youth. We were most particular friends. Dear Maria. She died very young." Lady Bertram fell silent then, no doubt thinking of another Maria almost equally lost to her.

Susan's flood of relief turned at once to concern. "Dear Aunt Bertram, may I fetch you anything? Tea? A glass of wine, perhaps?"

"Thank you, but no. Tell me, do you plan to see Mrs Lynd again soon?"

"She has asked me to call upon her tomorrow, if you have no objection."

"My dear, do you really think I should frown upon your intimacy with such a charming young lady? Although perhaps I should not say young, for I think she must be nearing thirty?" She gave Susan an arch look.

Susan blushed, and stammered, "I believe Mrs Lynd to be nine-and-twenty." She could only hope this information would not form the dreaded connection in her aunt's mind. She steeled her nerve, and looked her aunt in the eye. "And you truly do not disapprove of our friendship? You do not think it forward of me?"

For although she would not – *could* not – risk her aunt condemning Mary for the long-ago actions of her brother, neither would she willingly go against the wishes of a lady so dear to her, and to whom she owed so very much.

Lady Bertram met her gaze, an unaccustomed clarity in her pale blue eyes. "My dear, dear Susan. When you have lived as long as I have ... Although it pains me to admit it, I have all my life been privy to things I should rather not know of. My poor boy's wretched dissolution, even the very foundation of Sir Thomas's wealth, built as it was upon the backs of those I now know to be our fellow men and women ... And although I have lived to regret it, I stayed silent on all. My habit of indolence has been, I will admit, my refuge in times of strife. If I could not abandon it to save my fellow creature, to save my own dear son, do you truly suppose that I should leave it now, merely because your affection for Mrs Lynd may outstep common bounds? My dear, I cannot see that any harm is done to others – and as for yourself, I flatter myself I may trust in your conscience to be your guide."

To hear such a long and passionate speech, from a lady whom many thought incapable of deep feeling, left Susan chastened, and saddened, and deeply sensible that she was beloved; but all was outweighed by the hope that flared in her breast. "Then … You do not object to our continued intimacy?"

"By no means. Now, I find I am more tired than I thought. Perhaps you would assist me back upstairs?"

Susan did so, with even more care than was her wont.

The next meeting with Mary took place, not at her lodgings, but once more at Lady Bertram's residence, for before Susan was able to call upon her friend, that lady called upon her. She was in company with a lady and a gentleman of her own age who, she explained, were long-time friends of hers lately arrived in Bath for a stay of only a few nights' duration. The Gregorys had known each other all their lives, and married young, a state of affairs Susan found hard to imagine when she thought back to the rough boys she had been acquainted with in her days living in Portsmouth. Then again, had not Fanny known Edmund since childhood?

"You must forgive us," Mrs Gregory entreated in a manner that was quite disarming. "For Mary told us you and she had plans, and yet we insisted she spend the morning with us. In our defence, it has been an age since we last saw her."

Mary laughed. "Ah, Susan, do not listen to her! For I confess it was all my doing. Having not seen them for so long, I found myself unable to part so soon from my dear friends, for all that they would have had me keep our engagement. Now tell me, are you very angry with me?"

Anger, indeed, was the last emotion Susan felt upon receiving such a winning smile. "By no means," she said easily. "I would not keep you from your friends."

"Then will you come with us to the pump-room? For I have told Mr and Mrs Gregory that to visit Bath without taking the waters is simply unheard of."

Susan smiled. "Indeed, we should not do anything to outrage society. Let me first enquire of my aunt whether she can spare me."

She ran upstairs to her aunt, and received the expected blessing for the outing.

Although Susan chafed at the lack of privacy which prevented her from speaking openly with Mary, she rejoiced to see her pleasure in her friends' company as they strolled through the streets. They stayed above an hour in the pump-room, laughed at the Gregorys' description of the water as "perfectly horrid", and were about to take tea, when Susan was astonished to see her aunt arrive upon the arm of Mrs Slocombe.

"Aunt Bertram," Susan cried, hastening to her side. "Had I known you intended to visit the pump-room today I should of course have waited for you."

"Do not concern yourself, my dear. Indeed I had no such plan, but when my dear Mrs Slocombe called upon me I found I had more energy than I thought, and asked her to bring me here quite upon a whim."

Susan was all astonishment. Lady Bertram, act upon a whim? She could only, and with some discomfort, attribute it to a wish to examine Mrs Lynd once more – perhaps, to ensure that Mrs Lynd's and Susan's behaviour in public did not stray beyond the bounds of propriety?

Or, perhaps, because she had some inkling of who Mrs Lynd might be? The thought chilled her.

"May I fetch you some water?" she asked to cover her confusion.

"That would be most kind, my dear. But first perhaps you will introduce me to your friends?"

Susan did so, with not a little trepidation. There was conversation of the sort which greets all newcomers to Bath, and they sat down to take tea together. Susan's eyes were ever on her aunt, seeking any sign that Mary's appearance had sparked a recollection in Lady Bertram. Surely she could not have changed so much, in ten years?

And yet, Lady Bertram had known Mary Crawford only for a brief season, a period she now had every reason to wish to forget. Memories faded, whether one willed them to or no; Susan found to her chagrin she could no longer clearly recall her own dead sister's face. And the sophisticated widowed lady of today might appear very different from the fresh young girl of a decade ago.

Nonetheless, fear clenched at her stomach every time the conversation turned to Mary's and the Gregorys' shared youth, for fear they would let slip some clue that would make the connection in her aunt's mind.

At length, the Gregorys began to appear anxious to be gone, having seen so far little of the city. Susan could not repine at their parting – but her relief was short-lived, however. Smiling, and wishing them well, Lady Bertram remarked that it did them credit to have kept their old acquaintance in mind.

Mrs Gregory replied with feeling how glad she was to have seen her friend again, turning to Mary as she spoke. "It has been a joy. Why, it seems only yesterday that I was skipping down the lane to visit you and Henry at Admiral Crawford's house."

Susan's heart clenched painfully – for their secret to have endured so far, yet be betrayed at the last!

But there was no sign that her aunt had registered the name. No jolt of surprise, no darkening of her face in anger. Could it be that they had yet escaped?

Mary, her colour somewhat heightened, took her leave along with the Gregorys, after exacting a promise from Susan that she would call upon her "tomorrow, without fail".

No further incidents occurred to cause alarm, but nonetheless, Susan was heartily glad when they finally returned to the rooms she shared with Lady Bertram, and gladder still when she heard from Mary that the Gregorys had departed for Bristol.

In the weeks that followed, in which Susan and Mary spent as much time in one another's company as they could, there was still no sign that Lady Bertram had connected Mrs Lynd with Mary Crawford. She still smiled to see them together, and although Susan's conscience, when it pricked her, did so only gently, still it pricked.

But seasons end, even in Bath, and country estates must be returned to.

Susan was consoled by long, long letters from her dear friend, Mrs Lynd, that were, contrary to all claims from their author, not dull in the slightest. And indeed Susan could use the lift to her spirits they gave her very well. Lady Bertram had seemed, upon her return from Bath, to be improved in health, but it had been a false dawn, and now she faded daily.

"I dare say," said Lady Bertram one day, as Susan sat by her bed, "that when I am gone, you shall want to go and live with Mrs Lynd."

"My dear aunt, such an event is not to be thought of now." Susan coloured, for indeed she and Mary had discussed the eventuality in their latest correspondence.

"No, my dear, it should, for I should rest much easier if I knew you to be settled."

"Well then, I suppose I shall. But I hope such an event will be many years hence."

Lady Bertram smiled faintly. "I'm sure you're right, dear. But I am pleased to hear you will not be friendless."

"Of course I will not. For I shall have Fanny, and Edmund, and ..." Susan hesitated to add "Tom", because his health was no better than his poor mother's, or "Julia and Mr Yates", for in truth the thought of becoming beholden to cousins who were almost strangers to her made her shudder.

"Yes, of course, my dear. But Mrs Lynd is your *particular* friend, is she not? Now I think I must sleep."

Susan sat a little longer, watching her aunt's shallow breaths. She was about to rise and leave her when the watery blue eyes opened again.

"Oh, but one more thing, my dear. Perhaps it would be best not to mention Mrs Lynd's former name to your sister, or to Sir Thomas. At least not until you are settled. One wouldn't want them to cause any difficulties."

As Lady Bertram's eyes closed once more, Susan could only stare at her fondly, and marvel.

Author's Notes

I've always found *Mansfield Park* to be one of Jane Austen's most interesting novels. Not because I think it's the best – viewed objectively, I'd score it rather low on the list of her works, although of course any book by Miss Austen is still a very fine book indeed – but because of its very imperfections.

The most glaring of these for me is that the central couple, Fanny and Edmund, are in many ways the least interesting characters in the book, and their romance is hardly full of flights of passion. Fanny is no heroine for modern sensibilities: she never stands up for herself, and is a terrible prude. Edmund is decent enough, if dull and plodding, but gets his head turned entirely too easily by a pretty, confident woman – whom, it becomes clear at the end, he does not really love. Theirs is a complacent, quiet happiness, Fanny's and Edmund's, when at last they win it.

But oh! The other characters – the headstrong, immature, and ultimately disgraced Maria Bertram; the rakish, charming Henry Crawford; and the very worldly Mary Crawford – she is far too intelligent to be called pert – to name but a few. The latter two in particular are far more suited to modern tastes; indeed, in the book itself they are held up as examples of (albeit unwelcome) modernity.

It's common, I believe, when examining *Mansfield Park* for queer themes, to look at a possible attraction between Mary and Fanny—for example, the scene in which Mary coerces Fanny into rehearsing a love scene with her can very easily be read as flirtatious, and Fanny explicitly describes Mary as "so extremely pretty, that I have great pleasure in looking at her". But I can't see those two ending up together. Fanny is simply too set in her priggish ways – and just not *fun* enough for Mary.

Fanny's younger sister Susan, on the other hand, with her "fearless disposition" and "quickness in understanding" and above all, her human fallibility even as she strives to do what is right ... She's far more a heroine we can identify with and root for – and with whom Mary might fall in love. We scarcely get to know Susan in *Mansfield Park*, but I believe were we allowed more time with her, we'd have to agree with Lady Bertram (another character, by the way, who is more intriguing than she might at first appear) that Susan fully deserves to be "the more beloved of the two".

JL Merrow

JL Merrow is that rare beast, an English person who refuses to drink tea. She read Natural Sciences at Cambridge, where she learned many things, chief amongst which was that she never wanted to see the inside of a lab ever again. Her one regret is that she never mastered the ability of punting one-handed whilst holding a glass of champagne.

She writes across genres, with a preference for contemporary gay romance and mysteries, and is frequently accused of humour. Her novel *Slam!* won the 2013 Rainbow Award for Best LGBT Romantic Comedy, and her novella *Muscling Through* and novel *Relief Valve* were both EPIC Awards finalists.

JL Merrow is a member of the Romantic Novelists' Association, International Thriller Writers, Verulam Writers' Circle and the UK GLBTQ Fiction Meet organising team.

jlmerrow.com
twitter.com/jlmerrow
facebook.com/jl.merrow

About the Stories

A Charming Marine Prospect
Lou Faulkner

Birds of a feather flock together, they say, and William Elliot and Richard Musgrove strike up an instant rapport when they meet in the vicinity of Lyme, a few years before the events of *Persuasion*. But is their relationship any more to be trusted than the unstable landscape of the nearby under-cliff which they explore together?

One Half of the World
Adam Fitzroy

How much more romantic must it be to be stolen away in the night by a lady dressed as a man, to be thrown across the saddle of her horse and to be galloped off with across the moors by moonlight?

Hide nor Hair
Atlin Merrick

Adam Ashford Otelian began to suspect something when he saw Miss Mary Hay's beard. Though to be fair, Adam found Miss Hay's beard only the second most intriguing thing about her.

Outside the Parlour
Andrea Demetrius

Darcy is a single man of eight-and-twenty and in possession of a good fortune. Talk of marriage and prospects crowd in on him – as do reports in the broadsheets of convictions for 'unnatural' crimes. He knows his fate. A decision must be made soon.

Margaret
Eleanor Musgrove

The elder Dashwood sisters have long been established in their new homes and families, but now it is Margaret's turn to spread her wings, when Colonel Brandon asks for her help with a rather delicate matter.

The Wind over Pemberley
Fae Mcloughlin
Darcy's life changes forever when he happens across enigmatic Lint on Pemberley Cliff.

Cross and Cast
Sam Evans
Jonathan Darcy, ex-soap-star bad boy and runner-up in the latest celebrity dance contest, has reluctantly signed on to take part in another dance show, *Dance with Jane Austen*. His agent is sure it will be the making of him – but the ridiculous dance they've been asked to learn is titled 'Mr Beveridge's Maggot', the theatre they're rehearsing in is too cold, and most worryingly the show will bring Darcy back in contact with the man who rejected him so harshly months earlier, dancer Elvin Benoît.

Jonathan convinces himself that all he needs do is get through the rehearsals in one piece, avoid Benoît, and not split the breeches he has been given to wear.

It was going to be easy, right?

Know Your Own Happiness
Narrelle M Harris
Four years ago, Cooper West allowed his brother to persuade him that it was easier to pretend to be straight than admit to being bi. It was a stupid decision that cost him the love of his life, Archer Flynn. Now out, recently dumped and still harbouring regret for his lost love, Fate and Cooper's cousin Kate are about to intervene, via a book club meeting where the book under discussion is … *Persuasion*.

Thirteen Hours in Austen
Fae Mcloughlin
Ashley gets more than he bargained for when he visits the Jane Austen museum with his mother.

Man of War
Sandra Lindsey
Intent on making his mark as the newest lieutenant aboard HMS *Thrush*,

William Price takes on the task of tutoring an ordinary seaman, Robert Oakes, so that the young sailor may improve his chances of advancement.

Oakes, however, hides something which could see him unceremoniously dropped from the ship's muster list and left in the closest port with just a few coins to his name. When William learns Oakes's secret in the aftermath of a skirmish with a French frigate, he must choose between proving himself a worthy friend or a dutiful officer.

Elinor and Ada
Julie Bozza
Elinor Dashwood has fallen in love with her sister-in-law's cousin, Ada Ferrars, and dares to hope that Ada returns her feelings. But soon Elinor must move to Devonshire with her mother and sisters, in much reduced circumstances – and while there, she learns a devastating secret. How can Elinor pursue this rare chance of happiness, when even duty and honour are against her?

Father Doesn't Dance
Eleanor Musgrove
When George Darcy passes away, the women of Pemberley have to adapt. For one of them, however, what begins as a daring plan to save them all from destitution soon becomes a whole new lease of life.

A Particular Friend
JL Merrow
When Susan Price leaves Mansfield Park to accompany her aunt, Lady Bertram, to take the waters in Bath, she little expects to meet an old 'friend' of the family. Initially scandalised, Susan finds herself drawn to the former Mary Crawford, now a widow, Mrs Lynd.

But Lady Bertram will surely never countenance Susan's intimacy with a woman whose brother caused her daughter's disgrace – and Mrs Lynd's true identity cannot be kept a secret forever.

❖

Manifold Press

Life in all the colours of the rainbow

For **Readers**: LGBTQIA fiction and romance with strong storylines from acclaimed authors. A variety of intriguing locations – set in the past, present or future – sometimes with a supernatural twist. Our focus is always on the characters and the story.

For **Authors**: We are always happy to consider high-quality new projects from aspiring and established writers.

Our 'regular' novels are now joined by the Espresso Shots imprint for novellas and our New Adult line.

Visit our website to discover more!

 ManifoldPress.co.uk

Made in the USA
Charleston, SC
21 October 2016